Down Range

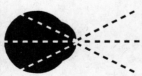

This Large Print Book carries the
Seal of Approval of N.A.V.H.

DOWN RANGE

LINDSAY MCKENNA

THORNDIKE PRESS

A part of Gale, Cengage Learning

GALE
CENGAGE Learning·

Farmington Hills, Mich • San Francisco • New York • Waterville, Maine
Meriden, Conn • Mason, Ohio • Chicago

GALE
CENGAGE Learning

Copyright © 2013 by Nauman Living Trust.
Shadow Warriors Series.
Thorndike Press, a part of Gale, Cengage Learning.

LIBRARY OF CONGRESS CATALOGING-IN-PUBLICATION DATA

McKenna, Lindsay, 1946–
    Down range / by Lindsay McKenna. — Large Print edition.
        pages cm. — (Shadow Warriors series) (Thorndike Press Large Print Romance)
        ISBN 978-1-4104-6799-7 (hardcover) — ISBN 1-4104-6799-6 (hardcover)
        1. Large type books. I. Title.
PS3563.C37525D69 2014
813'.54—dc23   2013047016

Published in 2014 by arrangement with Harlequin Books S. A.

Dear Reader,

Lindsay McKenna did a great job creating *Down Range*. There were times I didn't want to put her book down. It hit on some of the emotions that I had locked up for a long time. So it will be an ongoing healing process for me after reading it. A deep, reflective book is rare.

Jake Ramsey, the hero, had reached a point where he was able to express his emotions in a way few SEALs openly do. This would be a great educational book for SEALs to read, because, like many warriors, their emotions are locked up so they can perform their jobs. It would not be uncommon for warriors to leave the military after unlocking their hearts, like Jake and Morgan did with one another, because the killing would become more difficult.

In my opinion, this book will appeal to a broad range of people and interests. Plus, the book relays important life lessons, like love, fear and dealing with emotional and physical trauma. The action scenes are excellent and realistic, and I found myself, even with my background, engrossed in them. I didn't have to suspend my disbelief, which is what often shuts me down on most action scenes in books and especially movies.

This is one of the best books in any category I've read. It would be a great movie if it could capture and relay these points.

I hope you enjoy *Down Range* as much as I did.

Chief Michael Jaco, U.S. Navy SEAL (retired), author of *The Intuitive Warrior.*
www.MichaelJaco.com

To U.S. Navy SEAL Chief Michael Jaco, who gave twenty-four years of service to our country and is now retired. More than anything, thank you for your service. Thank you for your help with some of the technical aspects in this novel. And thank you for writing *The Intuitive Warrior.*

And

To the U.S. Navy SEALs. Thank you for your heart, your courage and your sacrifices. To the wives and children of a SEAL, who indeed sacrifice in their own way while their husbands and fathers are gone and protecting all of us as a country. You are ALL heroes in my eyes and heart.

CHAPTER ONE

What the hell? He had to be seeing things. SEAL Lieutenant Jake Ramsey froze as he climbed out of his rented red Jeep Wrangler. He'd just parked at the Pentagon, ordered here for an appointment with U.S. Army General Stevenson. He had no idea what this meeting entailed. It was top secret.

His heart thudded in his chest as he stared one row of cars up. A Marine Captain emerged from her black SUV. Jake removed his wraparound sunglasses, remaining motionless, watching her pull her black leather purse over the left shoulder. The gesture was all too familiar to him.

She wore her khaki summer uniform short-sleeved blouse along with dark green gabardine trousers that emphasized her long legs. In short-heeled, polished black pumps, she was all spit and polish. Morgan Boland had an hourglass figure, and though her clothes fitted her comfortably, Jake knew how beautiful she was without any clothes at all.

His mouth tightened. What the hell was Morgan Boland doing here?

Stunned, Jake wrestled with a lot of old feelings leaping to life within him. Oh, he remembered tunneling his fingers through that mass of silky red hair now softly framing her oval face and stubborn chin. The strands curled slightly across her proud shoulders.

She hadn't seen him — yet.

Two years ago they'd met in the Hindu Kush mountains near the border between Afghanistan and Pakistan. They'd collided like two comets, renewing their relationship that had started at the Naval Academy, Annapolis. His lower body tightened in memory of those three incredible days with her in his arms in that Afghan village. Three of the most incredible nights of his life since . . . He ruthlessly tried to crush the grief-stricken memories from when he was twenty-four years old. Jake had lost his wife, Amanda, and two-week-old baby, Joshua, in a car accident. They'd only been married a year.

At twenty-seven, Jake had unexpectedly met Morgan once again. And whether she ever realized it or not, she'd salvaged his

10

bleeding, wounded soul. Those few days had transformed him, pulled him out of a three-year depression. She'd breathed new life into him.

His mouth pursed, the corners pulling in as he watched her shut the door on the SUV. The May morning's breeze was inconstant, lifting a few gold-and-copper strands of hair across her face. He stared with a mixture of grief and longing as she lifted her long, expressive fingers and pulled the strands away from her cheek.

Morgan was still hauntingly beautiful to him. His mind spun with a hundred questions as to why she was here at the same time he was. Jake worked to suppress those unrequited feelings about their shared history. He'd had that impulse, of never allowing her to escape his arms again. But she had. And it had been his damned fault. For the second time in his life, he'd driven Morgan away from him.

There was a file beneath her left arm. She pointed the clicker at the SUV to lock it. Jake swallowed hard, trying to ignore his desire. It had been a lethal attraction from the first moment, in Annapolis, while going through the Naval Academy. They were a powerful match in bed, but dammit, she was bullheaded and wildly independent. She refused to be what he wanted her to be. When they came together in bed, it was like the Fourth of July every time. Yet, afterward, it always descended into a heated argument, hurtful words flying between them like bullets being fired from an M-4 rifle.

His breath jammed in his throat as he saw her lift her head, her green-eyed gaze meeting his. For a moment, Jake felt like a proverbial deer paralyzed in a set of car headlights. Her eyes narrowed. Of course, she recognized him. Her oval face with high cheekbones and a sprinkle of pale freckles tightened. Her mouth . . . *oh, God, her mouth . . .* Jake remembered hotly covering those full lips, feeling her hungry response, her sleek, athletic body pressed demandingly against his, wanting him as much as he wanted her. Now that soft, full mouth thinned with displeasure. He forced himself to hold her gaze. Even from this distance, he could see the spark of surprise and then anger flare in her green eyes.

What the hell were the chances of meeting Morgan two years later, here in a damned Pentagon parking lot? Jake decided he had to be a gentleman and walk over and say hello. He shut the door on his Jeep, locked it and shoved the key into a pocket of his tan Navy summer trousers. Pulling

12

the garrison cap from beneath his left arm, he settled it on his head.

Jake felt as if he was going downrange into a direct action combat mission. Born of a Navy SEAL, he walked with an easy, natural confidence toward the only other woman in his life who had held his heart — and he'd screwed it up both times. Now, as he closed the distance between them, tension was evident in her, but she was a warrior like him. Jake tried to prepare himself. Morgan was definitely not happy to see him. And he knew why.

"You're the last person I expected to see here in this parking lot," he said, trying to soften his normally hard expression. He came to a halt a few feet away from her, but he could still see her emerald eyes flash with what he interpreted as disgust. Or maybe, distrust. *Probably both.*

"Makes two of us, Ramsey."

"What business do you have here, Morgan?"

She quirked her lips. "It's top secret. How about you?"

He managed a sliver of a smile, appreciating the way the uniform hid her breasts. He knew those breasts well, and even now, his body hotly remembered their firm curves, too. "Same. Where you headed?"

"The E-ring. You?"

His brows rose. "Same ring." What the hell kind of cosmic joke was being played upon him? Jake saw confusion for a moment in her eyes, too.

The breeze blew enough to lift strands of her red hair across her flushed cheeks. He had the urge to lift his hand, catch those errant strands with his fingers and gently tuck them behind her delicate ear as he'd done on so many other occasions. Why the hell couldn't he erase Morgan from his body and memory forever?

He'd been in the military since he was eighteen. He'd gone to Annapolis and went into the Marine Corps. Later, he moved to the U.S. Navy to become a SEAL. At twenty-nine, Jake felt snared by a joke being pulled on him by Marine Corps god Odin himself. The last person he ever wanted to meet again was Morgan. And here she was: all six feet of woman warrior who proved him wrong about her being the weaker sex.

She glanced down at the watch on her right wrist. "I've gotta go, Ramsey." Morgan drilled him with a hard look. "And I can't say it's been nice seeing you again."

Jake watched her turn on her heel and walk toward the main doors of the Pentagon. It almost felt as if she'd physically slapped him. He stood for a moment, letting her quiet rage pass through him. It wasn't her fault, he sourly admitted. He'd been the one to hurl the indictment that women were weak. That they shouldn't be allowed into combat. He and Morgan had gotten into that very argument after making love on Christmas morning as a blizzard hit the Afghan village.

He and his SEAL team had holed up at the American-friendly Shinwari village to wait out the coming storm. To his everlasting surprise, Morgan had been there, too, with another SEAL team. The SEALs operated in small four- and eight-person fire teams throughout the Hindu Kush, rooting out the bad guys and taking them down. He hadn't been able to swallow his surprise or disguise his pleasure at discovering she was there. Morgan had been assigned as a linguist with another team on a separate black-ops mission.

Rubbing his recently shaved jaw, Jake saw her disappear inside the building. He had just enough time to make his appointment with General Stevenson of the U.S. Army. His emotions, no matter how he tried, burned bright and intense over meeting Morgan once again. She had stood out at Annapolis from the moment he'd seen her in their plebe year. They were in the same class, and for two years, Jake had fought to ignore the tall, assertive redhead. Morgan was as physically strong as most of the men going through the four-year military program. Jake had watched her begin to shine and bloom in her third year. She'd been at the top of the academic list, a champion fencer on the fencing team, and her keen intelligence had been recognized.

He quickly walked across the asphalt parking lot, in deep thought over her. When had he fallen under her charismatic spell at the Academy? *How* had it happened? Jake had accidentally met Morgan as a third-year student at a local civilian pizza parlor everyone frequented on Saturday evenings. There were plenty of guys who wanted her. She'd always been surrounded by them, but she didn't seem to care or notice any of them. Yet, when they'd met up at the bar to order pitchers of beer, something had happened.

"Damn," he rasped, scowling. They'd accidentally grazed one another's elbows. Jake remembered Morgan's gaze meeting his. Those deep green eyes that made his heart melt, made his body go hot and hard with longing. Her nickname at the Academy had been Amazon because she was tall, physically strong and she had a bruising, in-your-face independence.

Jake remembered taking Morgan's hand and leading her into the hall of the bar to be alone with her. He'd done something he'd wanted to do for years: kiss the hell out of her. Morgan, he'd discovered, had been watching him for a long time, too. He'd asked if she was protected, and she'd said yes, she was on the pill. They'd never made it back to the Academy until very early on Sunday morning. And their hearts and fates had been sealed, for better or worse.

He needed to stop remembering. Morgan wasn't in his life anymore. Jake scowled and climbed the stone steps of the Pentagon. Up ahead were soldiers with M-16 rifles. Since the bombing of the Pentagon on 9/11, security had markedly changed. He would go through an X-ray machine before ever being allowed into the military bastion.

Jake aimed himself toward the outer ring, the E-ring. It was the only level that had windows looking out into the civilian world. Only senior military officers got those posh office assignments. This was where many top secret and black-ops missions originated. Curious as to why he was called off PRODEV, sixty days of leave granted to him

17

after coming back from Afghanistan with his SEAL platoon, he arrived at the E-ring. Looking at the file he held, he saw the number of the office and turned to the right.

Captain Morgan Boland was sitting in a chair opposite the secretary's desk when the door opened. Her eyes widened. Jake Ramsey, again? Her lips parted for a moment. What was *he* doing here? He stopped when he realized she was sitting there staring up at him. He had a stunned look across his normally unreadable expression. Shock bolted through her.

Morgan lowered her gaze, and her heart sped up. Why couldn't she just ignore Ramsey's darkly tanned face? His rugged good looks and those stormy-looking gray eyes of his? Her fingers tightened imperceptibly around the file in her lap. The only other empty chair in the small, cramped office was two feet away from where she sat. She listened as Jake went to the fortysomething-year-old blonde administrative assistant and gave his name to her.

"Thank you, Lieutenant Ramsey. General Stevenson will see you in just a bit. Would you like some coffee or tea while you wait?"

Jake took off his cap. "No, thank you, ma'am." He hated having to sit next to

Morgan, who was staring at him as if he were going to bite her. His traitorous body and heart clamored over being so close to this fiery woman. Jake wanted to be close. Wanted, somehow, to undo the wrong he'd done to her two years earlier.

Sitting down, he glanced over at her. Morgan was staring straight ahead, her hands tense over the file in her lap. He relished viewing her profile and then realized her once-perfect nose now had a bump on it. Had she broken it? He almost asked but thought better of it. There was an assistant sitting six feet away from them, and Jake didn't want her to know how much Morgan hated him.

What to say to Jake Ramsey? Morgan felt heat radiating off his hard male body. The uniform showed how athletic and fit he really was. SEALs took exercise to a whole new level, plus six months climbing mountains in Afghanistan had honed his body into a dangerous weapon. She saw the SEAL gold trident on his well-sprung chest, rows of colorful ribbons beneath it. Jake was part of the best of the best black-ops teams the military had. She remembered those pale eyes of his going dove-gray as he'd made love with her. God, they were good in bed together. *Too good.* And above all, Morgan knew she had to keep a secret she would always carry from that last meeting they had. Jake would never know. Pursing her lips, she refused to say anything to him. Her mind churned with questions on why both of them were here, in the same office of the Pentagon. It made no sense to her.

A buzzer sounded on the assistant's desk. She looked over at Morgan. "Go right through this door, Captain Boland. General Houston will see you. Room two, please."

Rising, Morgan nodded, ignored Ramsey and opened the door. Inside, she saw two offices, one on either side of the hall. Turning to the left, she saw a frosted glass window with "2" painted in gold upon it and knocked firmly.

"Enter," a male voice ordered.

Morgan's heart picked up a beat as she opened it. Inside was a man in his late-fifties, fit, in a dark green U.S. Army uniform. The salad, or ribbons, across his powerful chest attested to his time and experience in the Army. There was silver on the sidewalls of his closely cropped hair. His eyes were sharp and intelligent-looking. Morgan came to attention in front of his desk.

"Captain Morgan Boland reporting as ordered, sir."

"At ease, Captain. Have a seat. We need to chat."

Indeed, Morgan thought as she took the only chair in front of the General's desk. The man smiled a little as he clasped his hands and rested them on the dark cherry-wood desk.

"What I'm about to tell you is top secret, Captain. But I already think you know what this mission is all about."

"I'm hoping it's an op to go after Sangar Khogani, sir. I've been pushing for it to find and kill him for the last couple of years."

A grin leaked through the hardened line of his mouth. He handed her a file folder. "We've been listening, Captain. Read along with me?"

Opening the folder, Morgan felt her spirits lift. Her emotions shimmered as she quickly read the one-paragraph synopsis on the mission. Looking up, she saw the General giving her a penetrating look. Morgan waited for him to speak, even though she wanted to tear through the rest of the assignment and read the details. She hoped like hell she had been assigned to it.

"You're a part of Operation Shadow Warriors," he began, opening the file. "Forty women volunteers from all the military branches were trained either in Ranger or

Special Forces schools and are now in ground combat to prove women have what it takes to do the job in the field. We're in the third year of a seven-year top secret experiment. I'm pleased to tell you, it's going very well in showing women can handle combat."

"Yes, sir." Hope rose in her breast. Morgan had never wanted an assignment more than this one. Was General Houston letting her have it or not? She couldn't read the man's deeply tanned face.

"You've been very active and vocal about mounting a mission to take out Khogani. He's an opium drug lord with the Hill tribe near the border area with Pakistan."

"Yes, sir, I have." She'd spoken to General Maya Stevenson, who had spearheaded women in combat, starting with the Black Jaguar Squadron down in Peru years earlier. Maya had put together a plan of an all-woman Apache combat squadron to halt cocaine shipments out of that country. It had been approved and had been a spectacular success. Then Stevenson had organized Operation Shadow Warriors three years ago. It was a program putting women's boots on the ground in various combat theaters.

Morgan wasted no time in pleading her

case directly to the General to mount a mission. She wanted to even the terrible score over in Afghanistan. Morgan had been caught up in the battle along with a group of Green Berets, wounded and one of the few survivors of Khogani's attack on a Shinwari tribe village.

Houston nodded. "You're going to get your wish, Captain. You've been a SEAL trained sniper for three years now, and you've exemplified yourself in that department. You've been downrange with SEAL and Special Forces units for the past three years."

"I have the background it takes to successfully complete this mission, sir."

"There's no question about that, Captain."

"I've lobbied hard to get this op on the board, sir."

Houston smiled a little at the brash woman officer. "If you could suffer a little more with me, Captain, let's talk about the mission details?"

Chastised, Morgan relaxed against the chair. She saw humor in his eyes, as if he were putting up with a petulant, pushy child. "Yes, sir, sorry, sir. I've got a few guns in this fight."

Houston nodded and sobered. He was

23

familiar with SEAL slang. "A gun in the fight" meant the person had a personal, vested interest in the undertaking. Morgan had never gone through SEAL training. Instead, she'd been working off and on with them for years over in Afghanistan. Their slang and lingo were bound to rub off on her.

"I understand. General Stevenson and I are responsible for the inception of Operation Shadow Warriors. We took your request seriously when you submitted this mission to General Stevenson. We've worked with SOCOM, Special Operation Command, up and down the chain of command to ensure this mission, which is now called Operation Peregrine, is successful."

"Thank you, sir. You don't know how much this means to me." Morgan held her breath as he slowly leafed through several pages of the mission. Would they let her be on the op? Just because they approved it didn't mean she was assigned. They had to allow her to be a part of it! Never had Morgan ever wanted anything more in life right now than to go after Sangar Khogani. She had two scores to settle with him.

At the same time, she knew Houston was well aware she was a sniper and a damned good one. She'd proved her skill out in the field many times over. Snipers weren't supposed to be emotionally involved in the hunting of their quarry. They couldn't do their job if revenge was uppermost on their minds. Emotions clouded a sniper's mindset; something no one wanted in the field during an op. Morgan realized she'd revealed her personal and emotional need to have a stake in this op. A stupid move on her part.

And now General Houston knew how badly she wanted Khogani. Would he overlook her passion? Or not? Unsure, Morgan forced herself to sit quietly and wait. After all, that was what snipers did best. Patience was a virtue among the sniper cadre, and ordinarily, Morgan had the patience of Job. But Khogani stirred up violent, angry emotions in her, and there was no way around it. She wanted that bastard dead. His head on a platter. And she wanted to be the one who put it there.

"Go to page four, Captain. This entails the guts of the op."

Morgan's gaze went to page four. There were two names chosen for the op. One was her, which sent a giddy emotion of joy through her. When her eyes dropped to the second name, her heart plunged with disbelief. Gulping, she snapped a look up across the desk at Houston. Struggling to speak, she rasped, "But — sir, I'm assigned to this op with Lieutenant Jake Ramsey?" For a moment, she felt as if someone had hit her with an armor-piercing round to her Kevlar vest, sucking the breath out of her.

"That's right," Mike Houston said. "General Stevenson and I want this to be a SEAL mission. You've worked well with them in the past. We needed a SEAL sniper who could be sniper leader on the op."

Morgan swallowed her disappointment. "Yes, sir," she barely mouthed. There would be no way in hell she could voice protest over Ramsey being assigned. On top of that, he had been designated as lead sniper. In the sniping business, they were both equally qualified, but one sniper would be the leader, the final decision maker. And it would be *him*! *Dammit!* The ramifications of the assignment whirled like a nightmare around her. Obviously, these generals did not know their long personal history. Maybe that was a blessing in disguise. Morgan was sure she'd never have been assigned to the op if General Houston realized what she and Jake had once been to each other.

Lifting her head, she said, "Sir? What led you to choose Lieutenant Ramsey?"

Mike sat back in his leather chair and said,

"His name was spit out by the computer, Captain. Any problems with that?"

"None, sir," she lied, her voice husky as she carefully closeted her roiling feelings. That was why she'd met Jake in the parking lot.

"General Stevenson is interviewing First Lieutenant Ramsey as we speak. If she feels he's the right man for the job, we'll be setting up the briefing tomorrow at 0900 here in this office. We'll all go over the details of this op at that time." He picked up a voucher and handed it to her. "You'll both be staying at this hotel located near the Pentagon. I know you just came out of Afghanistan, flying for almost twenty-four hours to make this meeting, Captain. Get a hot meal under your belt tonight and get a good night's sleep. I need you a hundred percent tomorrow morning. Understand?"

Quickly coming to her feet at attention, Morgan said, "Yes, sir. Thank you, sir."

"Dismissed."

Morgan forced herself to turn and walk to the door. Emotions clashed within her. She felt a little dizzy. As she left the office, she was grateful not to see Jake Ramsey. She kept walking toward the front doors, trying to deal with this new development. Closing her eyes for a moment, she dragged in an uneven breath, forcing all those feelings down into her once more. It didn't work.

Morgan fought the deep jet lag. She'd only been able to grab some sleep aboard the C-5 that had flown her from Bagram air base in Afghanistan to Rota, Spain, and then on to Andrews Air Force Base just outside Washington, D.C.

Pushing herself, Morgan left the Pentagon, glad to be out in the warm May sunlight once more. The breeze reminded her she was home, if but for a little while, not in the harsh desert mountains of Afghanistan with a hunter-killer SEAL team. Aiming herself at the rented SUV, Morgan looked at the voucher. She was so damned tired, she was weaving. Houston was right: she needed a hot shower and then bed. If she woke up sometime this evening, she'd get dinner to fortify herself. Because the turnaround on this op was immediate. The schedule had them leaving within twenty-four hours, headed back into Afghanistan.

As she opened the door to the SUV, Morgan wanted to check in to the hotel and make a call to her parents in Gunnison, Colorado. And even more, she wanted to talk to her two-year-old daughter, Emma. Just thinking about her family buoyed Morgan. She tried to force her thoughts away from Jake Ramsey. What did he think of the sniper pairing on this op? He had to be feeling like an IED had exploded beneath him. Morgan knew, without any doubt, the last woman Jake would ever want on a mission with him would be *her.* Correction, he'd never want any woman on a mission with him, believing they were incapable of operating in combat.

All hell was about to break loose. . . .

CHAPTER TWO

Jake Ramsey wondered what kind of bad karma was hanging over his head. When he opened door number one, he came face-to-face with an Army woman General. He snapped to attention in front of her desk and reported as ordered.

"At ease," General Maya Stevenson said, gesturing to the chair in front of her desk. "Have a seat, Lieutenant Ramsey. We have a lot to cover in a short amount of time."

Sitting, Jake got his first good look at the female General. His mind spun in shock, but somewhere, in his memory, he had heard this woman's name. Where? And he almost blurted, what is a woman doing mission planning on a black ops? But didn't. Judging from the serious look on her face, he'd keep his mouth shut. Her hair was black with some silver strands and barely brushed the shoulders of her green uniform. It was the burning intelligence in her large emerald eyes that warned him she wasn't some weak woman like his mother. Far from it; so he sat there on edge, trying to appear interested but not anxious.

"Lieutenant, you were chosen for Operation Peregrine by our computers." She leaned forward, handing him the mission brief. "We need two snipers to go after Sangar Khogani, a Hill tribe leader who is an opium warlord." She rested her hands on the file. "We have chosen a sniper team to go after him and remove his presence from the fight."

"Yes, ma'am."

"Are you interested in this type of op, Lieutenant?"

"Absolutely, ma'am." Jake felt himself sweat. This woman General had the kind of look that could cut an officer into so many ribbons. Why would she ask such a question?

"Open the file to page four, Lieutenant."

Jake opened it. His mouth dropped as he read who his assigned sniper partner would be: Captain Morgan Boland. He snapped his mouth shut, feeling shock bolt through him. "Ma'am," he said, struggling, looking at her, "this can't be right."

"What isn't right, Lieutenant?"

"This . . . this is a woman, ma'am."

The General's long, arched brows turned downward. Her once-relaxed facial features turned glacial. He knew he'd said the wrong thing but didn't care. There was no way he was going on a black op with a woman! Not even Morgan Boland. Especially not her. Adrenaline began to leak into his bloodstream. What kind of sick joke was this?

"You got a problem with that, Lieutenant?"

Wincing internally, Jake heard the frost in her husky voice, her eyes narrowed speculatively upon him. Okay, so he saw the choice: argue that a woman had no place being a sniper on a dangerous black op and ask for a man to be assigned with him instead. As Jake sat there in those seconds, he suddenly remembered Maya Stevenson. Scuttlebutt had circulated among the SEALs that a female Army General had formed an all-woman combat unit. The women had been divided among the black-ops community. The all-volunteer force had been trained in Ranger or Special Forces schools. They had then been assigned to a black-ops team to become a working part of it in combat. And he remembered hearing the plan was working very well. Dammit.

Mouth dry, Jake tried to temper his answer. "Ma'am, with all due respect, I honestly don't feel a woman could handle this kind of op. Just perusing some of the challenges on this mission, it's in the Hindu Kush mountains. We could be at twelve thousand feet on rocks and scree. I've been up in those mountains many times, and I know how brutal the elements and challenges are for a sniper."

"Which is why you were chosen for this mission, Lieutenant. You bring experience to the table. But so does Captain Boland."

There was a hard edge in her voice, and Jake felt trapped. She wasn't even going to discuss a woman being assigned to the op. It was a done deal to her, normal SOP, standard operating procedure. He held her unblinking gaze. "Yes, ma'am."

"There's a *but* in your voice, Lieutenant." She gave him a cutting look. "This meeting between you and me is to simply iron out any major problems before we meet at 0900 back here tomorrow morning to go over the details of this op."

Swallowing hard, Jake felt her power. He could see she was holding back her emotions. "Again, with all due respect, General, I will not allow a woman on an op like this."

It was the wrong thing to say. Jake felt as if a bomb went off in the small, cramped room. It wasn't physical, but invisible, as if he got slapped with angry energy. The General straightened, her face going hard. He tried to prepare himself against the anger he saw.

"We're not asking for your 'allowance,' Lieutenant Ramsey. I don't know what rock you've been hiding under, but women *are* in combat. And they've *been* in combat from day one of the Iraq War. They're in combat in Afghanistan. For the last ten years. Where have you been?"

"SEALs have no female operatives in their ranks," he shot back. This op assignment terrified Jake. He couldn't take Morgan as a sniper partner. No way in hell.

The General gave him a patient look. "Again, Lieutenant, for your edification, women have gone on SEAL ops. I suggest you study Captain Boland's training and background. That should change your prejudicial mind."

"Ma'am, it's not prejudice. I'm concerned for a woman's well-being." Jake's mouth thinned. He felt the beginnings of real threat to him by taking the op. He and Morgan had a challenging relationship. He was positive Stevenson knew nothing of their personal history. Otherwise, they would never have thrown them together in this op.

"Regardless of her gender, Lieutenant,

you should be concerned for your partner. Sniping is an art as much as experience to remain hidden so you can take out your target."

His palms grew damp, his heart pounding with adrenaline as it flooded his body. "I take care of my *men,* ma'am. They are my priority."

"Taking care of your personnel is expected of every officer. Well, this time, it's a woman, Lieutenant. And I can tell by the way you're looking at me that you think you just landed on Mars. Get over it. This is the twenty-first century, and there is a group of women out there who have been in combat for the last three years in Operation Shadow Warriors, Lieutenant. A very dark, deep SOCOM-produced experiment to see if women could handle combat beside their male counterparts." She leaned forward, her voice a rasp. "They've been proving it, Lieutenant. There are other SEAL teams that Captain Boland has been working with for the past three years. Successfully, I might add."

Mind spinning, Jake sat back, stunned. SEAL units were small and a tight-knit family. "I've been a SEAL for seven years," he challenged strongly, "and I've never heard anything about a woman assigned to a platoon for combat purposes." If there had

been a woman assigned to certain SEAL
units, word would have gotten around, for
damned sure. Jake saw the General's face
grow even harder, if that was possible. Sweat
dribbled down the sides of his ribs. He felt
under fire, in a combat situation.

"We've looked at your record. You've had
women assigned to your team on several
patrols, Lieutenant. They were there as a
linguist, an 18 Delta medic and a forensics
and FBI specialist. Were these not direct action missions?"

Jake felt trapped. He did remember
women being assigned. But that was different. "That wasn't as a principal shooter,
ma'am."

"The missions these women were assigned
to illustrate each woman was shot at and all
successfully returned fire, Lieutenant. The
selection of 'principal' members is beyond
your pay grade. Are you telling me that you
are refusing this op?"

"No, ma'am."

"Good to hear. I want your word, Lieutenant, that you will not treat Captain Boland
in a prejudicial manner. She's equally qualified as you."

Stunned, Jake jerked a look down at the
open file on his lap. He hadn't had time to
read anything about Morgan's sniper back-

ground. He didn't even know she had one. He knew she'd gotten a major in civil engineering and a minor in linguistics back at Annapolis in Pashto, but that was all. Working his mouth, sweat forming on his upper lip, he muttered, "I'll do my best, ma'am."

"That's not good enough, Lieutenant. And you damn well know it."

Stevenson's growling voice stunned him into silence. Jake sat stiffly, holding her glare. She was a General. He was a lowly Lieutenant. Refusing this op would end his career. "Yes, ma'am. I won't have a problem with Captain Boland being my sniper partner."

"You sure?" She drilled him with an intent look.

Jake felt as if she had X-ray vision, staring holes through him. His career was far more important to him than arguing women were weak to this Army General. The SEALs were his family; the men, his brothers. Maybe not by birth, but they'd spilled blood among one another on too many occasions. Mouth pursed, he gave her a crisp nod. "It won't be a problem, ma'am. I'll make it work."

Her nostrils flared as she sat up. "By God, you'd better, Lieutenant Ramsey. Or I'll have your career. This op is not about you. It's got a lot of other ramifications you aren't even aware of. And if other SEAL platoons can work well with Captain Boland, so can you. Dismissed."

Morgan had just given the waiter her menu choices when Jake Ramsey, in civilian clothes, entered the restaurant. It was 2200, or ten at night. She groaned. She'd hoped not to meet him until 0900 tomorrow morning.

As Morgan sat at the table for two in the corner of the busy hotel restaurant, she couldn't stop her heart from expanding with old, warm feelings. Jake was dressed in a light blue short-sleeve shirt, tan chinos and loafers. Even twenty feet away, she could tell he was a SEAL. He carried himself with a well-earned confidence, his shoulders back, his gaze always roving slowly around an area, checking it out. His black hair gleamed, indicating he'd probably just taken a shower. There was no question, he was a damned good-looking man. He was in control, powerful and intense.

Morgan's mouth quirked as his gaze moved her way. And then his eyes locked on hers. Surprise flared in his gray eyes for a split second, and then that hard, unreadable SEAL game face dropped into place.

She smiled to herself as she picked up the delicate china coffee cup in both hands and took a sip. Now what was he going to do? Pretend he didn't see her and get the maître d' to seat him on the other side of the room so he wouldn't have to talk to her? Or would he bite the bullet and invite himself to her table? Morgan wished Jake would disappear to the other side of the room. But when the maître d' approached, he pointed toward her table.

Friggin' great. She was barely awake, her lack of sleep so deep she was barely functioning mentally. Never mind emotionally. She forced herself to try to be more alert.

"Mind if I join you?" Jake asked.

Morgan said, "Sit down."

The maître d' left the menu with him after he'd taken a chair and sat down. Morgan stared across the table at Jake. Hell, if they didn't share such an awful history between them, she'd find herself drawn to the SEAL officer. His square face had been recently shaved, and that dangerous feeling that was always around him appealed powerfully to her.

"You look tired," Jake observed, trying to find some safe ground. Though he did notice, too, how beautiful Morgan was. She had on a pale lilac pant-suit and cream-colored tee with a dark purple scarf around her shoulders. Jake had forgotten just how she could take his breath away. Her hair lay like a gleaming red cloak about her proud shoulders. Morgan never wore makeup, but she never had to. Her green eyes were large and well spaced with thick red lashes to frame them. But he saw shadows beneath those eyes, and whether he wanted to or not, he became concerned for her.

"I just got hauled off an op in the Hindu Kush to make this meeting," she said. "Don't worry. I'm up for our mission."

His nerves nettled as he forced himself to look down at the menu. Jake still wanted her, dammit. His heart did, too, because a ribbon of happiness soared through him. He scowled, focused on the menu. "I was making conversation," he told her, lifting his chin and meeting her flat stare.

Morgan had the most arresting eyes he'd ever encountered. Jake could feel himself being lured into their depths, the forest-green mixed with glimmers of willow-green color. He remembered hotly that as they made love, there would be gold highlights dappled throughout them. Shifting uncomfortably, Jake felt himself responding to her, much as he wanted to remain aloof.

"You just came off an op? Where?"

"Same area where we met December, two years ago." It had changed Morgan's life in ways Jake would never find out about. In one way, it broke her heart and she felt guilty. In another, there was an unbridge-able chasm between them.

Ouch. Damn. Jake scowled, decided on something simple and straightforward to eat. The waiter came over and took his order for a hamburger and fries. He folded his hands, sensing how tense she was. Morgan's gaze was wary. And that delicious mouth he'd tasted and kissed was pursed. "Did you hitch a C-5 out of Bagram?"

"Yes." Morgan tried not to be swayed by Jake, but dammit, the toughest thing to do was ignore his blatant maleness. He was a man's man, a SEAL, and they had male charisma to burn. The expression in his gray eyes was neutral. She saw him struggling to try to find some purchase with her that wasn't argumentative or threatening. Truth be known, she was too tired to pick a fight with him. "I'm whipped," she admitted, sliding her long fingers around the china cup.

"Flights halfway around the world will do that to you," Jake agreed, keeping the edge out of his tone. "In fact, you don't look quite awake."

Snorting, Morgan sipped her coffee. "Understatement. I feel beat-up. As soon as I left my meeting with General Houston, I came over here and crashed and burned." She looked at the watch on her wrist. "I've slept since 1000 and it's 2200."

"You need another twenty-four hours of downtime to get your body and mind back on the same page," Jake agreed. In fact, because Morgan was exhausted, her normal defenses weren't in place. And for that, he breathed a sigh of relief. Anything he'd ever heard about red-haired women applied to Morgan ten times over. She was a risk taker, hotheaded and no-nonsense. Her feistiness had always drawn him. Even now.

The waiter brought over Morgan's meal, a hamburger and a large plate of French fries. She thanked him, and he left. She saw him eyeing her food. Good God, why did the man have to have such a sensual mouth? Morgan remembered kissing that mouth. He was such a damn good lover, a thoughtful one, despite how they fought outside the bedroom. That was the past. She had to let it go. Seeing Jake stare at the stack of hot French fries, she pushed the plate toward the middle of the table.

"Go on. I know how much you like them."

"Guilty," Jake admitted, grinning sheepishly and thanking her. She handed him the bottle of ketchup, knowing that was how he liked his fries. "Been six months since I tasted real French fries."

She fixed her hamburger, watching Jake through her lashes. "You just get back from Afghanistan and you're on PRODEV, professional development, with your platoon now?"

"Yes, I was supposed to be on my sixty days of leave." Jake's face melted with pleasure as he ate the first few fries. The man was so easy to read when he dropped his SEAL game face. He sat back in the chair, his eyes shuttering closed as he relished and appreciated the food. Some of Morgan's testiness dissolved.

Morgan understood that the SEALs pined for real American junk food when they were in their six-month rotation into a combat zone. As she bit into the juicy hamburger, she knew six months in combat wore on everyone. SEALs didn't go into any area that wasn't life threatening. Since 9/11, sixty SEALs had died in combat. Far too many, but it attested to the sheer dangerousness in their work. They were frontline warriors, black-ops commandos who hunted down the enemy to make this world a safer place for all Americans.

"Gawd," Ramsey whispered, opening his eyes, "who knew French fries could taste so damned good?" He reached for more.

"The hamburger is to die for, too."

Jake nodded. "Mine's coming." He met and held her green gaze. For once, there was no animosity in Morgan's stare. He absorbed the peaceful moment between them. God knew, there were never many. He wondered how they were ever going to get along on a sniper op. Would she be able to put her sword away? Could he? But tonight, Jake didn't want to address those concerns with Morgan. And he sure as hell wasn't going to bring it up tomorrow morning at the briefing with the two Generals, either.

"Here," Morgan muttered, cutting her hamburger in half. "Get some good food into your stomach." She handed half of it to him.

Surprised and pleased, Jake took the proffered hamburger. "Thanks . . ." Their fingers briefly met. The shock, the pleasure running up his fingers, amazed him. Trying not to be swayed by it, he bit eagerly into the hamburger. Maybe, just maybe, Morgan wasn't going to be hard to work with after all. It didn't necessarily mean the war between them was over.

CHAPTER THREE

Morgan girded herself for an intense hour of briefing on Operation Peregrine. Jake Ramsey sat opposite of her at a rectangular maple table in a large room deep in the bowels of the Pentagon. The two Generals arrived precisely at 0900. Both officers snapped to attention when they walked into the room.

"At ease," Maya Stevenson told them with a wave of her hand. She sat at one end of the table, Mike Houston at the other. Houston placed his leather briefcase on the table and opened it up.

"Here's the mission," he told them, distributing a thick red plastic folder to each of them.

Morgan saw an Army Sergeant, a woman with blond hair, enter with a tray that held a large pot of coffee, four white mugs, sugar, cream and a plate of Oreo cookies. She smiled to herself, knowing that General

Stevenson was addicted to Oreos. Even at 0900.

After the door closed, leaving the four of them in the soundproof, lead-lined room, Morgan tried to relax. She cast a quick look over at Jake. He was handsome, unreadable, his gray eyes somewhat narrowed. Tension radiated from him, but she didn't see it in his face.

Morgan wondered if he'd argued against her being on the mission. He considered women weak and incapable. If Jake had, there was no outward sign. Glancing at Maya, whom she knew very well because of Operation Shadow Warriors, Morgan saw the General was focused on thumbing through the briefing. At fifty-four, she was one of the youngest women ever to achieve the rank of General.

"All right," Maya said, "let's go to page five."

Morgan opened the red briefing folder, noting it was top secret.

Houston poured coffee for everyone and passed it around. "The cookies are for General Stevenson," he intoned, a grin coming to his face. "Off-limits to the rest of us non-Oreo lovers."

Maya smiled briefly. "Roger that."

Morgan couldn't help a small chuckle.

Right then, Jake looked up, confused, glancing first at Maya and then over at her for some explanation. None was forthcoming as Mike Houston picked up the plate and set it near the General's left hand.

Jake shifted uncomfortably, which made her wonder how he'd reacted to knowing she was his sniper partner. Sniper teams could go out in the field as a single operator, or as a twosome, depending on the mission. She couldn't read into his bloodshot gray eyes. Jake must not have gotten much sleep last night.

Houston looked over at Maya. "General Stevenson, want to tell them why this op has been initiated?"

Maya nodded, folded her hands over the briefing. She pinned both officers with an intense look. "Sangar Khogani is an opium warlord in Afghanistan. He's chief of the Hill tribe, and they are at war with the Shinwari tribe, next door. We couldn't care less about this except that the Shinwari are under our government's protection. We've given them millions of dollars in the past few years because they asked for our help. They want infrastructure, schools, medical clinics and help in creating a viable economy for the four-hundred-thousand strong in their tribe.

"The biggest reason why we're involved with them is that the Khyber Pass, between Pakistan and Afghanistan, occurs in their territory. They are the front door to all al Qaeda coming from Pakistan into their country. They've promised to give us intel, and they have. They are Pashtuns who live by a fifteen-hundred-year-old code where your word is your bond."

Jake nodded. He slipped a glance over at Morgan. She had turned her chair, fully facing General Stevenson. Maybe he should, too? A sign of respect?

"Questions?" Stevenson demanded.

Jake said, "Ma'am, it's my understanding, after being assigned to that region of the Hindu Kush, Sangar Khogani is a menace to everyone in the area." Jake opened his hands. "The Shinwari call him the Phantom. He's got two hundred men on horseback and literally strikes and hides in one of those thousands of caves in those mountains. This is the same man we're talking about?"

Maya looked pleased. "Yes, it is, Lieutenant Ramsey."

Jake relaxed a little, the General's smile easing some of his inner tension.

"But let's move forward to three months ago. Turn to page ten. You'll see a map."

Jake turned to the map, instantly recognizing the village of Margha. It was the same one where he and his team had holed up to wait out a blizzard two years ago in December. Heat tunneled through him. It was the village where he'd unexpectedly met Morgan. They'd shared three days of incredible sex and intimacy. Until he'd opened his big mouth about women being weak and everything had gone to hell in a handbasket. Gulping, Jake didn't dare look over at Morgan. She had to be thinking the same thing. *Damned karma . . .*

"Margha," Maya said, jabbing her index finger at it, "had a hundred and fifty Shinwari men, women and children. All pro-American. Captain Boland was in that village along with an Army Special Forces team a year ago. They were there rendering medical aid to the populace for five days and were going to leave the next day. Khogani descended at dusk and attacked the village." Her voice lowered. "The Special Forces team tried to protect the villagers, but it was eleven people against an estimated two hundred riders on horseback. Even they can't buck odds like that. And it was impossible to bomb the village with a drone or fighter jet or they would end up killing the very people we were trying to protect from

Khogani."

Maya gestured toward Morgan. "Captain Boland had a couple of guns in that fight, Lieutenant Ramsey. What you don't know is that the Special Forces team had to evacuate and hightail it to a rally point to be lifted out by the Night Stalkers MH-47 helicopter. Every person in that team was more or less wounded. So was Captain Boland. They fought until they ran out of ammunition, and only then did they run for their lives."

Jake sucked in a quiet breath, twisting a look toward Morgan. She refused to look at him, her attention on her clasped hands in her lap. His heart squeezed with pain for her. Unconsciously, Jake rubbed his chest, remaining silent but wrestling with unexpected emotions about her being wounded.

"The next day," Maya went on, "Captain Boland returned with reinforcements, but the damage had already been done. When Captain Boland landed with two SEAL teams and two Special Forces teams, they found a hundred and fifty people murdered." Her voice lowered even more. "Khogani slaughtered innocent people because the elders of the village had refused to allow opium transport through their valley. This is why we're initiating this op. We

51

feel it's best to send in a sniper team. And that's the two of you. You will have time on target for as long as it takes. Snipers know how to stalk. And they know how to track and be patient in finding someone like Khogani. Questions?"

"This is a SEAL op?" Ramsey demanded.

Houston said, "Yes, but you'll have any other military assets available you need via GPS satellite and/or radio communications. Camp Bravo, an FOB, has a squadron of Apaches on standby, a medevac squadron, the CIA is there with drones and so are a number of Special Forces teams. There are a number of Operation Shadow Warrior women combat operators who are already assigned to some of these teams."

Jake asked, "Who's my SEAL contact? Is he out of Camp Bravo or J-bad, Jalalabad?"

"Lieutenant Ramsey, let's starting thinking plural here, shall we?" Maya met his startled look. "You said 'my contact.' It should have been *our* contact."

Realizing his mistake, Jake nodded. "My apologies, ma'am. I meant *our.*"

Morgan almost felt sorry for Jake. He wasn't about to back up on a General, man or woman. He'd backed up on her in many a furious argument about women being weak. She saw the banked anger and confusion in his eyes for a moment, but being a SEAL, he moved on to the next important item.

"Who's running radio comms?" Jake asked.

"Captain Boland will," Mike Houston said. "She's taken SEAL schooling in every kind of communications gear you presently utilize."

Relief sizzled through Jake, because that was not his specialty. "That's good to know," he murmured, lifting his gaze and meeting Morgan's cool green eyes. He'd leafed through the report last night and seen her impressive list of training. If Morgan wasn't in Afghanistan with black-ops teams, she was stateside getting more training. He respected her for that. And it could save their lives out in the field.

"You're going to be working with Lieutenant-Commander Viera out of J-bad," Houston said.

More relief showered through Jake. He might be forced to have a woman on this mission, but at least he had a solid SEAL officer supporting it. "Yes, sir. He's the best." And Julio Viera, or Vero, his nickname in the SEALs, was a badass Puerto Rican from the slums who had worked his way up through the ranks. He was a mustang,

53

someone who started out as an enlisted person but eventually got to officer's school. With a decade of experience behind him, Vero's reputation in the community was as one of the best SEAL planners in the business. Vero would have their back, and Jake was grateful. His karma had just turned into dharma.

Houston looked at his watch. "You're wheels up at 1100 from Andrews. You'll be hopping a C-130 flight to Travis Air Force Base, California. From there, you'll fly across the Pacific and get a hop on a C-5 heading for Hawaii. You'll stay overnight at the Schofield Army barracks in Honolulu. The next morning, you'll grab another C-5 flight heading into Bagram Air Base north of Kabul, Afghanistan. From there, you'll meet Captain Khalid Shaheen, U.S. Army. He's an Apache combat pilot, but works closely with the Black Jaguar Squadron out of Camp Bravo. He'll fly you into J-bad. From there, the Night Stalkers will drop you into the valley where you'll meet our ground asset, Reza."

"Afghan local?" Jake wondered.

"He's more than that." Morgan spoke up, her quiet voice carrying emotion behind it. She quickly looked at General Houston, apology in her expression. She shouldn't have interrupted a briefing.

"Go on," Houston said, unruffled by her comment.

"Thank you, sir." Morgan turned her attention to Jake. "Reza is a thirty-five-year-old Afghan from the Shinwari tribe. He's worked with SEALs and Special Forces over the last seven years. He's pro-American." Her voice caught, and she cleared her throat, getting ahold of escaping emotions. When she spoke again, Morgan's voice was husky. "Reza lived in the village of Margha that Khogani attacked. The only reason he lived was because he was out with another SEAL team twenty miles south of the village at the time it was attacked."

"I see," Jake murmured. But maybe he didn't. He could have sworn he saw moisture come to Morgan's eyes. For just a split second. Her lips, full and soft, twisted. He knew that gesture. She was trying to hide emotions. And when she tucked her lower lip between her teeth for a second, Jake knew there was a lot more to this story.

"Reza," Morgan added, her voice low, "is the soul of Islamic kindness. He lives the Koran as it should be. He's kind, gentle and helps others. He was beloved by everyone in Margha. He was responsible for bringing in the Special Forces and getting medical help for the children seven years ago." Morgan blinked, pushing the tears away. She forced herself to go on. "He lost his wife and five children in the attack." Bowing her head, she muttered, "I couldn't even save one of his children. . . ."

An unexpected lump formed in Jake's throat. He swallowed a few times. There was pain mirrored in Morgan's face, even though the wall of red hair hid most of her expression from him. This time, she wasn't trying to hide anything in spite of the fact there were two Generals present. Her cheeks had gone pale.

Jake found himself wanting to reach out, touch Morgan's tightly gripped hands on the table. But he remained still, buffeted by her grief. And that was probably how she ended up getting injured during the attack, trying to rescue Reza's kids. She loved children with a passion.

Old memories began to rise in him. God, he had to contain them. He couldn't afford to relive that two years back at the Academy when they'd been lovers. It had been a mixture of incredible happiness, brutal sorrow and serrating pain.

"War sucks," Maya agreed in a quiet tone. "You did what you could. Sometimes, it's not enough, Captain."

Morgan nodded, blinking away unshed tears. "Yes, ma'am, you're right."

Jake saw the natural warmth between Maya Stevenson and Morgan. Clearly, they knew each other very well. For a moment, he wondered if the General was Morgan's sponsor. Every young officer hoped that a higher-ranking officer would take them under their wing and give them opportunities other officers would never get. They were groomed for leadership and put on a fast track for higher rank and responsibility. Yes, he would bet his right hand Stevenson was her sponsor and mentor. "Any other questions?" Houston demanded.

"No, sir," Morgan said.

"No, sir," Jake said.

"Good hunting out there," Maya told them, meaning it as she rose.

Both officers leaped to their feet, coming to attention.

"At ease," Houston murmured, standing and placing two folders into his briefcase. The other two would go with the snipers. "Do yourself a favor and take advantage of the chow in the Pentagon cafeteria." He smiled a little. "Pig out on hamburgers and French fries. Where you're going, there won't be any for a damn long time until you nail this son of a bitch. Stay safe out there."

Morgan smiled at the tall, broad-shouldered General. "Thank you, sir. We will."

"Makes two of us," Jake said, standing aside to allow General Stevenson by him.

"Better load up on Butterfingers," Maya called over her shoulder to Morgan as she left.

Morgan grinned, especially as Jake cocked his head. He knew her favorite candy was Butterfinger. For a moment, she felt happy. An emotion she hadn't felt since . . . Morgan's smile faded. She picked up her black leather purse and bucket hat. That spark of happiness died quickly in the wake of a wall of grief and loss. Her husband, SEAL Lieutenant Mark Evans, had been killed by Khogani five years earlier. She had two good reasons to hunt Khogani down, once and for all.

Jake gestured for her to leave the room first, his hand on the doorknob. His whole body responded when she managed a slight smile of thanks. Morgan's face and those mesmerizing green eyes of hers radiated such intimate warmth. It was a peek into the real Morgan when she didn't have to maintain officer and military decorum.

Morgan hesitated in the outer office where the secretary was busy. Jake was her sniper partner, and she should wait for him. A part of her wanted to run away as fast as she could. That was the wounded woman in her. The rest of her, the military officer, knew they needed time to go over the op, look at it, figure out the details, fill in any holes that could be found in it and get on the same page with the mission — together.

When Jake emerged, hat in hand, she felt a rush of heat blossom deep inside her. Startled by it, Morgan thought that two years would have ended their tempestuous on-again, off-again relationship. She pursed her lips as he walked up to her. It hadn't.

Morgan could feel raw male energy radiating off him like invisible sunlight. Did he realize how damned charismatic and sexy he was? She didn't think so. Jake's whole life, his entire focus, was about his SEAL fraternity. He never wanted a serious personal relationship standing between him and his SEAL career. A roll in a bed was fine with him, but he was Mr. No Strings Attached. As she'd found out too late, in her third year at Annapolis. Jake Ramsey had devastated her, sheared her world in half and never looked back. Never apologized. She should know better. How many times had she fallen for him? Twice. Twice too many times.

"Ready to rock it out?" he asked her quietly, looking down into her eyes.

"Funny you should use that word," she murmured, turning. It was a favorite SEAL saying when live fire or an attack was just about to be initiated against an enemy. "Let's go chow down."

CHAPTER FOUR

Jake sat opposite Morgan at one of the many lunch tables in the cafeteria. Most uniformed personnel who came in at this hour of the morning went for coffee, doughnuts or rolls. They sat with huge platters of hamburgers and French fries, plus a Pepsi on the side. Jet lag did wonders for the digestion.

"I don't know where to start with you, Morgan," Jake admitted.

"Makes two of us. I didn't know you were selected for this mission, either. It was a shock."

He watched her eat, and his lower body tightened, which didn't make him happy. Taking a deep breath, he decided to ignore their history together. And there was plenty of time in the next two days to get clear on the op. "I'm sorry for what happened to you at that Afghan village. It had to be tough."

The vibration of his voice, that whiskey

tone of his, sent a keening ache through her. Morgan lifted her head and met his tender gray gaze. Jake was really trying to be humble and caring. On occasion he could be so damn warm and persuasive, moving her from ice to fire.

She gave him a hard look. "Let's stick to business, Ramsey. It's the only place I want to be with you. I don't want to discuss that attack." It was too painful for her. She'd break down in tears, something Jake had never seen her do. And Morgan wasn't about to bare her soul to him in, of all places, the Pentagon cafeteria.

Jake sat back, his mouth tightening. His gray eyes going glacial as he stared into her stubborn-looking face. "This *is* business," he ground out. "I didn't know you were a sniper. When did you get your training?"

"Three years ago."

"As part of Operation Shadow Warriors?" He searched, trying to piece her training. Oh, he'd read her résumé, but he wanted a hell of a lot more.

"Yes, ten of the women from Shadow Warriors were sent to SEAL sniper school. Five made it through." Her heart fluttered, and she hated herself for wanting Jake. She could see through him like glass. He was twisting in the wind, not sure how to handle or approach her.

"Did either of your parents hunt?"

Mouth quirking, Morgan picked up a fry. "Since when did you ever want to know anything about my home life, Ramsey? Funny, you had a year at Annapolis to find out everything you ever wanted to know about me. But you never asked me once about my family."

He winced.

Served him right. Would Jake ever grow up? He was twenty-nine, same age as her. And he had the personal irresponsibility of a fifteen-year-old hormone-driven teenager. Relationships meant nothing to him. She'd meant nothing to him outside of the bed. Even if Jake hadn't grown up, Morgan had.

Holding up his hands, he rasped, "Look, that was a long time ago. I've changed." He smarted beneath her accusations. Morgan didn't know he'd married to settle down to raise a family.

"Really?" The word came out filled with derision.

"I'm waving a white flag. Can I surrender and we talk about the mission?" It was then Jake began to understand the depth of hurt he'd caused Morgan in the past. She couldn't hide anything from him, no matter how hard she tried. Running his fingers through his short hair in frustration, Jake sat back, staring at her.

"A SEAL surrendering." Morgan smiled a little, but it didn't reach her eyes. "Jake, you always say the right thing at the right time. The problem is, it doesn't stick for long. You're like the Velcro you use on your gear. Sticks when you want it to, rips off when you no longer need it."

"I've changed, Morgan."

She heard an edge to his voice, his eyes going a slate-gray. That color meant he was emotionally upset about something. Her, most likely. Morgan took the last bite of the delicious hamburger and wiped her fingers on a nearby paper napkin. "You haven't changed since I met you at Annapolis, Jake."

He shrugged his broad shoulders. "Well, I guess you're going to have to find out differently on this op, then." He paused for a moment. "Look, I don't even know anything other than you're a sniper. General Stevenson seems to think you're very good at it." He searched her hooded eyes. "Can we at least talk about that?"

"Sure," she said, wadding up the napkin and dropping it on her plate. "Since becoming a qualified sniper, I've been out nine months out of every year with either SEAL or Special Forces teams in Afghanistan. I would be assigned when a team lost one of their two snipers and would take over that position as a straphanger."

"You asked to go along? I'm trying to understand how this top secret Operation Shadow Warriors works."

She sat back, arms across her chest. "I was asked to volunteer for it the second year I was assistant commanding officer of a Marine Corps company in Kandahar."

Surprised, Jake's brows rose. "You'd always wanted to fill a billet in a combat company."

"Yes, and I got my wish." Morgan hitched a shoulder. "In part, it was because I had four years of Pashtun language under my belt. My CO, Captain Davis, was desperate for anyone other than an Afghan terp, interpreter, he had to use to speak to the elders. He was trying to make serious headway with a number of villages, and he felt the interpreter was not giving him accurate info."

"So, your minor in linguistics landed you in Kandahar?" he said, almost to himself.

"Yes. And when Davis found out I was a damn good executive officer for the company, he was a happy man. He gave me more and more responsibility. By the end of my first year I was running missions with the recon Marines. I'd rather be out in the field than in a stuffy tent at a hundred and ten degrees. At least outside, you can breathe in fresh, hot air instead."

He smiled a little, nodding. "You always wanted combat."

"I wanted a shot at what I knew I'd be good at, that's all."

"You must have been."

"Davis gave me rave reports for my leadership ability. I had three months left in my second tour when I was invited to volunteer for Operation Shadow Warriors."

"So, what does this operation do?"

"It takes volunteer officer or enlisted women who want to be in combat and they're trained up for it. Then a woman is rotated into a SOF team, special operations forces."

He shook his head. "You were with SEAL teams? I never heard anything about it."

Morgan rolled her eyes. "You weren't supposed to, Ramsey. It was, after all, top secret. The men in that platoon signed their lives away legally on paper to the Pentagon, never to breathe a word of it."

"Well, it's sure as hell worked." He couldn't help but look at her left hand. No wedding ring, though he didn't expect to see one. People in combat never wore jewelry. It could get hung up on a rifle and screw things up in a damned hurry. This didn't mean she wasn't married. He couldn't ask. Morgan was prickly with him anyway, and he couldn't blame her. He didn't deserve much respect for what he'd done to her. He'd been a first-class bastard. But damn, she was hot-headed, and when she got wound up, he felt overwhelmed by her intense, focused anger at him.

Morgan allowed her arms to drop to her sides. "My gear is in Hawaii, at the Army barracks. I want to use my sniper rifle on this mission."

Jake nodded. In a sniper op, there was one sniper rifle shared by both snipers. The other team member always had another weapon on him — or her, in this case — to protect the sniper and play rearguard action if they were discovered. "Okay. I'll take an M-4 with a grenade launcher on it with me."

"Good choice. Grenades come in handy upon occasion."

"Oh? You found that out?"

She grinned wickedly. "Yeah, but that's a story for another day. I've got a SIG Sauer 9 mm pistol. I'm assuming you're bringing yours along, too?"

His mouth dropped open, and just as quickly, he snapped it shut. "How in the hell did you get your hands on a SIG?" It was a special German pistol made only for active-duty SEALs. He saw her grow sad for a moment.

"It was a gift," Morgan admitted in a voice riddled with barely held emotions. "The Commander in charge of the SEAL squadron approved the gift to be given to me. He said I'd earned it even though I wasn't a SEAL." Her voice dropped, a hint of sadness in it. "He said I was a SEAL by proxy."

"That's —" Jake struggled for words "— a hell of a gift."

"It saved my life a few times. Every time it does, I write to the Commander and thank him all over again. He gets a chuckle out of it."

Morgan had always wanted to head into danger. It was in her genes. Now, from what she was saying, and Jake did believe her, she was in combat most of the time. "Look, let's get over to Andrews. I've got my gear in the Jeep, and I need to stow it on that Herky Jerky, a C-130, we're taking at 1100."

Nodding, Morgan pushed the chair away and stood. "I'm going back to the hotel and jumping in my SEAL work uniform and boots. I'll meet you at Andrews at noon."

"Sounds good," Jake said, standing there, feeling a bit overwhelmed. She was a woman. And she carried a SIG. And she was working in SEAL teams! Damn, what was the world coming to?

Picking up his cover, he left the cafeteria. No doubt, a lot had happened to Morgan, and she was closed-mouthed about it. If she was going to be his sniper partner, he needed to know a hell of a lot more, because right now, he didn't trust her with his back in a firefight.

Morgan had taken the opportunity to sleep, no matter how noisy and loud the aircraft around her was. She'd hung up her hammock in the rear of the C-130 and dozed off. By the time they landed in Honolulu, Hawaii, it was late afternoon because of time-zone changes.

Jake had slept a lot but had also worked on his Toughbook laptop, which every SEAL officer carried with him. When Morgan awoke, she figured he was probably trying to check up on her, find out what she was made of. Jake had such little belief a woman could be strong, resourceful or half as smart as he was.

As they walked into the terminal and requisitioned a military vehicle to drive to the BOQ, he seemed deep in thought.

They located the dark olive-green car in

the black asphalt parking lot; Morgan breathed in the warm, moist air. "I love Hawaii. It's one of my favorite places on earth."

Jake smiled a little, responding to her unexpected spontaneity. This was the Morgan he knew from his Annapolis days, and he wanted to see more of that side to her. But would she reveal herself? To do that she had to trust him. Not an easy issue to resolve in two days' time. Not with their spotty record. "They've got a nice pool at the BOQ."

"I want to grab my swimsuit out of my duffel bag and head for the beach." She gave him a droll look. "You're a SEAL. Water's your home."

"Is that an invite to come along?" His hopes rose. Maybe another six hours of sleep had put her in a better mood. The serious look on her face melted his heart. He wanted her so damn bad.

"Up to you. After all these flights, murderous jet lag, I need to move into Mom Ocean's arms and just be."

"I'll come along in case some nasty undertow starts to drag you away. Or some shark decides to think you're a delicious dessert."

She shook her head as she opened the driver's-side door on the military car.

Reaching in, Morgan sprung the trunk open so they could put all of his equipment, including his duffel bag, into it. "You SEALs own the water. But somehow, Ramsey, I don't need any rescuing or protecting." She slid into the car.

Jake felt his spirit lift a little. Morgan was more like her old self. The woman he knew. The woman who loved so damned hotly that he felt scalded inside and out by her raw sensuality. Climbing into the car, he said, "Maybe you'll have to rescue me, then."

She threw her head back, husky laughter rolling out of her. God, how he'd missed that laugh. And yet, Jake knew she was an emotional minefield. As badly as he wanted her to surrender to him, he knew she didn't dare. He couldn't break her heart the way he knew he would. Not ever.

"Mmm, I've died and gone to heaven," Morgan sighed, the warm ocean water moving slowly around her. She had swum out beyond the breakers with Jake, floating on her back. The sun was lower in the sky, dapples of light dancing around on the smooth, turquoise water.

Sharks were big in these waters. And by floating on her back, Morgan would look like a sea turtle to one of them. "The water was a good choice."

Barely opening one eye, Morgan saw Jake treading water nearby. He hadn't shaved since this morning, and the dark growth made him look dangerous in a sexy kind of way. "Your dad was a SEAL."

Jake nodded. "Yes, he was."

His shoulders were incredibly broad, tightly muscled, his chest darkly haired and well sprung. Morgan remembered his body as if it were yesterday, much to her consternation.

"Did he teach you a love of water, I wonder?" The water soothed her aggravation and always having to be on guard against Jake. The warmth lulled her, made her feel safe.

"No. I taught myself to swim. My father wasn't around much." He had died when he was twenty, killed by an enemy in a foreign land, but Jake had never told Morgan. Jake allowed the wave to push him closer to her. The dark purple bathing suit was one piece, but on her body, it made her look like a Titian or Raphael woman.

Morgan had a tall, proud frame. She was all legs, and Jake watched the water flowing sensually across them. Frowning, he saw what he thought were several new, pink

72

scars on her left, upper thigh. He couldn't see much, because most of the scarring was below the water surface. Were these the injuries she'd gotten when Khogani had attacked that Afghan village? He didn't like to think her beautiful flesh was scarred. Or that she'd suffered pain, because he'd made her suffer enough. Morgan didn't deserve it. She was a good person with a trusting heart. Well, she *had* been trusting. . . . He'd taught her to trust no man.

Lifting her head, Morgan forced her legs down into the water, gracefully moving her arms outward to steady herself. Jake was close and terribly handsome, the water running off in rivulets down his face to his neck and shoulders. His eyes went slate-gray again, as if realizing her question had probably dug up a lot of unwanted and hurtful memories from the past.

Morgan wanted to reach out and simply rest her hand on his shoulder and tell him it was all right. In some ways, Jake had been born behind the eight ball, and he'd had to struggle all his life for everything he'd earned.

A wave splashed her, and she wiped the stinging salt out of her eyes. Jake continued to be a big SEAL guard dog. "You think a Big White's gonna see me as a turtle out here, don't you?"

His mouth drew into a hesitant grin. "Something like that."

Shaking her head, she said, "Ramsey, you're a piece of work. You really are."

"What? Can't I make sure you can enjoy your swim? What's wrong with being watchful? There have been plenty of shark attacks on the beaches of the Hawaiian Islands."

Spitting out water she'd accidentally swallowed, Morgan shook her head. "Someday, I hope you stop being so damned overprotective, Jake. You were that way with me at Annapolis. You never thought I could take care of myself once because I was a woman."

"Look, I don't want to argue with you, Morgan. We got a job to do."

The growl in his tone was a warning. His face went blank and unreadable, a glitter in his icy gray eyes. "That's right — we do have to get along or we're both dead meat out there on some godforsaken, ass-freezing Afghan mountain." Morgan lifted her hand and flung off beads of water and pushed the wet strands off her face. "Your mother contracted multiple sclerosis when you were ten years old. I remember you were the one saddled with being her caregiver until you were eighteen." Her voice lowered with feeling. "Jake, I know you loved your mother, but you grew up fast in that family because your father was never there. You took care of her until she died when you'd just graduated high school." She noticed how his eyes went stormy. Morgan gave him a pleading look. "You think all women are weak because your mother was weak. You think because you had to take care of her 24/7, you have to burden yourself thinking you have to take care of me out here. You don't, Jake. You don't. . . ."

CHAPTER FIVE

They had just returned to the BOQ after having a Thai dinner at Morgan's favorite restaurant in Honolulu. The moon was rising in the east, the Pacific Ocean gleaming with a pale corridor of light across the darkened ocean. Jake put the car in Park, the low sulfur lighting revealing a crowded parking lot in back of the building. His hands tightened on the steering wheel for a moment. It was time.

Morgan released her safety belt when he said, "We need to talk."

When Jake's voice lowered to that intimate growl, she couldn't refuse to look at him. Her heart skidded in her breast. As Morgan turned and met his shadowy gaze, he placed one arm across the back of the seat, his hand less than an inch from her shoulder.

"What do you want to talk about?"

Jake compressed his lips. He moved his fingers lightly across her shoulder. It was the first time he'd touched her in two years. "There are some things we need to discuss. Get right between us. We're going down-range tomorrow morning, and we have to be focused."

"Yes," she admitted, her flesh needy as his calloused fingers barely brushed her blouse. Though aching to kiss him, to rekindle what they'd had before, Morgan fought herself. Jake would walk away again, like he always did. "What do you want to talk about?"

"Us," he said huskily, seeing confusion in her green eyes. "You've had an apology coming from me for nine years. Back when we were at Annapolis together. We were twenty years old then."

His fingers came to rest on her shoulder, as if to steady her in some small way for what he was about to say. With a mix of anguish and uncertainty in his gray eyes, he was being vulnerable with her. The only time she'd ever seen him like this was when they'd made love.

"For what?" Morgan managed, her voice tight with defensiveness.

Taking an uneven breath, Jake plunged in. "Your miscarriage . . ."

Bowing her head, Morgan shut her eyes, unable to look at him. She'd not seen this one coming. Her heart squeezed with old pain. His fingers became more firm on her shoulder. Steadying. "What about it?" she said in a broken whisper.

"Neither of us wanted it to happen. It wasn't anyone's fault." His mouth thinned, and Jake forced himself to go on. "Morgan, when you needed me the most, I wasn't available." He felt her tremble. "I'm sorry to bring this up, but I haven't liked myself very much ever since it happened. I should have stayed at your side after I got the call from the hospital."

Morgan went very still. He couldn't even hear her breathing. He braced himself for her reaction, knowing he had coming whatever she wanted to throw back at him.

Hot tears slipped beneath her tightly shut eyes. As much as she tried, Morgan couldn't control them. Jake moved his hand across her shoulder, as if to soothe away some of her raw pain. At least he wasn't running now. So many emotions flooded her: the grief over the miscarriage, needing him to hold her in the aftermath, his absence.

She could feel Jake watching her in the thickening silence. She fought with everything she had not to cry.

Finally, Morgan lifted her hands and covered her face. She took several broken breaths. The past overwhelmed her. "I never expected you to say you were sorry," she whispered bitterly. "Never."

Jake wanted to touch her hair, to touch her. He wasn't sure what Morgan would do if he tried. Pain moved through his chest. "I owe you the apology. I'm so damned sorry, Morgan. I've had a long time to think about my actions. I was dead wrong." He did not expect her forgiveness. When she raised her head, turned and stared at him, her eyes were marred with darkness, and he felt as if he'd been gut punched.

"Let me fill you in," she began hoarsely. "I was a twenty-year-old girl. You were my first and only lover. The doctor had me on the pill, which you knew. I was three months pregnant and didn't even know it. I felt odd on some days, but I just shrugged it off as the stress everyone was under at Annapolis." Morgan pushed tears angrily away from her cheeks. "It was February, Jake, and I contracted a horrible flu. I lay in my room with a one-hundred-and-five-degree fever. My roommate, Deanna, wanted to get me to the dispensary, but I refused. I was going to tough it out."

His eyes narrowed. "I — didn't know."

"Deanna wanted to call you, but I said no. All you wanted was a good time, Jake. You just liked me in your bed. That was it.

And God help me, I liked being there, too." Morgan sniffed and went on in a robot-like tone. "Deanna left for a date. I was hallucinating, moving in and out of the fever. I thought I was going to die. I remember going to sleep. I woke up sometime later, maybe near midnight. I felt this awful, tearing pain in my womb, and I doubled over on my side, screaming. The next thing I knew, I had blood pouring out of me. At first, when I looked at myself, I thought I was having a bad nightmare. Deanna came back from her date and found me. She called 911. I remember just before I blacked out she held my hand, telling me the ambulance was on its way and not to die."

Jake forced himself to hold her marred gaze. "You were taken to the hospital. I knew that much." Her eyes grew sad as more tears slid down her face.

"I woke up in E.R. A doctor was there and she was very kind. She told me I'd miscarried my baby, that my high fever had caused it. She said I'd be okay. She also said I was on too low a dose of birth control pills and that was why I got pregnant. She gave me a new prescription to ever prevent that from happening again." She sighed. "Physically, I was fine."

"Damn," he muttered, "I'm sorry, Morgan. . . ."

"Deanna called you when I was in the hospital. She told you what happened." Her words came out shredded with disbelief. "You never came. You told Deanna you had other important things going on and couldn't make it. I left the hospital the next morning feeling hollow, feeling lost." She held Jake's guilt-ridden gaze. "I needed you, Jake. That was *our* baby! On the way back to Annapolis, I figured out why you refused to see me. You thought by me being pregnant, I would become like an anchor around your feet like your chronically ill mother had been, someone you had to take care of for the rest of your life." Her fingers trembled as she wiped the tears from her face. "You didn't want a pregnant girlfriend. You weren't going to get trapped by another weak, sick woman, were you?"

Sitting back, Jake removed his hand from her shoulder, a mass of grief and misery overwhelming him. Morgan looked like he felt. "It was the biggest mistake I've ever made," he managed, his voice low with apology. "I shouldn't have abandoned you, Morgan. And I did."

She sat there stiffly, struggling to grapple with all her grief and put it in a box once again, deep down inside herself. Jake's gray

eyes were stormy-looking, filled with remorse. Now that he had finally apologized
nine years too late, it didn't make her feel
as good as she thought it would. If anything,
she saw an answering grief in his expression. How would he know what it was like
to lose a baby?

"The only reason you're apologizing now,"
Morgan said in a quavering tone, "is because we're going downrange tomorrow. You
don't want anything to make us lose our
edge." She leaned against the car door, as
far away from him as she could get. He
withdrew his arm from the top of the seat.
As Jake lifted his gaze, she could see how
miserable he was over her story.

"No," he rasped, his voice tight with emotion. "Whether you believe me or not, Morgan, I've matured since our last encounter."
His eyes grew dark with sorrow. "I've carried this guilt over my actions toward you.
As much as you believe I didn't care, I did."
Jake's mouth tightened. "This was a chance
for me to tell you to your face, I *am* sorry. I
was screwed up, Morgan. This doesn't
excuse my choices. I wish in some way I
could make up for it, but I know I can never
do that." He held up his hands. "I just
wanted to be honest with you, Morgan,
because I never was before."

Morgan absorbed his admission. The silence thickened between them.

"At least you're finally being emotionally honest. That's new."

Wincing internally, Jake sighed. "Morgan, I hope I've matured a little bit more."

His gaze fell to her abdomen covered by the pink skirt. She'd held their child in her body. *Their* baby. Misery drifted through Jake in a new and unfamiliar way. He'd already lost his son, Joshua. This new grief hit him doubly hard. He'd made so many mistakes with her. "I thought you didn't want a family until you were thirty or so?"

"That's true, but when I accidentally got pregnant, I knew I'd want to have the baby," she muttered defiantly.

"So you would . . . Would you have kept the baby?"

"In a heartbeat, Jake." Morgan stared at him. "And if I hadn't miscarried, that baby would be mine, not yours. You weren't ready to settle down. You didn't want to marry me or be responsible for what we created."

Mouth thinning, Jake tried to absorb her icy anger. "You're right. I wasn't ready to settle down." He would now, but it was far too late.

"Well, things got handled differently," Morgan said, her voice quavering. "We were both set free to pursue our military careers."

"Damn," he whispered, holding her gaze, "I wish . . . I wish I could go back and change what I did to you. You didn't deserve it, Morgan."

She grew quiet. Morgan held on to an even bigger secret. One that Jake would never, ever know about. When they'd had a brief affair two years ago, fate had intervened once again, even with protection. This time, she'd left her team and gone stateside. Emma Boland had been born with black hair and gray eyes, the spitting image of her father. Morgan didn't dare tell Jake since he might prove twice that he wasn't ready to be with her. Protectively, she placed her hand across her abdomen. "Don't try. You cut and run when things get serious relationship-wise."

"I don't have a good track record with you, Morgan." Feeling sad, Jake added, "That was then. This is now."

Shaking her head, Morgan opened the door and climbed out of the car. "I'll see you at 0600, Jake. I'm done going over the past with you. Thanks for the apology." She slammed the door shut and walked off.

Sitting alone in the car, Jake wrestled with so many damned emotions. His SEAL father had died in combat that very evening when Morgan needed him the most. Jake was overwhelmed with paperwork because he was the executor of his father's will. He'd been at the personnel office wrestling with so many decisions, funeral arrangements and his own grief; he couldn't handle Morgan's plea to come to the hospital, too. It wasn't an excuse. Jake knew he'd been too young, made some bad decisions on that night. If he'd had it to do all over again, he'd have gone to see Morgan, regardless.

As he rubbed his jaw, the prickle of beard against his calloused fingers, his conscience ate at him. In the SEAL community, family, wife and children were just as important as the operators out in the field to the command structure.

SEAL ethos set the family as much of a priority as they did the men going downrange. Studying the light and dark shadows across the parking lot, Jake realized it had been SEAL culture that finally had brought him back into the fold. Made it possible for him to stop running away from relationships. He'd met Amanda and fallen in love with her at twenty-three years old. He'd spent six months in Afghanistan and arrived home just in time to be there for the birth of his son, Joshua.

Jake shut his eyes, remembering the loss

of his wife and baby two weeks later to a car accident. He couldn't share his past with Morgan. It wouldn't be right under the circumstances. He understood as never before what it was like to lose his child. Just as she'd felt the devastating loss with the miscarriage that he'd run away from. What a mess. All of it his own doing.

As he climbed out of the car, Jake resolved to say no more. He'd done what he could to clear the decks between them. He felt deeply, the past overlaying the present. This was an unresolved situation and he was still trapped within it. God help him, he wanted Morgan. Needed her as never before. But after their long history, he knew she'd never come back to him again.

Jake wasn't prepared next morning to see Morgan in SEAL gear as he entered Operations. She was in desert cammies, the SIG pistol riding low on her right thigh in a drop holster, a SOG SEAL knife in a sheath in the same position on her left thigh, and wearing dark leather Merrell hiking boots. She looked like a SEAL from a distance. Earlier, he'd found out Morgan had checked out of the BOQ and gotten a separate ride over to Operations.

Her gear sat near the door as she waited

to be called out to the C-5 now parked in the revetment area. Setting his gear down next to hers, Jake wore desert cammies, as well. Although dressed similarly, every SEAL liked his gear in certain places. Jake preferred his knife on his left side of his waist.

Still torn up over last night's conversation, Jake removed his utility cap and walked over to her. Worse, he'd made Morgan cry, and she'd never cried in front of him before. His heart felt like so much pulp, the ache deep and constant.

"How are you doing?" he asked quietly, catching Morgan's sideward glance. Her profile was beautiful. She was a strong, confident woman.

"I'm fine, Jake. Don't worry. I'll hold up my end of this op whether you believe I can or not."

Okay, the old, defensive Morgan was back. Her eyes were clear, but he could still see remnants of sorrow deep within them. Grief he'd caused. Nodding, he gestured to a sheath on top of her third-line gear, a large desert-camouflaged rucksack with about sixty-five pounds of gear contained in it.

"That's your AW Magnum?" It was one of the sniper rifles chosen by SEALs to use on certain types of ops. The rifle was covered with a tan nylon fabric sleeve to protect it from weather, dirt and dust.

"Yes." Still raw, Morgan didn't want to talk to Jake. She'd barely slept, reliving their conversation all over again. Most humiliating of all, she'd cried in front of him. She wished with all her heart he'd apologized because he cared about her, not because they had to trust each other for this assignment. She pursed her lips, wishing the C-5 would hurry up and allow passengers to load. Then she could get away from him, grab some desperately needed sleep and get her act together.

"You look tired," he observed, remaining at her side.

"I didn't sleep much."

"I didn't, either." Jake felt her tension. "Plenty of room on this flight to catch some shut-eye. It will be empty except for the crew of doctors and nurses going over to Bagram to pick up another group of soldiers who are wounded."

"I hope those guys all make it," Morgan whispered, thinking of them and their families.

"The U.S. has the best-trained medical teams on the planet," he told her, resting his hands on the H-gear pockets around his waist. "Those grunts and soldiers have the best chance in the world to survive."

"When we get on board, I'm finding a hole to bunk into and sleep," she said. As she searched Jake's face, Morgan saw the darkness beneath his eyes. He was growing a beard, which was common among the black-ops groups. Without a beard, the men stood out like sore thumbs to the Taliban and al Qaeda.

"Me, too. We have to get rested."

Jake didn't want to leave her side. He sensed Morgan's feelings; he always had whether she shared them with him or not. SEAL sixth sense, he supposed. Or . . . his heart whispered, it was something more. Something beautiful and profound. And he instantly suppressed those feelings. He'd loved twice in his life, and both times, it had turned into a life-numbing tragedy.

Turning away, Jake ambled over to his equipment sitting on the polished white floor. No, he couldn't risk his heart a third time. He simply didn't have the strength to reach out and try to love again. The potential losses were just too great. And no one knew better than he, there was no promise of happily ever after. . . .

He hefted his ruck, swung it easily across his broad shoulders and then belted it up. An M-4 rifle, barrel downward for safety reasons and safed, chamber empty, was strapped on the outside of it.

He watched as Morgan walked over to her gear, not at all surprised she could lift a sixty-five-pound ruck and make it look light as a feather. Yesterday, as she'd walked into the Pacific Ocean in her purple bathing suit, he'd seen just how fit she really was. Maybe a little too thin, he supposed, but she was all firm muscle, not an ounce of fat. He'd winced when he'd seen those recent pink scars on the back of her left thigh.

Jake was sure those were shrapnel wounds she'd received at that village three months earlier. He wanted to touch them, kiss each of them and remove the pain and memory of how she'd received them. Jake knew he could heal Morgan with his touch, his voice and his hands, if she'd give him a chance. He could be tender toward her. She brought out the best in him, made him feel like a man. Leaning down, he grabbed his eighty-pound weapons bag, slipping it into his right hand. An airman opened the glass doors for them, gesturing for them to go to the parked C-5.

The sunlight was bright, the sky a pale blue. A few clouds were in the distance as Jake walked toward the ramp at the rear of the C-5. A number of nurses, doctors and medics were boarding the largest transport aircraft in the U.S. military. Following Morgan, who walked with an incredible confidence, he compared her to the other women ahead of them.

Morgan stood out. Her red hair was caught up in a ponytail, the strands moving between her shoulder blades. There was just something so damned different about Morgan compared to any other woman Jake had ever known. There was no question, she was a combat warrior. It was in her stride, the way she squared her shoulders, her chin tilted slightly up. Despite the bulky cammies, she didn't look like a man. Not with the sway of those hips of hers and her natural grace.

Once on board, they stowed their gear in a storage locker below the cockpit area of the C-5. The rest of the crew had already boarded. Jake stood near Morgan. Lights went on overhead, revealing three tiers of litters along both sides of the fuselage. Jake wondered what she was thinking as she watched the medical teams prepare to take on newly wounded men once they arrived at Bagram.

"Morgan," he said quietly, "let's crash. We need all the sleep we can get."

Barely turning her head, she absorbed

Jake's calm, steadying presence. His low voice soothed that anguish they'd shared last night. All Morgan wanted to do was turn around, throw her arms around his solid, powerful shoulders and seek solace against him. It wasn't protection she had ever sought from him. Jake knew how to hold her.

"Yes," she managed, her voice husky and sounding far away to her. "We're going downrange. . . ."

Chapter Six

Morgan tried to tame her excitement as the Night Stalker pilots landed the MH-47 helicopter at the Afghan village of Margha. It was barely dawn, and out the window, she spotted thin Reza in his wool cap, baggy pants, vest and coat, waiting near the few mud houses still left standing. Her heart broke for the Afghan. This had been his home. The place he lost his wife and five children to Khogani's raid. It had to be painful for him to stand where his life had once been.

Within minutes, the helo was down, kicking up clouds of dust, grit and small rocks into the air as they rapidly disembarked with their weapons and gear. Once they cleared the helo, Jake gave the pilot the okay to take off via the radio. The helo powered up, the thunder of the powerful engines heard for miles across the long, fertile valley that was just awakening for the day.

"Reza!" Morgan shouted, hauling her gear to where the Afghan stood. Reza was five foot six, lean, his skin tobacco-brown from thirty-five years spent in these rugged mountains. The Afghan's face was deeply etched, smile lines deepening around his eyes and mouth as he stepped forward.

"*As-Salāmu 'alayki,* Wajiha," he said, bowing to Morgan as she dropped her gear. The ancient greeting meant "Peace be upon you." He formally hugged her and then chastely kissed each of her cheeks. Long ago, he'd given her the name of Wajiha, which meant "beautiful one" in Pashto.

His greeting was a very warm, loving welcome bestowed upon family members only. Morgan had been injured trying to save his family. A man was never supposed to hug a woman in Islamic culture, but Reza felt strongly she should know how grateful he was for her willingly putting her life on the line to try to save his youngest child from Khogani's slaughter.

"*Wa 'alaykumu s-salāmu wa rahmatu l-lāhi wa barakātuh,* Reza." Morgan returned the ancient greeting in Pashto. It meant "May peace, mercy and blessing of God be upon you." She hugged him and placed a kiss on each of his bearded cheeks. And then she grinned, threw her arms around him and squeezed the hell out of the wiry Afghan. He pounded her happily on the back of her Kevlar vest, enthusiastically welcoming her.

Jake walked over, watching the warmth between them. He smiled, glad to see Morgan happy. Her face, even in dawn light, was suffused a pink color. It was her eyes, wide with affection for the Afghan guide, that touched him the most. Jake dropped his gear and Reza released Morgan.

"*As-Salāmu 'alayka,* Lieutenant Ramsey," Reza greeted him, placing his palm across his thin chest. "Welcome. I am Reza. I will be your guide."

Jake returned the proper Pashto greeting and then thrust out his hand to the short, wiry man. Reza eagerly took it, pumping it up and down with unbounded earnestness.

"Come, both of you." Reza gestured for them to follow him into the nearest mud home that had a huge hole blown through one side of it. "We must hurry. Taliban watch us from the mountains."

Morgan entered and saw four small, hardy horses munching on some dried grass. One of them had a Western saddle on its back. The other two had the typical Afghan saddle made of wood and nails covered with a rug. The fourth animal was a packhorse.

"Hey, you remembered," she told Reza,

pointing to the Western saddle.

"Of course, Wajiha. You told me to look after your saddle, and I did. You promised to return, and here you are."

Morgan choked up as she saw tears of gratefulness come to Reza's eyes. He was the only survivor of his destroyed village. Her smile disappeared as Jake entered. Moving to the Afghan, she pulled the Velcro pocket open on her Kevlar vest and retrieved a number of photos.

"Just a minute, Jake," she called.

Jake nodded his response, leaving them as she went to Reza's side and spoke to him in a low voice. He couldn't hear what she said in Pashto, but the look on the Afghan's face was one of surprise. Tears began to trail down his high cheekbones as he took the photos from Morgan. She placed her arm around the man's shoulders, pointing to each one, telling him something about it.

Jake felt like an outsider and busied himself appraising the four animals. They were small bay horses with black manes and tails. Horses in Afghanistan always looked short and stocky, but then Jake knew they ate whatever the barren, rocky mountains gave to them, which wasn't much.

He heard Reza sob. Turning, he saw the man clasping the photos to his breast, his other hand pressed against his face, crying openly. He gave a quizzical look, but Morgan held up her hand into a fist. It was a signal that said, "stop." Jake respected the sign and remained with the animals.

Reza got ahold of himself after five minutes, carefully tucking the plastic bag of pictures inside his dark brown wool vest. His eyes were bright, his face in anguish as he bowed and profusely thanked Morgan.

The Afghan picked up the lead rope of the packhorse and led him outside, wiping his eyes with the back of his sleeve.

"What was that all about?" Jake asked, concerned. Morgan wiped her eyes and then turned to face him.

"I had taken pictures of his family and many others who lived here," she said in a strained tone. "I always take photos wherever I go. I thought Reza would like photos of his five kids and his wife." Her voice broke. "It was the least I could do. . . . He loved his family so much. . . ."

Morgan drew in an uneven breath. "I was in this area with two different black-ops teams. Reza doted on his children, and my God, how they loved him in return. His wife was the sweetest, kindest person you would ever meet. If a widow who was starving and begging for a meal came to their door, she'd be welcomed and fed. A lot of the villagers won't feed widows because food is so scarce." Morgan rubbed her cheeks dry and gave him a broken smile. "It feels good to do something kind in return for him, Jake. Reza is the epitome of the Islamic belief of living your life through your heart."

Jake nodded, far more touched than he expected. The fact Morgan would think to bring photos back to Reza made him want to reach out, pull her into his arms and simply hold her. A well of suffering rose through Jake as he stood on the brink of doing just that. Dragging in a breath, he shoved all his needs down deep within himself. In an effort to lighten the moment, Jake said, "Sounds like you read Rumi, the Sufi poet?"

Her brows rose. "You know about Rumi?"

"Sure," Jake said, pretending his pride was hurt. "I might be a country bumpkin of sorts, but I am widely read." SEALs tended to be voracious readers about foreign countries they worked in.

Morgan felt his warmth and care in that moment. "Now it's my turn to apologize."

"Don't worry about it." Jake gestured to the three horses. "That one has an American saddle on it."

Morgan saw him eyeing it with great interest. "Yes, and it's mine. I brought it over three years ago. I got sick and tired of my butt being carved up by nails and wood splinters in my behind from those damned Afghan saddles."

He put his hands on his hips and nodded. "Why didn't I think of that?"

"You didn't ask me," Morgan pointed out, untying the reins to her gelding and leading it out of the house.

Jake grinned. He untied the other two horses and led them outside. To the east, the Hindu Kush sat like silent, powerful giants, a pink dawn outlining the very tops of the snow-covered peaks. Reza had just finished packing their gear and threw a dark brown tarp over the contents. With more light, Jake could see it was a long, narrow valley, green and fertile. A river ran through it, providing irrigation so that the villages would have water for their crops.

Reza smiled and tied the lead line of the packhorse to the back of the saddle on the horse he was going to ride.

Jake saw Morgan already on the sat, satellite, phone to J-bad, calling in and letting Vero know they'd made contact with Reza and were now going to head south through the valley. She was efficient, he decided, watching her place the sat phone in the leather saddlebag behind the cantle of her saddle.

Jake gave Reza a radio headset to wear. They would each wear the headgear and be on the same frequency so they would always be in contact. The send-receive was good for up to a mile.

"We good to go?" he asked, walking over to her.

"Four square. Vero sounded relieved."

"I imagine." Jake looked around, always uneasy about being out in the open. Taliban and al Qaeda operatives lurked and hid in the scree slopes of every mountain that surrounded this valley. The only thing that they couldn't do was shoot at them because the distance was too far. Jake was sure they had glass, binoculars, on them. The Taliban would pass the intel along to other Taliban spotters in the area via radio transmissions.

Reza walked up. "You must know that a goat herder from Dor Babba —" and he pointed south "— saw Khogani yesterday at the snow line with twenty men."

Jake nodded. "And we're headed that way?"

"Yes," Reza said. He had a huge pile of clothes draped over his saddle. "Now, you and Wajiha must wear these Afghan clothes. It will fool our enemy." He handed Jake a set of dark brown clothes to wear over his cammies and H-gear.

"Ah, we're going hajji," Morgan teased Reza, taking the black wool cape, brown vest and black turban. They were large enough to fit over all her gear. *Going hajji* was slang the operators used when they wore Afghan clothing. It would help them fade into the population, harder for the Taliban to spot them at a distance.

Reza put his hands on his hips, critically assessing them. He went over to Morgan and adjusted the black turban covering most of her red hair. Along with it was a woven blue-and-white Shemagh scarf, identifying her as a Shinwari tribesman, which she would wear over her lower face so she couldn't be recognized so easily as a woman by the enemy. "A man would wear the turban like this. . . ." He grinned in apology as he tweaked how it was to sit properly on her head.

Morgan nodded and thanked him. Jake definitely looked like an Afghan. His beard was well started and the dark brown color of the rolled cap on his black hair would fool everyone. Reza checked him out carefully. He arranged the vest a little more across Jake's powerful chest. Probably trying to hide it, Morgan thought.

"You pass inspection," Reza told them. He pointed to the packhorse. "We go under-cover, Wajiha. If the enemy sees us through their binoculars, we look like a family sell-ing shoes." He tapped the tarp, a black silhouette of a shoe that had been painstak-ingly hand painted on the material. It had his name above it, announcing he was a cobbler. "They will think we repair and sell shoes, going from one village to another."

"Brilliant," Morgan said. Reza had been a cobbler all his life. And he regularly rode from one end of this valley to the other, stopping at each village along the way once a month. In the winter, he remained home and fashioned shoes and boots he would sell to villages the following spring.

Morgan checked the tightness of the cinch on her fourteen-hand-high horse. Every-thing seemed okay, and she mounted and arranged the long, draping cape and vest that would hide her uniform and her pistol. Over her left shoulder, she carried an AK-47 in a sling so it was readily available if she needed the weapon. The disguise wasn't perfect, but it would fool the enemy at a distance. "Let's go," Reza said. "We have twenty miles to reach the first village."

Jake mounted, grimacing. He hated these wooden saddles. The Special Forces guys rode them all the time. They had scarred asses, too. He shoved some of his wool cape beneath the saddle to give him some added padding and protection.

"God, I don't think I'll be able to dismount by the time we get there," Jake groaned. He heard Morgan's husky laugh. She seemed very comfortable in her leather saddle, back straight, shoulders squared, riding like someone who had done it all her life.

"Don't worry," Morgan said, chuckling. "I'll haul your sorry ass off that saddle tonight."

Jake grimaced as they started out at a leisurely walk beside one another. "Hey, this isn't funny. The last time I had to ride in one of these damn torture traps, I got a nail puncture right there." He jabbed a finger at his right cheek.

"Oh," Morgan said, trying to look serious, "did you have your tetanus shot updated before we left Hawaii?" She saw Jake grin a little. She enjoyed the unexpected camaraderie. Who else got nail wounds in their butt? No Purple Hearts were given out for them, either.

"Yeah, I got another shot, plus a round of antibiotics for my ruck. I also got rid of that damn saddle I had to ride last year and traded it in for a better-made one. Cost me five hundred U.S. dollars from an Afghan horse trader, but it was worth it. I should have held on to it."

Morgan laughed and then relaxed as they rode. She was back into swiveling her head, paying attention to the least little thing that seemed to be out of place, and she constantly perused the dirt road for any suspicious IEDs or wires that might have been strung across it to kill them.

Morgan felt at home, in a way. Pressing her hand to the pocket on her Kevlar vest beneath the Afghan clothes, she felt the one photo she hadn't shown Reza. She always carried a photo of her daughter, Emma. Maybe later, when they were alone and Jake wasn't around, she would share it with her dear Afghan friend. There wouldn't be many opportunities because a sniper team was joined at the hip.

That night, in the first village, they spent it out in a goat barn. Jake hated the odor. There were no windows in the building, and the potent goat-dung odor was choking him, making his eyes water. He wanted to go outside, but Morgan cautioned against it. Reza was sleeping just outside the door of the mud building, their horses' lead ropes tied to his ankle, snoring away.

Jake sat up on his bedroll, cursing softly. Morgan was six feet away, sleeping near the door. "How the hell can you sleep in this stink?"

Drowsily, Morgan opened her eyes. "Ramsey, shut the hell up, will you? I'm whipped. Isn't your ass tired enough to fall asleep?"

Jake sat up, scowling. The goats were all lying down, crowded next to one another in a small, wooden corral a few feet away from him. One bleated at him. He never took off his boots, but he had laid his Kevlar vest next to his rifle in case he needed them. "Hell, no!"

"Gawd," Morgan mumbled, rubbing her face. "We've got friggin' jet lag, we haven't slept in twenty-four hours and you're wide-awake. If you're going to bitch all night, get out of here. Go sleep outside with Reza."

Amazed she could handle the foul, intense odor, Jake got up, jerked his sleeping bag off the dirt floor and muttered, "I'll do that." He headed for the door. He could barely see Morgan, milky slats of the full moon leaking light into the barn.

"You need to stay in here," she growled, throwing out her hand and grabbing his lower pant leg so he couldn't leave. "You know better, Jake. Now, get a grip, will you?"

He halted, her hand strong on his pant leg. Looking down, he snorted. "I'll die of asphyxiation by dawn if I don't get out of this hellhole. Then you'd feel guilty."

"Oh, stop the drama, Jake. Sit down. We'll talk. Maybe that will make you drowsy. Once you're asleep, you won't smell this crap." She jerked twice on his pant leg. "Sit!"

After he dropped his sleeping bag next to hers, Jake walked over and picked up his rifle and Kevlar. Placing them near his head, he lay down. Morgan was six inches away. He swore he could feel her body heat. He placed his hands behind his head and muttered, "This sucks."

"What a whiny baby," she grunted, sitting there cross-legged, looking down at him. Jake's face was deeply shadowed, but she could see those icy gray eyes and saw he was really upset. "I thought you'd be griping about your ass, not the goat smell in here."

Mouth quirking, Jake enjoyed looking over at Morgan. The moonlight was soft. He could barely see the freckles sprinkled across her cheeks. "My butt aches like hell, but who's going to listen to me bitch about that? And —" he raised one brow, his voice deepening "— just for the record, SEALs don't whine."

Morgan shook her head. "I swear. A man can be eighty years old and still be a sulky fourteen-year-old teenager when he wants to be."

"I'm not sulking."

"Are you going to be like this the rest of this mission, Ramsey?"

There was a teasing glint in her eyes. Her mouth was soft and relaxed, more like her old, feisty self. Had Morgan rebounded from the emotional meat grinder he'd put her through in Hawaii?

On the flight here, Jake had run out of options on how to try to atone for his past behavior. His way of helping would be hauling her into his bed and loving her. He knew Morgan wouldn't approve of those tactics at all. In fact, she'd fight him. He smiled a little. "This barn and the goat smell isn't a five-star quality hotel over here in the badlands, is it?"

Clasping her hands around her drawn-up knees, Morgan shook her head. "There isn't even a one-star in this poor country. At least you have a roof over your head. If it was raining, you'd be happy to be in here."

"Well, the sky's clear and it's not raining."

She sighed. "I love rain. . . ."

Hearing the wistfulness in her soft voice,

Jake decided to make a daring request. "Tell me a bedtime story, Morgan. And then I'll let you go back to sleep."

She tilted her head, as if seriously considering his request.

"What kind of story? *Jack and the Beanstalk,* so you can visualize yourself climbing out of this barn?" She gave him an evil laugh.

Her laughter went straight through his heart. Morgan rarely laughed, and in truth, there hadn't been much to be happy about, either. "You know, I've missed hearing you laugh. It's the most beautiful sound I've ever heard."

Morgan's smile instantly dissolved as she heard the sincerity in his voice.

For a moment, Jake wanted to reach out and graze her clasped hands wrapped around her knees. Her hair was loose, framing her face. She looked so damned feminine in such a rough, godforsaken place. And yet, he was glad she was here. "Okay, the story I want to hear is about your family. Tell me about your mom and dad."

Morgan instantly scowled, suddenly wary. "Why?"

"There you go again. Accusing me."

"You *always* have a reason for any question you ask, Ramsey. Remember? I know you too damned well."

He held up his hands. "Okay, guilty." He tucked his hands behind his head once more. "Seriously, I'd like to know, Morgan."

"Why?"

"Because I want to understand you better is all." That was the truth, and Jake could see she was surprised by his honesty. "Look," he argued equitably, "you accused me of never asking you about your growing-up years or your folks. Now I am. Are you going to gig me on that, too?"

Morgan rubbed her brow. "Ramsey, I never know when to trust you or not," she griped, moving and lying down on her sleeping bag. She used the saddle for a pillow. Laying her head on it, facing him, Morgan jerked the thick wool cape over her body. He was giving her that little-boy look she could never resist. And she knew damn well he was doing it on purpose. So, what was the downside of telling him? Morgan didn't see any.

"Okay," she growled, "but so help me God, Jake, if you fall asleep in the middle of my telling you, I'll *never* say anything about my family again to you."

"Fair enough," Jake murmured, grinning and meeting her dark, serious gaze. For a moment, he thought he saw laughter in her eyes. Morgan sighed loudly. "Nothing has changed about you."

His grin increased. "Thank you. Now, tell me about your growing-up years. I want to know." And Jake really did, but he didn't ask himself why. Why was it so important to him now?

CHAPTER SEVEN

"My mother is Cathy Fremont. My father is Jim Boland. They were part of a military grand experiment two decades ago." Morgan tilted her head. "Do you remember that conflict between Laos and Thailand that erupted?"

"Yeah, tempest in a teapot, as I recall."

"It was more than that." Morgan frowned. "The military wanted to see if women could handle combat. Major Louise Lane, a woman Marine, had a senator who sponsored her ideas. He had enough power to persuade the Joint Chiefs of Staff to create a volunteer group of military women to form a company. It was called the WLF, Women's Liberation Forces. They then went over with a brigade of Marines out of Camp Pendleton."

"I vaguely recall something about it," he said, searching his memory.

"My mother was a Marine Corps Corporal. My father was a Force Recon Marine Captain. My father's company commander, Colonel Mackey, felt that Lane was screwing up. He didn't think she was an effective enough leader to place women into combat. Mackey, with some hawk senators in Congress, concocted a plan to get one of the women in the WLF to testify against Lane's methods and expose her weaknesses as a leader." Her mouth turned down.

"Your mother got caught in it?"

Nodding, she sighed. "So did my father. Colonel Mackey tricked my dad into believing he was helping a number of women in the WLF company who were being overworked. Major Lane was running them on two patrols a day."

Brows rising, Jake said, "That's insane."

"No kidding. To make a long story very short, that's how they met. My mother was nearly killed in an ambush. My father rescued her with his Recon team and he sustained a bullet wound to the base of his skull."

"He must have lived or you wouldn't be here." Jake tried to lighten the tone because Morgan looked stressed. Maybe he shouldn't have asked about her growing-up years. Why would he ever think Morgan had a normal childhood?

"Yes, my father was in a coma for a while. He woke up in Hawaii, happened to catch a television broadcast of my mom in front of a congressional fact-finding committee be-ing torn apart by that senator who had sup-ported Major Lane." Her mouth tightened. "My mother is a very brave person, Jake. She's a fighter. And that senator was trying to blame her for everything going wrong with the WLF. He called her a coward. . . ."

He sat up, hearing the anger in her tone. Morgan was so close. He could reach out and slide his hand over hers. Forcing all his selfish needs aside, he said, "I remember a huge five-day television circus orchestrated by Congress."

"My father rescued my mother from that senator. He set the record straight before that congressional committee."

"Your mother must have been very good at what she did in the WLF despite what that senator was trying to saddle her with." Just the tilt of Morgan's head, the softened expression on her face, made Jake ache to reach out and touch her cheek. He took a deep, uneven breath, remaining where he was.

"They called my mother the Valkyrie." Pride leaked into her husky voice. "My mother showed Congress and the military

113

that women could handle combat. They were just as good as any man. They needed more experienced leadership, was all."

"And so," Jake said, putting the dots together, "Operation Shadow Warriors is predicated upon that initial trial that took place over in Thailand?"

"Yes. General Maya Stevenson has picked up the gauntlet for women who want to volunteer for combat and being allowed to do it provided they met the strict physical standards."

"And you're the daughter of the original woman in that program." Jake said it more to himself than her. Morgan was created by two people who had a strong military background. "Did you get appointed to Annapolis because of that?"

She smiled a little, resting her brow against her knees. "My father petitioned one of our state senators and I was given the choice of any military academy I wanted."

"Did you want to be in the military? Or were you fulfilling your parents' wishes?"

Lifting her head, Morgan said, "I was fulfilling my desire to have women's boots on the ground. I didn't want some man telling me I couldn't pick up a rifle and fight for my country. I'm just as much a patriot as the next guy. As long as I can haul ass on the ground, carry my gear like they can, who cares? I'm a gun in the fight. That's all that counts with these operators out on the front lines, Jake. I can shoot back and hit what I'm firing at. Once I proved I can, they're more than happy to have me in their team."

"You raised hell at Annapolis. I remember you banging down doors and demanding to be allowed into combat classes at the Academy."

"And I won." Morgan straightened, rolled her shoulders and added, "You never thought I would be a combat soldier."

"Don't go there. We're only talking about your growing-up years. Remember?"

"Okay, truce. You know the rest. We were in the same class at Annapolis. I was able to push through women being assigned into Marine Corps companies in Afghanistan after graduation. It was a real victory and a step forward for women who wanted to go into combat slots."

"Yes, it was." Jake remembered how much of an intense firebrand Morgan had been at the Academy. Her communications skills, her passion and belief that women should be given the opportunity to volunteer for combat slots and careers, persuaded the brass at higher levels. "How did General

Stevenson get wind of you?"

"Oh, she'd been quietly cherry-picking women like myself from all branches of the military for over a year. When she got forty of us, she pushed through Operation Shadow Warriors three years ago. It's a seven-year trial, and so far, the women are showing they can get the job done."

Jake saw how exhausted she was becoming. "Look, why don't you get some rest? We've got a full day's ride ahead of us, and dawn isn't far away."

"You gonna stop whining about the stink and let me sleep?"

"As long as I can lie here next to you, I'll be quiet." Jake pointed to the door. "There's fresh air coming in around the door."

Grinning, Morgan drew the wool cape across her shoulders. "And you just figured that one out, SEAL boy?"

Jake gave her a sheepish smile. Her back was to him, her face inches away from the fresh air leaking in between the door and the jamb. Damn, she was smart. As he lay down, he thought of the years of being in Afghanistan and being in one too many smelly goat barns, and Morgan had learned this little secret. Jake couldn't stop grinning for a long time over that discovery. She was damned bright, full of common sense and far too beautiful. Closing his eyes, he hoped they wouldn't get assigned to another goat barn in Dor Babba. Maybe Reza had more influence than he did here. . . .

Jake watched with some amusement and awe as they entered the village of Dor Babba late the next afternoon. Word had been passed from one goat herder to another that they were coming. The human telegraph was fast in this part of the world. As they dismounted in the square of the massive mud-building village, children of all ages came pouring out from all directions. They had been waiting for their arrival.

And they all focused on Morgan, who had handed the reins of her horse to Reza as she walked out to meet them. Jake watched with curiosity as they kept shouting, "Wajiha" to her. They danced around her, touching her, smiling up at her, joyous.

The Pashtun name certainly fitted Morgan. She had removed her hajji clothes and had reached into a deep pocket on the right side of her cammies.

The children quieted, all eyes focused on her hand as she brought it out of the pocket and opened it up in front of them. She spoke warmly to them in Pashto, kneeling down in the circle of children. In her palm were small Butterfinger packets.

Jake felt his chest tighten with emotion. A very young boy, perhaps four years old, with black hair reminded him of his son, Joshua. Pain flitted through his heart. He would have been four this year. Jake pushed the grief away and focused on the happy children as Morgan passed out the candy among all of them. From the appearances of Morgan's bulging calf pockets, she'd brought a ton of candy along to share with these children who knew her so well. A group of elders walked slowly down the main street toward them. They were to meet Hamid, the tribal leader of this village, upon arrival.

Lifting her head, Morgan spotted Hamid walking down the rutted street along with six other elders who flanked him. He was smiling. So was she. By the time they'd arrived, every child had Butterfingers clasped in their hands and disappeared like the wind.

Jake moved to her side. He'd removed his hajji clothes, too.

"You have a new name," he said, grinning. "Wajiha?"

"Yes. Reza christened me with it three years ago." Morgan touched her mussed ponytail across her shoulder. "He thought my freckles and red hair made me look beautiful. I guess my spotted skin inspired his imagination." She smiled fondly.

"How many times have you been in this area?"

"Too many to count."

Jake needed to catch up on how well Morgan knew this region. That was a definite asset to their mission. "That's why the kids know you so well?"

"Yes. As you know, I'm a trained paramedic from my days at Annapolis, so whenever my black-ops team came through a village, I'd set up a clinic for the women and children. The male combat medic, always a guy, set up a clinic for the men. I always gave the kids candy if I had to give them a shot. They all wanted a shot then." She grinned. "These kids are not stupid."

Morgan never met a child she didn't like, Jake decided. Or maybe, her beauty, kindness and generosity left an indelible mark in each child's memory and that attributed to her popularity. That was probably closer to the real truth. He was grateful to see her interact without any of her defensive walls in place. Morgan was vulnerable and open with the children, her maternal side showing. Clearly, they loved her, their eyes bright with affection, wriggling like excited puppies, happy to see her once again.

Their collective focus shifted to a tall, thin man in his forties. Hamid had a long black beard peppered with gray. He wore a cream-colored wool cape, baggy black pants and a black turban on his head. His light brown eyes sparked with welcome. Jake got ready to make the customary greetings with the Pashtun leader.

"Welcome," Hamid intoned, giving the greeting in Pashto to them.

Morgan wasn't surprised when the leader stepped forward, placed his hands on her shoulders and fondly kissed each of her cheeks. She did the same, having great respect for the Afghan leader.

Hamid greeted Jake and shook his hand.

Reza approached and greeted the elder with respect, as well. He seemed surprised as Hamid extended his hand to him, his face alight with pleasure at being recognized by the village elder.

"Will you do me the honor of coming to my humble home?" Hamid asked Morgan and Jake. "My wife has known of your coming for a day, and she has been working with all the wives of the village to greet you properly with good Afghan food."

Morgan glanced over at Jake, and he nodded. "We'd love to, Hamid. Lead the way."

Chuckling, Hamid said, "Oh, you lead the way, Wajiha. You know this village as if it were your own." He opened his hand and made a grand gesture toward the rutted road.

"It is an honor," Morgan whispered, meaning it. As she walked past the elders, she was joined by at least ten children who all wanted to claim her hands and escort her to the elder's home. They laughed, skipped and clung to her clothing. One little girl, no more than four, ran up to Morgan, arms open, begging her to pick her up.

Morgan instantly recognized the child. "Duniya! Where have you been?" she asked, leaning down and scooping the terribly thin child into her arms.

Duniya laughed, threw her arms around Morgan's neck, kissing her cheek again and again. "My mother is coming, Wajiha. We missed you! We're so happy to have you home!"

Touched, Morgan settled the small girl against her hip, giving Duniya a kiss on the noggin. "Were you out in the fields?"

"Yes. We heard shouting. My mother wouldn't let me run across the fields."

"Wise choice," Morgan murmured, rubbing her hand gently down the child's back, feeling her protruding ribs. "There's buried

121

IEDs out there. You have to be careful, little one." Morgan spotted Duniya's mother standing between two of the mud homes, a shy smile of welcome on her darkly sun-burned face. Morgan lifted her hand in greeting to the mother, Roya, whom she was close to.

"Do you have candy for me, Wajiha?"

Chuckling, she said, "Yes, I saved some for you, Duniya."

"Ohhhhh, good! Thank you, Wajiha. You are truly an angel! Mama prays for you every day in her prayers."

Morgan squeezed the girl gently and said nothing. As she looked around her, more and more of the village's children had returned, and they were a ragtag group hollering around her, the older boys racing up and down the street, proclaiming Wajiha's return. Happiness flooded Morgan's heart as they made their way to a three-story mud-and-stone home where the leader of the village lived.

Morgan gently placed barefoot Duniya on the ground. She dug into a pocket in her H-gear and produced two Butterfinger packets for the shy little girl with the long black hair. Duniya held out her hand to receive the gift.

"One is for you. And one is for your

mama," Morgan instructed her, giving her a kiss on the head and gently nudging her toward her waiting mother on the other side of the street.

"Thank you, Wajiha. I love you!"

Straightening, Morgan smiled softly as the child ran like a deer to her mother's side, giving her the candy. Roya's face brightened with surprise, a smile of thanks coming to her oval face. Morgan lifted her hand and then returned her attention to Hamid.

Jake followed the entourage of six leaders and Morgan into the three-story house. On the first floor there was a large central room. The dirt-packed floor was covered with beautiful Persian carpets. The wife and daughters of Hamid enthusiastically welcomed them. Hamid asked them to sit on either side of him, at the head of the jirga, or meeting. It was a place of honor. Women were not to attend an all-male jirga but Hamid wanted Morgan at the meeting.

Jake noted that Hamid gestured for Morgan to sit at his right hand. That was considered the most important place to sit next to the leader. She waited until he had sat cross-legged on the pillow before sitting down next to him. Jake was familiar with Pashtun customs and fitted easily into the ceremony.

The women served the three of them first. They brought silver trays with bowls of cool water and a towel beside it. Jake appreciated the gesture. They'd ridden all day, sweated and smelled like hell. There were no showers out here. No water to take a dip in, but the bowls of water were a start.

He remained patient, knowing it would be a while before they got around to discussing Sangar Khogani. Did Hamid have any updated information? Jake hoped so, but patience was the key. Afghan jirgas were long, with many cups of tea in between serious conversation.

CHAPTER EIGHT

Near sunset, Morgan and Jake strolled through the village. He needed to acquaint himself with the two hundred people who lived within the five-foot mud walls that protected them. Morgan showed him the only gate in and out of the fortress. The heat of the day was easing, but sweat ran freely down their faces as they walked outside the massive wooden gates that were always manned by a young boy during the day and an armed farmer at night.

"Up there," Morgan told him, pointing at a twelve-thousand-foot mountain rising to the south of the village, "is where the boys herding the goats the other day saw Sangar Khogani and his men."

Jake studied the rocky slopes of the mountain, which were part of another chain farther to the south. He had a map in hand, studying the terrain of it against what he saw. Over the years since 9/11, SEALs had done much of the updating of mapping terrain in these isolated regions. Their work, combined with updated satellite imagery, gave him a much better picture of the Hindu Kush in this area. "That's a rugged mother of a slope," he said.

Morgan rested her hands over the waist belt of her H-gear. "Yes, it is. The boys take the goats up there on five different paths across that slope. It's steep but not impossible."

"I hate working at twelve thousand feet. It sucks oxygen-wise," he grunted, studying the map again.

Morgan continued to look around. The Afghans were coming in from the fields to the west of the fortified village. They were done for the day. All the men wore sandals. The soles were fashioned out of cutting up old car tires, wood or anything else they could find. Nothing was wasted out here. They carried a rake, hoe or shovel across their shoulders. Older boys also accompanied their fathers into the fields, learning agricultural practices to keep their crops alive.

The big problem was that Khogani and his men rode through every three months during the dead of night. His men would plant IEDs outside the gate and in their fields. Her mouth twitched. Her hatred of Khogani was intense. He never left her mind. All Morgan had to do was see the ten children in the village who had lost legs to his IEDs or see the sadness in Reza's eyes, and she wanted the bastard permanently removed from this planet.

"Okay, I've seen enough." Jake looked over at Morgan. She seemed far away, unreachable. "What are you thinking about?"

"How badly I want Khogani's head."

"These people have really suffered under him," Jake agreed, turning and walking back to the gate.

"I want to call in Captain Shaheen's charity organization. His wife, Emma Trayhern, who used to be an Apache combat pilot, now flies a CH-47 for their organization. I want to ask Khalid to bring in a medical and dental team to the village tomorrow."

Jake slowed his pace, considering the request. "Isn't that dangerous? Khogani's been seen up there. He's well-known to kill NGO teams coming in to help a village."

Morgan shrugged. "I've worked with Khalid and Emma before. They're U.S. Army and a little wiser to how things work around here. Emma can get flyovers by an Apache gunship, so she knows whether it's safe to land or not. Khogani isn't going to show his presence when an Apache is around."

"Aren't you afraid it will chase him off?"

"It might draw him in. In which case, we'll be able to find him easier. There are a lot of people in the village who need medical attention." She rubbed her sweaty brow. "The Apaches might be able to spot him. You never know. They have all kinds of avionics equipment, including thermal imaging to seek out human body heat. If he's still around, it might pin him down and help us pick up his trail."

"As long as it doesn't slow down our operation."

"It won't," she assured him. "We were planning on staying here for two days anyway. With Khogani being sighted, we have to get satellite flyovers and drones on station 24/7 to see if they can find him and his men. That can take twenty-four hours or more."

It sounded reasonable to Jake. "Okay, call J-bad and get Vero to authorize the request. Then give Captain Shaheen a call and see if he'll bring in the teams."

"Thanks, Jake." Morgan gave him a hesitant smile and finally said, "This is one of those rare times I like you. It tells me you really do have a heart."

Her whispered words made his throat tighten. Jake hadn't expected a thaw between them, but it had happened. All he wanted right then was to bring a rare smile to her beautiful face. Rolling his eyes, he grinned. "Give me a break, Boland. I'm a *nice* guy and you know it."

She couldn't help melting beneath that sudden, boyish smile and seeing his hard mask drop away. Her heart beat a little faster. "Sometimes, like right now," Morgan agreed, huskily, "you're a 4.0 guy." Four-oh was a Navy expression for someone who was squared away and knew what they were doing.

"God, a compliment from you." Jake dramatically pressed his hand against his chest. "Next, you'll be rewarding me one of those Butterfingers you got stashed in your pockets." He chuckled.

Laughing softly, Morgan said, "You don't like Butterfingers, remember?" Most SEALs had a stash of junk food in their gear that they would bring over with them. She was sure Jake had packages of his favorite candy, Kit Kat, stored away in his third-line gear, his rucksack.

Shrugging, Jake placed his thumbs in the waist belt of his H-gear. The M-4 was slung in a loop across his left shoulder. They went nowhere without weapons. "I know . . . but it's the thought that counts," he teased, seeing the smile in her eyes. Eyes he could get lost in and never return from. Despite the sweat, the dust, her hair coated with it across her shoulders, Morgan was beautiful.

A deep ache began once more in his heart and lower body, like it always did when he was around her. Jake could never logically figure out what his response was all about. And when Morgan's lips drew into a soft smile, it made him feel powerful and special. Being with her once again was bittersweet. If only he could have a third chance with her. This time, he wouldn't screw it up because of lack of maturity, misunderstandings and terrible mistakes he'd made.

Halting at Hamid's house, they would sleep at different levels within Hamid's home. Women slept with women. Men slept with men. That was Islamic law. Jake would be on the third floor, Morgan on the second.

Tiredness washed over Morgan. "I'm going to see if I can scare up some water and take a spit bath." She wrinkled her nose and touched her cheek. It felt gritty beneath her fingertips. "See you tomorrow morning?"

"Yeah. This is an upgrade from the goat barn last night."

Morgan nodded. "Indeed it is, Ramsey.

But I didn't smell any of it. . . ."

"Classic gotcha," Jake agreed, grinning. And then he sobered. "You keep the radio on, though?" She and Jake had a headset communications with one another. If something happened, he wanted them to be able to talk to her, as well as react immediately as a team.

Hamid had confirmed things had been quiet at the village for the past month. Jake felt they would be very safe within the walls. As a SEAL, he was fully aware that if Khogani's men wanted to attack, a five-foot wall wasn't going to stop them. The wall was a psychological state of mind for the villagers as far as he was concerned, not true protection against the bad guys.

"Yes," Morgan agreed, patting the radio snapped to her H-gear harness on her left shoulder. "See you tomorrow morning." She lifted her hand and took the steps into the house.

Much to his chagrin, Jake woke up very late the next morning. It was 0800! Sunlight was pouring into the window of the men's sleeping room. Hurrying through breakfast, he got his gear, rifle and headed outdoors. The morning was coolish as he loped easily down the road.

Hamid was out and about, and Jake stopped a man with a donkey and cart hauling wood to ask if he'd seen Morgan. The farmer told him she was out in the fields with the elders. Hurrying out the gate, Jake saw the village was up and moving. Women were doing washing outside their homes, children were playing, dogs were yapping and most of the men were already in the fields for the day.

Morgan was standing with Hamid and several other elders at a ditch when she spotted Jake coming around the wall of the village. She gestured for him to come join them. After giving the Pashto greetings to the elders, he came to Morgan's side.

"Good morning," she murmured. "You overslept, Ramsey. I didn't have the heart to wake you at 0530 like you wanted."

Scowling, he said, "You should have." When he looked around, Jake saw at least fifty men in the fields, hoeing, picking out weeds or guiding the water from the river down a ditch into the narrow rows to water the corn, beans and other vegetables.

"It's one of the few times you can sleep in. No harm, no foul. I contacted Captain Shaheen and they'll be here in about an hour with two medical teams."

"Good," Jake said, staring up at the huge

mountain to the south. His neck prickled with warning. Khogani was up there. He was sure. Watching them? Probably. Turning, he asked, "What are you doing out here?"

"Working with Hamid and the elders. They wanted to know if they could improve their irrigation techniques." She pointed to the fields. "You see how hard they work to get that water down into each of those rows?"

"Yeah," he said, rubbing his chin and studying the problem. Morgan was a civil engineer, which had been her major at Annapolis. It was evident how good she was at it. "Do you have a plan?"

"I think so," she said, enjoying the moment with him. She pointed along the parallel edge of the long field that was at least a football field in length. "I was telling Hamid if we could get some guys out here to dig another ditch, create a second channel for this river water, that they would have water coming in both ends of every row. That way, when they pulled up the wooden gates to allow water into the fields, it would irrigate twice as fast with a lot less work for the men."

"I'm impressed," Jake said, catching her gaze. Her eyes grew warm over his compliment. This morning, Morgan wore the boonie hat that all SEALs wore on an op. She had her SIG riding low on her right thigh, her H-gear on and a shovel in her left hand. The M-4 wasn't far away from her reach.

"You like the idea?"

"Yeah. It should work."

Hamid tapped Jake on the shoulder. Jake turned to the elder.

"You need to consider her for a wife, Sahib Ramsey."

Morgan's mouth dropped open, and she stared disbelievingly at Hamid, who usually said little. And then she shifted her glance toward Jake. His mouth was still open, too. Laughing, she said, "Hamid, we do things a little different in America. Women aren't assigned a husband to marry. We choose who we want to marry."

Hamid smiled a little, stroking his long, well-kept beard. "If you lived here, I would order you to marry this fine man. He would be a good husband for you, Wajiha. He's strong." Hamid pointed to Jake's upper arms beneath his cammie sleeves. "And he has a good heart. What else could you want?"

Hiding her smile, Morgan knew Hamid was giving them high praise. "My Lord Hamid, you are too generous and kind with your praise."

"Then you will consider my words?"

She gave Hamid a teasing look. "You're a wily wolf, my lord. I will give it thought." But nothing more. Jake appeared like a deer frozen in oncoming headlights. Despite his growing beard darkening his face, he was still ruggedly handsome, virile, and appealed to her on every level. Wily Hamid had sensed or seen their connection and camaraderie. Or maybe he saw something neither of them did? That last thought scared the hell out of Morgan.

Hamid grinned beneath his beard and bowed toward her. "You are a fine, fine woman, Wajiha. Any man would be proud to have you as his wife."

Jake swallowed and struggled to hide his unease. "My lord," he said, trying to remain serious, "Wajiha is her own woman. She chooses who touches her heart. I'm not that man." He wanted to be, but he'd screwed his chances up a long time ago.

Hamid nodded. "That is a pity, Sahib Ramsey. You are a fine leader."

Jake thanked him. He was desperate to get Hamid off the topic. Even worse, Morgan seemed to enjoy his discomfort. So he picked up a shovel. "Morgan, why don't you go measure the length of the ditch so we can start digging it?"

"Easy enough to do," she answered. Pushing her shovel into the ground, she picked up a coil of nearby rope.

One of the younger sons of the elders came up and asked if he could help. Morgan said yes and sent him down the field with her holding the other end of the thick rope. In no time, they had a perfect line to build the new ditch. Once the line was created with a bunch of rocks, Morgan came back and picked up the shovel. Wearing Kevlar always made one sweat like a pig because it was so damned heavy. And she couldn't take it off because they were out in the open. Everything looked bucolic and peaceful now, yet Morgan knew it was an illusion. She gestured to Jake, who was going to walk down to the other end of the ditch that had to be dug. "Hey, Ramsey, why don't you start at one end with your crew and I'll start up here with mine? We'll meet in the middle."

Jake lifted his hand. "Sounds good." He called five waiting men with shovels to follow with him.

Hamid's brows rose. "Wajiha, you are going to dig a ditch?"

Merriment came to her eyes. "Absolutely,

Lord Hamid. In our country, women do work that they choose to do."

Scratching his beard, the other elders whispering in his ear, he said, "Are you sure? You are a woman."

Laughing, Morgan pulled the field hat down a little tighter and slipped on her wraparound sunglasses. "Don't worry, Hamid. I won't break. I'd like to get this ditch finished by sunset tomorrow."

Hamid shook his head. "What strange customs Americans have. . . ."

Then they all heard a helicopter coming from the southeast. Jake looked up, squinting into the light blue sky. There was a CH-47 transport helicopter being escorted by two Apache gunships. He grinned and looked down the field. Morgan was systematically digging up dirt along with her five-man team. "Hey," he called into the radio mic near his mouth, "we got company coming. Looks like the charity helo at ten o'clock."

Morgan wiped her brow with the back of her arm. "Okay, I'll switch channels, contact them and we'll go meet them."

By the time Jake walked back to where Morgan stood, she was in contact with all three helos coming quickly down the throat of the valley. Morgan directed the CH-47 helicopter to a flat area outside the gate that the children had cleared earlier of stones, brush and anything else that might fly up from beneath the whirling blades of the helo as it landed. IEDs had already been searched for by the farmers at dawn. It was a safe, clear landing area.

Hamid appeared to be very happy, and he and the other elders went toward the landing site located out in front of the gates of the village to meet the incoming teams. Jake waited until Morgan ended the transmission.

"Let's go meet them," he urged Morgan. And then he grinned. "Unless you want to keep digging the ditch? I'm impressed with all your dirt building skills."

Morgan put the shovel into the dirt, a feral smile on her mouth. "Yeah, I took Ditch Digging 101 at Annapolis. Looks like you did, too, SEAL boy. I'll go play paramedic for a while and help the medical team set up the child-and-woman clinic." Lifting the hat off her head, Morgan wiped her brow and settled it back into place. Jake had his sunglasses on, and she couldn't see his eyes. Which was why SEALs wore them. If a person couldn't see their eye movement, they couldn't tell which direction they were going to move. In a gunfight, that was an advantage.

"I like it when you're feisty, Boland. You must have gotten a good night's sleep." He met her grin with one of his own. Jake gestured toward the village. "I'll go and help set up the men's clinic." He rubbed the back of his neck, felt the danger. Damn. It had to be Khogani watching them.

Lifting his chin, he glared up at the gray, rocky slopes of the mountain. At twelve thousand feet, he and his men could be hidden anywhere. Chances were, however, if Khogani was around, he was probably hightailing it into one of the hundreds of caves up there to hide from the malevolent eyes of the Apache gunships escorting the charity helicopter.

Morgan seemed happy. She was alert, always looking around, never taking anything for granted. The villagers did, but they did not. His neck prickled again. Jake's mouth thinned as he walked toward the front of the village. Something was wrong. . . .

CHAPTER NINE

Sangar Khogani felt every sharp rock biting and sticking up through his clothing as he lay flat on his belly on a ridge. He followed the activity below at the village of Dor Babba. The binoculars showed a CH-47 that had just landed. *What* was going on? He felt Droon, his second-in-command, drop quietly to his side.

"Are the men in the cave?" Khogani demanded, watching developments below. They had heard the hard, puncturing beats that signaled an Apache in the area. Sangar had ordered his twenty men and horses to hide in a nearby cave so they did not become targets.

"They are, my lord."

"Apaches!" he spat. "Demons of the air!"

Droon wiped his mouth. "Too bad our Stinger missiles can't reach them." That was, if the battery still worked. No battery, no ability to fire the Stinger at any aircraft.

And a battery had a shelf life.

Snorting, Sangar growled, "With those Apaches around, we'll wait."

"What do you see?" Droon asked, watching the two Apaches peel off after the CH-47 had landed. He was familiar with their pattern of operation. One would make a wide circle around the village, ever watchful with their instruments in their cockpit that could locate their body heat or actually spot them with a television camera on board. The second combat helicopter rose until it would be higher than the twelve-thousand-foot mountain they hid upon. Then it would turn on its camera and infrared and hunt for them. They had a few minutes before the second Apache was able to gain the elevation it needed. Then they would have to quickly escape into the nearby cave. Fortunately, Apaches had no ability to look inside a cave to see the twenty horses and soldiers hiding within it.

"It's a charity," Sangar growled. He handed Droon the binoculars. "Hamid has nerve. He knows I hate infidels. You'd think the IEDs we plant once every three months out in their fields and fruit orchards would be enough of a warning." He tapped his fingers, the nails dirty and broken, and then stroked his unkempt black beard. Hatred welled up inside him.

Droon studied the helicopter. "Looks as if there are two groups coming off it. Not military."

"Probably medical teams."

Droon handed the binoculars to his leader. His whole family had been wiped out like Sangar's by an American drone that carried a missile. Since then, they had sworn allegiance to the Taliban, increased their numbers until more than two hundred men, mostly from other countries, rode with them. The fact that Khogani was the lord of the Hill tribe put him in a good position with the Pakistanis. They wanted all the opium he could bring across the Khyber Pass to them.

Sangar looked up. The Apache was nearly level with the mountain they were on. "Let's go." He pushed up on his hands and knees. They quickly moved off the scree, their clothing black, brown and cream-colored, blending in perfectly with the surrounding landscape. Running into the cave, Sangar saw all his men sitting on their haunches, reins of their horses in hand, waiting for their leader.

"Make camp," he ordered. "Move as far back as you can. The Apache is hunting us!"

The twenty men quickly rose and did

Khogani's bidding, leading their horses down a tunnel. The tunnel was getting smaller, but they knew it eventually opened up into a large cavern big enough to hold Sangar's army of two hundred. There, they would make camp, start a small fire and rest. The smoke would easily dissipate through the many holes in the Swiss-cheese-like ceiling overhead. They would remain undetected.

"What do you want to do about Hamid?" Droon asked, walking at Khogani's shoulder. His leader was tall for an Afghan and towered over him. Sangar's narrow, deeply brown face turned into a snarl.

"When the Apaches leave, I will send Hamid a message he won't soon forget."

"There were two commandos down there with that group," Droon cautioned. "SEALs." They knew their enemy well by what they wore. And Droon was far more scared of SEALs than Army Special Forces, Rangers, Delta Force or any other black-ops units who operated in the area. The binoculars weren't strong enough to pick up faces, only the color of their uniforms and the way they wore their pistols low on their right legs. SEALs were famous for that.

Shrugging, Khogani picked up the reins on his bay gelding. "They're more than likely with that helicopter. They will drop these teams in, guard them and then fly off with them." He smiled, showing his yellowed teeth. Two of his front teeth were missing because of the nearby explosion from the drone that had killed his entire family. He'd been the only survivor. The blast had knocked the teeth out of his head, burned his left shoulder and upper back.

"I wish we could watch and make sure," Droon said, worried. "That way we'd make sure those SEALs aren't staying behind in Dor Babba."

Waving his hand, Sangar growled, "It doesn't matter!"

Yes, Droon thought, it did. But he remained silent, following the soldiers down the narrow, twisting passage. The cave smelled of bat feces and dry earth. There was no water in this cave. The snort of horses soothed his worry.

"Hamid's going to regret this," Sangar promised softly.

"I'm sad to see everyone go," Morgan confided to Jake as they stood near the gates watching the CH-47 lift off. Above them flew two guard-dog Apaches, guaranteeing they wouldn't be shot at by the Taliban while leaving the valley. Dust and pebbles kicked up in furious, billowing yellow clouds in every direction. The sun was setting, the last long rays in the west as they silently stole across the valley, touching the tips of the Hindu Kush in the east.

"Those two teams did a lot in a short amount of time," Jake agreed. Both had spent the day providing medical aid and helping the doctors and nurses tend villagers with medical issues. It made Jake feel good to do something for these people who lived on the harshest edge of survival every day.

"I'm going to stay with Duniya and her mother tonight," Morgan said, looking up at him. Jake's eyes were narrowed, the palm of his hand resting on the butt of his SIG. The M-4 was looped over his broad left shoulder. "She's invited me over for dinner. It will give me a chance to have some quality time with them. You okay with me not being at Hamid's house tonight?"

"Not a problem. We have radio contact."

"Right." She was very tired. The sun had set, the clouds on the horizon starting to turn pink along the peaks of the mountains. It was a beautiful sight. *Eden in hell. So damned beautiful but so friggin' deadly.*

"Tell me about Duniya."

Morgan wiped her cheeks dry of perspiration. "Three years ago I was here with a SEAL team. Duniya had tuberculosis. She was dying. Luckily, we had antibiotics and some other medicines to pull her out of it."

"I noticed she had a pigeon chest," Jake said. He heard the emotion in Morgan's husky voice, savoring this alone time with her.

"Yes, typical body build of a tuberculosis patient. Her mother had just lost her husband to an IED. She was a grieving widow and her child was dying in her arms. The SEAL OIC had a lot of cash on him. You know how we buy things over here with greenbacks?"

"Can't do without them," Jake agreed.

"I persuaded him to give the mother enough money to survive on. Most women, when widowed, die of starvation and so do their children." Morgan sighed. "There just isn't that much food to go around. Everyone is always on the edge of starvation here, Jake. *Always*. I don't know how they survive. I couldn't."

"And so you pick up the slack here and there whenever you go into a village?"

"Yeah. Every SEAL team I've been assigned to has been generous with their time, food and money. I know money buys loyalty among the Afghans, but it also buys children

146

time to grow without their legs bowing because of scurvy. When I first came over here three years ago and realized so many of the children were bowlegged, I started carrying bottles of vitamin C tablets in my third-line gear. I'd give the bottle to the mother."

"Otherwise," Jake said with a slight smile, "the kids thought it was candy and gobbled it down in a night's time."

She joined his quiet laughter. "Oh, yeah, and the next day those kids had the worst diarrhea you've ever seen."

Jake wanted to reach out and move his index finger down the clean line of her jaw. Morgan's profile was classic. "Hey," he said, "tell me how you broke your nose. Two years ago, it was straight. What happened?"

The unexpected question shook Morgan. She licked her lower lip, mind spinning. She decided to tell Jake part of the truth. "I was visiting my parents about a year after I saw you in Afghanistan. The bathroom door near my old bedroom always hangs ajar. My dad hadn't gotten around to fixing it yet. I got up one morning, leaned down to turn on the faucets for a bath. As I straightened and turned, I slammed my face into the edge of the door." Morgan forced a smile she didn't feel and rubbed the bump on her nose. "I remember reeling backward, stunned. It nearly knocked me unconscious. When blood gushed like a faucet out of my nose, that's when I groggily realized I'd broken it."

"Helluva way to break it," Jake murmured, frowning. There was something else in the recesses of Morgan's eyes as she glanced in his direction. He couldn't decipher it, but he felt there was more to the story. Shifting from one foot to another, hands resting relaxed on his H-gear belt, he said, "And you never got it fixed?"

The corners of her mouth pulled inward. "No. I don't like surgery. You know that. If I could get away with never being cut on, it would be fine with me." Morgan struggled not to tell Jake the rest of the story. She had just been hit with the first contraction while carrying Emma as she'd straightened to turn around. The excruciating pain had caused her to strike the edge of the bathroom door with her face. It had broken her nose. She'd started to fall, caught herself, reeling in shock and pain. Fortunately, her mother had been in the next room and heard the commotion and had run to help her. Morgan had ended up with a swollen nose and black eyes while delivering Emma the next day at home. Swallowing hard,

Morgan wavered.

Right now, Jake and she were in that zone where trust was present. She could see it in his eyes. He enjoyed her nearness and so did she. This was one of those times, when it magically occurred, that made Morgan question her decision to keep Emma's birth from him. She wanted to tell him, but she couldn't. He always ran. She didn't want Emma to know her father and then have him disappear for years at a time. She didn't want her child's life emotionally torn up as her own had been by Jake. As his gaze narrowed on her upturned face, Morgan felt genuine care radiating off him toward her. *Damn it.* Life was torture. This was one of those times.

"Well," Jake said, giving her a teasing look, "you sure as hell picked the wrong career field, didn't you? In our business, the surgeon is only a step away if we get wounded."

She held up her fingers and crossed them. "So far, so good. Three years with boots on the ground and all I have to gripe about are a few shrapnel scars and bruises." And then Morgan added in a wry voice, "And a few puncture scars in my butt from those damned Afghan saddle nails."

Jake's brows fell as she pointed to her

darkly tanned lower arm with its visible thin, white scars. Reaching out without thinking, his fingers barely grazed her arm. "I know. And it hurts me to see you having suffered, Morgan. . . ."

His huskily spoken words flowed through her. Jake's gesture surprised her. It wasn't sexual, but sincere and caring. Kindness. Her skin tingled and warmed beneath his unexpected touch. This was something new between them. Where had Jake developed this side to himself? Certainly not with her. Maybe he was maturing after all? Dropping her arm to her side, Morgan whispered, "Listen, in the black-ops business, this is part of the price you pay to be in the game."

Nodding, Jake absorbed her nearness, their intimacy strong as they watched the sunset deepen, the light pink of the clouds hanging on the peaks of the Hindu Kush turning a fiery orange. "Yeah, one of many things we pay for the price of admission."

"I don't regret it."

"Neither do I. I can't conceive of myself doing anything else in my life. Being a SEAL is all I ever dreamed. I'm happy where I'm at."

It felt as if a stake had been driven into Morgan's heart. If she'd had *any* doubts about telling Jake about Emma, she didn't now. SEALs rotated on a two-year turn-table. Eighteen months of continuous, non-stop training and schooling in the U.S. and then six months of combat duty in Afghan-istan for Team Three SEALs. Other teams were assigned to far-flung locations where SEALs were needed elsewhere in the world. Jake was with ST3, and they were always focused on Middle East assignments. She managed to say softly, "I know you're happy."

Hearing the strain in her tone, Jake looked over at her. "You're not?"

"I didn't say that." If things were differ-ent, if Jake wasn't in the SEALs, Morgan might have revealed that he was a father. Emma deserved a father in her life, although her own dad, Jim Boland, was the closest her daughter had to a father figure. For that, Morgan was grateful. Emma was doted upon, deeply loved and cared for by her parents. They gave her a steady, affectionate foundation, and she was thriving beneath their care.

Looking up into Jake's eyes, seeing the light of conviction in them, her spirits sank. Even if she told him Emma was his daugh-ter, he'd run from that responsibility again, just as he'd run from her at Annapolis when she'd miscarried their first child. Anguish

151

moved through Morgan along with frustration. It was a terrible secret to carry. Sometimes, at moments of weakness like this, with Jake at her side, attentive and caring, she was guilt-ridden.

Desperate to change topics, she said, "The Apaches found nothing up there." She pointed toward the twelve-thousand-foot mountain south of the village. "Hamid is sending the boys with the goat herds up there tomorrow morning to snoop around."

"Yeah, but Apache infrared can't shoot into a cave to locate and confirm warm bodies. I think we need to have ground assets, people on the ground to do the hard work. Maybe one of those boys will spot Khogani again." Jake rubbed the back of his neck, still uneasy. All day, he'd been tense and alert as the medical teams had gone about their work in the village. Even with two Apaches flying overhead and watching to keep the teams safe, he hadn't felt good about the situation. Finally, he muttered, "I don't have a good feeling about this, Morgan."

"You feel Khogani around, too?"

"Do you?"

"Yeah, the last two days." Morgan grimaced. "I think Khogani is up there. We might not see him, but he's there. Watching."

Releasing a breath, Jake dug the toe of his boot into the dirt. "Good to know."

"It's our sixth sense that keeps us alive out here."

Jake scowled at the mountain, now turning dark and shadowed. The cape of the night drew silently across the sky. "We've got a request for a drone to monitor that mountain in the night hours with infrared capability, but they can't spare us one."

Just as frustrated as he was, Morgan nodded. "Drones are great, when they work. Vero was saying that the CIA drones out of Camp Bravo were broken. Both of them. He said it was a software problem. They've got an Air Force team flying in from Bagram to fix them and get them back into the air to provide us support."

Jake whispered a curse. "That doesn't help us now."

"I wish we had a Raven."

Ravens were very small, handheld drones. Jake had his team carry one in their third-line gear. They could fly the drone, the size of a real raven, and it would give them real-time camera intel into his laptop that he carried with him. The small drone was able to fly above an area where they were hunting the enemy and locate them. "Yeah, well, they're in short supply, too," he grumbled. American drone makers were building drones as fast as humanly possible. All black-ops groups used them. But so did the rest of the military. It had become critical when an adequate supply of drones couldn't be produced fast enough to help the troops out in the field. It left teams like his open to attack.

"What do you want to do?" Morgan asked, feeling Jake's energy change. She sensed his worry and was concerned, too. A five-foot wall was no match for an enemy who wanted to infiltrate a village like this one.

"Nothing. Stay alert is all." His brows drew down as he almost said that he wanted them together in an abandoned house somewhere else in the village. Jake didn't like being separated at a time like this, yet he knew Morgan wanted to see the child and mother. She had powerful ties in this village with the people, and he wasn't at all surprised. There was a strong maternal side to Morgan he'd always been aware of. Now he was seeing it in action.

"We'll have one more day here tomorrow," she said, speaking in a quiet tone. Voices carried. It was darkening now, and she saw most of the villagers were inside their homes for the night. Even the few stray dogs were sitting or lying on the doorsteps, hoping for a scrap of food being handed out to them later after the family ate dinner.

"Yeah, I want to get going, but there's no sense making a move unless we can pick up Khogani's trail."

Morgan heard the frustration in his deep timbre. Her arm still tingled warmly from his brief touch. "We'll dig ditches tomorrow and get that done for the village. Service work by U.S. forces always makes for friendly villagers."

Jake laughed a little as he pushed the toe of his boot through the dry soil. "Yeah, we've converted to ditchdiggers. I'm sure that will look good on my résumé. Someone will be impressed by it."

Morgan knew he'd rather be on the hunt, have a focus and be on the mission. So would she. But it would do no good to start climbing that mountain in search of Khogani unless they had a trail to follow. If they had one, then all bets were off. Like a bomb-detection dog and handler, they'd be on the scent. Both of them knew how to track and find their enemy. And she lived to find Khogani. "Patience, Ramsey."

"Normally, I have plenty of it," he griped,

giving her a good-natured smile.

The corners of her mouth tipped upward. In the dusk, her wide beautiful eyes were accentuated. Though aching to touch Morgan, to love her, Jake pushed all those selfish desires deep down within him. They had no real trust. He'd destroyed it. And this mission was their focus, not their broken relationship. "Okay, I'll see you tomorrow at 0530," he said, lifting his hand and placing it briefly on her shoulder. "Good night."

His hand came to rest on her shoulder. Turning, she whispered, "Good night . . ." before heading toward the wall where there was a well-worn path.

CHAPTER TEN

Jake picked up his shovel. The morning sun was just crawling over the Hindu Kush as he and his five-man Afghan team went to the opposite end of the field where the ditch needed to be dug. Morgan was at the other end with her five volunteers. The morning was cool, and he was glad to have his Kevlar and cammies on. They carried so much gear usually that jackets weren't worn unless it snowed or rained.

Children began to gather along the ditch after breakfast, helping Jake and his men. They threw out large clods of dirt and rocks, removing them from the growing ditch. Jake liked the kids' laughter; it raised his spirits. The stray dogs came and ran after the clods of dirt the children threw for them to fetch. Every now and again, he'd looked up to catch sight of Morgan working. If her team of men found it odd a woman would be digging a ditch, it didn't show. Every now and again, he could hear her laughter. That made him feel good, too.

As he dug, watching Morgan, his mind revolved back to his chronically ill mother. She couldn't lift a glass of water, much less do what Morgan was presently doing. Mouth quirking, Jake thought maybe he needed to stop seeing her and his mother in the same light. They were direct opposites. And Morgan's impassioned plea to him in Hawaii to see her differently was sinking in.

Sweat ran freely down his face as he worked with his Afghan crew. A pang of intense emotion moved through his chest. Jake thought about Amanda, his late wife. She had not been helpless like his mother, but she had relied on him emotionally for strength. Jake hadn't felt imprisoned by Amanda's need to be protected; rather, he'd expected that from a spouse. His wife had willingly accepted him being the strong one in the family. From the time they'd met in a bar in Coronado, he'd known Amanda was enamored with him because he was a SEAL. To her, he'd been a hero. Jake realized she'd seen life through rose-colored glasses. And she'd loved him with everything she had. All Amanda had wanted was a family and to be a mother. He had been ready to settle down and take responsibility for a family.

Jake swallowed the sadness from his past.

On a break near 1000, Jake walked up the half-finished ditch toward Morgan. She was sitting down on the ground, sucking water out of the CamelBak that she carried. He came and sat down inches away from her. Morgan's red hair was dusty, and strands clung damply against her perspiring skin. Her eyes were shining with happiness. She'd been an incredible athlete at Annapolis, reveling in her physical strength and endurance.

"Looks like we're making good progress," he said before taking a drink of water.

Morgan removed her boonie hat and pushed the dusty strands away from her face. "I figure by evening, we'll be done."

Jake studied the sunlit slope of the mountain. Early this morning, five boys had herded their goats up across the boulder-strewn slope. None was visible now, each herd having taken a different trail along the nine-thousand-foot level for their goats to find sparse grass or brush to eat. The children had been told to keep alert for Khogani. If any of them spotted him or his men, they were to drive their flock back down the mountain to the village and tell Hamid.

"I don't see any kid coming back with his

goats yet," Morgan said, watching as Jake stared darkly at the mountain. Earlier, she'd contacted Vero at J-bad and found out the drones were still unavailable.

"This is something I never knew about you," he teased. "Being a ditchdigger. Or is that your civil-engineer passion to artfully push dirt around expressing itself?"

Grinning a little, Morgan silently absorbed Jake's nearness. They sat on a raised dirt dike between the fields and their ditch. The other workers and children were taking a break, as well, the wives coming out with jars of water to refresh them. "My parents work with a Catholic mission down in Sonora, Mexico. From the time I could remember, we would drive down once a year and stay at a village for two weeks and help dig rows in the fields to help them out." She dusted off her hands. "My dad is a civil engineer, and I used to follow him around and he showed me how irrigation was important to farmers. By the time I was ten, I was digging ditches alongside my parents."

Jake considered her information. "Your parents are good people. Not many families would drive down to Mexico to help dig ditches in fields." Tractors weren't available down in the poor parts of that country, Jake knew. It was shovels, pickaxes, rakes and hoes to create the long rows and then plant the seeds for the coming year.

Morgan nodded. "My folks have always believed in helping the poor. My mother was abandoned at birth, handed over to a priest at a Catholic church. She never forgot the church's generosity to her."

"Your mother is a strong woman to come out of that kind of adversity." Jake thought about his own life. He'd had a mother and father. Both had been absent. He'd been abandoned in a different way, although growing up, he'd never seen himself like that. Only later, as an adult, did he understand the feelings he'd had as a kid.

"My mom went through five or six foster homes by the time she was eighteen," Morgan said. "It was really hard on her. I don't think I could have survived something like that."

"What did she do at eighteen?"

"Got two jobs and went to college. She wanted to be a registered nurse to help others. Only, she didn't have enough money to finish college, so she joined the Marine Corps to save money. And when the WLF got formed, she volunteered because her best friend, Lisa, enlisted. Her original plan was to sock the money away for three years, finish her commitment to the WLF and then go back and get her degree."

Jake wrapped his hands around his drawn-up legs, hearing pain in Morgan's tone. "After the WLF was disbanded, did she get her degree?"

"Yes, eventually she did. My dad got a dishonorable discharge from the Marine Corps because he fraternized with my mother, who was enlisted."

"Ouch."

"Really." Her mouth puckered. "My dad was philosophical about it. He said love didn't recognize officer rank or enlisted ratings. He started an engineering and construction business, which became highly successful. It enabled my mom to go back to school and get her degree as an RN. By the time I came along, she worked at a Gunnison, Colorado, mission helping the poor at a medical clinic."

"So, you're driven to help the underdogs of life?"

Meeting his gaze, his eyes contemplative, Morgan said, "Yes."

"And you're doing the same over here." Jake gestured toward the village. "You're using your paramedic skills whenever you can to help the Afghans?"

"Always. I don't believe we have to be regarded as killers just because we're in black ops." Morgan sat up and moved her shoulders as if to relieve the tension in them. "Nation building and education are the only way to get the poor lifted out of this hellish abject poverty. I love working with the black-ops groups, no matter what branch of the military they come from. When they come into a village, they bring medicine, food and money, and it makes everyone feel good. I haven't met one guy from any team that doesn't want to help these poor people."

"You're right." Jake felt his way through her background. He found himself wishing he'd been a helluva lot more interested in Morgan's history when they'd been twenty years old or even later when they'd reconnected briefly. He'd had a year to explore her family story at Annapolis and get to know her, and he hadn't. They'd shared sex. Great sex, really, but he hadn't been mature enough to look beyond his own self-gratification. Morgan was so much more than Jake had ever realized. He was beginning to understand her commitment to the military and to the struggling Afghan people who were trying to survive. She realized she could be a positive role model to the Afghans in many ways.

"You always put your money where your

mouth is, Boland?"

Morgan met his glinting gaze. "Does it show, Ramsey?" Her heart expanded as she saw something else in his eyes. It felt good to Morgan, but she couldn't interpret it. Jake's mouth softened, the corners pulling up. A powerful emotion, an intense yearning for him, tunneled through her. If only . . . oh, God, if only they could go back and rewrite the script of their moments together. . . .

CHAPTER ELEVEN

The sun was setting low in the west as Morgan sat with Jake on the first floor of Hamid's home. Earlier, she'd laid out a cloth and field-stripped her AW Mag. It was something she did every evening. All the working parts would get dusty, and when in the field, it was imperative that the rifle be kept as clean as possible.

Jake was sitting cross-legged nearby, helping to clean each moving mechanism, the parts spread between them on the protective canvas.

"Did you get local oil?" Jake asked, picking up the 32X Night Force scope.

Morgan nodded, drying her hands on another cloth she kept in a plastic bag in her third-line gear. "Reza gave me some."

"Good." SEAL snipers had learned long ago to use local oil to clean their rifles. Taliban, if they came across the odor on the air, would smell it. If it was a foreign oil, they knew the difference. And then they would know an American or another foreign sniper was nearby and take action. Something as simple as this could make the difference between life and death for a SEAL sniper remaining hidden or being found.

Jake tried to ignore Morgan's nearness. This turned out to be his favorite time of day with her. Hamid's wife was gracious enough to give them the large room on the first floor to clean their equipment. He glanced over as she dried her hands, making sure they were not damp before picking up the Night Force scope. She pulled out a baby wipe to gently clean the light film of dust off the body of the scope.

Jake would occasionally glance over at her, noticing how relaxed she was when cleaning her rifle. The warmth of the sun through the windows made the room stuffy, but he didn't mind. His heart moved with a lot of mixed emotions. The more he found out about her background, the more he chastised himself for his past behavior. If he'd known about Morgan's history, would that have drawn him even closer to her? Hell, yes, it would have. Jake respected people who helped others who were less well-off than himself. The SEAL community had it in their bones, too. The first aid, the medicine, food and anything else they could give to the villagers were always priorities. SEALs were human. They didn't like to see people suffer, either.

He cleared his throat as he reached for another baby wipe. "How did you survive SEAL sniper school?"

Morgan lifted her chin. She studied Jake's expression and saw real curiosity there. "It was the hardest school I've ever attended. But the instructors were incredible."

"In your childhood, did your parents hunt?" Often, Jake found men who became snipers had been hunters in their youth. With Morgan having a set of military parents, it was a real possibility. He was fascinated to see how her unusual childhood had molded her into the woman she was today.

Morgan's mouth quirked. "My mother, in the last foster family who took her in at twelve years old, had a father who hunted. They had six foster kids and he hunted nearly every day to put meat on the table for them. My mother was the oldest, so he taught her at age twelve how to use a 30.06 to drop a buck."

Surprised, Jake muttered, "A 30.06? For a twelve-year-old? That would knock any kid on their ass from the recoil."

"It did, and often. My mother hated killing anything. Especially animals. But the family was poor and couldn't feed the six children properly, so the foster father pushed her into hunting with him."

Shaking his head, Jake muttered, "Your mother had a hell of a childhood."

"You didn't exactly have a good one, either," Morgan noted drily, running the baby wipe down the long length of the scope cradled between her fingers. She looked up and saw the corners of his mouth tuck inward, a sign Jake was feeling emotional pain. She was glad she knew him so well because he always hid how he really felt from everyone. A SEAL trait.

"I'm beginning to think my childhood was a piece of cake compared to your mother's. That must have been hell for her."

"It was, but that's why she stood out in the WLF. She was a sniper-quality shooter."

"Did she teach you, then?"

"No, my dad did. He was the hunter, and I grew up in the Rocky Mountains, nine thousand feet, and he'd take me out with him." Morgan smiled softly. "I loved learning how to track. My father had been a Recon Marine and had gone through Marine sniper school. He was a natural for it, and he taught me to track an animal even on scree, across rocky slopes. I was really good

168

at it." Her brows fell. "I didn't like shooting a deer or elk, though. My mother had a soft spot for animals, and so do I."

"But you did it anyway?"

"Yes. My dad explained that we'd use the meat. It wouldn't be wasted. He has some Cherokee blood in him, and he taught me to pray for the release of the spirit of whatever I shot. There was a respect for the animal and its spirit. That made me feel better about it."

"So, when you were sent to SEAL sniper school, that background probably served you very well."

"It did. The SEAL instructors were tough, but they really wanted us to graduate. Five women didn't make it. In the end, they just didn't have the kind of patience it took. There were times I lay eight to ten hours out in a field, with the instructors watching through binos, binoculars, to try and locate us. I remember waiting five or six hours for a buck to pass by close enough to take him down as a kid. For me, it was easy to remain unseen."

"You've always been a patient person," Jake noted. And then he grinned. "Even with your red hair."

Snorting softly, Morgan appreciated his praise. These quiet times with Jake were going to end shortly, and she would miss them. "My red hair symbolizes my passion for life, for what I feel is worth fighting for."

"A banner for sure. What's the longest sniper shot you've ever taken out in the field?" Jake knew everyone graduating from SEAL sniper school was expected to hit a target at a thousand yards and nail it. However, school shooting and then taking those skills out into the real world were markedly different. Wind direction, weather, the barometric pressure and so many other variables all fell into whether a sniper could hit his or her target. One shot, one kill, was the maxim, although it might take two shots. Or even three.

"I nailed an al Qaeda regional leader at eleven hundred yards." She lifted her chin and held his gaze. "What about you? What's your longest shot?"

"I took out a Taliban leader at twelve hundred yards. The wind was a key player. I missed the first shot but dropped him on the second round."

"The wind," she muttered. "God, how I hate the wind. It's the worst variable of all. And in these mountains, it makes getting a shot ten times tougher."

"Yeah, that's the truth. Mountains make their own weather, and wind patterns change in a heartbeat. In school, what was your final graduation score?" There was a possible one thousand points a student sniper could earn. In Jake's class, no one got close to that number. He was curious about the women going through the training. Had they been better or worse scores than the men?

"I made nine hundred. The other women were in the high eight hundreds."

"That's a damn fine score, Morgan." And it was. Very few male students made the nine-hundred range. It spoke of her abilities and Jake began to understand why she'd been picked for this op.

"What was your graduation score, Ramsey?"

"Eight seventy-five. Nowhere near yours."

"That's a good score."

Jake shrugged. "I wanted it to be better, but things happened in the class. I had one sniper student on a stalk move suddenly in front of me. The instructor watching the field where we were hiding and stalking. He caught movement of the taller grass. He didn't sight the student, but he found me instead. I was so pissed."

"That doesn't seem right," Morgan said, feeling for him. She knew how important those scores were. The best snipers got the best assignments. And Jake was a relentless type A who always strove to be the best. It was simply in his genes.

"It wasn't," Jake growled. "After the stalk, I cornered the guy, a Marine, and I told him if he ever tried anything like that again on me, I was going to field-strip him like a sniper rifle."

"And?"

"He took my threat to heart. By the end of the schooling, we were good friends. We are to this day."

"So, you must have picked it up out in the field? Otherwise, you wouldn't have been chosen for this op."

"Yeah, once I got out in the field, I excelled."

"Does it bother you to shoot a human?"

Hearing the guarded emotion in her tone, Jake held her serious expression. "No. I'm taking out a bad guy who's killing a lot of innocent people, not to mention, our military people. You?"

Shrugging, Morgan put the finishing touches on the scope, satisfied it was as clear as it was going to get. "I've always looked at it this way, Jake. If I take a bad guy down, that means he's not going to threaten another village, kill the men and bury IEDs for the children to step on." Her mouth compressed as she thought about the next words. "Like you, if I take out one of these monsters, it means American soldiers may get to go home to their wives and children. I'm the fulcrum point between the bad guys and the good guys."

Nodding, Jake rasped, "It's the same for me."

Morgan laid the scope aside after putting it back into the protective pouch that was padded as well as rainproof. "I want Khogani. I want to take the shot that kills that murdering son of a bitch." She stood up, slid her hands against her thighs and looked out the window. "I'm going to stay with Roya again. You okay with that?" The sun had set and darkness was nearly complete.

Jake nodded. "Go ahead, but wear your helmet and NVG gear? It's dark outside."

"I will. Too bad the boys coming back earlier with the goat herds didn't spot Khogani."

Jake grimaced. "Yeah, but I can feel the bastard is nearby. Watching."

"I'll get my gear and leave. My radio will be on. Have a good night," she said, rubbing her neck.

Jake would reassemble the rifle shortly. Everything was clean. He knew that Roya and Morgan were very close, and he wanted her to be able to spend one more night with the woman and her sickly daughter. "Stay safe out there. . . ."

Night had fallen. If not for the grainy green that Morgan could see through her NVGs, night-vision goggles, after turning them on, she wouldn't be able to see her hand in front of her face. The problem with NVGs was that there was no depth of perception, so when she saw a deep rut, she knew it was deeper or wider than it appeared and would slow her stride. As she walked quietly down the center of the street, heading for the wall where there was a path to cut quickly across two streets to Roya's house, Morgan keyed all her senses.

The night air was cold and humid. She wore her cammies but not a jacket. Maybe she should have. Far off in the distance, she heard the hoot of an owl, the sound carrying from the fields. What she didn't hear were crickets. They always sang at night around the village. Slowing as she made a left turn between the last mud house and the wall, Morgan wished she had better hearing. She stood and waited. It was her sniper's patience coming forward to serve her.

No cricket sounds.

Morgan barely turned her head, listening for the three feral dogs that lived in the village. If someone was sneaking around outside the walls, the dogs would hear them first, and they'd start barking. They were a first line of defense.

Nothing.

The palm of her hand came to rest on the butt of her pistol. No dogs barking meant all was well. Or, as her lips thinned, considering the odd lack of night noises, the enemy slit the dogs' throats before they could bark and give away their position. All of that ran through Morgan's mind. She wasn't going to take chances and spoke in a quiet tone into the mic near her lips.

"North wall, end of Hamid's street. No night sounds. Going two streets over. Out." It was a precaution, one that always paid off to let Jake know her location. Just in case.

"Roger."

His voice was equally quiet in responding. Voices carried a hell of a long ways, and a short few words. A whisper could be heard more easily by the enemy than speaking in a low tone. Without thinking, Morgan unsnapped the retaining strap across the SIG, in case she needed to draw the weapon. There was never a time that the pistol wasn't unsafed. It didn't have a safety on it. Morgan made sure a bullet was always in the chamber. She would not have time for those two actions in a firefight as it would slow her down. And it could get her killed. Her fingers automatically closed around the butt of the pistol as she walked very quietly down the well-trodden dirt path parallel to the wall.

She had just reached the second road, where Roya lived, when she heard a sound. Morgan turned on her heel, her heart suddenly banging in her throat. Her eyes widened as she saw three men leap up onto the wall, rifles in hand, dressed with bullet belts across their chests.

They saw her, and all hell broke loose.

Morgan's hand went to pull the SIG swiftly out of the holster. Everything slowed down. Her breath caught as she saw the one man stand up on the wall, aim his AK-47 at her and fire.

She fired simultaneously.

The bullet struck her Kevlar, high and to her right shoulder, spinning her backward, knocking her off her feet. Stunned, Morgan slammed into the ground. She rolled, hearing the snarls of the men scrambling over the wall. She knew they were Khogani's men. They dressed differently than the Shinwari men at the village.

As she rolled and leaped to her feet, two more bullets snapped and popped close to her head. She crouched, hands on the SIG, firing as one more man struggled over the wall. He cried out once, toppled forward, landing in a heap on the path inside the wall.

The third man lifted his weapon. Morgan shot first, the bullet finding his head.

Gasping for breath, her heart thundering in her chest, she managed to rasp out her position to Jake. Her chest hurt like hell. With one hand, Morgan frantically felt and touched her upper right chest. *No blood.* The thick Level 4 ceramic plate in her vest had done its job. Damn, it hurt to breathe! How many more Taliban were outside that wall?

Turning, Morgan heard a number of doors opening, men running toward her, ancient rifles in hand. Gasping, she didn't dare fall. But she wanted to as dizziness slammed into her. Right now, she wished she had an M-4 instead of the pistol. Morgan warily glanced at the heap of three men piled below the wall. None of them moved. Her shots had been clean and deadly.

Jake raced to where she was staggering and watching the wall, her pistol pointed at it. He skidded to a halt, nearly stumbling over the dead men. Leaping over them, his

M-4 at his shoulder, he moved swiftly to her side.

"You all right?" Jake asked, breathing hard, watching the wall. He moved silently along the corner of the mud house, taking his thermal scope and moving it across the mud wall. *Nothing.*

Jake was worried about Morgan. She didn't sound right. Terror raced through him as he silently stepped past her and kept his scope moving along the wall in the other direction. *Dammit!* His warnings, his sense of an impending attack, had come true. Worse, as Jake remained fully focused on the threat, deep down inside him, he realized Morgan could have been killed.

"Answer me," he ordered. "Are you okay?"

"Yeah," she croaked. "Three over the wall. There could be more outside it." Morgan continued to observe the wall for as far as she could see it in both directions.

Reza ran up to them, gasping and out of breath. He had a rifle in his hand. His eyes were wide with terror.

Morgan pleaded, "Reza, get the men of the village to stand guard along the wall. There could be more of Khogani's men on the other side ready to attack."

"Yes," Reza said, turning and quickly speaking in Pashto to the gathering, shaken farmers standing warily with rifles in their hands.

Morgan felt as if the area of her right shoulder was on fire. Every breath was damned painful. She wanted to collapse and struggle to draw in some air. Jake came back to her side, NVGs down, M-4 raised and ready to take on anyone else who was stupid enough to clamber over the wall.

Morgan tried to steady her breathing. "This might not be over. Can you get the sniper rifle with a thermal imaging scope up on Hamid's roof? It's the highest roof in the village. We need to see what's out on the other side of these walls." The scope would detect body heat, making them easy targets to shoot.

Jake nodded, unsure of leaving her alone out here. "I'll get the rifle up on the roof and let you know when I get there."

"Be careful," she said, pressing her hand against her right shoulder, the pain excruciating. Her shoulder was locking up on her, making it difficult to move her arm.

"Call Vero. We *have* to get a drone up here or we're dead meat." Jake turned on his heel, running as hard as he could down the wall to get back to Hamid's house.

Hand shaking, Morgan changed channels on her radio and made the call.

CHAPTER TWELVE

For two hours, the village remained tense and on high alert. Jake saw nothing through the Night Force scope. It would pick up any movement in the darkest of nights because of its thermal imaging capability. Morgan got Hamid to set out a watch of ten men along the walls and gate. They would be relieved every two hours by another group of men. The arrangement would go on until dawn. Hamid ordered everyone else to go to bed.

Morgan walked over to a group of farmers. They'd laid out the corpses, beginning to search them for identification, letters or anything else that would give them intel. She spoke into the mic. "I'm coming up."

"Roger."

She told Reza, who was in charge of the search for anything important on the dead men, she would be up on Hamid's roof. Morgan could see how scared he was with perspiration dotting his wrinkled brow. Everyone was frightened. They now knew Khogani had ridden down on another village forty miles away and decimated it during the night hours. It could happen again and they knew it.

Holstering her SIG, Morgan ducked between the wall and the houses, making her way toward Hamid's house, two streets over. Darkness closed in on her. She heard the voices murmuring in Pashto behind her. Candles had been extinguished in the many homes, the darkness complete except for the sparkling stars that seemed close enough to reach up and pluck out of the sky.

Suddenly, Morgan felt her stomach lurch. Bile filled her throat, coming up fast. She fell to her hands and knees, and her body convulsed and she violently heaved. With her head hanging, breathing hard, Morgan's eyes were tightly shut. It was a visceral reaction to the firefight. Her stomach convulsed again. She dry heaved, arms wrapped around her stomach, retching. Panting for breath, saliva dripping out of her mouth, Morgan waited for another wave to strike her. Finally, it passed. Dazed, she grabbed the CamelBak and sucked water into her mouth, swished it around and spat it out. Shivering, she forced herself to her feet. A fine tremble sang through her. Morgan leaned against the wall of a house. Gasping, trying to hang on, she tried to suck in large drafts of air. The pain in her right shoulder reacted and she groaned, bending over, hand pressed against her Kevlar.

Finally, Morgan calmed down. This wasn't the first time she'd vomited after a firefight. The shock of combat often brought down many a soldier. Wiping her sweaty brow and mouth, Morgan forced herself to stand. She drank some more water, knowing she would become dehydrated from loss of so much fluid.

It felt as if an hour had passed, but when she looked at her watch, it had been only five minutes. Of hell. Pushing forward, she hurried to be with Jake up on the roof.

Morgan lay on the top of the roof, slowly moving the AW's Night Force scope across the land outside the village. The air was cool and she shivered. Snipers had to get used to being miserable in any number of climatic conditions. Their job was to hunt and find the enemy.

Jake was next to her, using the thermal scope on his M-4, slowly searching the area for heat signatures. He made her feel safer than usual. There was something quiet, steady and solid about him since the attack. She'd never seen Jake in action, never fought with him at her side. But he was a SEAL, and his reactions to the attack were the same as the men she'd fought alongside on other teams. Safety . . . there wasn't any. A night breeze made her fingers cold and numb as she moved the stock of the rifle toward the south. Her right shoulder ached like hell, and it hurt to push the stock into it as she needed to. That bothered Morgan because when setting up to shoot, the fiberglass stock had to be jammed deep into the sniper's shoulder. Right now, she could barely stand anything against her swollen, aching flesh.

"Nothing," she whispered into the mic.

"Not a damn thing," Jake groused.

Morgan moved quietly, reorienting her long body on the rooftop, slowly scanning the next area. Vero had called back. There were no drones available. The Air Force crews were working nonstop to figure out what kind of software malfunction had occurred in the two based at Camp Bravo. They had no eyes in the sky to protect themselves or this vulnerable village.

"Tangos," she rasped. "Nine o'clock." *Tango* was military speak for *enemy*.

Instantly, Jake quietly changed position,

aiming his M-4 scope to the south where hers was pointed. Toward that mountain he knew Khogani was hiding on. "Got 'em." Jake saw at least ten men running toward the slope, rifles in hand.

"It has to be Khogani's men," Morgan gritted out, her hands tightening on the sniper rifle. "I'd love to take those bastards out. . . ."

The distance was too far away for a clean shot. "Better to let them show us where they're going."

"Yeah," she grunted. Her adrenaline continued to course through her body, making her heart pound. Pulling out her wheel book, a small computer every sniper carried, Morgan knew Jake had a bead on them. She tapped in what she saw. How many men. How many weapons. And then she rolled back onto her stomach, pulled the AW Mag stock against her cheek, scope near her eye and continued to follow the group. They took one of the goat paths and she was amazed at how quickly the fleeing group moved at that altitude. Morgan reminded herself these men had been born at high altitude and could handle the thin air and still move like swift goats up that scree slope. Neither of them could ever move that quickly; their bodies were simply not attuned to working in rarefied air.

"At least now," Jake muttered, at her elbow, "we know they're here. And we know where they're going. The kids will know that path and where it leads." It was the break Jake was hoping for.

Morgan heard someone climbing the rickety wooden ladder that led to the roof where they were. Automatically, she turned the rifle in that direction, looking into the scope. She took no chances. Reza popped up on the roof, waving his hand.

"Don't shoot me!" he called, panting.

Lowering the rifle, Morgan called, "Over here, Reza. Stay low. . . ."

Reza came and hunkered down between them, breathing hard. "Hamid's men have confirmed those are Khogani's soldiers. They're Hill tribesmen."

"Have they found any intel on them?" Morgan demanded.

"Yes, one of them had a map." He waved it in his hand. "I took it. It could be valuable. It might show us where Khogani is hiding in these caves. I haven't had time to look at it yet."

"Okay," Jake murmured, "good job. Go back and make sure those bodies are searched thoroughly. We need every scrap of intel they can provide us."

"Yes," Reza whispered. "Did you find them?"

"Yes, we did," Morgan muttered, still following the green dots that were men climbing the goat trail. "There won't be any more attacks tonight."

Jake turned and sat up, facing the Afghan. "Go tell Hamid that Khogani's men have run back to the mountain. There's no enemy around the village. Have them stand down and put out the guard watch."

"Yes, sir," Reza murmured, scuttling quickly across the roof to the ladder.

Jake rolled back on his stomach, pulling the M-4 scope to his eye. "They're gone."

"Yeah, they disappeared over the ridge," Morgan said. The shot would be too far away, and Jake was right: better to let the survivors of this attack flee back to Khogani. She was sure the Hill leader was going to be pissed. A dark feeling ran through Morgan, a sense of primal satisfaction she'd taken out three of his men. It would be three less for them to fight.

"We're going to have to ride at dawn and go after them," Jake said. He watched as Morgan continued to slowly scan the ridge of the mountain. If he had any doubts she knew her job, he was satisfied now. Her movements, her skills, were as good as any

SEAL team member who had his back. She was solid. That took the question that always hung at the back of his mind out of the equation between them. It still stunned him that she was a woman doing a man's job. And doing it professionally and as an equal.

Sitting up, his mouth compressed as he laid the M-4 between his arms, Jake knew he had to stop looking at Morgan as less than a man in combat. Tonight, it had been three against one, and she'd dropped all of them with her SIG. That impressed him. Morgan's behavior was cool, calm and collected. Yet, as he sat there, gazing up at the bright stars of the Milky Way that looked like a river of light across the cold heavens, he worried for her on a personal level.

Jake struggled not to care for her. He avoided giving his feelings any label. There was no time or place for them. Not right now. Glancing down, he studied her profile, the stock tight against her cheek, still watching. Still waiting. Solid. Morgan was solid.

"Let's get down," Jake told her roughly, his hands numb against the rifle because of the cold. "They've hightailed it. Khogani will know we'll be looking for him at dawn. If anything, he's planning to leave the area right now. He knows we have drones, and

187

his only escape is under the cover of night."

Morgan sat up, crossing her legs, their knees brushing against one another. She rested the AW Mag in her arms as if cradling a baby. "Khogani knows we have drones up 24/7. He knows he can be spotted at night, too."

"Yeah," Jake said wryly, "but we have no drones. No eyes in the sky."

"He doesn't know that." Morgan stared, frowning at the mountain she could see in the grainy green of her NVGs. "He'll take to the caves, go through connecting tunnels and probably try and get out of the area that way."

Jake nodded. "Yeah, let's get down. I want to see if they found any more intel on those bodies."

It was only midnight, but to Morgan, it felt as if days had passed as she unrolled her sleeping bag in a room of a deserted home. Jake had insisted to Hamid that they remain together from now on to deter any new threats. They were a team and had to remain together for the protection of the village. She was too tired to argue, taking the room on the left. There was a central room between the two smaller rooms. Jake would probably sleep in the other room on the right.

Morgan slowly peeled open her Kevlar. Her right shoulder hurt like hell. Shedding the heavy vest, she dug into her H-gear and located a pen flashlight, pulled her dark green T-shirt downward and away from her neck in order to expose her right shoulder. Morgan's eyes widened as she caught sight of it. Her entire shoulder was heavily swollen from where the bullet had struck the Kevlar. The bright purple-and-red bruising spread out from where the bullet had punched into one of the protective curved ceramic chest plates that fitted into the vest pocket. It looked to Morgan like a huge splat of purple paint as large as Jake's hand. Grimacing, she released her T-shirt and shut off the light. There was nothing to be done about it. Morgan desperately needed sleep. She pulled herself down into the bag, boots remaining on. She'd use the rucksack as a pillow. The sleeping bag was warm.

Exhausted, her shoulder aching, her stomach still rolling off and on with nausea, she tried to relax. Jake would arrive soon, and a sense of safety descended around Morgan. She heard the door open and close.

"Jake?"

"Yeah, it's me. Where are you?"

"Room to your left. You take the one on the right."

Morgan heard him grunt, the door close and the brush of his boots against the hard packed dirt floor. It was the last sounds she heard, dropping off an abyss into blackness.

Jake snapped awake when he heard Morgan moan. Or was he dreaming? Instantly, his hand went to the SIG he kept next to his ruck. Silently rising to his feet, he keyed his hearing. Morgan groaned more loudly this time. What the hell was going on? Pistol raised, Jake could see slats of moonlight around the wooden door. It gave him just enough light to see the room ahead of him was empty. The small window in her room shed plenty of light.

Jake's eyes narrowed as he saw Morgan clearly. His gaze fixed on her slender neck. What the hell was that on it? He moved to her side, knelt down and gently placed his hand over her left shoulder.

Instantly, Morgan awakened, gasping.

Jake grabbed her right hand before she could reach her pistol near her head. "Easy," he breathed, "it's me. Jake." The wild, startled look in Morgan's eyes disappeared as she jerked into a sitting position, pushing his hand off her shoulder.

190

"What's wrong?" she demanded, her voice low and raspy.

"I heard you moaning," he said, remaining in a kneeling position above her.

"I was asleep!"

"Yeah, well, so was I until you woke me up. What the hell is that, Morgan?" He jabbed his index finger toward the right side of her neck.

"What?" She frowned and placed her hand protectively against her neck. It was swollen and painful to touch.

"Did you get hit out there tonight?" Jake demanded, worry evident in his eyes.

"Yes," Morgan sputtered defiantly. "I took a slug to the right shoulder but the plate protected me. I'm *fine,* Jake. Let me go back to sleep, will you?" She glared up at him, shaken by his attention. He reached down to his left thigh and pulled out the SOG knife from the sheath. Sucking in a breath, she snarled, "You are *not* going to slit my T-shirt in half, dammit!" She scooted away from him. Morgan knew from combat first aid, everyone wore a tan T-shirt and if there was an upper-body wound, the medic took his knife and slit it up the middle to get a good look at the injury.

"Why not?" he growled. "Dammit, Morgan, you're *hurt.* Or does that not compute?"

"It's just a damned bruise, Jake! Jesus, you're acting like a friggin' mother hen! Put that SOG away before you hurt somebody!"

His nostrils flared. He saw her anger and that stubborn set come to her mouth. "Okay, then you pull it over your head. I want to look at that bruise. It could be a hematoma, Morgan. And that could cause a blood clot and you could die. It needs to be checked out. You know that."

"I already looked at it before I went to bed. It's fine, Jake!" His face hardened even more. He wasn't taking "no" for an answer.

"Your choice, Morgan." Jake held the knife up in a warning position.

"Damn you! I don't have anything on under this T-shirt!" Her voice broke, and she stared malevolently back at him, just daring him to try cutting the fabric. It was her T-shirt, and she wasn't about to strip naked in front of him! And then he got a crazy smile on his face. He chuckled as he slipped the SOG back into the sheath on his waist.

"What the hell is so funny?" Morgan demanded angrily, pulling her knees up against her chest, arms wrapping around them. The care burning in his eyes never left, but she could see another emotion in them she couldn't interpret. Her heart was pounding, but it wasn't because she was afraid. It was because Jake was too close and she felt incredibly vulnerable after the night's action.

Jake sat back on his heels, resting his hands on his thighs. "You. It isn't like I haven't seen your breasts before, Morgan."

Shocked, she blinked once. And then she started to laugh. Jake's laughter joined hers. Pretty soon, she was laughing so long that she started hiccuping. It was a release, and she knew it. Hand across her mouth, she felt tears running down her cheeks, she'd laughed so hard. Morgan saw Jake wipe tears from his eyes, too, his mouth pulled into a silly grin.

Finally, she stopped. Her stomach hurt. The silence settled around them. "I guess we needed that."

"Yeah, been one helluva night." Jake reached out and pushed some of her red hair behind her ear. "All laughing aside, I need to examine your shoulder, Morgan." He saw her eyes go wide, and Jake finally got it. She felt vulnerable in a way he'd never seen her before. Combat did that to everyone. Especially after a firefight like tonight. And she'd been on the tip of the spear and taken a bullet. Reaching out, he leaned over and murmured, "Babe, you keep your T-shirt on. All I'm going to do is slip my fingers beneath your neckline and ease the fabric to one side and take a look at the area." He pulled out a penlight from his cammie pocket.

His breath warmed her cheek and jaw. His roughened fingers gently curved beneath the material. Carefully, Jake pulled the fabric away from her neck just enough to expose her upper shoulder. He was so close to her. Inhaling his male scent, Morgan closed her eyes, tense. Jake smelled good, despite no shower, fear sweat and dirt on his flesh. With his other hand, he pulled the T-shirt aside even more and carefully observed the area. The bruise was located well above her breast.

Morgan opened her eyes looking up at him. Her pulse was twitchy. Jake was so close . . . *oh, God, too close.* She felt blood rushing to her lower body, desire keening through her like an out-of-control flood. Her chest tightened with so many emotions. The urge to lean upward a few inches, tilt her head and close her mouth over his nearly unstrung her.

"That's a hematoma," Jake muttered, barely turning his head, meeting her eyes.

Morgan's lips had parted, her eyes trained on him. Instantly, his body responded. And so did his heart. Jake's hands froze in place on her T-shirt. Her mouth was bare inches from his, and he inhaled her feminine fragrance. Her expression was shadowed with wariness and longing. For him. And God help him, he wanted her just as badly. What was he going to do? What did she *want* him to do?

CHAPTER THIRTEEN

Jake released her T-shirt, holding Morgan's mutinous gaze. Damn, every cell in his body ached for her. It had to be different this time. He couldn't do what he'd done in the past. Before, he'd have just taken what was his, kissed her, loved her. He'd never asked permission from Morgan before, just assumed she wanted him as much as he wanted her. His voice came out husky as he asked, "Morgan, can I kiss you?"

Swallowing hard, she whispered brokenly, "Jake, I can't. . . ." And she couldn't. Emma needed a father who would be at her side no matter what happened in her life. Jake ran when things got piled up with too much responsibility. If she gave in, she'd be lost and never keep control over protecting her daughter. Never break the cycle between them that served neither of them any longer.

His face changed, sorrow coming to his eyes, his mouth a hard line. But she also saw something else. Maturity. Jake eased back, as if understanding.

"Okay," he rasped. "You got your blow-out kit in one of your leg pockets?"

"Yes, right lower pocket," she said, her voice unsteady. Every cell in her body screamed to kiss Jake, make love with him. Morgan felt tortured as never before, cursing whatever it was that made them like sex-starved animals around one another. And it would be great sex, but Morgan couldn't handle the aftermath.

Swallowing his remorse — and his frustration — Jake leaned over and carefully peeled back the sleeping bag and pulled the Velcro open on the right thigh pocket of her trousers. Every SEAL had two blow-out kits, medical supplies that could save their life. There would be a battle dressing, nasal-pharyngeal tube, Celox, a blood coagulant and other items needed to treat a gunshot wound or a sucking chest wound. He placed the items he needed in a row on her sleeping bag.

"You need two things for that hematoma," Jake went on, trying to sound casual. His body throbbed, and he gritted his teeth, trying to will away his physical hunger for Morgan. It was more than physical pain. Jake couldn't stop the grief he felt in his heart over her telling him no. He hadn't come in here thinking of kissing her or making love to her. He'd wanted to hold her after seeing she was injured. Yeah, his body wanted sex, but his heart was guiding him elsewhere: to give Morgan genuine care, something he'd never afforded her before. Amanda had taught him that a woman needed to be held, cared for, and that it wasn't always just about sex. She'd drawn him out of his selfish shell and made him see that love had a hell of a lot more facets, a much broader and deeper landscape. And she'd taught him how to hold their son, Joshua, in his arms.

New feelings Jake had never realized he'd had came to the surface as a result. That tiny baby boy, so innocent and vulnerable in his large arms and hands, had made him aware of his own ability to nurture another human with pure love. Between his wife and his son, they had changed him for the better. But that wasn't the man Morgan knew. She only saw the immature boy, and she didn't realize how much he'd changed and grown.

Jake had never seen Morgan as anything else other than a sex partner. Sure, he knew how to pleasure her, make sure she enjoyed it just as much as he did. But he'd never extended himself to hold her afterward, to feed her emotionally in another, less physical way. Now he wanted to, and Jake knew he could, but she'd turned him down cold. Their past always hung between them. He'd grown; he'd changed; he'd become more sensitive to a woman's needs, but Morgan wasn't about to let him through that barrier from their past to prove it. Jake couldn't blame her.

"We'll start with ice and a pain reliever," Jake said.

Warily, Morgan watched his expression in the shadows. Jake seemed tense, and she could tell why. But she couldn't make love with him now. Her shoulder was a mess, and she was in constant pain. Compressing her lips, she watched him pull out the chemical ice pack and a bottle of ibuprofen. His hands shook slightly. Hell, she felt like so much jelly inside herself right now, too.

It hurt to see the disappointment cross Jake's face. What amazed Morgan the most was that he was allowing her to see how he felt. In the past, any time he'd felt threatened, that game face would settle into place, completely unreadable. Detached. Maybe Jake *was* changing. He'd never asked if he could kiss her before. They'd always come together like hungry, primal animals in the midst of heat. It was volatile, earthy and utterly satisfying to both of them. Afterward, he'd roll out of the sack, get dressed and leave. Morgan needed more.

Jake handed her two ibuprofen and pulled over her CamelBak and placed it into her lap so she could suck some water after popping the pills into her mouth. When his hand touched her palm, heat seared up her fingers. His touch always brought her pleasure, igniting her lower body, triggering every hungry sexual need she possessed. Morgan thanked him, her voice barely above a whisper. Dutifully, she took the medication, drank water and laid the Camel-Bak aside.

"I don't know why I didn't think to put the ice pack on this," she uttered, lying down and pulling the cover of the sleeping bag up to her waist. She needed to put something between her and Jake. Her pulse was rapid and rising. He was so damned male that she could feel the grating sensation of longing deep within her. Jake was a consummate lover, and now, of all times, she wanted him for all the wrong reasons. He was a hunger she could never satisfy. *Damn.*

Jake gently slid the pack beneath her T-shirt and positioned it over the worst of the swelling. "None of us think clearly after being shot at. Don't be hard on yourself, Morgan." He tried to ignore the way her hair created a halolike effect around her head. There was confusion in her eyes, her gaze never leaving his. Without thinking, he eased several errant strands away from her brow.

"How's it feel now?" It usually took about a minute or two for the chemicals in the bag to produce the icy coldness. The pack would remain cold for about thirty minutes, able to markedly reduce swelling. It would allow a SEAL to keep walking after wrapping the ice pack around his ankle and using dark green duct tape to hold it in place. Plus, the duct tape would provide support to the weakened area, as well. With her shoulder, it would be impossible to rig it up.

"I feel it," Morgan said, relief in her voice. Her brow tingled where he'd briefly grazed her with his index finger. Jake's touch had startled her. Frowning, she dug deep into his dark gaze as he knelt on one knee above her. "Thanks. The ibuprofen will reduce the blood-clot-forming possibility."

"Yeah," he said, resting his arms across his knee. Jake felt starved for intimacy with Morgan. He felt driven almost beyond his massive control. Maybe it was triggered because she could have been killed out there tonight. "The ice pack will reduce the swelling."

She grimaced. "I couldn't position the butt of the sniper rifle against my shoulder up there on the roof tonight. Pissed me off."

"I knew something was wrong. I saw you grimace once, and it isn't like a sniper to keep repositioning the rifle against their cheek and shoulder once it's set in place." He knew Morgan wouldn't have told him about the pain or swelling. In the SEALs you didn't bitch when you were hurt. You just kept moving with the team to complete the mission. There was no whining. It was just part of the price that was paid out in these badlands.

Morgan touched the ice pack. "God, this is beginning to feel good. Thanks, Jake. . . ." She gave him a grateful look and forced her hand to remain still no matter how much she wanted to touch him. She could feel that powerful, sensual animal energy of his invisibly embracing her. Despite the pain throbbing in her shoulder, the ache building in her core was devastatingly painful to her in another way. Morgan felt needy, like a cat in heat looking for action. It was Jake. *Only him.*

"You'll probably quit moaning in your sleep now."

"And waking you up."

Jake smiled a little and slowly rose to his full height. "You didn't mean to. I just wish, Morgan, you'd have told me earlier you'd been hit."

Seeing real concern in his eyes, she whispered, "Jake, I'm so used to being hurt on missions, I just didn't think."

Understanding, he started to turn away. "Wait . . ."

He halted and slowly turned his head, meeting her shadowed eyes. "What?"

Morgan took a deep breath. "Why did you ask to kiss me, Jake? You've never asked me in the past."

A grimace pulled at one corner of his mouth. "You always accused me of being self-centered and never caring about anyone but myself, Morgan. That and running when things got too hot to handle." Weariness coursed through him. "I don't know. . . . I wanted you to want the kiss as much as I did."

A ragged breath escaped her. "Why the change, Jake?"

He shrugged. "I've never seen you wounded before, Morgan. It pulled on me in ways I'd never felt. I . . ." He raised his gaze to the low, dark ceiling, trying to find the right words. "I wanted to comfort you, was all." And then he dropped his gaze to hers. "When I asked to kiss you, it wasn't about sex, if that's what you were thinking. I just wanted to take your pain away. Maybe hold you for a while and maybe you'd feel better." Just as he'd held Joshua when he cried in his crib at night and Jake would go in, slip his hands around his tiny son and hold him against his chest. Joshua always stopped crying and Jake began to understand the value of human touch, human compassion.

"I . . . didn't know . . ."

"I don't want to make you feel any more miserable and upset than you already are with me being around." Jake lifted his hand. "Get some sleep, partner. Tomorrow is coming early."

Morgan lay there alone in the silence for a long time before sleep overtook her. Something remarkable had shifted between them. She was too exhausted and emotionally strung out to figure out what it was. Whatever had happened was new. And good.

The last thought Morgan had as she dropped off to sleep was Emma needed a father. One who would not run if she got sick and needed his continued support. Had

Jake stopped running from personal responsibility? If she could believe the care that
burned in his eyes, the raw emotion in his
voice that said all he wanted to do was hold
her, comfort her, then Jake had made a
monumental shift and change.

Time would tell, but as Morgan plunged
into sleep, her heart reacted with intense
love for him. Because she'd always loved
him. She'd never stopped loving him. But
now that feeling was intensified by his
tender concern toward her. It wasn't just
about sex. It was one human responsibly
caring for another and wanting nothing in
return for it.

Morgan jerked awake when she heard the
door creak open. Sitting up, her hand
automatically going for her SIG, she saw
Jake come to a halt in the doorway. Wiping
the sleep from her eyes, she realized sunlight
was pouring brightly into her room.

"What time is it?" she muttered, throwing
off the sleeping-bag cover. The ice pack
slipped down through her T-shirt and
flopped out onto her lap.

"0900," Jake said, coming over with a
plate in his hands. "I let you sleep in." He
knelt down and handed her the plate and a
fork. "Here, breakfast. Eat." He noticed the

confusion in her eyes, her hair tangled, making her beautiful to him. Jake quieted his need for her.

"But we were supposed to ride at dawn!" Morgan protested in a strained husky tone, looking up at the window. She took the plate, their fingers touching momentarily. "Thanks . . ." There were five fried eggs, some goat meat and thick, dark slices of hot bread on the plate. Her mouth watered. Crossing her legs, she set the plate in her lap, starved.

Jake sat down, one leg tucked beneath him, the other pulled up to his chest, his arms wrapped around it. "I got a call from Vero at 0400 this morning," he told her, seeing how her cheeks were flushed. The night's sleep had helped. Morgan's green eyes were clear this morning, not muddy-looking like last night. "They got one drone up and working."

"That's good news!" She used the warm, fresh bread to mop up the broken yolks on the plate. Jake's thoughtfulness touched her deeply.

"Yeah, because right now, that drone has spotted Khogani about twelve miles south of us up on that mountain. He's continuing to head south, moving in and out of caves and tunnels. The drone is catching him out in the open, but not long enough to launch a missile at him and take him out of the fight."

"Thank God, they got one drone up and working," Morgan whispered, relieved. "Why aren't we going after them, then?"

Jake twisted his head so he could get a good look at the side of her neck. The bruising darkness was still present. "Let me look at that hematoma when you're finished with breakfast?" He waited for her to give him permission. She had finished off the meal and set the plate and flatware aside.

"Go ahead and check it out." Morgan found her voice, sounding husky. She sat relaxed as he eased his fingers beneath the collar of the fabric. Her skin reacted hotly to his grazing touch. And then her breasts tightened. Worse, her nipples hardened, and she groaned to herself. She knew Jake would see them pucker against the fabric. *Damn.* And when Jake stood up on one knee, his face so close to hers, she unconsciously held her breath for a moment. Morgan felt the material being gently moved aside. The ache in her breasts increased. He was being extremely gentle, and it affected her deeply. Looking up at his solemn face, Jake's eyes narrowed as he assessed the hematoma, she released a softened breath, trying to hold on to her escaping emotions.

"What do you think?" she managed. Morgan was going to die of embarrassment. She'd turned down his kiss, but she couldn't keep her traitorous body from telling him differently.

Jake brought her T-shirt back into position, easing the material back into place along her shoulder. Jake sat back down on his other leg and said, "The swelling's reduced by about fifty percent. That's good news." It took everything he had not to stare at her nipples pressing against the T-shirt. Her cheeks burned a bright red, a hue he'd never seen on her before. Jake didn't want to humiliate Morgan or make her feel embarrassed. And, yeah, he sure as hell wanted to cup those beautiful breasts of hers, feel their firm roundness in his palms, place his mouth over one of those nipples and send her into another world of heat and wanting.

Getting close to Morgan was like touching fire, and his damned body had a mind of its own. He swallowed hard, kept his game face in place, as if nothing were wrong.

Jake placed the medical items from her blow-out kit nearby. He reached for it, hoping Morgan didn't see the fine tremble of his hands, and said, "You need two more ibuprofen" and handed them to her. Dragging over her CamelBak, Jake placed it in her lap.

This morning, Morgan appeared fragile. He'd never seen her this way. Getting shot deeply affected everyone. It was just a question of how much and for how long. The fire that was usually in her green eyes was extinguished. It seemed that the small things he did for her made a difference. He'd seen the warmth and gratefulness in her eyes when he'd brought her breakfast. And when he'd come so damn close to her, he'd seen vulnerability in her face, as if she needed him close to her, as if he represented safety to her right now. He knew he could give this to Morgan.

SEALs were great at protecting others even though he knew Morgan didn't want that from him. She'd felt smothered by him two years ago when he'd tried to protect her, and she'd fought it. Morgan didn't need a man like that. Jake was beginning to understand the finite difference between him being tender toward her versus being protective. Every human, he was finally beginning to understand, needed another human being when they were hurt or down. Being sensitive, being tender and solicitous, was different from being an overbearing guard dog. And he clearly saw Morgan responding to his care. It made him feel damn good about himself. And her.

Jake knew from experience that coming so close to death wasn't a pleasant or easy place to go. No one wanted to die. And he knew how important it had been for his teammates to be more solicitous toward him when he'd been hit, knocked six feet backward, slamming into the ground, taking two bullets to his chest. Only the Kevlar plates had saved him, but Jake got a whole new perspective on the fact he wanted to live, not die. That one time had changed him forever. Every day became precious and to be lived to its fullest extent. More important for Jake, it was to be lived honestly, unselfishly.

Morgan took the ibuprofen and drank the water. "What is the plan now? Are we going after Khogani?"

He barely shook his head. "Vero wants us to stand down for twenty-four hours." He saw Morgan cock her head, confusion coming to her eyes. "I gave him your medical status report."

"Dammit, Jake. You shouldn't have. I can ride with this hematoma. I want Khogani!"

Grinning a little, he enjoyed the fire in Morgan's eyes. The way she set that mouth of hers, he braced himself for more heated arguments. "I'm the sniper team leader. If I think you can't push the butt of that AW Mag into your shoulder correctly, it means you can't get off an accurate shot. Vero agreed with me. There are very few of us SEALs who haven't taken bullets to our Kevlar, Morgan. This is the first time for you and you're going to have to trust me . . . trust *us,* on this decision. Today, I want you to ice pack that area. I've got three packs in my third-line gear we'll use, too. It will reduce the swelling enough, I think, so that we can leave tomorrow just before dawn."

"Damn," Morgan whispered, angry and helpless. Of all things! Frustrated, she muttered, "I'm *not* going to be bedridden, Jake!"

His mouth quirked. "Far be it from me to force you to stay in bed."

His eyes gleamed, and Morgan caught the implication. All her anger dissolved. "I'm just worried Khogani will get too far away. That we won't be able to catch up to him, Jake." Giving him a pleading look, she reached out and gripped his hand resting on his long, hard thigh. "Please, let's go after him? I can ride! We have to close the distance gap on him."

He felt the warmth of her strong fingers across his. Morgan could be damned persuasive when she wanted to be. Picking up her hand, he held it gently between his own and pressed a chaste kiss to the back of it. "Sorry, babe, you're grounded." Jake reluctantly released her hand, saw the shock of his kiss registering on Morgan's face. Did he see desire in her eyes? Jake couldn't be sure, and he forced himself to his feet. "Every woman in the village has been boiling hot water all morning and filling that copper tub at Hamid's place for you. Let's get you over there. You can take a hot bath, relax and then I'll tape that ice pack on your shoulder. Okay?" He held out his hand toward her.

A bath . . .

Morgan was stunned. She knew Hamid's wife had the hand-beaten copper tub, but it took hours and many kettles and buckets of water for a bath. Not only that, it burned up precious wood supplies that were always in short supply. The women had probably worked since dawn so that she would have a warm bath. She could wash away all the crud, dirt and fear sweat off her body. She could wash her dirty hair. "Th-that was so kind of them," she said, her voice mirroring her emotion.

"Yes, it is. You're a heroine around here this morning, Morgan. The people wanted to thank you. I think every house has been boiling water in their largest kettles, walking them up to Hamid's house." He smiled tenderly down at her. For a moment, Jake saw tears in her eyes. And then she looked away. He had been touched by the people's generosity of this village, too. Morgan had earned this gift from them.

"Did you know," Jake said in a quiet tone, "that they found ten grenades on each soldier's body? They were climbing that wall last night to wreak havoc on this village. Khogani's men were planning on running down each of the streets, popping the pins on those grenades and launching them into the houses. If they'd killed you, Morgan, they might have gotten away with it." He saw the information sink into her, her eyes widening with shock over the possibility.

"My God . . ." Morgan managed, her voice going hoarse. "I didn't know. . . ."

He smiled a little. "So? Are you ready for a hot bath with real soap? I always keep a bar of it in my ruck." Morgan's face went soft, her lips parting as she took it all in. She lifted her left hand and wrapped it into his strong fingers. The many calluses on Jake's hand matched her own as he easily lifted her to her feet. She stood close, feeling light-headed for a moment. His hand tightened firmly around hers.

"Okay?" he demanded softly. Morgan had been through a lot. Vero was right: they needed a twenty-four-hour stand-down in order to get her back. The Commander wanted to medevac her to Camp Bravo, but Jake knew Morgan would throw a shoe on that order and adamantly refuse to allow it to happen. He'd argued Morgan's case and had won her a semi-reprieve. She'd never know, however. Right now, all Jake wanted was for Morgan to have a low-stress day. And out here in the badlands, that was damn near impossible, but he was going to see to it she was protected. He wasn't about to let anyone or anything get close to her. Even if Morgan hated his protection, he was going to be that damned big guard dog whether she liked it or not.

Chapter Fourteen

The last thing Jake did that night was check on Morgan. She was fast asleep, lying on her side. For a moment he stood in the doorway, feeling the drive to simply lie down at her back, hold her close against his body. Protect her. Let her heal. Scowling, he knew it wasn't meant to be. He walked through the darkened, silent house, the mountain winds blowing furiously across the valley.

The bath had worked miracles for Morgan. Jake was profoundly touched when he was called to take a bath, too. It was dirty water, but, God, it was warm and he didn't care. Anything to get the stink off him was great. The unscented soap had come from his ruck. It was better to smell like soap than stink. He wearily pulled off the Kevlar vest and dropped it next to his sleeping bag.

Tonight, Morgan didn't have to wear the ice pack. With cold packs and ibuprofen, the affected area was healing, the swelling down by a good 60 percent. She showed him earlier she could jam that AW sniper rifle into her shoulder, stock tight against her cheek, no problem.

Smiling a little, he placed his SIG next to his ruck, the M-4 next to his Kevlar. Everyone was relaxed because with the drone up in the sky watching and tailing Khogani, the villagers knew he would not attack tonight. A quiet, safe night. For once. Jake shrugged out of his cammie shirt, wearing his clean, tan T-shirt, trousers and boots to bed.

Jake lay awake, his head resting on his ruck. His mind whirled with so many details. At dawn, they were leaving with Reza to ride up the southern flank of the mountain, heading into harm's way. Only one drone was on station for a fixed time. A drone could stay on station a helluva long time, but not forever. He was uncomfortable with the situation, but there was nothing he could do.

He worried about Morgan. She wasn't herself. It was no wonder since she was still fighting through being shot and not dying as a result. Jake had seen fellow SEALs' Kevlar vests take a hit for them, and it took days, usually weeks, to work out of the terror of nearly dying. Finally, Jake dropped

216

off to sleep, feeling safer than he had in a long time, the drone giving him that space.

Morgan screamed, "Emma! Emma!" The sound jerked her out of her sleep and upright. A sob broke from her lips as she automatically reached for her pistol.

"Morgan?"

Jake's worried voice sheared through the darkness and her confusion. Still trapped within the insidious nightmare, vulnerable, she sobbed again, fingers wrapping around the pistol. As she started to raise it, she felt a man's strong, firm fingers grasp her wrist.

Jake dropped to one knee, gently guiding her hand and the pistol downward, away from them. Morgan's sobs tore at him. Dammit! She was reacting to the shooting. Oh, he'd cried, too, after getting shot. Jake had walked far, far away from the team compound, found a place to hide and sob out his fear of dying. No one had heard him. But now he heard those same raw sounds clawing out of Morgan's throat and recognized them for what they were.

Easing the pistol out of her fingers, Jake whispered, "It's all right, Morgan. I'm here. You're okay. . . ." And he unchambered the round in the pistol and set it aside where she couldn't reach it.

Torn between the virulent nightmare and Jake's hand on hers, Morgan gulped unsteadily. Her hair was mussed, strands sticking to her drawn cheeks, tears dampening her skin. "Emma . . ." The sound came out strangled. Taut.

"Come here, babe . . ." Jake sat down next to her, pulling her into his arms. He was alarmed at how badly Morgan was trembling. Was it a nightmare combined with reaction? And who was Emma?

Without a word, Morgan buried her face against his chest, her fingers in a fist against his shoulder. "Shhh, it's all right, all right. . . ." Jake kissed her hair, inhaling the clean scent among the strands. And then Morgan lifted her tear-stained face and looked him in the eyes.

"Talk to me," Jake coaxed thickly, framing her face, digging into her marred, confused eyes. "What were you screaming about?"

Jake's hands anchored Morgan, brought her back from the edge. She'd never been shot before; it shook her to her soul. Clinging to his glittering, dark eyes, she kept trying to speak. Kept trying to form the words. Only rasps, half cries, rose out of her constricted throat.

With a shaking hand, Jake pushed the hair away from her face, his palm wet with her tears. "Hold on, Morgan. Hold on." The wild look in her eyes scared him. Jake had never seen Morgan like this. "Dammit, focus!"

His order slammed into her roiling, destabilized emotional state. Blinking, Morgan took a deep, ragged breath. Her nightmare was of Emma being abducted by terrorists. Of her husband being killed by the Khogani. Oh, God. Oh, God . . . Mark . . . Mark was never coming back.

Jake's hands pressed more firmly against her jaw, his gaze riveted to hers. Literally, she could feel him willing her back from a place she'd never been before, and it had rocked her soul. He kept repeating the word "focus" to her. She listened to Jake's deep voice, his tone moving through her, giving her purchase. Morgan struggled out of the violent netherworld.

Finally, she closed her eyes, felt herself coming back together. Coming . . . home . . . to Jake. He must have sensed her grit, her inner strength returning, because he whispered her name and hauled her into his arms, holding her tightly against him.

Her fingers moved unsurely across his chest toward his broad, capable shoulder. Morgan could hear his slow thudding heart beneath her ear, the calm rise and fall of his powerful chest. It was almost like being rocked and held like a frightened child in his arms. Eventually, she calmed down. Morgan didn't know how long Jake held her, but at some point, he'd stopped breathing unevenly and so did she.

Opening her eyes, she surrendered to Jake. He was presently strong where she was weak. He was holding her and slowly rocked her in his arms. "This has never happened to me before," she managed in a strained voice.

"Morgan, you've got to walk through that hell of being almost killed. We all go through it. I'm glad I'm here to help."

She flattened her hand against his chest. "So am I. . . ."

"What was the nightmare about?" Jake continued to move his hand slowly up and down her spine. He knew her body intimately, a burning, memorized map written across his heart and mind. Now he was wanting to learn about what drove her, what frightened her so badly. Morgan didn't scare easily.

Sure, every SEAL was afraid. You just didn't let the fear control you. And you did your job, regardless, because your team was counting on you. Jake pressed a kiss to her hair, feeling its silkiness and strength. Morgan knew fear. But she'd never let it stop her before. She sure as hell hadn't let it stop her from taking down three bad guys last night.

Choking, a lump forming in her throat, Morgan pressed her face more deeply against his shoulder, wanting to hide, needing his arms around her. "I — Jake, I married Lieutenant Mark Evans when I was twenty-four."

Scowling, Jake knew the name. The SEAL community was small. "Mark?" he demanded, looking off into the darkness. "OIC of Echo platoon?"

"Yes." Wearily, Morgan opened her hand and closed it against his taut, hard flesh. The T-shirt was damp, and she was sure it was from her tears. "I was assigned to his platoon as a linguist. We fell in love. . . ."

Jake shut his eyes. He froze for a moment, letting the information sink into him. Why should he be surprised? He'd gotten married, hadn't he? Releasing a painful sigh, Jake whispered, "I didn't know him personally, Morgan, but his reputation was that of a solid officer."

Barely nodding, Morgan squeezed her eyes shut, her voice turning hoarse. "We were married when he came out of deployment. And then . . . less than a year later when he should have remained stateside, they pulled him for a top secret mission and he came back over here." The next words hurt so much, she could barely get them out. "Mark was a sniper, and he was sent in to hunt down a high-value target, Khogani. H-he took a shot, missed and then he was too close. Another soldier fired an RPG at his position, and it killed him." She sobbed, absorbing his tightening arms, holding her even closer if that was possible.

Reeling with the information, Jake remembered the SEAL loss. And then he remembered Mark Evans. He'd been a Cornell graduate, intelligent, compassionate, and he'd had a fierce reputation for looking out for his men. Jake's mind skipped over so much. He hadn't heard of Mark marrying. Maybe it had all been top secret because of Operation Shadow Warriors? Morgan had never told him, either. By the time he'd met her the second go-around in Afghanistan, she'd been twenty-seven by then, a widow for two years. Had her wanting him really been wanting Mark back? It put a whole new perspective on their three days of frantic lovemaking in that Afghan village two years ago. Jake had no answer.

Shattering inwardly, Jake viewed that second time they'd come together in a whole new light. He'd lost Amanda and Joshua at twenty-four. Morgan had lost Mark near the same time. They were each still hurting from their loss. Had they crashed into one another, hurt, wounded animals seeking, what, sex? Yes. Something more? Protection? From the ugly world they lived in? Probably.

At that time, Morgan had needed his tenderness, but Jake had none to give, taking everything she'd given him, emptying himself, burying himself in Morgan to forget his terrible, heartrending losses. She had helped him heal from his grief even though she'd never realized it. Worse, he'd given her nothing in return like she had given him . . .

Jake drew in a serrated breath, feeling Morgan trust him. He held her full weight, aware of her shallow breath, content to remain in his arms. Resting his jaw against her temple, he said, "I'm so damn sorry, Morgan. Evans was a hell of a SEAL officer. One of the best in the teams. Did you have a child?" he wondered.

She shook her head, saying wearily, "No . . . no children . . . We wanted them, but it didn't happen." Morgan felt Jake squeeze her gently, placing a kiss against her wet cheek. His tenderness was a salve to her broken heart. She'd never expected this from him, but now he was healing her.

In an effort to pull herself together, Morgan reluctantly eased out of his arms, clinging to his shadowed gaze. Jake's face was tense, and she felt so many raw emotions swirling around him but it was impossible to sort out what, exactly, he was thinking right now. "I thought I could tough it out, but getting hit by this bullet changes my whole world." Morgan lifted her hand to touch his hard face. He caught her hand, pressing a kiss to her opened palm. The warmth of his lips, his breath flowing across her sensitized flesh, left her breathless once more.

"You aren't running, Jake."

"I stopped running two years ago. You just didn't know it." *I didn't show you, either.* Jake placed her hand on his chest, holding her wounded gaze, her lower lip trembling. "I'm here for you, Morgan. I'll *always* be here for you from now on. I have your back. . . ."

Morgan moved close, her hands sliding over his shoulders, leaning up . . . up to kiss Jake. Something had changed between them. Something that drove her to connect with him on every level of herself. Her heart tore open, the scar from so many years ago dissolving. Her mouth curved hotly against his, greedy, wanting him.

A groan tore through Jake as he felt her sob, the sound captured between their clinging mouths. Her scent flowed through his starving soul, and he inhaled her deeply. Arms tightening, his mind unhinged, his fevered body responding hotly, he placed a steel grip on himself. Jake understood Morgan's driving need to prove that life trumped death. Her palms flattened against his chest, and he felt her irregular, warm breath against his face. Oh, God, he wanted her so badly he could hardly control himself. Her mouth sent blistering waves of heat down through him. His erection was so damned swift and hard, he tensed.

Morgan sank against Jake, his mouth taking hers gently, not hard. In the past, it had been frantic, rough sex shared between them. He had always been in a hurry, and so had she. This time, it was completely different. Inwardly confused, Morgan was too shaken to figure it out. Her heart urged her to accept the pace, that things had changed between them. Maybe good changes; she didn't know.

Jake's mouth skimmed across her lips, memorizing her once more, and it sent a scalding heat shattering straight down to her burning womb. He captured her and eased her down beside him. His breath was irregular as he propped himself up on one elbow, looking deeply into her eyes.

"Is this what you want?" Jake demanded, his voice guttural with emotion. Because he sure as hell wanted her. But this had to be her decision this time, not his.

"I need you, Jake. . . ."

The steel trap surrounding his heart began to melt. Jake dissolved beneath those pleading eyes and begging lips. "Let me undress you. . . ." Her right shoulder looked like hell, and he knew the area was sore. Jake wanted to show her tenderness. It was what she needed right now. It was what he could give her.

Morgan had given so much to him two years ago when they were hurting over the loss of their families. She'd loved him with an incredible tenderness he never thought was possible. And it had been something new shared between them at that time. Now Jake wanted to show her he could be just as gentle, giving and loving to Morgan as she had once been with him.

CHAPTER FIFTEEN

As Jake slid naked beside Morgan, he said, "I didn't bring any condoms."

She managed a wry look, understanding that neither of them had thought they'd ever find themselves in this position with one another again. "It's okay. It's a safe time in my cycle."

"Good to know," he said.

Morgan closed her eyes, absorbing Jake's lean, powerful body against her. His mouth sipped at hers, and she felt exquisite fire bolt downward as he rocked her lips open, his tongue moving against hers. His hard, calloused hand moved downward, cupping her breast, his thumb lightly feathering across her hardened nipple. She moaned, arching against him, the sound absorbed beneath his deep kiss. Wanting more, Jake held her captive, his leg over hers, so she couldn't move, open and available to him in every way. Barely aware of the deep ache in her shoulder, Morgan clung to his mouth, lost in the teasing movement of his thumb encircling her nipple, driving her crazy. Frustration thrummed through her tense body, her thighs damp, her womb clenching with need. It had been so long. So long . . .

Jake eased from her soft, wet mouth, his eyes narrowing, watching Morgan for reaction; her chest was rising and falling sharply, her moan of need vibrating through her. God, she was so hot in his hands, so damned sensitive, willful and hungry. The arousal in her eyes sent white-hot fire screaming through his lower body. This time, it was about healing Morgan, helping her to hold herself together and start the long road back from nearly being killed.

As Jake tilted her head, deepening their hungry kiss, Morgan became aware of the gentleness of his mouth upon hers. Something broke in Morgan as he eased his fingers across her jaw, framing her face, holding her so that he could breathe his life into her, breathe his maleness into her tortured, twisted emotional soul. This was not the Jake she knew. It was someone better, someone who cared, who was reaching out beyond himself to help her.

Morgan relinquished all of herself to Jake for the first time in her life. There was a trust that had somehow been built since meeting for this operation, and she desperately needed the gentleness he was offering to her with every touch of his mouth; his hands and body could feed her.

Jake left her mouth, gently placing nips along her slender neck, licking her flesh and feathering a kiss upon it before moving downward once more. Her hips twisted as his thumb moved languidly across her nipple, the shower of electric impulses rocking through her body, making her thighs slippery with need. Morgan felt his lips lightly touch the area of the bruise, the pain disappearing beneath his ministrations. His mouth drifted lower, caressing the curve of her breast with his tongue. Her skin grew taut and achy, a groan tearing out of her as his lips claimed the aching peak, suckling her.

Morgan arched as Jake drew more deeply upon the nipple, a craze of fire exploding in her body. A whimper tore from her as she felt his other calloused hand moved down the center of her damp, straining body. Her mind shorted out as his roughened palm enclosed her other breast. When he suckled her, she moaned, a deep yearning building powerfully in her lower body, hips twisting toward him, wanting him. All of him.

His kisses moved lightly between her breasts, and she felt him kissing each scar she'd collected over the years. As his mouth wove wet, languid patterns across her abdomen, moving downward, Morgan felt herself melt between his hands and mouth, felt the nightmare fear finally release her. Focused on his mouth as he lightly kissed her mound, his moist breath flowing across her, his fingers curved downward, finding out just how wet she was. Morgan heard him give a low growl of satisfaction as his fingers found her entrance. Breath jamming in her throat, she arched hard against his fingers, wanting Jake so badly she wanted to scream. The ache in her increased tenfold as he moved against her core, testing her, teasing her. She was lost in the blistering heat of him suckling her and his fingers creating streaks of burning heat up through her.

Gently, Jake eased open her right leg, his hand settling firmly between her taut thighs.

Panting, crying softly for him to enter her, Morgan savored the feel of his roughened hands as they gripped her hips, holding her in position. His shoulders widened her thighs, and she trembled violently as his mouth found that sweet spot. She pressed her fist against her mouth, her scream of pleasure nearly silenced. His tongue probed her, causing her body to spasm and contract, her juices to increase.

He found that group of nerves, the pearl at the entrance to her core, with his tongue. A shudder rippled through Morgan, and she grabbed at the sleeping bag, clenching the fabric, mewls of satisfaction tearing out of her. Aching, she felt the explosiveness building quickly inside as he pleasured her in such an intimate way. And when he slid his fingers inside of her, her world exploded into lights and violent heat.

Jake had barely touched her, and the volcanic ripples of an orgasm erupted, her muscles wildly contracting around his fingers, deluging him with the sweet fluids of the gift he'd given her.

Her entire body arched, paralyzed as he milked her body again and again with his mouth, tongue and fingers. And like the hunter he was, he stalked that spot deep within her. Morgan could feel herself flying apart, dismantled and utterly trusting herself with Jake. She glowed like a furnace raging out of control, responsive and violently reactive.

It had been so long since Morgan had had sex. Two years. And the last time was with this same man. Now he was loving her on a whole new level that made her sob with pleasure.

Jake eased from Morgan and teased her with his breath, his tongue, a low groan vibrating through her. Morgan could take no more and whimpered, calling his name, her fingers digging into his damp shoulders. In moments, Jake rolled over, easing her on top of his more-than-ready body. He wasn't going to put his weight on Morgan if he could help it since he wanted to protect her injured shoulder.

Her hair fell across his face as she hungrily found Jake's mouth. He absorbed her moan, and she moved her wet, slick core against his erection. His hands splayed across her hips, guiding her so that she could enter him. Morgan became lost in the fiery haze of wanting Jake within her aching, needy body. He arched his hips, lifting her ever so slightly, then eased her down upon himself.

Morgan tore her lips away from his, uttering a cry of throaty contentment. The burning sensation clashed with the blistering heat of her body welcoming him. As Jake slowly filled her, she felt the burn, stretching to accommodate him. He slowed her down. Nothing had ever felt as good as this, Jake in her, becoming one again, melting. Morgan thrust her hips, forcing him to sheathe deeply into her.

Tipping her head back, eyes tightly shut, Morgan absorbed his power, her muscles fitting like a very tight glove around him. And then he slowly brought her into a rhythm with him, his hands guiding her hips. Her damp palms lay flat against Jake's dark-haired chest. She felt the thudding power of his heart, his roughened breath, his thrusts taking her into another cauldron of boiling heat that swiftly rose within her. The pressure was great, and Morgan gasped, feeling him groan beneath her.

They were good together; they always had been, and this time was no different. Morgan unraveled as he expertly positioned her, thrusting deeply, teasing her into joining him in a rhythm that dissolved her mind and fused them together. Nothing had ever felt so right to her. She imploded into another soul-burning orgasm beneath his cajoling hip movements designed to tease her.

Morgan tensed against Jake, a cry tearing out of her mouth. He was overwhelmed by her heat, her wetness, the powerful contractions gripping him. He had to control himself, he had to try to be present, not lost in the swift-moving fire enveloping them. This time was for Morgan. He allowed her all the pleasure she could possibly want.

When she suddenly weakened, like a bow that had been pulled too taut, and collapsed against him, gasping, her breath fanning moistly across his neck and chest, he knew his wait was over for him.

Now Jake could take her, and he thrust several times, so deep within her that his world came apart. He surrendered his steel grip, filling her, drowning in the fiery heat of her soft, giving body. His teeth locked as he strained against her. Lights flashed behind his tightly shut eyes, his entire body quivering. It had been two years since he'd touched a woman. And now, as Jake felt the sudden release and the satisfaction following it, nothing had ever been so right as loving Morgan in this moment.

Jake didn't know how long they lay there, spent by their actions. He kissed Morgan's damp face, the silk of her hair beneath his mouth. She was warm, sweaty, and her heart hammered in time with his own. Gently, Jake eased her off him and he tucked her beside him. Pulling up the cover, he nestled Morgan fully along his length, holding her tight, holding her as the warmth of the sleeping bag enclosed them.

She stirred against him, her fingers tangling in the soft damp hair across his chest. It was as if she was reacquainting herself with him. Jake felt a peace he'd never before experienced. They had always been good together. This time was over the top. He couldn't ever remember having felt this happy or satisfied after having sex.

Morgan nestled her cheek against his shoulder, face tilted upward. He looked down into her drowsy gaze. The tension in Morgan's face was gone. Her fingers traced the line of his hard jaw. So many potent emotions swept through him as their gazes met and held.

"You feed my soul," Jake rasped, sliding his hand over hers as she cupped his cheek. There was a tremulous smile playing across her well-kissed lips as Morgan closed her eyes, content to simply be in his arms.

"You feed my heart," she whispered against his heated skin.

"You needed this. I needed it."

Morgan whispered, "You've changed, Jake." When had it happened? Morgan didn't have the strength to follow the thought, her mind just so much mush, her heart expanding with new, deeper feelings toward him. A chuckle rumbled through his chest. Jake lifted her hand, opened her palm and placed a kiss to the center of it. Wild, tingling sensations radiated outward to her fingers.

"I hope that's a compliment," Jake whispered against her hair, pressing a kiss into the clean strands.

"You know it is."

"How are you feeling?" There was veiled worry in his deep voice.

"I'm okay." *More than okay.* Her body was flooded with the aftermath of their lovemaking, glowing like a tide slowly moving in and out deeply within her.

"I didn't have a condom on me." Jake's voice turned wry. "I honestly didn't expect to have sex with you on this mission."

"Makes two of us," Morgan admitted. "It's okay," she reassured him. She lay there wanting to tell him that she'd already carried his daughter in her womb. Jake lifted his hand to stroke her back and hips. The guilt surged through her. Jake had changed for the better. He could care for someone other than himself.

Stirring, she pulled away from Jake just enough to catch and hold his hooded gaze. Morgan could see the fire of desire still burning in the recesses of his stormy gray eyes. There was something magical and unexplained that had always drawn them helplessly to one another.

"Jake, what happened to change you like this?" Her whispered words had a profound effect on him. His eyes suddenly went dark, his mouth moving into a painful line. "Tell me?" Morgan coaxed softly, lifting her hand and cupping the side of his bearded face so he couldn't pull away.

In a low voice, Jake told her about marrying Amanda at twenty-three, her having his son, Joshua, weeks after he'd returned stateside. The hardest part for him was telling Morgan how he'd lost both of them in an auto accident two weeks later. As he did, her eyes flared wide with shock, and then she forced herself up on her left elbow. There was genuine devastation on Morgan's face. And when tears formed in her eyes, Jake felt his heart rip open. Morgan whispered his name, holding him. This time, he was the one who clung to her.

Shaken to her core, Morgan tried to absorb some of Jake's pain. As she moved away and held his sad gaze, felt his anguish in every line of his face and in his eyes, she felt numbed. Jake had been married. *Oh, God, he'd had a son!* Morgan couldn't wrap her head or emotions around his losing Joshua so soon. She didn't know what she would have done if Emma had been torn out of her arms two weeks after she'd been born. How had Jake survived? He had been carrying the tragedy all those years since then. *Alone.*

Looking deeply into his eyes, Morgan saw moisture in them. It was then that she understood so much more about Jake's life. By marrying Amanda, Jake had been ready to take on family responsibility. He'd grown up. Morgan threaded her fingers through his short, dark hair in an effort to try to assuage the sadness she felt around Jake. The loss of a child was something no parent ever got over. She couldn't find healing words enough to help him. All Morgan could do was lie in his arms, touch his face and watch as each small ministration took a little more of the grief out of his expression.

"I didn't know, Jake," she finally forced out. Pressing her brow against his cheek, she whispered brokenly, "I'm so sorry . . . so sorry for your loss. . . . I don't know how you survived it. . . ." And Morgan didn't.

"Time helps," Jake finally admitted, holding her tightly. Morgan made the world go away for him. Just her gentle touch, her woman's strength she possessed, made the heartache recede a little more. "It's been five years now. There have been days, Morgan, when it all comes back to me in spades. And on those days, I feel so damned torn up, like I'm in pieces and I'll never find all of them ever again, put myself back together and mend." Jake's voice flattened. "When I see Afghan kids that are four years old, I sometimes see Joshua in them instead. I wonder what he'd look like now. Would he have that wildness in him like you see in the Afghan boys? What would be his interests?" Shutting his eyes, Jake felt Morgan's arms tighten around his shoulders, her brow pressed silently against jaw. She was holding him, sponging away some of his grief.

Morgan lay there, wanting to tell Jake about Emma. But her mind, her experience in war, warned her to say nothing. Jake was vulnerable right now, just as she was. They had to go after Khogani at daybreak. They had to focus on the op, or they'd make mistakes because they weren't emotionally together. Distraction was always a killer. His attention would be diverted in terrible ways that could get either himself or her killed. He'd want to see Emma. Hold her in his arms.

Plus, Morgan wasn't sure how Jake would react to her withholding the information from him for so long. It was complicated. And there were layers of entanglement that would take days, weeks, even months to straighten out between them. Closing her eyes, Morgan sighed raggedly, guilt eating her alive. Jake had lost so much . . . much more than she had. He deserved to know. But not now . . . God, not now. . . .

"Here," Morgan told him the next morning, before they mounted their horses. "Can you keep this, Jake?"

Jake turned, making sure the cinch on the horse's saddle was tight. The entire village had surrounded them to say goodbye. Reza was already mounted, the packhorse tied to the back of his saddle, waiting near the gate. It was barely a gray dawn, the winds cold off the Hindu Kush. He looked down at the white envelopes Morgan held out toward him in her gloved hand.

He gave her a startled look. When going downrange, SEALs would give their CO a death letter. That letter, if the SEAL was killed, was carried by two of the team's SEAL brothers to his wife or parents. It was always a letter that would, in some way, help those left behind and ease their grief.

"Please, take them." She'd written it this morning after Jake had dressed and left. Her heart twisted in her chest. Morgan noticed his hesitation. No doubt, he didn't want to admit that where they were going, she could die. His mouth tightened as he stared at it, as if it were alive. Morgan's heart overflowed with love for Jake.

This morning, as she'd written the letters and wept between the sentences, she'd known without a doubt, her love for Jake had deepened over time, not lessened. It was a cruel sentence, especially if they didn't survive this mission.

Swallowing hard, Jake took the letters, opened up the pocket on his Kevlar vest pocket just below his chin. There, he folded them into the small area, pressed the Velcro closed with his gloved hand.

Morgan stepped a little closer, lowering her voice so only he could hear. "There are two letters, Jake. One is for my parents." Her voice caught. "The other is for you. . . ."

Jake scowled. He still felt raw from last night. So much had been laid out on their respective tables with one another. There was love burning in her eyes. Love for him. Despite this, Morgan was okay this morning, back where she needed to be for this op. He wasn't. At least, not yet. He would be soon enough because their lives depended upon it.

"You're not going to need them," Jake told her in a growl. "I didn't give you one, did I?"

Her mouth stretched into a partial grin. "No. But you've always been the optimist in our relationship, Ramsey. What else is new?"

Morgan turned away because if she didn't, she would cry.

As she told Hamid and his wife goodbye, lifted her hand to the silent, huddled villagers, Morgan mounted her horse. The letter to Jake told him that he had a daughter. Emma couldn't replace Joshua. But she could fill his grieving heart with new love and hope. He would at least have her.

She had included the photo of Emma that she always carried with her into combat. For Morgan, her daughter was like a guardian angel. Now she wanted Emma's sweet spirit to watch over Jake. The other letter was to her parents and to her daughter. Kicking the flanks of the horse, Morgan trotted the frisky gelding toward the opened gate where Reza patiently waited for them.

Cursing softly, Jake shook Hamid's hand and told his family goodbye. Many of the children waved to him. The grim looks on the adults' faces mirrored what Jake knew. Where they were going, there was a strong chance they might not return. It might be the last time the villagers saw them alive. Jake lifted his hand to them, mounted and kicked his horse into a gallop to meet his team.

They trotted across the valley, long before the sun rose over the rugged, shadowed peaks. Jake had spent thirty minutes on the sat phone with Vero much earlier and gotten the latest drone intel. He'd filled in Morgan as they rode, the cold air making the horses eager to run.

Khogani was wily. The drone would circle and briefly spot him with seventeen men out on a goat trail. But not long enough to send a missile into the group, obliterating them off the face of the earth. No doubt, Khogani automatically assumed a drone was watching their every move.

By early afternoon, they were at nine thousand feet, their horses snorting and laboring up the thin, rocky goat trails. Above, Jake saw the white snow that would never leave the peaks. He had the M-4 slung over his shoulder, hanging at his left side in case he needed it. Morgan carried the sniper rifle, strapped upside down, outside the ruck on her shoulders.

The winds were erratic and changeable at this high altitude. Finally, Reza found a cave near the ten-thousand-foot elevation, and they dismounted inside the shelter. He quickly tied the horses together and made a small fire from wood he carried on the pack-horse.

Jake moved to the front of the dry cave. The sunlight lanced strong and silent into the mouth, high above them. They'd been riding for eight hours. Morgan joined him where he knelt, the Toughbook laptop open, receiving real-time intel signals from the drone via the satellite. She looked over his shoulder, squinting to see the images.

"Khogani is still moving south," she muttered.

"Yeah, he knows he's being watched." Jake turned, her face inches from his. That calm and reserved game face Morgan had was in place. She was all business now, and it made him feel good. Sometimes, for whatever the reason, one teammate was not as focused as the other. There was an automatic shift to the partner who was steadier. He wanted to be, but their conversation about Amanda and Joshua had torn open an old, festering wound he'd never wanted to revisit. In truth, Jake was glad Morgan knew. He'd seen the difference in her since letting her in on his married life.

Morgan moved around to where he was kneeling. She remained just inside the cave so as not to become a target for a sniper. She waited until he closed the laptop.

"How are you doing?" she asked him softly, seeking out his gaze. Reaching out, she placed her gloved hand on his shoulder, feeding him strength, letting him know she cared.

Jake studied Morgan's serene expression. "Up and down," he admitted.

"This was a bad time to ask you, Jake. I'm sorry."

He reached out, barely brushed her ruddy cheek with his gloved fingers. "Having you here is helping, whether you know it or not."

Her cheek warmed beneath his unexpected touch. Morgan gave him a tender look. "We're not going to engage Khogani today." She stood up, which was good because if she didn't, Jake was going to kiss her. Wrong time. Wrong place. Worse, he couldn't afford to fall in love with her again. It would never work.

Jake said nothing and rose to his full height, tucking the laptop beneath his left arm. He walked with Morgan toward the rear of the cavern. For all the trauma she'd gone through, he was amazed by her resiliency. She walked confidently, shoulders back, head high. Amazed by her woman's strength, Jake shook his head. Few SEALs ever recovered as quickly as she had. It occurred to him as they crouched down around the small fire Reza had made to boil tea that his perspective on women being weak was completely wrongheaded.

Chapter Sixteen

They huddled near a small fire as night fell, in another cave, ten miles south of where they'd been in the early afternoon. It was nearly 2200, ten at night, and Morgan laid out her sleeping bag in a tunnel. Reza would sleep near the cave opening, about a tenth of a mile away from them. It was the only entrance/exit point. He'd unsaddled the horses, given them dried grass and water. This cave, miraculously, had a small pool of water near where they would sleep.

Jake laid his sleeping bag next to Morgan's. He didn't remove the Kevlar but did place his SIG near his rucksack that doubled as his pillow. She had done the same. The grimness of their mission was landing four square on them.

Ten miles away, Khogani and his men had slipped into another cave right at dusk. The drone was doing its work by tracking them. If, for any reason, Khogani moved during the night, which Jake felt they wouldn't, Vero would call Morgan on the radio and awaken them.

With the tension building, Morgan could feel Jake watching her face in the firelight. The small fire didn't do much except to heat food and water. They chose to sleep near the wall of the tunnel, and the drip, drip, drip of water from overhead was from snow melt far above them. The horses had eagerly drunk their fill. After putting purification tablets into the water, so had they.

It was a luxury for them to get clean. They both had stripped down as much as they could to wipe off the sweat and dirt. Morgan had kept on some clothes since she didn't want Reza to accidentally walk in and see her naked.

As they settled down next to one another, the sleeping bag warming them, Morgan lay facing Jake. The fire was slowly going out, but she could still see the hard planes of his face. A hell of a lot was going on within him. All day, he'd seemed to become more alert and present. He was working through his emotions just as she had back at the village.

"Khogani is always going to stand down at night," she told him in a soft voice.

"I know. I've been turning in my mind the best way to nail him. Dawn or dusk? Those are our two opportunities." His eyes went flat and hard.

"Look, today was getting back into the saddle. Getting locked into the mind-set of this op. I think we need to ride hard tomorrow and catch up with him. We need to be there at dawn the next morning, to surprise him when he comes out of the cave."

Jake nodded. "Exactly what I was thinking. We can set up the sniper scope above wherever he's going to be hiding." His nostrils flared. "I just hope like hell we get a decent angle to shoot from." That wasn't always possible with the wind, the ambient temperature, the time of day, all of which conspired to work against a sniper, not with him. Or her.

"I'm on the same page." Morgan wanted to reach out, touch his hand, but she stopped herself. Jake was so easy to love, and so damn hard to live with afterward. "We need to tell Vero about the plan. We'll have to get authorization, like always."

"Yeah, he's going to have to get assets in place." Assets like an F-15 loaded with smart bombs, Apache helicopters from Camp Bravo on standby . . . and Jake didn't want to go beyond that. But he knew a medevac would automatically be on call, as well, in case one or both of them got wounded.

He scowled. He did *not* want Morgan harmed. But dammit, it could happen. It bothered him she'd given him those death letters. It was SOP, standard operating procedure. Still, Jake had a bad feeling about the coming mission.

"If we can get a clean shot," Morgan said quietly, "killing Khogani is going to throw his men into an immediate hunt for us. They'll want revenge."

"And if we miss him," Jake said grimly, "all hell will break loose, too. Either way, we know they're coming after us."

"If we get lucky, we'll take him out with a second shot." Morgan knew in these mountains, the one shot, one kill maxim didn't always work. The wind was their nemesis. A spotter worked closely with the sniper. SEALs were trained to be sniper and spotter, but on a mission like this, each would have their duty and responsibility. Spotters knew the direction of the wind, speed and any wind shifts. Sometimes, they could pull it off. Other times, they couldn't. Then it came down to Kentucky windage. It was a sniper term that meant the sniper relied on his or her experience to make the correct adjustments to the rifle.

Jake sighed and moved on his back. He

slid his arms behind his head, glaring up at the shadows dancing on the tunnel's ceiling of jagged rocks. "Taliban soldiers are damned good at knowing what direction a bullet's come from. We're going to have an exfil planned, big-time."

Exfil meant exfiltrate or get the hell out of the op or mission, their escape plan. Morgan felt his worry and knew the situation only too well from her own experience.

"All we can do is try. We'll have exfil, a rally point, and the assets will be ready to come in and pick us up," she said. Even all of that could go to hell in a handbasket, and Morgan knew it. Jake knew it, too. They were on rocky, steep mountain slopes. Anything could happen. Anything . . .

They lay there for a long time, the silence thickening. Morgan fought herself. Fought touching Jake again. It would not help them with this coming op. She heard his breathing settle down and closed her own eyes. *God, let Jake survive this. Let him be able to hold Emma in his arms. . . .* It was the last thought Morgan had as she surrendered to her exhaustion. Tomorrow would up the ante. Tomorrow, they moved into sniper mode. Tomorrow, their world changed. . . .

◆

Morgan lay on her belly next to Jake just

below a rocky ridgeline. The sun was setting, the wind sharp and cold as Jake moved the Night Force sniper scope toward a cave to the left of them. Because her shoulder was not fully healed, Morgan gave up the right to be the sniper. Instead, she volunteered to be his spotter.

She held her scope, watching as the last of the seventeen Taliban rode into a cave. Her heart beat slowly, her breath even. Now they were stalking. Every hour, they traded off the sniper-spotter position because the amount of intense energy and mental focus could only be held so long.

Jake had the AW Mag sitting on a bipod that kept the rifle barrel aimed and steady. The stock was tight against his shoulder and cheek. They'd just missed Khogani riding into the cave after they'd scrambled up the slope behind them to locate the enemy horsemen. The drone, however, had identified him going into the cave earlier.

Jake watched through the scope, the rocks biting into his prone body, causing discomfort here and there along his hips and legs. He was used to it. The Kevlar actually protected his chest and torso from the rocks, which was good.

Morgan remained where she was. It appeared the Taliban were in for the night.

Their cammie jackets blended in with the rocks and scree around them. She lowered the scope and studied the cave entrance. They had a high, angled shot, one chance, to kill Khogani. Her mouth turned down as she studied the surrounding area.

Khogani and his men had come up and over a goat path right where they lay now. The path was steep and vertical, and even the horses would have a hell of a time sliding down the winding trail to the cave below.

Darkness fell. The wind picked up, howling toward them, the temperature below freezing. Their voices would not carry down to the cave with the present wind direction. His eyes still trained on the cave, Jake whispered, "Exfil?"

Morgan grimaced. "We miss that shot this morning, and they're going to come boiling up and over this goat path we're lying on."

"Not good," Jake agreed. He moved the scope slowly, studying the rocky brown, black and cream-colored terrain around the cave. "Only one exit point out of that cave. And that's back up this goat path we're on."

"Reza said that particular cave is big, but there are no connecting tunnels to it. Khogani has to come back up this scree slope tomorrow morning. He has no choice."

They were in for a long, brutal night on

the ridge. Reza was about a quarter of a mile down below them, in another, smaller cave. Tonight, he'd feed the horses, give them some water from the large five-gallon tins they carried on the supply horse and keep them saddled. Jake watched through the AW Mag's scope. A sniper never left his target unobserved. One or the other of them would have to watch that cave like a hawk all night long.

Morgan gazed behind them on the scree slope. The goat path was a thousand feet long, and at the bottom, it split and went north and south. To the north part of the path was a wadi, or ravine. The wadi was shaped like a lightning bolt, a zigzag ravine, a good two thousand feet in length. She studied the scraggly trees eking out an existence in the wadi. There was a lot of six- to ten-foot-tall brush clogging the ravine, as well. It would be easy to hole up in the wadi and not be seen.

If Jake missed the shot or shots, and Khogani survived, the Taliban leader would be coming after them to kill them. Those hardy mountain horses could climb like goats, acclimatized to the high altitude. They wouldn't have much time to escape. It was seventeen Taliban against the two of them.

Neither of them wanted Reza caught up in the melee if it happened. The man had already lost his family. That was enough. Jake had given Reza orders yesterday evening to leave at dawn, no matter what happened. To head north, back toward the valley and to the safety of Hamid's village far below.

They settled on the ridge, the wind blowing toward them, well below freezing. Morgan had the spotter scope set up next to where Jake lay prone on his belly, the AW Mag's barrel draped with camouflage netting and pointed down at the cave. The drone was somewhere overhead, watching. Always watching. It was on the western side of the mountain, circling, its eyes on the cave where Khogani and his men had holed up for the night. They lay next to one another, body warmth important for the long night ahead of them.

"Another thirty minutes and dawn will break," Jake told Morgan quietly. The wind was raw, and he was glad for the thick jacket, hood and gloves. Still, he was freezing his ass off. No one could lie out on a rocky slope, motionless for hours, and not get numbingly cold.

Morgan nodded and lay nearby, her spotter scope on the cave below them. They'd traded off positions every hour. She'd take the rifle and he'd become her spotter. As dawn rose, it was Jake's turn at the sniper rifle to make the shot.

Grimacing, Jake knew as a sniper, being cold and uncomfortable came with the territory. This wasn't his first gig at hiding up on a mountain waiting for his HVT, high-value target, to appear at dawn. "I hope Reza is right about that cave where Khogani's holed up."

Morgan rubbed her hands, trying to warm them. She had on gloves, but the wind was sharp, gusting and sporadic. "What? That there are no tunnels to this side of the mountain?"

"Yeah," he muttered. Because if Reza had been wrong, a tunnel could lead to their location. They could be blindsided, surprised and have seventeen of those bastards climbing up after them to kill them.

"He doesn't think there is."

"Reza doesn't know this area as well as north of Hamid's village."

"I hear you." Morgan continued to watch through the spotter scope. Having used the laser scope earlier, she gave to Jake the closest distance estimation she could get on where Khogani would emerge. Jake set the dials and all they could do was wait. There was only one place where he had a shot.

Morgan saw light to the east, behind them. The dawn glowed behind the highest peaks, announcing the coming day. The drone would let them know if Khogani moved. They'd have time to set up a shot, albeit a very badly angled shot. It would be their only chance. Morgan had already received authorization from J-bad to take the shot. The exfil plan was to get an Apache in the air from Camp Bravo, as well as a medevac following it. Other than that, they'd ride their horses down the mountain and meet a Night Stalker MH-47 Chinook on the valley floor and fly away. That was if everything went according to plan. And like the SEALs always told Morgan, Murphy was always around: what could go wrong, would go wrong, and plan for plan B, C and D. Murphy's Law was real to them. They'd seen it in action way too many times.

Jake's mouth turned down. They were vulnerable. Up on a scree slope, just below the ridgeline, they had no cover whatsoever. The wadi was too far away to reach by foot. Reza had tied their two horses below, but that was a thousand feet down this slope in order to reach them. A very bad feeling washed through Jake. He'd gotten this feeling before, and it always came true. Dammit, he'd just reconnected with Morgan. Something pushed him to speak.

"Listen, when this is over, I want to stay connected with you, Morgan." He waited, afraid that she might not have the same idea.

"I feel the same, Jake. We're older."

"I've matured a little bit. . . ." Jake wanted to laugh but his focus was on the cave through the scope.

Morgan smiled, but Jake couldn't see it. "We've been through so much together and individually."

"Life is hard, babe." His eyes narrowed as he watched the entrance to the cave, seeing nothing, but always on guard. "We're getting it at both ends — personally and career-wise. There's nothing easy about being a SEAL."

"You're right about that. Like you guys say, the only easy day was yesterday."

"I'm so damn proud of you, Morgan. You've changed my mind about women in combat."

"If you didn't have to care for your chronically ill mother, I don't think you'd have been so bullheaded about women being the weaker sex, Jake."

"Yeah, after twenty-nine years, I finally realized that."

"Where will you be sent after this op is

completed?"

"I get PRODEV. I'll be stateside with my new platoon in Coronado. Do you think General Stevenson will send you back over here?"

"No. I've petitioned her to let me take 18 Delta medical training."

Jake was surprised. The U.S. Army medic course was the best in the world. Hand-picked male medical corpsmen from every military branch spent eighteen months learning battlefield medicine that would save men's and women's lives when it counted: under fire. "Will you get the billet?"

"I'm hoping so. I've been a paramedic since Annapolis. General Stevenson has a lot of power. I'd be the second woman allowed to go through 18 Delta training. You know there aren't any women field medics because that puts them directly into combat."

He heard the derision in her husky tone. "Well, that would mean you'd be stateside if you get the school."

"Yes."

"I'll be on the West Coast. You'd be on the East Coast." Jake took a deep breath. Sure, he wanted to reconnect permanently with Morgan, but he couldn't. His life as a

SEAL was one of constant danger. He could die. Jake wasn't even sure Morgan would agree to have a relationship with him. She was gun-shy just like him.

"That's the story of our lives." Always on opposite sides with one another except when they made love.

Morgan thought about how she was going to tell Jake about Emma. If everything went right, as soon as they killed Khogani, they'd be sent home to Washington, D.C., for the debrief. And Morgan was sure they'd each get sixty days' leave. That would be the perfect time to ask Jake to come home to Gunnison, Colorado, to meet his daughter for the first time. Provided that Jake forgave her. A deep love for him welled up in her. And then she took the biggest risk in her life. "You know, we've never said we loved one another, Jake. Not through all these years." Morgan took a deep breath and whispered, "I've never *not* loved you, Jake. You need to know that. But our past scares the hell out of me, and I'm not sure of our future."

Jake was about to reply when he spotted something through the scope. His radio beeped a warning that the drone saw movement in the cave. "They're moving."

Instantly, Morgan focused on the cave

through the spotting scope. There was just enough gray light now to see the cave opening. Her heart rate remained slow. Snipers could control their breathing and remain calm. Tension amped up as she analyzed all of the data. The wind was inconstant. The other problem was their position would be given away, regardless. Adrenaline began burning into her bloodstream.

Jake settled in, the fiberglass stock pressed to his cheek. There was a natural still point to the breath. And to the body. He lay with his legs spread. In this kind of light, his head would look like one of a thousand rocks peppering the ridgeline. The sniper scope was draped with material so that the barrel wouldn't shine or glint and catch the Taliban's sharp-sighted attention. He felt confident in his position.

"First rider out," Morgan spoke quietly. "Not Khogani."

Jake realized he had a second to fire. His mind was running over a thousand variables on the shot. The bullet, when fired, would actually arc up at supersonic speed and then down toward the target, slowing as it went. He got a clear view of the first rider coming out of the maw. The other problem was riders and horses. They were both unpredictable. It wasn't something a spotter could call or control. Wind and animals. His mouth tightened.

Morgan would have a millisecond to identify Khogani. And he'd have a millisecond to fire. He might not get down to that still point between the inhale and exhale. That was ideal as to when to squeeze the trigger. But he wouldn't have that luxury. And it made them damn vulnerable as a result.

"Khogani!" Morgan whispered.

Jake caught the Taliban leader riding his horse in the crosshairs of his scope. He fired.

CHAPTER SEVENTEEN

The sniper rifle bucked hard against Jake's shoulder, the power of it rippling through his entire body. The harsh bark of the bullet echoed around the area after it left the barrel. It had no muzzle suppressor, and the Taliban would see the flash and easily locate them. Jake held his breath.

There was a rider coming out of the cave at the same moment Khogani did. He trotted his horse right in front of the leader. And he was knocked off his horse by the bullet, dead before he hit the ground.

Morgan gasped softly. "No good! You hit the guy next to Khogani."

"Dammit!" Jake seethed. The echoing sound of the bullet sent Khogani wheeling his horse around and escaping back into the cave. There would be no second chance. "Exfil!" he snapped, shouldering the rifle across his back. Jake quickly slid back down off the ridge.

Morgan grabbed the spotter scope. She leaped down, boulders and smaller rocks loosening on either side of her boots as she slid, causing minor landslides. She jammed the scope into her jacket while moving. They were going to need help. And fast. Morgan grabbed the radio, made the urgent call to Vero at J-bad. He would launch two Apache combat helos and a medevac from Camp Bravo. Her call was acknowledged.

Already, as Morgan slid, fell, bruised her backside, she could hear angry screams, yells and orders erupting from the other side of the ridge. They'd just stirred up a hornet's nest, and now seventeen Taliban were going to romp up over that ridge and come after them.

Jake slid down on his butt, feeling the rocks biting into his legs. It was Morgan's job as the spotter to protect him. She had the M-4 rifle and would initiate rearguard action if they were attacked. Jake was vulnerable as the sniper because the rifle had only three shots to a magazine. And a sniper rifle wasn't good in a close-quarters fight like this. All he had was his SIG Sauer pistol, his second line of defense.

His breath tore out of him as he fell again, rolled headlong, slamming the rifle into the rocks. Cursing, Jake realized there was nothing he could do about it. He would never leave the rifle behind. Not ever.

When he heard Morgan sliding above him, he twisted around, watching her skidding to a stop, her gaze fixed on the ridge, the M-4 rifle jammed into her right shoulder, ready to fire. Thank God there were five grenades in that grenade launcher on a slide beneath the barrel. They were going to need them to get out of this alive. Jake saw one of the horses rip its reins free of the bush they'd tied them to. Panicked, the animal ran off down the goat trail, reins trailing in the wind.

Dammit!

The second horse was rearing, whinnying and trying to get loose to run after the other fleeing horse. Jake leaped and jumped over larger rocks, trying to steady himself down the slope. Above, he could hear Morgan coming down behind him. Small rocks pelted him as she continued to slow her descent, playing rearguard action.

By the time Jake hit the bottom of the slope and grabbed the reins of the frightened horse, he heard Morgan fire the M-4 above him. Jerking a look over his shoulder, he felt his heart slam into his ribs. Three Taliban were riding hard up and over the ridge. The echoing shots of bullets being fired rang throughout the area.

Morgan knelt, fired systematically at the three horsemen who rode over the top toward her. All three men fell. The horses, wild-eyed, scattered, barely missing her. Her bravery, her courage to hold the position, to protect her sniper partner, was what a spotter was supposed to do. Jake feared for her life.

"Exfil!" he roared into his mic. Leaping up on the horse, he landed in the Western saddle Morgan had been riding. Jake yanked the animal around, then swiftly reached for his SIG and brought it up. Morgan turned, leaped and slid down the last three hundred feet.

Another rider crested, firing wildly down at them with an AK-47. Jake snapped off one, two, three shots. The bullets landed in the Taliban rider's horse instead. The animal's legs collapsed beneath him, the rider thrown over his head. Jake watched as the man cartwheeled through the air, his head striking a huge boulder. He collapsed on the ground, dead.

"Come on!" Jake yelled, hauling back on the reins to stop the horse from leaping around.

Morgan threw the M-4 strap across her back. She grabbed Jake's extended hand,

and he hauled her upward in one single motion. She landed hard onto the back of the horse, behind the saddle.

"Exfil!" she gasped, sliding her arms around Jake's waist.

Jake whirled the frantic horse around once again. Above, they heard more cries. Glancing upward as he sank his heels into the frenzied horse, Jake noticed two more Taliban riders cresting the ridge. They began firing wildly. The bullets screamed by them. Mouth tight, Jake leaned forward. There was just enough light to see the goat path leading down toward the wadi. It was their only chance!

Breathing hard, his breath coming in gasps, Jake felt Morgan's arms tighten around his waist as they galloped toward the wadi. The wind tore past him, his eyes watering as the horse ran hard, his hooves pounding along the narrow, rocky goat path. Jake's mind was clicking over the variables. It would take the Apaches fifteen minutes to arrive on station. It would be way too late! They'd have to make a stand. He estimated how much ammo they had between them. The sniper rifle would be useless in a close-quarters gunfight. They had an M-4 grenade launcher and two SIGs and plenty of mags for both. Maybe . . . just maybe, they could fight and hold them off. Maybe. . . .

The wadi appeared around the curve of the mountain. Jake hauled back on the horse's reins. The animal grunted, slid to a stop, panting, its sides heaving.

Morgan slid off, jerking the M-4 off her back.

Jake slapped the horse's rump. It went galloping panic-stricken down the goat path. What he hoped was that as the Taliban rounded the corner, they'd see the horse in the distance and follow it. He wasn't that sure he could fool them.

"Come on!" he said, pointing toward the wadi. He held the SIG in his hand, watching the corner of the goat path above them. "We've got to get in deep and as high as possible."

Breathing unevenly, the high altitude making her lungs burn, Morgan nodded. She ducked into the cover where the brush was thick, tall and poked savagely at her body. The boulders were large and small, making climbing hard and slippery. They were in trouble. As she scrambled, Morgan radioed the coming combat helos with their present GPS position. But their position would continually change as they climbed.

Brush swatted at Morgan as she turned

aside, allowing Jake to move past her. His face was gleaming with sweat, his gray eyes nearly colorless. This was going to be a fight to the end. There would be no survivors, one way or another.

Morgan had the M-4, and it was her duty to hang back, provide cover fire for Jake, who only had a pistol and a useless sniper rifle. The trees around them were short and spindly. It was the brush that would give them cover. At the same time, it rendered the sniper rifle useless. A twig could turn a bullet enough to deflect and miss the enemy target. Jake was reduced to just his pistol. That wasn't good odds for them. Two rifles and one pistol against sixteen AK-47s.

As Morgan allowed him to move above her, she heard the thunder of approaching horses. Her adrenaline was pumping, burning through her bloodstream. Everything was slowing down; it always did in moments when she could die. She'd been at this point before. But never did she ever feel this kind of overwhelming dread. Death was breathing down their necks. Their number was up.

Jake managed to climb a thousand feet up into the center of the ravine, finding several large boulders. They could hide and make a stand of sorts. Rocks were better cover than tree limbs and brush. Morgan was laboring upward just as he was. By the time they reached the boulders, Jake heard the screams, shouts and horses below them. They hadn't fooled the Taliban at all. From his vantage point, Jake could see the horses and riders milling down below the wadi, soldiers excitedly pointing upward, pointing at them, even though they couldn't see them yet. Khogani knew they were in here. And he was coming after them.

Morgan sobbed for breath, her lungs burning, as if on fire. Jake grabbed her hand and helped her the last few feet up to the other boulder. Between them, the rocks would act as a shield. They would have minutes to settle their breathing, take their positions and wait.

"Apaches on station in ten minutes," Morgan reported, breathless.

Jake hissed a curse. There was no way for the Apaches to send missiles or Gatling gun bullets into the wadi now. Both the hunter and hunted were mixed together somewhere in the undergrowth. Apaches had infrared ability to see body heat on a human. But they wouldn't be able to identify which was the enemy and who were the friendlies. His mouth flattened. He knelt, finding as comfortable a position as possible to rest his wrist on a rock to steady the aim of the SIG.

He kept his sniper rifle across his back. This was going to come down to an old-fashioned shootout. The Apaches would not be able to help them. *Son of a bitch!*

The screaming and cries of the Taliban sounded closer and closer. Morgan hunkered down on one knee, resting her right arm against the cold, gray boulder. There was a narrow area that had no brush below them. They would funnel in that way because it was easier than fighting through the thickets. And that was where they had to pick them off, one at a time.

Breathing hard, sweat trickling down her ribs, her heart feeling as if it would leap out of her chest, Morgan looked behind them. Worried, she continued to search up above the brush. Was it possible that Khogani would send men on either side of the wadi above their position? Or come in from the sides at them? *Yes.*

"I'm taking the area above us," she told him, instinctively reacting to the possibility.

"Roger that. I'll take below us."

Her chest heaved with exertion. The brush snapped and shattered. The sounds of the approaching soldiers grew louder. The Taliban would appear any second now. . . .

Jake saw the first soldier pop up into the area. He snapped off a shot. The man screamed, toppled, his AK-47 flying into the air. He spotted a second soldier, but instantly, he moved back into the brush to hide. Jake's mouth was tight, hands gripped around the SIG, the perspiration running off his face. The light was better, and he could see more deeply into the brush below them.

Suddenly, he heard a scream. It had come from his left. Surprised, Jake turned, swinging his SIG toward the sound. Out of the brush a soldier came firing at him. The bullets snapped and popped around his head. He fired once, twice, three times. He felt a sudden numbness in his right calf. The soldier's twisted, angry face suddenly took on a look of surprise. Jake's third bullet hit him in the chest. The man was jerked backward, off his feet.

There was a sudden commotion above them. The Taliban had not only paralleled the wadi where they were located, but had climbed above their position! They were firing from the brush, their bullets singing and ricocheting all around the boulders where they were hidden. Morgan had to move. She couldn't hide behind the boulder because the Taliban were down below, throwing every kind of lead their way they could. The bark of the AK-47s was deafening. She crouched, trying to find the men who were making the noise above them. To her left, she heard more soldiers coming in to get them.

Jerking a look to her left, she saw Jake go down. For a second, Morgan caught a glimpse of the blood on his lower right leg. *No!* There was nothing she could do to help him. It sounded as if the rest of the Taliban had climbed far above them and were coming down.

Morgan shouldered the M-4 and popped off a grenade. It thunked, the heavy, bruising recoil of the stock against her shoulder. It flew into the thick brush. The explosion occurred, the invisible pressure-wave reaction pounding against her body. She fell to her knees, watching the fire and brush, soil and rock erupt. Screams and shrieks pierced the dust-laden air. And then more bullets flew into the position where she was kneeling.

She heard Jake systematically firing the SIG. They were in a pincers with the Taliban closing in on all sides of them! There was no place to hide. Mouth tightening, sweat running down her temples, Morgan turned and fired a second grenade off to the left of where Jake was located. And then she fired a third one down below where six Taliban struggled to reach them on foot.

The explosions were loud and concussive. Her ears hurt, and she could barely hear anything afterward. She was firing dangerously close, meaning they could be injured in the grenade explosions, as well. Above the fray, for a second, Morgan could hear the Apache helicopters circling above the wadi. Their rotor blades punctured the air like huge kettle drums being beaten above their heads. The pilots didn't dare fire into the wadi because it could kill them.

More movement came from Morgan's left. Just as she was going to fire a grenade into the side of the wadi, a bullet struck her in the chest. She cried out, thrown back off her feet. Morgan landed hard against the boulder, momentarily stunned. Without thinking, she triggered the grenade into the brush. Burning pain floated up through her chest. Scrambling to her feet, Morgan spotted two more men to her right, aiming at Jake. She fired the last grenade, the M-4 bucking against her shoulder.

The explosion rocked the area. It was so close to them! Hundreds of pounds of rocks and gravel exploded upward, showering them. Morgan realized she was down to bullets only. The brush moved above her. Jake was down but still firing prone, keeping half the enemy at bay. Gasping for breath, Morgan moved to the left, exposing herself to anyone that might still be below them. Two men were in the brush above her. For a second, she recognized Khogani. Hatred flowed through her. She jammed the M-4 against her shoulder. Morgan wanted that son of a bitch!

A bullet struck her Kevlar from behind. Morgan was flung forward, off her feet. She gasped in pain. Jake turned, firing the SIG at two men coming up to finish her off from behind. Rolling, she saw the two Taliban above her leap out in front of her. She lifted the M-4, firing multiple times at the first man who charged her.

Everything slowed down to a crawl. The man's eyes widened in surprise as her bullets struck him three times in the chest. The AK-47 he was firing arced upward, spewing bullets up past her and into the sky. Then came his scream of rage. But her focus, her entire life, was zeroed in on the man coming right behind him. It was Khogani. *Bastard!* Morgan's lips drew away from her clenched teeth. Burning pain consumed her torso where she'd taken a bullet to her Kevlar vest.

Morgan leaped to her feet, crouched and aimed. Khogani screamed at her, raising his

AK-47, firing at her at the same time. Morgan didn't move. Her whole life was through the scope of the M-4. She had his head in the sights, and she pulled the trigger. As she did, her left leg suddenly became unstable. Surprised, she watched as her bullet went an inch left of the Taliban leader's head. He was no more than ten feet away when her left leg collapsed beneath her.

Grunting, the M-4 slamming into the rocks, her hand still gripping it, Morgan saw Khogani suddenly give her a feral grin. He had glee written across his bearded face as he pulled his scimitar from the sheath and held it in his left hand. He was going to decapitate her.

She'd been hit and hit bad. Her eyesight started graying. Morgan felt herself bleeding out. The last thing she was going to do before she lost consciousness was kill Khogani. He'd killed Mark. He'd murdered Reza's village of a hundred and fifty Shinwari people.

Her gaze held his baleful one. He was triumphant now as he slowed down, seeing she was lying on her back, helpless. He didn't think she had the physical strength to pick up the M-4 lying useless in her right hand. He moved the scimitar, slinging the AK-47 over his shoulder, wrapping his hands around the handle of the curved blade. His eyes gleamed with excitement as he approached her.

Morgan felt her heart pounding in her chest. Felt the warmth of blood spurting out of her thigh. Her fingers closed around the M-4. Khogani was six feet away, smiling down at her, his eyes filled with malice.

No doubt, he didn't think she had any fight left in her, and she was counting on this. She used every ounce of her hatred to lift that M-4 and aim it at Khogani. With superhuman effort, black dots dancing across her vision, Morgan hauled the M-4 up, aimed and pulled the trigger. She watched the bullet strike Khogani in the face.

The Taliban leader was thrown backward six feet. He landed in a heap, the scimitar flying out of his hand, falling on the nearby rocks.

Gasping for breath, Morgan tried to listen for more Taliban. It was suddenly quiet except for the Apaches thunking heavily overhead, watching through their avionics the carnage and bloodbath below.

"Jake!" she yelled. "Jake!"

"I'm here. Where are you?"

Morgan sank to the ground, breathing hard, feeling pain starting to move up her leg and into her gut. "Eleven o'clock. I'm hit. . . ."

"Hold on. . . ."

The M-4 slid uselessly out of Morgan's fingers. She blinked, trying to hold on to consciousness. Jake appeared, limping badly, his face hard and unreadable. A lot of blood oozed from his lower leg. His eyes widened as he stared down at her. That look told her everything. Morgan suddenly felt very weak, no matter how hard she battled against it.

Jake fell to her side, holstering his SIG. He ignored the pain of his leg wound and quickly jerked the tourniquet off the position it was held on her left shoulder. Her left leg had been trapped beneath her body.

He gently moved her so that he could carefully straighten out her leg. It worried him how pasty Morgan's face was.

"Lie still, babe," he rasped, opening the tourniquet and quickly placing it high, around her left thigh.

Morgan had taken a bullet, and it had not only hit the flesh of her thigh, but it had shattered her femur. The white bone stuck up out of the raw flesh and scared him as little else ever would. Gulping, Jake quickly tightened the tourniquet down so hard that she screamed and lost consciousness. The blood spurting out of the torn area stopped. He called on his radio for medevac. They had to get out of here! A medevac would never be able to land near this ravine.

Jake looked down at Morgan, her eyes shut, her mouth slack. With shaking fingers, he pressed them against the carotid artery located on the side of her slender neck. There was a pulse. But very weak and slow, indicating just how much blood she'd already lost. The tourniquet would slow down most of the bleeding. Did he have a chance to get her out of here alive or not? He didn't know.

Turning, Jake grabbed some green duct tape out of his gear and quickly wrapped it around his lower leg and knee. A bullet had passed through the meat of his calf. If he could just use the duct tape to support that leg, he could carry Morgan out of the wadi and to help. He heard the Apaches circling. They'd heard his desperate request for the medevac to land on the goat path, just clear of the wadi.

Had they killed all the Taliban soldiers? Jake didn't know. He thought so, but he couldn't be sure. It was a terrible risk. Leave Morgan here, alone and unprotected, and go see if there were any more bad guys left alive in the wadi hunting them down, or not?

His mind moved through how many were killed. Pain was affecting his thought processes. Jake savagely willed himself to think clearly and gut through his pain. Yes, all seventeen were accounted for. There was no one left.

Jake heaved to his feet, testing the duct tape around his wound. Looking down, he realized he could never put Morgan in a fireman's carry. Not with the bone of her femur sticking out like that. He'd cause her more injury, probably kill her by ripping another artery open. Breathing hard, shaking with adrenaline from the battle, Jake leaned down, sliding his arms beneath her shoulders and her knees. *God, help me get her out of here. Just give me the strength. . . .*

CHAPTER EIGHTEEN

Jake shielded Morgan in his arms, turning his back toward the Black Hawk medevac landing on the goat path south of the wadi. Rocks, dirt and dust exploded around him as the rotors tore up the area and the helo landed. He fell to his knees, leaned over as far as he could, pulling Morgan close, trying to protect her from the flying debris kicked up by eighty-miles-an-hour gusts.

Gasping for breath, Jake wasn't sure he could rise out of the kneeling position due to loss of blood. The helo was less than a hundred feet away. Every time he looked down at Morgan, her head tipped back, throat exposed and her lips parted, her flesh whitened a little more with every passing minute. Jake desperately willed his life back into hers.

The two combat medics leaped out of the helo, running hard down the goat path toward them. The aircrew chief, Jackson, a man in his forties, looked grimly down at her wounded leg. The white femur stuck out of Morgan's bloodied trousers, stark and jolting.

"We got her," he yelled to Jake over the roar of the rotor wash. Jackson gripped Jake's shoulder and then barked orders over at the younger combat medic, Tennison.

"She's critical, a nine liner!" Jake yelled, his voice cracking. He looked up into the man's eyes. Jake knew what he knew: Morgan could die in transit. His mind whirled, he felt dizzy, and he held on tightly to her limp body.

"Let her go," Jackson ordered, gripping his hand and prying Jake's fingers away from beneath her bloodied thigh.

"He's wounded, too," Tennison called, spotting blood on the SEAL's lower leg.

"Goddammit!" Jake yelled at the younger blond medic. "You take care of *her*!"

In moments, the medics had lifted Morgan carefully between them. Jake fell to his hands and knees, gasping for air. He wasn't sure he could make that torturous climb out of the wadi. His legs felt like jelly. Even as toughened as he was as a SEAL, he'd pushed far beyond his own physical limits. Terrified for Morgan, he gritted his teeth, pushed up to his knees and, somehow, staggered to his feet.

Jake picked up the M-4 and his ruck that had the sniper rifle strapped to the back of it. Turning, he forced his cramping legs to move into a trot. Ahead, the rotor wash violently buffeted him, flinging up dirt and pebbles. Jake shielded his eyes with one hand and bowed his head against his chest, weaving at a run toward the opened door of the Black Hawk.

It was Tennison who hauled him on board, gripping his shoulder, helping him in the rest of the way. Jake spun down past the medics, avoiding the litter strapped to the deck where Jackson was feverishly working over Morgan.

Sinking to his knees, Jake twisted around and shrugged off his ruck. He brought the two weapons down between him and the wall of the chopper. He squeezed into a corner, sitting down and drawing up his legs against his body so both medics had as much room as they needed in order to help Morgan.

The Black Hawk spooled up, broke earth, the thunking blades pulling strongly, heading straight up. Jake felt woozy but shook it off. He watched as Tennison fitted an oxygen mask over Morgan's face. Jackson ripped open several packages of Celox, a blood coagulant, and poured it into her torn thigh to stop all the bleeding. He quickly cut off the left sleeve around Morgan's arm, inserted an IV. The other medic pulled out the whole blood from a nearby cooler, handing it to Jackson. The life-giving blood would flood her cardiovascular system. It would start to make up for the loss of blood, and it *could* make a difference by getting enough fluids into her body. It would stop her heart from going into cardiac arrest.

Jake felt helpless. All he could do was sit there as a witness. The medics quickly placed a large field dressing over her leg, carefully covering the exposed bone. And then they drew on a set of trauma pants. The LSP air trauma trousers fitted from her ankles to halfway up Morgan's torso. They pumped air into the pants to force blood from her lower extremities back into the center of her body so her heart had enough blood to keep it working. The pants would also stabilize the open fracture and slow down the shock eating away at her.

Jackson was pushing one syringe after another of drugs into the IV line, dropping them wherever they landed around him on the deck. He was snapping orders to Tennison, who appeared shaken. His eyes had gone huge when he'd realized Morgan was a woman, not a man.

Pushing the sweat out of his eyes, Jake saw a nearby crew helmet, grabbed it and pulled it on. Above his head, he inserted the jack into an outlet that would allow him to hear inter-cabin communications.

"Lieutenant," Jackson snapped, looking up toward the cockpit, "you get this bird red lined. This patient isn't gonna make it. Fly straight to Bagram. I want to be switched over to the E.R. trauma surgery channel at the hospital, stat."

Jake's heart raced with dread. The older combat medic's mouth was flattened, his eyes narrowed and focused solely on Morgan. Pulling the mic closer to his lips, Jake said, "She's type O positive blood. She's lost close to two and a half pints from what I can estimate."

"Dammit!" Jackson barked, grabbing another IV. He thrust it across Morgan to Tennison, ordering him to cut off her other sleeve and insert the second IV of saline fluid in her other arm. It would give Morgan twice the amount of fluids as before. It was a desperate rush to stabilize her.

The helo was roaring, shaking and shuddering as it climbed over the twelve-thousand-foot mountain, straining at the highest possible forward speed in the thin air. Jake sat tensely, his eyes never leaving Morgan's face. Once the IVs were inserted, Jackson, as gently as he could, removed her Kevlar vest. He threw it across the helo, and it landed at Jake's feet. He pulled the vest next to the weapons at his side.

"Any other wounds?" Jackson demanded of Jake.

"I don't know," he said, swallowing hard. "We got separated." Jackson nodded and with a pair of scissors quickly cut open the front of her shirt. There were no bloodstains on her tan T-shirt. But when Jackson cut the fabric in half and pulled it open, Jake gasped. Morgan had sustained a bullet to her Kevlar. The huge purple bruise appeared below her right breast.

My God, how had she managed to fight on? And she hadn't let the hit stop her from returning fire. Jake had seen her bring down Khogani. There had been nothing he could have done directly to help Morgan, as he'd been killing the last Taliban soldier coming up at the same time behind her to shoot her in the head.

Jackson, despite his size and his large hands, was gentle as he and Tennison worked to pull off Morgan's clothing and inspect her back to examine it for bullet exit wounds. They handled her as if she were a fragile, broken doll.

Jake couldn't believe what he saw as they eased her over just enough to inspect the back of her body. Morgan had sustained a second hit to her Kevlar vest. Another purple bruise just beneath her left shoulder blade stared back at him. Tears jammed into Jake's eyes as he sat there, realizing what she'd done. Morgan had exposed herself on both flanks, trying to protect him after he'd been wounded and gone down. He'd tried to get up, but his leg had kept buckling beneath him. The Taliban had fired at her repeatedly. The vest had saved her life twice. How could she have continued to fight with two hits to her Kevlar like that?

Jackson pulled a dark green wool blanket across Morgan's upper body and gently placed each of her arms outside of it. He put the stethoscope to her heart, head bent, listening . . . listening. . . .

Jake struggled to take a deep breath. He kept praying they'd get enough fluids into Morgan soon enough to stop her heart from cavitating. The monitors hanging on the back of the copilot's seat showed that her blood pressure was in the basement and her pulse was dropping. She was borderline. Any second, Morgan could go into arrest.

The expression on Jackson's face was

tense as he was patched through to Bagram air base near Kabul. The man wasted no time in telling them to have a surgical team with a gurney waiting for them. He described Morgan's medical state in stark detail, giving them the stats and ordering an ortho surgeon to be heading up the surgical team because of her broken femur.

Jake's gaze moved to Morgan's face. Her lips were slack, her skin translucent, dark purple crescents beneath her closed eyes. Rubbing his face savagely, all Jake could do was wait. He loved Morgan. He loved her so damn much, and she was lying critical on the deck of a Black Hawk. He could do nothing else to help her. Her life was measured by the amount of fluids flowing into her arteries. And her will to live.

He prayed as he'd never prayed before. He'd trade his soul to the devil if Morgan would be allowed to live.

Eventually, Tennison crawled over to him.

"Sir? Will you let me look at your wound?"

"Take care of *her*," Jake ground out, glaring up at the young medic.

The combat medic reared back, as if struck. SEALs had a bad reputation out in the field. And most combat medics knew a lesser wounded SEAL would ignore their own injury in favor of another teammate's more serious wound.

"Tennison, get over here," Jackson ordered tightly.

Jake looked out the window. There was blue sky. It was morning. He pulled the cover off his watch, his fingers trembling. They'd been in the air for almost an hour.

"ETA to Bagram?" he asked Jackson.

Jackson was checking Morgan's blood pressure, which had finally stabilized at a very low setting. "Another twenty minutes."

"What's her status?"

"Past critical."

The way Jackson said the word scared Jake even more.

"What's a woman doing out here?" Tennison asked, turning to Jake.

"It doesn't matter," Jake snarled.

"But . . . you're a SEAL."

Jake wanted to scream. Why the hell did it matter at all? Morgan was as close to death as anyone could get without outright dying. "Keep your head in the game," Jake yelled. He jabbed his index finger down at Morgan. "Focus on *her*!" Breathing raggedly, Jake almost wanted to get up and put a fist into the kid's face. He was young. This was probably his first tour in a medevac. Thank God Jackson was here. The older man was fighting every mile to stabilize Morgan against all kinds of odds stacked against her.

"Tennison, strap her in," Jackson ordered him sharply. "We'll be landing shortly."

The aircrew chief nodded slightly to Jake, as if to apologize for the kid's badly timed questions. Jake drew up his knees and rested his head against his arms, exhausted.

They couldn't land too soon. Jake breathed a sigh of relief as the Black Hawk landed at the hospital, cutting the engines, the shaking and shuddering slowing down. Jackson unhooked the inter-cabin connection, ordered Tennison to slide the door open on the helo. Jake remained where he was. Four men came forward with a gurney, the blades whipping their green scrubs and hair. It was Jackson who was in charge, and he barked orders at the doctors and nurses who assisted. Together, they gently moved Morgan out of the helo and onto the gurney. In moments, they had her strapped in and were trotting toward the open doors that led directly into the surgery unit.

Jackson leaped back on board, his eyes boring into Jake's bloodshot gaze. He reached out, gripping the SEAL's arm, pulling him forward toward the door. All the life, the urgency, bled out of Jake. He looked down to see the huge pool of blood that had leaked out of his duct-taped leg wound.

Jackson was strong and guiding. Jake moved slowly, every effort draining him more and more.

As the second gurney was moved to the lip of the open door, Jake hesitated. He grabbed the combat medic's arm. "Thank you . . ."

"Any time, sir. Good luck. Godspeed."

It was the last thing Jake remembered as he fainted from blood loss.

Jake snapped awake in the E.R. A team was prepping him for surgery. An orthopedic surgeon came over.

"I'm Dr. Jonas. I'm going to be operating on Captain Morgan Boland. You were with her, right?"

Jake shook off his dizziness. "Yes, sir, I was." He saw the surgeon frown. "Why?" His heart sped up with fear.

"Her leg wound is very bad, Lieutenant. I'm probably going to have to amputate it."

Hissing a curse, Jake willed himself up on his elbows, grabbing the surgeon's green scrubs. "Like hell, you will! You do whatever you can, Doctor, to save her and her leg!" His glare burned into the doctor's widening eyes. "Don't you dare take her leg!" His voice cracked. "Give her a chance! You hear me?" His fingers tightened into the material at the surgeon's throat. Desperation, grief, soared through him as he saw the ortho surgeon tense.

"Okay, Lieutenant." He pried Jake's fingers off his scrubs. "I'll do what I can."

Breathing hard, Jake snarled, "You'll do better than that. I'll hunt you down if you don't save her leg."

The surgeon scowled. "At ease, Lieutenant. You're wounded and you're going into surgery here in a few minutes yourself."

There was anger in the surgeon's eyes, and, somehow, Jake didn't feel he could trust him. Maybe it was his own weakness that caused this paranoia, but he had to do something. When the surgeon left, Jake struggled off the gurney, much to the chagrin of the nurse who was trying to help him.

"Get me to a phone," he growled, drilling a hard look into her eyes. *"Now."* He pulled the IV out of his arm, dropping it on the gurney.

The nurse nodded. "Come with me, sir." She led him to an office just off of E.R. Opening the door, she pointed to a phone on a desk. "Do me a favor? Once you finish your call, come back to the cubical so I can prep you for surgery?"

"I will," Jake grunted, limping heavily. He

ignored the pain, closed the door and went to the desk. Grabbing the landline, he called General Maya Stevenson at the Pentagon. Jake was going to move heaven and hell to get Morgan's leg saved. If anyone could help, he knew the General would.

Jake jerked awake. He sat straight up, gasping for breath. Looking around, his heart pounding, he realized he was in a drug haze. He was in a private room. Perspiration rolled off him, dampening the material of his blue hospital gown.

The walls were washed light green. There was a window with venetian blinds across it near his bed. The beeps and sighs of monitoring equipment finally caught his attention. A dark-haired, brown-eyed nurse in dark green fatigues quietly entered his room.

"You're at Bagram air base, Lieutenant Ramsey. How are you feeling?"

Jake swallowed, his throat hurting. "Where's Morgan? How is she?" he demanded, his voice hoarse.

The nurse stopped and pulled his chart from the bottom of his bed. "Captain Morgan Boland?"

"Yes." His heart started to pound; his head ached like hell.

"She's still in surgery, sir." And then she

gave him a sympathetic look. "You passed out from blood loss in the E.R. shortly after you got done with your phone call. Dr. Thornton, your surgeon, repaired your right calf. You're going to be fine."

His emotions roared through him. "How long has Morgan been in surgery? Did they save her leg?"

The nurse checked the IV and said, "Seven hours, now. And I don't know about her leg."

Closing his eyes, Jake felt anxiety. "I need to see her, then." Had his call to General Stevenson worked? Panicked, he hoped she'd been able to get to the right people here at Bagram in time.

"That's impossible, Lieutenant. I'm sorry."

"I need to be with her. Even if it's the damn lounge on the surgery floor. Get me up there." Her cheeks colored at the hostile tone in his voice.

"I'll ask Dr. Thornton."

"Screw all of you," Jake growled, throwing off the covers. He saw his lower right leg bandaged. Sitting on the edge of the bed, he quickly pulled the IV out of his arm and dropped it on the bed

"Lieutenant! You can't do that! You can't take out your IV! It has morphine in it to stop your pain."

"SEALs deal with pain all the time. Where are my clothes?" Jake demanded, standing in the light blue gown that hung to his knees. The pain in his heart wasn't something he could combat, his love for Morgan transcending any physical pain he might have. Someone had washed him, all the dirt and grime gone. The nurse started to panic.

"I, uh . . . I have to get the doctor!" She ran out of the room.

Muttering a curse, Jake limped unsteadily over to the closet. Jerking open the door, he found a clean pair of desert cammies in there. His dirty boots were on the floor beneath them, still bloody. Morgan's blood. His blood. He grabbed the gear and headed to the bathroom, urgency pushing him to get to her side. He worried they'd amputated her leg.

By the time Dr. Thornton arrived, Jake was sitting on the chair, lacing up his second boot. The doctor was in his forties and pushed his wire-rimmed glasses up on his dark hair. "Lieutenant Ramsey? You in a hurry?"

Jake noticed the young nurse peeking out from behind the tall doctor. "Either you tell me what floor surgery is on and which surgery theater Captain Morgan Boland is in, or I'll go find her myself."

He smiled a little. "Nurse, get Lieutenant Ramsey a wheelchair? We don't want him opening up that bullet wound that I just worked so hard to close for him."

Jake met the man's dark blue eyes. "Thanks, Doc."

"She was your partner?" Thornton guessed.

"Yes, sir."

He nodded, pursing his lips. "Just to warn you, there's FBI and CIA crawling all over that surgery floor. They're telling everyone they cannot discuss the fact a woman in combat gear, wounded in a firefight, is here at our hospital."

Jake stood, feeling pain drift up his leg. "That's right," he ground out. "It's top secret."

The nurse brought in a wheelchair. Thornton thanked her, dismissed her and brought it over to Jake. "Lieutenant, I'll take you up there. Normally, I wouldn't do this, but we'll go up to the observation room in that surgery theater. That's as close as you can get to her. Fair enough?"

Grateful, Jake nodded. He didn't trust his voice. He felt as if he was going to cry. Fighting the urge, he sat down. Without a word, Thornton turned the wheelchair around. The nurse opened the door and he pushed Jake out into the long, busy hallway.

Jake's heart started to pound hard as Thornton eased the wheelchair into the observation room above the surgery theater. A lump formed in his throat. Below, he could see Morgan, her bright red hair against the white cradle where her head rested.

She was on oxygen, an anesthesiologist monitoring her functions. Her body was draped in blankets and sheets. There was a medical team of ten people around her. Anxiously, his gaze moved to her thigh. Relief showered through Jake. Morgan still had her leg! No longer was the bone sticking out.

Tears stung Jake's eyes, and he fought them back down deep inside himself. General Stevenson had reached out and made sure the surgeon wouldn't amputate Morgan's leg. He was grateful to the woman.

"What's happened while I was unconscious?" he demanded of Thornton, who stood behind him. "I'm a combat medic for my SEAL platoon, so can you give me her medical lowdown?"

"She coded two hours ago, Lieutenant Ramsey."

Jake's breath jammed in his throat. That

meant Morgan's heart had stopped beating. He stared at her, desperation mounting in his chest.

"They worked hard to bring her back," Thornton quietly assured him. "She'd lost nearly three pints of blood. No one really knew just how much blood she'd initially lost. They've been replenishing her blood type ever since then."

"And now?" Jake croaked, leaning forward, unable to tear his gaze from her.

"Stable." Thornton patted his shoulder. "She's going to make it, Lieutenant. We weren't so sure two hours ago, but we are now. Jackson, the aircrew chief on your medevac, really saved her life. I don't know if you knew this, but he's an 18 Delta combat medic. The best we have. He used two IVs to replace missing blood. If he hadn't . . ."

"What's going on now?" Jake demanded, his voice strangled with emotion.

"Cleanup. There are probably twenty or so bone splinters and fragments they have to find and then remove before they can close her up. She's lost about thirty percent of her femur, but with time, physical therapy, the bone will grow back. Tomorrow, you'll both be on a C-5 flight to Landstuhl medical center in Germany. She'll undergo further surgery there. We've saved her leg, but there's a lot more to be done and they have the facility to do it. We don't." The surgeon's voice dropped. "She'll never be able to do what she did today again, Lieutenant Ramsey."

Leaning back, Jake felt utterly exhausted. He closed his eyes, gripping the wheelchair arms, his knuckles whitened as he tried to keep his emotions in check. Morgan would live! And her leg had been saved! He didn't give a damn if she ever saw combat again. He loved her. He wanted her safe, dammit. And as far away from Afghanistan as he could get her.

"Listen," Thornton said, breaking the silence, "I need to place a call to Jim and Cathy Boland. They know their daughter was wounded, but they don't know if she is going to live or die. Would you like to speak to them instead? I think you're a lot more involved with Captain Boland than most people would guess."

Jake opened his eyes. He twisted a look up at the doctor, who smiled slightly. "Yes, I would like to talk to them. I'm sure they're worried sick." He wanted to personally reassure them.

"I'll take you down to my office so you can call them."

Morgan was going to make it. Jake felt like a dying man who had been granted a new lease on life. With a deep, uneven breath, he muttered, "Yes, let's go."

The doctor smiled and turned the wheelchair around. "You SEALs are something else. You know that?"

"SEALs stick together," Jake muttered defiantly. "They're our family. . . . We leave no one behind. . . ." And he'd have willingly given his life for Morgan's. In a firefight, they were an unbreakable, unstoppable team. And they would always take care of their own, no matter the life-and-death consequences. All that mattered was that Morgan was going to make it. *Oh, God, thank you . . . for everything. . . .*

Jake tried to compose himself in the doctor's office. Thornton had left him alone so he could make the call to Morgan's parents. He stared at the black telephone, the number for the Bolands before him. Never having met them, he tried to think what he was going to say. He knew Jim and Cathy Boland had been in the military, been in combat. Cathy Boland had nearly died in a firefight, if not for Jim coming to rescue her in time to save her life.

As he rubbed his face tiredly, Jake felt exhaustion so deep he could barely think beyond his wildly fluctuating emotions. Thornton had told him that the Marine Corps had called her parents to say she'd been gravely wounded in combat, but nothing else.

Jake took a deep breath and dialed the number. It would be seven in the morning at the Boland household. The phone rang. Jake's fingers tightened around the receiver, his eyes closed, trying to steady his emotions.

"Jim Boland speaking."

"Mr. Boland? I'm Lieutenant Jake Ramsey. I'm calling about your daughter, Morgan." His heart started to pound, and tears threatened to overtake Jake. He heard the wariness and worry in the man's voice at the other end. "I want to tell you your daughter is going to live. She's going to make it."

"Thank God . . ."

"Yes, sir. I know you were expecting to talk to the surgeon, but I wanted to call you myself." Jake took in a shaky breath. "Sir, your daughter and I were out on an op I can't discuss. She sustained a very bad leg injury, her left femur broken by a bullet." The scenes played out behind Jake's tightly shut eyes. And the tide of feelings roared up through him as he remembered the blood spurting out of a severed artery in her leg.

Compressing his mouth into a thin line, Jake thickly added, "She's critical but stable. The ortho surgeon said we'll be flying by C-5 tomorrow morning to Landstuhl medical center in Germany. Morgan will undergo more surgery at that time." He wouldn't go into the details about how her leg had almost been amputated. They didn't need to know it at this point.

"Is she conscious, Lieutenant Ramsey?"

"No, sir. They're inducing her into a drug coma until they get her past the second surgery at Landstuhl. Once that is done, she'll become conscious."

"I see. . . ."

"She's going to live, sir. That's what I wanted you and your wife to know."

"That's very kind of you to call us, Lieutenant Ramsey."

Jake heard the silence grow on the line. He wondered if Morgan had ever talked to them about him. He took a chance. "Sir, you probably don't know this, but I care very deeply for your daughter. We've had an on-again, off-again relationship for the past nine years." His voice lowered with emotion. "I love her, sir. And I will do everything I can to be by her side through all of this."

Jake knew in his heart that he could never

have the relationship he wanted with Morgan. Even if his heart wanted, his head knew better. They were fated to remain apart.

"Lieutenant, my daughter has spoken a great deal about you to us."

Jake didn't hear any censure in the man's voice, and relief fled through him. "That's good to know, sir."

"I don't know if you knew this, Lieutenant Ramsey, but our daughter never stopped loving you. We know you two have had a rocky relationship."

Tears leaked out of his tightly shut eyes. Jake drew in a ragged breath. "Sir, if I could have given my life for hers, I'd have done it. I wish I could tell you more, but I can't. You were in the Recon Marines. You know black ops."

"Yes, I do, Lieutenant. Listen, stay with Morgan. Can you call us after she comes out of surgery at Landstuhl? We're trying to arrange flights to get there to be with her."

"Yes, sir, I will. I won't leave her side, sir. Things are moving fast here." Jake blinked, wiping the tears away with his hand. "I heard one ortho surgeon say that as soon as Morgan is stabilized in Germany, they're looking at sending her home, to the U.S., to the Bethesda medical center on the East Coast. I'd hate for you to fly to Germany and she's already gone. Let me see what I can find out as things unfold? In the meantime, I'll be in touch with you."

"Sounds like a plan," Jim Boland said. His voice grew emotional. "Thank you for saving her life. Morgan couldn't have had a better partner than you. I hope, someday, we can meet and I can thank you in person, shake your hand."

Jake tried to steady his voice, the exhaustion making him vulnerable to his normally suppressed feelings. "If it had been me who got hit, she'd have turned around and saved my sorry ass."

Jim Boland managed a chuckle. "Well said, Lieutenant. How are you doing?"

Jake hadn't expected such concern or care from Morgan's father. It made him choke and pull the phone away for a moment. Desperately, he collected himself. "I'm good, sir."

"You're a SEAL. Why would I expect any other answer?"

It was Jake's turn to grin a little. "Yes, sir, I guess that says it all."

"Just know Cathy and I will be forever in your debt and grateful to you. And thank you for calling us. You have no idea how much better we'll feel now. We won't be worrying and wondering. My wife, Cathy, is still sleeping, so I'll tell her the good news when she wakes up."

"I'll be in touch, sir. Goodbye."

Jake hung up the phone, rubbing his hands tiredly across his face. His beard was rough, and now he could shave it off. He slowly rose, feeling the stiffness and deep bruising his body had taken during combat. Maybe he could find the doctor and persuade him to give him a watertight bandage around his calf so he could stand under a hot shower and get rid of the bone aches and stiffness.

CHAPTER NINETEEN

The world was full of sounds, but Morgan couldn't identify any of them. Her consciousness came and went. She was vaguely aware of pain drifting up her left leg. Mouth dry, she moved her lips. They felt cracked and sore. Her throat, when she tried to swallow, hurt like hell. The only thing she could focus on, despite the sounds, smells and moments of nothingness, was a warm, strong hand holding hers.

And sometimes, she'd feel him lace his fingers between hers. It was intimate. Tender. Morgan felt cold, and he felt so warm. Moving her head slowly, she wanted to open her eyes, but her lids were so heavy. Voices intruded. A man. A woman. No one she recognized. She recognized Jake's low, deep voice. He was so close. People were talking around her.

Their excitement was evident even though they were whispering to one another. Her attention remained on his hand as Morgan struggled to surface from the drug state. Jake's fingers closed gently around her own, as if to silently reassure her. Her anxiety began to dissolve. *Jake.*

Her mind wasn't working. Just bits, pieces, but his hand was her only anchor.

The voices left, and something squeaked, perhaps a chair? The hand would shift around hers, which made her panic. And then his fingers gently stroked her hair, moving strands away from her cheek. Her lashes fluttered; the gesture was one she knew so well. Jake was so close to her.

Morgan thought she could feel his moist breath flowing across her brow. As he pressed a light kiss on her forehead, her anxiety ebbed even more. She sighed and relaxed, still unable to surface. But Jake was with her and nothing else mattered.

Jake was sleeping, his head resting on his arms against the bed where Morgan slept. It was nearly three in the morning, and he was exhausted.

They'd flown Morgan out of Bagram the next morning and he'd been on the flight with her. At Landstuhl medical center in Germany, she'd undergone another six more hours of surgery to repair her shattered femur. He'd been allowed to wait in the lounge until they'd wheeled her out of surgery. He'd been grateful that they'd had a chair waiting for him at her bedside in a private room at the military hospital. Morgan had been heavily drugged, and the doctors had assured him, she would slowly become conscious.

Jake had paced the room for hours. Thinking. Remembering. Replaying the firefight. The terrible flight in the Black Hawk back to Bagram, never knowing from one moment to the next whether Morgan would go into cardiac arrest and die before his eyes or not. And there would be nothing he could do about it. Absolutely nothing. The emotional phone call to Morgan's parents had gutted him in a new way. They *did* know about him and their relationship. Jake had heard no censure or judgment in Jim Boland's voice toward him, which had been a huge relief for him.

The hours in flight from Afghanistan to Germany had made Jake take a hard look at his life. At his love for Morgan that had been there from the very first time he'd laid eyes on her at Annapolis. He'd always loved her. He'd been too full of himself to realize it. Until it was almost too late. Finally, at two in the morning, he'd pulled the chair over to her bed. Jake had placed his arms on the bed near her right hip. The moment he laid his head down he'd fallen into a weary, tense sleep.

At one point, Jake had jerked awake. Like any SEAL, he awoke instantly, completely alert. Sitting up, he heard Morgan moan. She was moving her long fingers across her stomach. Taking a swift breath, Jake pushed the chair out of the way. He placed a hand on her shoulder. Her lashes fluttered. Her lips moved, incoherent sounds slipping from them. Looking over at the monitors on the other side of the bed, Jake noticed her blood pressure, pulse and temperature were all normal. A smile cracked his exhausted features. Morgan was becoming conscious. *Finally . . .*

When Morgan's lashes slowly opened, even with the bare light from the monitoring instruments, Jake could see her eyes were murky-looking. He gently massaged her right shoulder. "It's all right, babe. It's Jake. And you're coming out of anesthesia. You're all right. Just keep fighting to come back to me. . . ."

Jake's words rang around in her head as if it were an echo chamber. Morgan released a sigh of relief. His hand resting on her shoulder oriented her. It became a focus to fight out of the cottony world that tugged at her. Finally, an hour later, Morgan lifted her lashes and looked up . . . up into Jake's darkly shadowed face. It was his gray eyes, glittering with tears, that sheared through her world of morphine. He tried to smile but failed, his hand tightening on her shoulder.

"Welcome back, babe. You gave us one hell of a scare. . . ."

By the time dawn arrived, Morgan was fully conscious and aware. There had been a parade of nurses and doctors coming in to check her, run the light across her eyes, monitor her heart, listen to her lungs. Jake remained quietly in the background as Morgan was informed by her ortho surgeon, Dr. Ruth Cramer, about the state of her broken femur.

Morgan stared up into Dr. Cramer's blue eyes. "What do you mean I won't be able to do what I was doing?" Panic ate at her. The doctor's eyes turned kind.

Reaching out, she touched Morgan's shoulder. "Captain, thirty percent of your femur is gone. It's going to take it a while to regrow. And even if it does, it will never be strong like you need it to be to do what you were doing out there before this injury occurred."

Morgan digested the sentence. "But with physical therapy?"

Dr. Cramer shook her head and patted her hand. "Morgan, your combat days are over. I'm sorry to have to tell you this, but it doesn't matter if you were a man or woman, it would be the same diagnosis. You'll need physical therapy, for sure. And we'll make sure you get it. For ninety-nine percent of whatever you choose to do with the rest of your life, your leg will be strong and reliable." She lowered her voice, seeing Morgan's face grow pale. "We'll talk more about your recovery plan tomorrow. Right now, Lieutenant Ramsey is going to be your big, bad guard dog. He's been with you every step of the way."

Morgan rested wearily against the slightly raised bed. Her left leg was beneath a tent. There were metal screws holding the bones together, and anything that touched the pins sent her through the roof with excruciating nerve pain. She gulped a few times, her breathing uneven as she considered the doctor's diagnosis.

"How are you doing?" Jake asked, coming over to her bed after the surgeon left. Morgan's hair glinted with copper highlights in the early-morning sunlight lancing through the blinds at the window. The slats threw themselves across her bed. To Jake, they looked like symbolic prison bars after hearing Dr. Cramer's diagnosis. He knew it had rocked Morgan's world in a way she'd never expected.

Morgan laced her fingers with his. "Not so good," she whispered, trying to choke back her emotions.

"I know. . . ." Jake tried to put himself in her place. What if he'd been so badly wounded that he was told he could never be a SEAL again? It would devastate Jake because his ego, his whole life, was centered around being one. He squeezed her fingers, seeing the anguish deep in her shadowed green eyes. "I'm sorry, babe . . . so sorry. . . ."

Morgan lay there wrestling with this news. His voice quieted her, soothed her. Jake was steady when she was not. She loved him. She drowned in his softened gray gaze. "I never thought we'd get out of there alive, Jake. I really didn't."

"Neither did I, babe." Jake compressed his lips for a moment, watching her wrestle with the bad news. "You know what? You're the bravest, most courageous fighter I've ever met. You saved my hide. You took out Khogani." He squeezed her hand. "You've done so much, Morgan. The world will never know about it, but the Generals will know, and I'll never forget what you did. Maybe —" Jake tried to smile but failed "— you've done enough? Other things are coming full circle in your life, and they should take on more importance now?"

If he only knew the whole truth. Her mind and emotions clashed. How badly Morgan wanted to tell Jake about Emma, but she wasn't thinking rationally. She needed to talk to her parents, whom she'd call for the first time in the afternoon. They would let Emma talk to her on the phone. Of course, her daughter couldn't know how badly she'd been wounded. But just to hear their voices would ground her. Maybe Jake was right. Morgan felt incredibly weak and overwrought. The trauma had stolen her normal mental toughness and powerful physical endurance. Jake was her strength right now.

"I think you're right," she whispered. And then Morgan ventured a bold request, understanding Jake would never be a permanent part of her life. "Kiss me? I've missed you so much, Jake." She raised her hand, slipping it upward across his chest.

Without a word, he leaned over, searching, finding her mouth as she raised her lips to meet his. Her lips brushed across his

mouth. Morgan was very fragile. Jake eased
his hand along the line of her jaw, gently
angling her to deepen the contact.

The warmth of Jake's breath, his roughened hand against her cheek, made Morgan
moan and hungrily kiss the man whom she
loved with every cell in her body. She craved
his closeness, his love. The trauma had
broken her in a new way, one that she'd
never experienced before. Jake had been
wounded before. He knew the ups and
downs a person went through after surviving intense combat. Jake was here for her in
every way.

He moved his mouth gently against hers,
nothing rough or jolting. Just . . . tenderness. His fingers eased upward, caressing
her clean hair, inhaling her scent as he
continued to slowly worship her lips and
welcome her back to the land of the living.

As Jake eased his mouth from hers, he
drowned in the green and gold of Morgan's
eyes. Moving his thumb across her eyebrow,
he whispered unsteadily, "I never got to
answer you out there on the ridge. You told
me you'd never stopped loving me." Jake
smiled brokenly, holding her gaze. "I've
never stopped loving you, either." He laid
his lips against her mouth and breathed his
breath into her. "I love you, Morgan. I'll

love you until I take my last breath." And that was the truth. Jake just didn't know if they could ever, really, be together.

His arms slid around Morgan, gently holding her. It was the first time they'd had time to be alone. He pressed her face against his chest, and his solidly beating heart saturated her with hope. "We have so much to talk about, Jake."

"I know, babe. I know. . . ."

The door opened.

Jake released Morgan and instantly went on guard. It was his nature. His eyes widened.

"Sorry, I didn't mean to intrude," General Maya Stevenson said, quietly shutting the door. She stood in cammies, a cap in her left hand.

Blinking twice, Morgan couldn't believe the General had come to visit her. Yet, the tall, black-haired woman who stood before her smiled. "General Stevenson . . ."

Jake came to attention, his hand leaving Morgan's gowned shoulder.

"At ease, Lieutenant Ramsey," Maya murmured, coming over and standing on the other side of Morgan's bed. "Officially, I'm not here." She gave Jake a pointed look that spoke volumes.

Jake relaxed. In a way, he wasn't surprised

the General had turned up because he was positive she was Morgan's mentor. "Yes, ma'am," he murmured.

Maya reached out and gripped Morgan's left hand. "You've had a tough haul. How are you doing?"

Morgan lay back, her heart beating hard in her chest from the interlude with Jake. "I'll make it, ma'am."

As she released her hand, Maya's smile disappeared and she looked across the bed to Jake. "And you, Lieutenant Ramsey?"

He managed a sour smile. "I'm good. A bullet in my leg hasn't slowed me down much at all, ma'am."

Nodding, Maya rested her hands on the side of the bed. She returned her attention to Morgan. "Has he told you what happened after you arrived at Bagram?"

Confused, Morgan glanced over at Jake. His face went dark, his mouth becoming a thin line. Something was afoot. What?

"I've said nothing to her, ma'am," Jake growled. He worried about the timing and saw the General was going to tell Morgan anyway. "She's fragile," he warned the General in a low voice. Jake didn't want Morgan thrown into another emotional storm.

"Hmm, so I see." Maya nodded. "Lieutenant Ramsey, I have your report. It's very thorough, and I appreciate the time you took on it. You left no stone unturned on this op. Well done." The woman's green eyes glittered with warmth toward him.

"Thank you, ma'am." Jake moved his head slightly in Morgan's direction. "She saved my ass. Literally."

A smile pulled at Maya's lips. "So she did. She's saved a lot of people out there." Maya held Morgan's gaze. "I'm putting you in for a Silver Star, Morgan. You've earned it." She pulled two small boxes out of her left pocket. Opening the first, she pinned the medal on Morgan's pillow. "And you've also earned a Purple Heart."

Jake came to attention as the General moved around the bed. She pinned on his medal.

"Lieutenant Ramsey, you've done your country a great service. Thank you."

"Thank you, ma'am."

Maya stepped away. "Lieutenant Ramsey, would you give us a few minutes alone? My two assistants are outside the door. Why not invite them down to the cafeteria for some coffee? They won't want to leave, but make them. Use your SEAL persuasion?"

Jake glanced over at Morgan. Her face was flushed, and she appeared wan. He didn't want to leave her, afraid the General didn't understand the extent of Morgan's emotional instability. "Yes, ma'am," he said, opening the door and leaving.

Maya pulled up a chair and sat down, facing her in the quiet. "How are you really doing, Morgan?"

Folding her hands in her lap, Morgan admitted, "Up and down, ma'am."

"I've been wounded before. I know what it's like to come back out of hell." Maya searched her face. "I didn't know you and Lieutenant Ramsey had a relationship?"

Morgan chewed on her lower lip. "We go back a long ways, ma'am. Nine years, to be exact."

"And it didn't interfere in this op?"

"No, it didn't." Morgan cleared her throat. "We've loved one another through hell and high water. Never could make it work until . . . now . . . maybe. . . ." Nothing was forever, Morgan knew from too much experience with Jake.

Maya sat back, studying her. "Secrets. There's always secrets, aren't there?"

"I guess so, ma'am."

"There's some things you need to know," Maya said quietly. "Lieutenant Ramsey sent in his report by email to me and General

Houston. That's why I'm unofficially here today."

What had Jake written to bring a General to her bedside? Morgan wasn't sure how to take the news. "Yes, ma'am?"

"You've more than shown beyond any doubt that a woman can handle combat," Maya began. "Lieutenant Ramsey clearly outlined your influence in the op. I'm very proud of you, Morgan. You have what it takes and then some. You come from a set of military parents. You two survived a fire-fight that, by all rights, should have brought both of you back here in body bags."

The chill ran through Morgan. She closed her eyes for a moment, clearly remembering every second of that desperate escape and being trapped in the wadi with Jake. Opening her eyes, her voice roughened, Morgan said, "Neither of us expected to make it out alive, either, ma'am."

"Well," Maya said, straightening in the chair, "you two pulled off the impossible. You had a lousy sniping shot position in the first place. The Apaches couldn't shoot anyone in that wadi. They had no idea who was who. You were up against a force four times larger than your own. I'm damned proud of you, Morgan."

"You need to be proud of Jake, too,

ma'am. We were a team. It took both of us to survive that firefight and kill Khogani."

"Understood," Maya murmured. "But you're one of the women proving to the JCOS that women can handle combat. You did that."

"Ma'am, with all due respect, I really don't think I deserve to be put up for a Silver Star. Jake was just as brave and courageous as I was in that wadi. You weren't there. I was."

Maya nodded. "Well, a couple of things set you apart from Lieutenant Ramsey during that firefight," she said. "You took a bullet to the front *and* back of your Kevlar. Once Lieutenant Ramsey was down, you deliberately exposed yourself to Taliban fire in an effort to protect him. Lieutenant Ramsey received no hits to his Kevlar." Maya's voice dropped to a growl. "You aren't in a position to see your courage, Morgan. General Houston was the one who suggested putting you up for a Silver Star, not me."

Gulping, Morgan sat back, feeling stunned. A Silver Star was for meritorious bravery under fire. "I . . . didn't know, ma'am. This is the first day I'm fully conscious. I haven't written my report yet."

"No hurry," Maya reassured her. "But I

don't think it's going to deviate from what Lieutenant Ramsey wrote, do you?" She drilled a hard look into Morgan's eyes. "Don't conveniently leave out any details, Captain Boland."

"No, ma'am, I'll be thorough," Morgan promised, her voice low. She could see the hardness come to Stevenson's expression. "I just don't want a medal because I'm a woman in combat is all," she challenged the General.

Maya smiled. "Fair enough. I understand now where you're coming from."

"My mother's CO, Major Louise Lane, tried to do that. She wrote up every woman for a medal who fired a rifle in that conflict over in Thailand. It was purely political."

"That won't happen here, Morgan. I can promise you that. That is why there is a male and female General running this covert operation. Two sets of eyes. Both genders. There tends not to be the skewed results that Major Lane managed to manipulate, this time around. It's a different time and place, Morgan. I have no desire for female volunteers to step into the arena unless they're clear about the consequences of making that decision."

Morgan watched the tall General rise to her feet. "That's good to know, ma'am. I don't want publicity or press, either."

"Won't happen. This is top secret. Goes directly into the Pentagon vaults and is kept that way." Maya smiled a little, walking over to her bedside. "Maybe, a hundred years into the future, the Pentagon will bring this operation out from under the covers. By that time, we'll all be dead and gone. It will then become a piece of history."

Morgan nodded. "That's good, because I don't want to be a celebrity like my mother was forced into becoming."

"Major Lane was a publicity hound who didn't care about her women or their courage under fire. No one is going to know on my watch, Morgan."

Releasing a breath, she whispered, "Thank you, ma'am."

"How's your leg?" Maya pointed toward the tent over her legs.

Mouth quirking, Morgan told her what Dr. Cramer had said.

"There's a silver lining to this. You need to know that Lieutenant Ramsey, after regaining consciousness inside the Bagram hospital, did something you should know about. And knowing him, he'd never tell you."

Puzzled, Morgan asked, "What?" Jake had said nothing about Bagram.

"The ortho docs at Bagram assessed your injury. They were going to amputate your leg, Morgan. Luckily, the head surgeon came to Jake to ask him some questions. When he found out that the surgeons were going to merely stabilize you and send you here to Landstuhl to have it amputated, all hell broke loose. He came off that gurney, I guess, and grabbed the surgeon by his scrubs and told him he was not going to amputate your leg."

Maya grinned, reaching out to cover Morgan's hand. "The surgeon backed down, obviously in shock over Ramsey's attack. The Lieutenant then, bleeding and limping, found an office, got to a landline and called me at the Pentagon. He told me the situation, upset and angry. I then placed a call to my friend and surgeon, Colonel Waltrip. He's head surgeon here at Landstuhl. I asked him to reevaluate your injury once you arrived.

"At Bagram, they did the hard work to save your leg. By the time you arrived here, Colonel Waltrip said they could save it." She patted Morgan's hand, seeing her eyes widen with shock. "That's quite a big guard dog you have in Lieutenant Ramsey. Now I know why he went to such efforts — that's love."

She considered the General's explanation. "My God," Morgan managed, automatically reaching out to touch her left leg. "They were going to amputate it?"

"Yes. Lieutenant Ramsey fought a different kind of battle for you, Morgan. Another kind of front. I can't award him a Silver Star for his courage under a different sort of fire, but I have a feeling he'll never tell you about this. SEALs are notorious for being close-mouthed and humble. They think it's bragging, so I'm telling you so you know the rest of the story. He'd take that info to his grave."

Shaken, Morgan whispered, "Thank you, ma'am."

"On to business," Maya said brusquely. "You're scheduled on a C-5 flight back to Bethesda medical center near Washington, D.C., two days from now. There, I'll make damn sure you've got the finest ortho and physical-therapy team they can assemble, to help you get back on your feet. And I'll make sure Lieutenant Ramsey is there, at your side, every step of the way." Maya reached out, resting her hand on Morgan's shoulder. "We'll be monitoring the situation, Morgan. If you need anything, you know my phone number."

Grateful, Morgan nodded. "Thank you, ma'am. It means a lot to me. . . ."

CHAPTER TWENTY

Jake quietly entered Morgan's room once General Stevenson and her assistants left. Morgan was resting, eyes closed. What had they spoken about? "How are you doing?" he asked, concerned.

Morgan opened her eyes, hearing his low voice. "Tired," she answered and held out her hand toward him. She wasn't disappointed as Jake limped over, his large hand engulfing hers. In as few words as possible, she told him what had happened, sidestepping the information about the leg-amputation confrontation he'd had with the surgeon at Bagram.

Jake leaned over and tucked several strands of crimson hair behind her ear. "I was worried the General was going to upset you. Right now, you need rest, not a parade of well-wishers." He framed her face and looked deeply into her shadowed eyes.

"She called you a big, bad SEAL guard

dog," Morgan whispered, meeting his descending mouth. "She was right. . . . You are. . . ."

She drowned in his tender kiss. Morgan hadn't experienced the nurturing side of Jake until this mission. As he eased his mouth from her wet lips, she looked up into his clear gray eyes that glinted with happiness. Was this how Jake had been with his chronically ill mother? Caring? Thoughtful? Morgan had so many questions for this man, and she didn't know where to begin.

"This afternoon I'll get a landline phone in here so you can call your parents," he said, pulling the chair over, sitting down and facing Morgan.

"I can hardly wait," Morgan said, suddenly emotional. And she'd finally be able to talk with Emma. My God, how much she missed her daughter. Especially now, realizing she had almost died. "We need to talk, Jake. You think I'm a fragile egg that's going to break."

"You've been through a lot," he warned, holding her gaze. Her cheeks were flushed from their kiss. It was so easy to care for Morgan because he loved her.

"I'm not that fragile, Ramsey." She managed a partial smile. "The General said we're heading home in two days. I don't know about you, but it's going to feel good to be back on U.S. soil."

Jake couldn't disagree. "I don't know how General Stevenson is going to get the SEAL command to let me stay with you for thirty days at Bethesda medical center. If she can do that, she's number one in my book. I'm glad I can be there for you, Morgan. The doctors have been filling me in on your recovery."

Jake knew it would be a long, painful road for Morgan. She'd find out soon enough. Right now, he wanted to give her time to absorb the trauma she'd survived. He was glad to play rearguard action to give her the downtime she so desperately needed. He would always have her back.

"I called your parents when we were at Bagram," he confessed. "Dr. Thornton figured out you and I were close, and he asked if I wanted to do it. I told him I did."

Morgan gave him a startled look. "You talked to them?"

"Actually, twice. The first time, I talked to your father. Your mother was asleep. I told him you were alive and going to make it."

Pressing her hand to her pounding heart, Morgan felt some trepidation. Had her father mentioned Emma? Feeling guilty enough, she didn't want to deal with that situation right now with Jake. "What did you talk about?"

Jake held her hand, feeling the strength and firmness of her fingers. "You. It was a short call. I told him I'd call once you were out of surgery here at Landstuhl, and I did. I know how parents worry, and I wanted to keep them updated on your condition. The second time, your mother answered, and I got to talk with her. They're relieved, to say the least. I told them as soon as you were conscious and felt better, you'd call them."

"Thank you for doing that."

He shrugged. "You'd do it for me if I had parents to call."

She felt a little sad for Jake, and he was trying to make light of the situation. "Yes, I would have," Morgan told him softly, squeezing his hand.

Jake stood up, releasing her fingers. Leaning over, he pressed a kiss to her brow. "Get some rest, babe. I'll drop in and see how you are in a couple of hours."

Giving him a weary smile, Morgan murmured, "Sounds good. I feel like I'm going to drop through a hole."

"I know," he said. "It's normal after getting wounded. Get some sleep. . . ."

Jake waited patiently outside Morgan's

room as she made her call home. She was stuck in bed, unable to walk or move around. The metal pins holding her femur together made her bed-bound for a minimum of six weeks before they would allow her in a wheelchair. He thought of ways to keep her engaged after they flew to the States. Morgan would go stir-crazy at the Bethesda medical center if she had nothing to engage her mind.

When the red light went on outside her room, meaning she had pressed the button for a nurse's help, it was a signal for him to come in. Jake rose from the chair and opened the door. Morgan's face was flushed from crying. His heart contracted. She gave him a sheepish look of apology and wiped her reddened eyes with a tissue. He knew how much family meant to her. He had none to look forward to when he went home. An ache rose in his chest as he limped over to her bed.

"Doing all right?" he asked huskily, picking up her damp hand. Morgan sniffed.

"It was good to talk to my mom and dad," she said, squeezing Jake's hand. "I told them about us, how we were mending our fences. They were happy to hear that."

Jake leaned over and, with his thumbs, brushed the tears from her cheeks. Morgan's green eyes were marred with sadness. "Why are you crying?"

Shrugging, she muttered, "I miss them. . . ." Barely able to hold the words back, she wanted to say, *I miss Emma so much. I want to hold her, kiss her, watch her smile, and I want to hear her laugh again. I want Emma to meet you so badly. . . .*

Swallowing, a lump in her throat, Morgan had confided her dilemma to her parents. She wanted to tell Jake about his daughter. Her father had counseled her to wait until she was further along in her healing process. She would have to pick the right time and place outside of the military hospital to take Jake aside and tell him the truth. Morgan had reluctantly agreed.

That meant waiting a minimum of six weeks to hold on to the terrible secret. Jake deserved better than that. Right now, Morgan was emotionally shattered and lacked the necessary strength to deal with his reactions. And she was sure he'd have many. She knew she would.

Seeing the concern grow in his gray eyes, she said, "My mother was shot in the left thigh during the Thailand conflict. Did you know that? And she suffered a compound fracture like me, only not half as bad as mine. Talk about genetic accountability."

She shrugged.

Jake sat on the edge of the bed on the right side so her left thigh would not be disturbed. "Your mother was a fighter when she was down and out. You are, too."

"I don't know, Jake." Morgan looked at the ceiling. "Things are sinking in. I'm going to be bed-bound for six lousy weeks. Six! I'll lose all my muscle tone. I'll suffer from muscle atrophy. . . ."

Jake reached out and cupped her chin. "Take a deep breath. You've been through a lot, multi hits to your Kevlar, getting shot in the leg and two surgeries. You haven't had time to absorb and process any of it yet. It takes time." Jake smiled tenderly, holding her tearful gaze. "I'm going to call General Stevenson tomorrow, before we board that C-5 back to the States. I think she can keep you pretty busy with paperwork on Operation Shadow Warriors. If she'll let you assist her in different ways, it might help her out, and you won't be bored out of your skull."

Morgan felt twinges of pain beginning to roll up her leg, like an ocean tide coming in. Most hours she felt pain, but it was bearable. When it rolled in like this, she had to release a lot more morphine into her system. And when she did, it knocked her out. Morgan hated drugs, but the bone pain could become so crippling, she'd scream with agony if she didn't press that pain-med button to put the morphine into her IV.

"Pain coming back?" Jake guessed, seeing darkness come into her eyes.

"Yes," she muttered. "I'm sorry, Jake —"

"Never be sorry," he growled, holding Morgan's cloudy gaze. "The more you're in pain and you don't take the morphine, the longer it will take for you to heal up." He saw her wrinkle her nose and press the button three times. The morphine drip was combined with her other IV. In a little bit, she'd be unconscious. At least she wouldn't feel that breath-stealing pain.

"You're right," she said, lying back against the pillows.

"Go to sleep, babe. Dream of us. . . ."

CHAPTER TWENTY-ONE

The next time Morgan awoke, she was in a private room at the Bethesda medical center near Washington, D.C. Sunlight was lancing through the window in the room. She slowly reoriented, feeling dull pain in her left leg. She immediately saw the blue covers in a tent over her legs.

The door quietly opened. Jake. He was clean-shaven, the beard gone. His gray eyes were alert, and he was wearing civilian clothes. Morgan thought he looked incredibly powerful and athletic in the black T-shirt, olive-green cargo pants and boots. Just the way Jake held himself, shoulders squared, she would have spotted him in a crowd of hundreds. SEALs walked with a natural confidence that was unmistakable and never duplicated.

"Hey," he called, seeing she was awake. "Welcome to the world of the living." Jake leaned down and kissed her lips, seeing the murkiness in her eyes. "You were out for the flight from Germany to the States. We arrived here at Bethesda medical center five hours ago. How are you feeling?"

Morgan felt thirsty. She struggled to sit up, and Jake brought the bed up. She pressed her hands to her face, trying to wake up. "I need some water, please," she muttered.

Jake poured her water from a nearby pitcher on a rolling tray near her bed.

Morgan took the glass in both hands, not trusting her strength. "You look upbeat," she noted, drinking.

Jake pulled up a chair. "I am. I've been in touch with General Stevenson. She's agreed to have you help her with paperwork. She doesn't want you feeling bored, either." He grinned, took the glass from her hands and set it on the tray. "Hungry?"

Morgan lay back on the inclined bed. "I guess I should be, but I'm not."

"You have to eat to keep up your strength, Morgan." Jake said the words softly, though he noticed how she grimaced at the idea of eating. Morphine depressed a person's appetite. "General Houston has buttonholed me while I'm here recovering for thirty days. He wants me over at their office at the Pentagon while I'm around. I won't be able to babysit you like I did before. I'll be able to see you before 0900 and after 1700. I get weekends off."

Morgan's eyes became clearer, more alert. Her hair was mussed, and he longed to pick up the brush and tame those crimson strands into place.

"That's good news for you," Morgan whispered, rubbing her face again. "You won't get bored, either." SEALs were about action, about taking the fight to the enemy. Jake was never one to sit around for more than a few minutes. He'd lived on high-octane energy for as long as she'd known him.

The pain in her leg was achy, but not the screaming pain it could become. Morgan felt pretty good with Jake sitting on the edge of her bed, holding her hand. Even in civilian clothes, he looked dangerous in a quiet way. He'd lost some weight, too, she realized, looking at the deeper hollows of his high-boned cheeks. "How are *you* doing? You were wounded, too."

"I'm good. The worst is over," Jake assured her. "I didn't lose the amount of blood you did, Morgan. And the bullet going through muscle is night and day different from having a bullet shatter the most major bone in your body."

"You're not in pain?"

He grinned carelessly, sliding his fingers slowly up and down her lower arm. "Motrin takes care of it." It didn't, but Jake, like every other SEAL, moved forward whether they were in pain or not. They'd learned in BUD/S a man could be in excruciating pain and still operate at a high level, despite it.

She groaned and closed her eyes. "SEAL candy."

Chuckling, Jake murmured, "Guilty as charged."

She sighed, feeling suddenly exhausted. "Jake . . . I need to sleep. I'm sorry. . . ."

"Don't be, babe. I get it."

The last thing she remembered was Jake warmly squeezing her hand, keeping her chilled fingers warm. Morgan had to fight to get better, to focus her energy on Emma.

Where had thirty days gone? Jake pushed his emotions very deep within himself as he walked down the hall to Morgan's room at the medical center. How was she going to handle the news? He was upset, not wanting to leave her. She'd made remarkable progress, much to her doctor's surprise. Jake gripped the cap in his left hand, trying to gird himself for her reaction. Neither of them had seen this coming. . . .

Morgan was sitting up in bed, the nurse bringing over the wheelchair. She was dressed in a dark blue one-piece swimsuit, a light blue robe over her shoulders when Jake entered. She never heard him coming, but that was the way SEALs walked. *Stealth.* Her eyes widened as she saw him dressed formally in military desert cammies. Before, Jake had always been in civilian clothes. The look in his gray eyes was guarded as he caught and held her stare.

"I'll come back in twenty minutes," the blond-haired nurse said with a smile. She nodded hello to Jake, who stood just inside the door.

After the nurse left, Morgan said, "Look, my first day in the physical-therapy pool. It's time to celebrate."

Jake gave her a heated smile. "You always look good in less clothes, babe." He moved to her side, kissing her awaiting lips. Morgan had bounced back strongly. Far more quickly than the doctors had anticipated. She was a week ahead of the normal healing curve, but Jake wasn't surprised. Easing away from her lips, he slid his hand across her shoulders. "I've got some news," he warned her. He saw worry come to her eyes.

"You're being called out for an op, aren't you?" Morgan's heart contracted with fear.

She'd known this day could come. Jake's bullet wound was pretty much healed, and he was ready for active duty again. He had been anticipating going back to his platoon as OIC in Coronado to hook back up with SEAL Team Three.

"Yeah," he muttered. "I thought I was going to get reassigned back to my old platoon. But General Houston has been working with the SOCOM Admiral on a special black op. They're pulling me in for it." Even though he could see the anxiety in Morgan's expression, Jake could tell she accepted the reality of their situation. In their business, there was no downtime. He moved his hand gently across her red hair.

"Okay," Morgan whispered, feeling as if hit in the chest with a fist. "I know you can't say anything about it, but I'm assuming Afghanistan?" *Again. Always.* That was SEAL Team Three territory, big-time. They were always called in as small, mobile teams, to hunt down HVTs among the Taliban and al Qaeda leadership.

Nodding, Jake said, "Yeah." He couldn't say anything else. But he saw her eyes focus, and he could see her thinking.

"Probably a direct action mission because of Khogani's death. A new warlord emerging from the Hill tribe near the Khyber Pass to take his place?"

He moved his mouth but said nothing. Morgan, he discovered, could read him like a proverbial book.

"Two SEAL fire teams?"

He shook his head.

"You and another sniper?"

He nodded.

"Are you getting someone you know? A fellow SEAL sniper?"

Jake nodded.

Licking her lower lip, Morgan felt some of her fear ease. It was essential teams worked well together. If they didn't . . . She didn't go there. "Same area?"

"More or less," Jake replied. He pulled up a chair next to her and eased his arm around her. Morgan laid her head on his shoulder. He could feel her breath, moist and warm, against his neck.

"Damn, I knew this would happen," she muttered, frowning. Raising her eyes, she saw the hard line of his mouth. "How long?"

"As long as it takes. There's no deadline." Jake looked down and drowned in her green eyes. "What I want you to do is *not* worry. Okay?" Her mouth tugged into a grimace. *Right.* Morgan was going to worry. "I'll be okay. I've got my sniper partner back. He's being pulled out of my platoon to go over with me. We're a good operational team, Morgan." Jake embraced her gently, trying to reassure her.

"At least it's July. It will be as warm as it can get up in the Hindu Kush. Are you utilizing Reza?"

He nodded.

More relief flooded Morgan. Her mind spun with shock because she had just reached the stage of being able to get out of bed and move around in a wheelchair. She had planned to call Jake, and they would go to a nearby hotel for a night where she could tell him about Emma. Now that plan was shattered. *Again.* Jake had to remain focused. Telling him about Emma right now would be the stupidest move she'd ever made. He wouldn't be able to focus, and that would get him killed.

"Will you stay in touch by email and Skype when you can?"

"You know I will, babe. But it's going to be sporadic at best."

"Who's running the mission from J-bad?"

Jake gave her a pained look. Morgan knew he couldn't say.

"Okay," she whispered, "it's Vero. I can feel it."

He grinned. "You're damn good at this twenty-questions stuff. Ask the question and have the answer, as well."

"I was in SEAL Intelligence for Team Three for a while. I have to be. I know the key players, Jake. Your life depends upon it. Vero's the best. He'll get your ass through this op alive. That's all I care about."

"Listen," he rasped, "all I want you to do is fight to get better. By the time I get back, I want to be able to take you out of here. I have dreams of reserving a room at a hotel and making love with you until we're so damned exhausted neither of us can move."

A pang of anguish and longing moved through Morgan as she met and held his eyes. His gaze was one filled with love and desire for her. "I want the same thing, Jake," she managed, her voice low with emotion. Morgan sat up, wanting to crawl into his arms, wanting to stretch out beside him and be held.

Jake eased his arm from around her shoulders and turned the chair, facing her. He framed her face with his large hands. "Your love will keep me safe, babe. I don't want you to worry. . . ." He curved his mouth hotly against hers. It was a kiss that would have to carry them for however long the op lasted.

As he lifted his mouth from hers, Jake saw tears shimmering in Morgan's eyes. He forced his own tears deep down inside himself. Right now, he had to be strong for both of them.

"Listen," he rasped, looking deep into her glistening green eyes, "I'm as close as that laptop computer of yours. I'll Skype you when I can. I'll be in touch as much as possible. I don't want you to worry."

Choking back a sob, Morgan barely nodded, lifting her hands and moving them across his capable shoulders that carried so many loads. "I hear you, Jake. I'll keep on getting better."

"Promise?"

"I promise. . . ."

"I love you. You hold on to that. . . ."

Closing her eyes, tears beading on her lashes, Morgan whispered brokenly, "I will, Jake. . . . I will. . . . I love you so damn much it hurts. . . ."

"I know. I'm worse than a bullet wound." He managed a partial, teasing grin.

Laughing brokenly, Morgan shook her head. "You've got the blackest humor at the worst times, Ramsey."

Jake cherished her smiling mouth, always wanting to remember this moment, the joy in her eyes, the love shining through her worry for him alone. It was bittersweet. Anguish soared through him. Jake had to leave Morgan and didn't want to. As a SEAL, it was his job to go back into harm's way. "Just be here waiting for me at Andrews Air Force Base when I get back," he growled, brushing his mouth against her tear-wet lips. Tasting the salt, tasting the sweetness that was only her, Jake kissed her deep and hard, branding the memory of this last kiss into his heart and mind forever.

CHAPTER TWENTY-TWO

Pain drifted up Morgan's leg as she was wheeled back to her room after the intense hour-long therapy. Three weeks had passed since Jake had left on the black op. She could count on one hand how many times he'd been able to contact her. Morgan felt as if she'd been reduced to little more than a desperate, needy sponge for any information. God, just to hear his voice, see his face, on that one Skype session had lifted her spirits, her hope, as nothing else ever could. Morgan knew he had been in J-bad SEAL headquarters; only they and SEALs at Bagram air base had capacity for satellite video transmissions. That had been two weeks ago. He was somewhere now in the Hindu Kush, hunting down another warlord.

Despite her continued, low-grade worry, this afternoon her parents were arriving from Colorado with Emma. She was going to be able to meet them at the hotel near the medical center. Morgan didn't want her daughter to see her in a hospital bed. Emma might be two years old going on three shortly, but her daughter would understand enough and she didn't want her thrown into anxiety.

The nurse drew out her civilian clothes, a set of white summer slacks, a dark green short-sleeved blouse, a leather belt and simple, serviceable brown leather shoes. Morgan was glad she could now dress herself. She could walk for short distances with the help of crutches, too.

"I'll call the staff car for you," the nurse said, hesitating at the door. "Twenty minutes, Captain Boland?"

"That's fine," Morgan called. "Thanks."

The nurse smiled. "I'll come back and get you."

Grateful, Morgan sat down, pulled off the wet bathing suit and dropped it on the plastic seat of the wheelchair. Her leg ached like hell, but she took ibuprofen, and the pain started to go away as she dressed. With crutches, she hobbled to the bathroom, brushed her teeth and combed her hair. She'd just gotten her hair cut and shaped two weeks earlier, the ends curling naturally against her shoulders.

Her worry for Jake gave way to her excitement over seeing her daughter and her parents once again. Right now, Morgan needed their support. It was hell lying in bed every night imagining the challenges Jake and his sniper partner were up against. Nightmares came every three or four nights. And as Morgan moved out of the bathroom, she was grateful to her parents for having come to be her moral support.

She took the bathing suit off the plastic seat of the wheelchair in one hand and dropped it in the bathroom sink. By the time she came back out into the room, the nurse had arrived. Her heart took off in an unsteady beat as Morgan carefully positioned herself in the wheelchair, holding her crutches and resting them on a footrest.

Morgan arrived at the fourth-floor hotel room, a suite that had three bedrooms, enough for a family, before her parents arrived. Nervous and feeling emotionally vulnerable, Morgan hadn't seen her daughter in nine months. Her mother always sent her photos of Emma nearly every day to her laptop. She was seeing Emma grow up without her, and it hurt Morgan in a way she never thought possible.

As she carefully sat down on the chocolate-colored velour couch, Morgan began to question what she was doing with her life. At twenty-nine years old, she had done more than most women would ever do. She'd been part of a volunteer group of women who had proved without question that they could go into combat and be successful alongside their male counterparts. But Morgan missed Emma. The ache deep in her womb for her daughter never went away.

Someone knocked and the door opened. Morgan sat up as Emma walked into the spacious room. She was dressed in a white cotton dress with a pink satin ribbon around her tiny waist. Her black hair was drawn into a long ponytail, captured in a pink ribbon, too. Morgan choked back tears as she realized Emma had Jake's square face, his dark gray eyes and black hair. It was as if she were staring at a shadow of him.

"Mommy!" Emma cried, spotting her. She raced toward Morgan, her arms open, flying across the room.

Morgan had purposely sat at one end of the couch, her wounded leg protected by the arm. Emma launched herself at Morgan. The impact caused Morgan pain, but she didn't care, wrapping her arms around her joyous daughter.

"Emma," she whispered, kissing her

daughter's hair, brow and cheek, tears leaking out of her eyes. She felt Emma wriggle like an excited puppy in her arms. Her daughter smelled of sunlight, fresh air and a hint of apples in her hair. The girl loved her apple shampoo.

Raising her head after kissing and hugging her daughter, Morgan saw her parents walk into the room. Her father, Jim Boland, was in his mid-fifties, a bit of silver at his temples, mixed in with his short black hair. He wore dark gray slacks, a white short-sleeved shirt and dark blue sport coat. He smiled over at her, his hand on Cathy's shoulder. "Hey, you're looking good, Kitten."

Kitten was her childhood nickname. Morgan smiled brokenly. "I'm okay now, Dad. Come on in. . . ."

Cathy Boland sniffed and wiped tears from her eyes. Her red hair was short, emphasizing her wide green eyes as she met her daughter's gaze. She pushed her damp palm against her light pink slacks. She wore a dark purple tee. "You look well, honey."

Lifting her hand, Morgan met and tightly held on to her mother's long, thin hand. When Cathy leaned down and pressed a kiss to her hair, Morgan closed her eyes. Family was everything. And they'd strongly supported her throughout her military career. She opened her eyes as her mother stepped aside.

Jim Boland leaned over, gently curving his arms around his daughter, and felt her tremble. Morgan leaned against his broad shoulder, a ragged sigh issuing from her lips as he hugged her. "Welcome home, Kitten."

His gruff, deep voice moved through her, made the fear for Jake go away, if but for a while.

Emma tried to climb into her lap, but Cathy quickly picked her up.

"Honey, your mama has a sore leg. You can't sit on her lap just yet."

Emma pouted, wriggled and wanted down. "Mommy. . . ." She thrust her hand out toward Morgan.

Laughing brokenly, Morgan held Emma's outstretched hand. "Mommy is a little fragile right now, Punkin'." Morgan pointed to her left leg. "I hurt myself a little while ago." Emma was staring at her left leg. Morgan wore a special soft black brace outside the slacks to keep her thigh stabilized. Emma's tiny black brows moved down, studying the device from Cathy's arms.

"That's funny-looking, Mommy."

They all laughed.

Emma stared at it. "Does it hurt?"

"No, honey, it doesn't. It gives my leg support when I get up to walk is all."

Emma seemed satisfied.

Cathy sat down with Emma in her lap next to Morgan. "You look good. You've lost a lot of weight."

Nodding, Morgan touched Emma's small, flushed cheek. Her gray eyes were wide, alert and reminded her sharply of Jake's. When Jake finally met his daughter, he'd immediately recognize her as his child. They were almost spitting images of one another. Morgan's heart broke a little more because she knew nothing in life was guaranteed.

Jim Boland stood nearby. He'd been a Marine Corps officer and had the stance of one. He was a ruggedly handsome man, and she thought that her mother's own natural beauty complemented his. Her father was athletically fit, deeply tanned from his outdoor work as a civil engineer, his hair always military short. Morgan smiled over at her father, so proud of him.

Emma touched Morgan's hair, running her fingers through the recently washed strands. "Mommy, can we stay? Are you coming home this time?"

"You'll stay here with us for three days, Punkin'," Morgan said, leaning over and kissing Emma's brow. "Mommy has to stay here and get her leg well."

Pouting, Emma said, "How long, Mommy? I miss you. I don't like you gone so much. . . ."

Her heart twisted in her breast. Morgan forced a smile, grazing Emma's hair and fussing with her pink bow. "I know, Emma. I feel the same way. Mommy has been thinking about a lot of things lately. I'm going to see what I can do. Okay?"

Jim Boland sat down on the couch, a few feet away from his daughter. Cathy had taken Emma down to the pool to play in the water. Emma loved the water. She was part fish. Those were Jake's genes at work.

"How is Jake?" he asked quietly.

Morgan sat back, carefully stretching her right leg. She could see the worry in her father's expression. He'd been the Rock of Gibraltar in their family. Morgan felt his strong, calm presence and she was able to pull herself together. That same energy was around Jake. They were the only two men in her life who could settle her down, help her gather her strewn, wild emotions and focus. She found her voice. "I haven't heard from him in two weeks."

Jim nodded. "He's out on the op, then. That's a special kind of hell." He knew about the hell of waiting. Many years earlier he'd been kept in Hawaii after coming out of a coma from his head wound. Days later, he'd accidentally found out Cathy was being used as a scapegoat in front of Congress for everything that had gone wrong with the WLF. It had been torture to discover the woman he loved so fiercely was being systematically slaughtered by the politicians, placing the blame at her feet, when nothing could have been further from the truth.

He knew his daughter was battling valiantly to appear unworried. Jim Boland understood, as few would, how being wounded and nearly dying made a person feel horribly vulnerable for months afterward. And just when his daughter needed Jake the most, he'd had to leave her side. That placed Morgan under special pressure, the kind no person should ever have to endure alone.

"It's hard, but he's going to come home to you, Kitten. I know that. Just hold on to that even if you don't believe it yourself. Just believe me?"

Her father's encouragement did more to support her than he could ever imagine. Morgan clung to his hand. "Oh, Dad, he doesn't know Emma's his daughter. . . ." A sob of remorse rose in her throat. "I couldn't tell him before he left. It would have devastated him. He wouldn't be able to focus on his mission."

Boland released her hand and moved carefully next to his daughter. She was strong, like her mother. Resilient. A fighter to the end. He placed his arm around her shoulders and allowed her to lean against him, her face buried against his shoulder. "It's all right to cry, Kitten. We're here. . . . We'll help you. . . . And when Jake gets home, you can tell him then. You were right not to tell him before he left. You made the right decision. . . ."

Morgan finally released the pent-up tears she'd held in ever since being wounded. She couldn't cry in front of Jake. She knew how worried he was for her. Sobbing against her father's broad shoulder, his arms holding her gently, she released a backlog of hurt, anxiety, fear of almost dying.

Emma was in bed for the night in the hotel suite. Cathy stepped out of the room and quietly shut the door. They'd had room service earlier, their dinner spent around a table as a family together for the first time in a long while. She worriedly assessed her daughter. Morgan was exhausted. She knew Jim and Morgan had had a long talk earlier when she'd taken Emma to the pool. Cathy was grateful Morgan had a special relationship with her father, glad to act as a diversion for Emma so they could talk privately.

Morgan sat in a leather chair opposite the coffee table and the couch.

Cathy went to sit down next to her husband. It was the first time she'd been able to talk with Morgan. With Emma around, they kept the conversation light and happy. Her husband slid his arm around Cathy's shoulders. Holding Morgan's dark eyes, seeing how pale she'd become, she said, "Do you want to go to bed? You look so tired."

Morgan roused herself. "No. I'm just let down, Mom. It's been rough . . . but you know that." Her mother's incredible blind courage to gut through the Thailand conflict as a combat soldier, and then to go stateside after nearly dying from her leg wound to take on Congress, was nothing short of heroic in Morgan's eyes. She met her mother's warm, understanding look.

"What can we do for you, Morgan?"

She grimaced. "I want Jake home, Mom. Safe. I want him to meet Emma." Opening her hands, Morgan added wearily, "Life is so damned complicated sometimes. . . ."

Jim gazed at his wife and then over at his daughter. "You're going through a real test,

Kitten. But you have our genes and your mother's strength to get through this. Jake will come home alive."

"I wish," Morgan whispered, giving her father a glance, "you could promise me that, but I know you can't." She pressed her hand to her heart. "I feel like a lost, scared little child inside, Dad. I feel so inept. I don't know what I'll do if Jake doesn't make it home."

Jake *had* to meet his daughter, if nothing else. Morgan loved him, but she had no illusions that Jake would want a permanent relationship. He'd told her more than once he didn't want her to be a widow again. That in his line of business it was easy to get killed, leaving a family behind without support.

"Don't go there," Cathy urged strongly. She sat up. "Morgan, look at me?"

Her mother was like steel when she needed to be, and Morgan could hear it in her husky voice. Opening her eyes, she held her mother's sharpened green gaze.

"Don't ever give up. I never thought I'd ever see your father again. I know what it's like to be alone and the world is caving in around you. I didn't have Jim to talk to, to listen to his counsel, to cry on his shoulder. I wanted to do all of that. But I was alone in a way that I never would wish on anyone. But you're there now, just like I was. . . ." Her voice lowered with feeling. "Morgan, you just have to have faith. You have to believe that Jake will be okay, that he'll return to you. And to Emma."

Morgan nodded. "There are minutes and hours when I know that, Mom. And there are days that are so black that I feel like I've fallen into a hole I'll never dig myself out of. I worry so much for Jake. . . ."

"I know. I've been there, honey. It's all right to feel what you feel, but you can't let it stop you. You have to keep fighting. You have to hold the faith for Emma, yourself and Jake. You have the heart to do that. I know. You're my daughter."

Morgan stood looking out of her hospital room window while leaning on her crutches. It was midday. Her heart felt bruised and beat-up. Her parents and Emma had just left after their healing four-day visit. With them, Morgan had felt strong, capable and positive. Now . . .

Feeling depressed, she ached for Jake's arms around her. He had always fed her strength, fed her his love, whether he knew it or not. Turning, Morgan moved slowly on her crutches to a chair near her bed. She

356

hated the bed, having been trapped in it for so long.

There had been no word from Jake. She wished with all her soul Vero could contact her, let her know what was going on. But she knew he couldn't. It was a top secret op, and no one outside of the SEAL world would know anything about it. Not even her.

Wearily, Morgan sat down, feeling lost, feeling torn apart on so many levels. With her parents nearby, they'd helped her make some life-changing decisions. Would Jake ever stop bolting from her life? Would he care what her plans were? What she wanted for them more than anything? Would he walk through those glass doors of Operations at Andrews into her arms? Or would Jake come home in a coffin?

Not knowing was the worst stress Morgan had ever tangled with. Being out on the op, she knew the focus was on killing the enemy. There was little room for thoughts about loved ones. A child. A parent. Every cell in her body was oriented toward that op and surviving it to return home. Now, Morgan decided, looking out at the blue sky dotted with white clouds, she understood how the wife of any black-ops soldier felt. The wife and family were left completely out of the loop. Alone with wild, crazy, insane thoughts of the man or woman dying in battle. No one to tell her whether her loved one was alive or not. It was a special hell, and she hated it.

CHAPTER TWENTY-THREE

"Everest Main, this is Everest Actual. Over." Jake spoke quietly into his mouth mic, getting ready to set up for the sniper shot. He waited to hear Vero's Puerto Rican accent over the radio from J-bad. To his right was his sniper partner, Petty Officer Lance Bigelow. Everyone called him "Big" because he was barely five foot six inches tall and weighed one hundred and forty pounds. Big was the smallest SEAL to make it through BUD/S. But he was one hell of a sniper and the only man he'd want as a partner on this op. Big lay prone beside him, a spotter scope in hand, watching and assessing conditions in the early afternoon. The sunlight was bright at eleven thousand feet. It was below freezing.

"Everest Actual, this is Everest Main. Over."

It felt good to hear Vero's voice. Jake lay prone, the AW Mag on a bipod, pointed at his target. "We've got Red Mountain spotted. An eleven-hundred-yard shot. We need approval."

No sniper op went down without authorization from higher SEAL command. The man who'd taken over as warlord when Sangar Khogani had been killed was his brother, two years younger, Anosh Khogani. He was riding below them on a goat path. They were on a scree slope just below the ridgeline. It was a simple shot compared to the one Jake had tried and failed with Sangar Khogani.

The summer sunlight was bright overhead. They wore their ghillie suits, having built a hide, and remained in position, waiting. Just waiting. Reza had ridden up into the mountains, found Anosh and his twenty soldiers on horseback. He'd been able to find out from a villager, who'd overheard the group talking one night, that they were coming this way. Ground assets like Reza were invaluable.

Jake never left his gaze off the target through his Night Force scope. Anosh was tall, bearded, wearing a dark brown turban and clothing. He was just as murderous as his older brother, having already killed a number of Shinwari villagers on their way down to the cave region south of where they were hidden. Jake was dying for some water but didn't dare take a drink right now.

"What's the holdup from SOCOM?" Big muttered into his mic, focused below.

"I screwed up another shot a couple of months ago," Jake said in a low voice. "They're probably wondering if I can hit our HVT this time around."

Chuckling softly, Big grinned. His close-cropped blond hair was covered with a gray, cream and black headdress. "Well, if that's the truth, Ram, you wouldn't be here on this op. Would you?"

Grinning a little, feeling exhaustion because they'd only gotten two hours' sleep before being awakened to stand watch, Jake said, "No, I s'pose not."

"Everest Actual, do you have a clear shot? Over."

"Everest Main, roger. No deflections or impediments. Wind is gusting to thirty miles per hour. Over."

"Everest Actual, you said an eleven-hundred-yard shot? Confirm? Over."

SEAL headquarters in J-bad was probably going nuts with that info. AW Mag accurate shots were good *up to* one thousand yards. Beyond that, it became the skill of the sniper, luck and a crapshoot of sorts. It really rested on the sniper to make up the difference. Jake knew he could take the shot and make it good. The only obstacle was always the wind. Mountain shots were notoriously difficult.

"Think they're peeing their pants about now?" Big asked, unable to keep the laughter out of his low voice.

A tired smile stretched Jake's mouth. He wanted to rub his scratchy beard with his dirty fingers. No bath for nearly three weeks, and he reeked. His skin continually itched. He would remain focused on his target instead. "More than likely."

"Everest Actual, you're cleared to take the shot. Exfil has been alerted."

"Roger that, Everest Main. Out." Jake glanced over at his partner. "Let's mount up."

Big gave a feral smile and went back to his spotting duties. He assessed the wind, the temperature, the altitude and so many other variables that all played into a successful shot.

Jake settled down on the rocks, the points biting into his Kevlar and his lower body. His head was below the ridge, the scope on Anosh Khogani, who rode at the head of the column. This time, it was a clear shot. Jake breathed out. His finger was on the trigger. All sounds, all sensations dissolved as Jake focused, Anosh's head in the crosshairs of his scope. The fiberglass stock was pressed tight against his cheek, his right hand extended, finger on the two-pound trigger. His left hand was tucked across his chest. Calm settled over Jake as he hit his still point. Squeezing the trigger, he heard the snap of the bullet leaving the barrel, the stock jamming into his shoulder as it recoiled. He knew Big would follow the vapor trail of the bullet through his spotter scope.

"Bull's-eye!" Big crowed triumphantly.

Instantly, Jake shimmied up over the ridge, taking the sniper rifle with him. Big quickly followed. Now time was of the essence. The shot had killed Anosh Khogani. One more bad guy was down.

Jake slid down the slope on his ass feeling the pounding and bruising to his flesh. Below them, Reza waited tensely, holding the reins on three nervous horses. Big played rearguard action. Halfway down the slope, Jake called into J-bad and gave the report they wanted to hear. Four weeks and they'd finally nailed the murdering bastard.

Jake threw Reza a thumbs-up as he landed on his feet. He quickly took off his ghillie suit, jamming it into his pack. Big tumbled ass end over teakettle, falling in front of the horses, who jerked around, frightened.

Big leaped up, jerked off his suit, jammed it into the ruck near the bushes.

There were three goat paths leading up to where they had taken the shot. The Taliban was not stupid; they'd figure out the direction of the shot and know it was courtesy of a SEAL sniper team. And then they'd come after them.

Glancing back at the ridge, Jake leaped into the saddle, his ruck across his shoulders, the AW Mag, barrel down, strapped to the outside of it. Reza handed Big the reins to his horse.

"They're here!" Reza cried, pointing up at the ridgeline two thousand feet above them.

Jake snarled a curse, jerked his thumb over his shoulder, a sign for Reza to take the lead.

"Here!" Big yelled, throwing him the M-4 rifle with the grenade launcher on a rail attached beneath it.

Jake caught the weapon and whirled his horse around as the other two took off at a gallop down the path. He was the officer; it was his duty to take care of his men. There were Apaches on the way from Camp Bravo. And a medevac.

As Jake yanked his horse to stand still, he jammed the M-4 to his shoulder and fired a high shot with a grenade. The Taliban riders were sliding and slipping down the rocky slope. He watched the grenade arc below where the leader was. The blast blew up tons of material, soil, rock and gravel flying in all directions.

Jake didn't wait to see the devastating results. He whipped his horse around, digging his heels into the flanks and yelling at the animal. Instantly, the horse bolted, crazed by the noise and rocks, galloping in panic down the goat path. Wind whistled past Jake. His eyes watered as his gallant little horse sped nimbly downward. Ahead, he saw Reza and Big. All they had to do was make it down a five-thousand-foot slope to the valley below. There, a Night Stalker MH-47 would pick them up, and then they could get them the hell out of Dodge.

The snaps and pops of bullets passed close to Jake's head. He rode low, urging the horse on, praying it wouldn't stumble. If it did, he'd be thrown over the horse's head. They rounded another curve on the mountain. The goat path became a very steep descent after that, a good two-thousand-foot drop to the valley below. Jake could see the Chinook helicopter landing. He changed channels on his radio and called to the pilot.

"Everest Actual to Fox One. We're two thousand feet away. We're coming in hot!"

"Roger, Everest Actual. We're touching

down now and will wait."

The horse was laboring, stumbling as Jake sent it flying full speed down the steep path. He leaned back. Way back, as the horse suddenly skidded on its rump, front legs thrown outward as it tried to negotiate the gravel path. *Damn!* Jake felt the horse slipping.

He threw his weight the other way, helping the horse to right itself. Instantly, it slid sideways and then made crowhopping movements to regain its balance on the path. On either side of them were nothing but huge boulders and smaller boulders. If they hit them at this speed, Jake knew they'd both break their necks.

More bullets popped and snapped by Jake. One thousand feet to go! Reza and Big were dismounting, letting their horses run away as they raced for the MH-47 kicking up yellow clouds of dust.

And then his horse grunted.

Jake realized in a split second a bullet had found the animal. His eyes narrowed, and he gripped the M-4 as he went sailing over the animal's head. Just as he hit the path and rolled off of it, banging over boulders the size of bowling balls, Jake had the air knocked out of him.

He landed with a thud against a huge boulder ten feet high, momentarily gasping and dazed. More shots sang around him, striking the nearby rocks, sparks igniting as the bullets ricocheted off them. Jake scrambled for safety behind the boulder. He swung the short barrel of the M-4 around the gray granite and fired a second grenade toward the Taliban wildly galloping down upon him. The grenade landed near the end of the group. Horses and riders went flying into the air as it exploded.

Cursing, Jake made a call directly to the Apaches, asking for help. Where the hell were they? He gave his GPS location, methodically firing the M-4 at the approaching tribesmen. The hatred on their faces was evident. He could die if he didn't kill all of them. It was one against twenty. Good odds for a SEAL, he thought, squeezing off shot after shot. The Taliban soldiers were flying out of the saddles as he hit the mark every time.

Ten men were left. Jake heard another sound over the roar of gunfire. The Apaches! Relief avalanched through him as two of the ugly-looking predators flew over the ridge, their rockets aimed at the Taliban. *Dammit!* He was dangerously close!

Jake dived for the ground, lying prone, opening his mouth, closing his eyes and holding his hands over his ears. When explosions went off this close, if a person didn't open their mouth, the air in the lungs had no escape and massive injury could result. By opening his mouth, he equalized the air between his lungs and the outside air around him, dodging severe, even lethal, injury.

Four rockets dived into the area, not a hundred feet in front of Jake's position. A flurry of rocks soared, flying in all directions, the hits accurate, taking out the last group of riders.

Jake shook his head, stunned by the close proximity of the rockets. His ears rang. He couldn't hear anything. Dirt and debris showered down on him. Rolling up against the boulder, he hugged it, burying his head, praying like hell a huge rock would not land on him and kill him.

In moments, it was over. Jake waited for just a second before stumbling to his feet. Dirt and rocks were flung off his shoulders and back as he stood up. M-4 in his hand, he peered warily around the boulder. There was carnage on the goat path. Every horse and rider was dead.

Wiping his mouth, he called the Apaches, thanking them. And then he called the MH-47, letting them know he'd be a few minutes late getting on board. He saw both Apaches moving in large circles around the MH-47 below, guarding it.

Nose bleeding heavily, Jake wiped the blood away with his dirty sleeve and heaved himself up on the goat path. He stumbled and reeled from the blasts. The more he moved, the quicker he hit his stride. The ruck was banging heavily against his back, some of the straps torn off in the explosion. All those years of training played a part in him making the last thousand yards to the valley floor.

Big met him, helping him because he was limping. Jake practically dived into the helo, landing and rolling hard across the metal ramp, M-4 still in hand. Big hopped in after him and the crew chief quickly closed the ramp, giving the pilots the signal to lift off.

Jake felt faint as he lay on the deck, gasping for breath. At nine thousand feet, his lungs felt on fire, his breath coming out in tearing sobs. Big knelt over him, his expression worried as he stripped off Jake's ruck and then quickly, with shaking hands, pulled off his Kevlar vest. Jake was grateful to just lie on the deck and feel the shudder of the helo around him. He saw Big pull out his SOG knife to cut open his T-shirt.

"I'm good," he yelled over the thunderous sound of the rotors.

Big rolled his eyes, slit the material anyway and pulled the T-shirt open. "Christ, Ram, you've got three friggin' bullets in your Kevlar! Your chest looks like hell!" A Level 4 Kevlar vest could take three armor-piercing rounds before it shattered. He'd taken the limit.

No wonder he was having trouble breathing. Jake didn't fight Big as he rolled him over, examining his back for exit wounds from bullets. There were none.

Jake pulled on a helmet and plugged the connection in so he could hear communications within the helicopter. "I'm good, Big. Nothing's broken. Just hurts like hell to breathe." Jake gave his partner a silly grin.

Big pulled his cut T-shirt closed, helped him back on with the vest and then fastened the Velcro on his Kevlar. "You're the luckiest damn bastard I've *ever* seen, Ram. You know that?"

Jake grinned wearily, exhausted. He lay motionless, trying to take in a full breath. "Big, check my Kevlar pocket?"

Big leaned over him, pulling the Velcro open at the top of his vest. "Why?"

"The engagement and wedding rings for my gal are in there. They didn't get hit, did they?"

Grinning, Big held up the small plastic

Ziploc with the rings in it. "You're good to go, partner. Rock it out." He stuffed it back down in Jake's vest and pressed the Velcro shut.

Wiping the blood away from his nose and mouth, Jake managed a cocky smile. "Damn straight I am. First, J-bad, and then I'm getting the hell home and asking that red-haired woman to marry me."

Chapter Twenty-Four

Morgan's landline phone in her apartment rang just as she hobbled through the front door. Exhausted from the hours of physical therapy at the medical center, she picked up the phone.

"Hello?"

"Babe?"

For a moment, dizziness swept through her along with incredible relief over hearing Jake's voice. "Jake?" Morgan sat down on the couch, her knees going weak, heart hammering.

"I'm coming home. I've got to finish writing up my report and then I'm going to grab a flight from Bagram to Andrews. How are you doing?"

His voice was like life being pumped back into her, flooding her with joy and unimaginable relief. Closing her eyes, Morgan held the phone tight against her ear. Jake sounded incredibly tired. She could hear him slurring his words; it happened when weeks of sleep deprivation occurred on one of these ops.

"I'm fine, fine. Are you all right?"

Morgan knew all these calls were monitored and recorded. They couldn't get personal, but, God, how she wanted to! Her heart thudded with unparalleled joy. Jake was safe! He was coming home!

Jake laughed. "Well, first things first. If I don't get a shower, throw away my cammies for a new set, no one around here is going to allow me to stay here for five more minutes."

His laughter lifted her. Morgan chuckled softly, tears jamming into her tightly closed eyes. "You're never going to change, Ramsey. What time does your C-5 land at Andrews? Do you know?"

"Not yet. I'll call you in transit. Can you meet me?"

There was worry in his tone. He had no idea how far she'd come with her wounded leg. "Yes, I'll be there," she promised, her voice turning husky.

"Gotta go, babe. I love you. I'll be in touch."

"I love you, too. Goodbye, Jake. . . ."

Morgan sat there, stunned in the aftermath of the unexpected call. Jake was coming home after being gone a full month on the op. Her mind whirled with things she needed to do. First, call her parents. They would want to know, too. Second, the apartment she'd just rented needed cleaning. It would take Jake approximately twenty-four to forty-eight hours, depending on what flights he could catch, to make a connection back to Andrews Air Force Base.

Morgan knew Jake loved her. But how much? Enough to consider a relationship? Some of her joy was shaded with knowing at some point, after Jake was rested, she had to tell him about Emma. It was something she looked forward to but with trepidation.

Jake had matured in ways she'd never anticipated. Were his running days over? Some things about him might never change. Looking down at the watch on her right wrist, Morgan had time to prepare for Jake coming home. Grateful he was alive and not wounded, Morgan picked up the phone to tell her parents the good news.

Jake wiped his watering eyes as he stood with a group of Army Rangers and a couple of Special Forces A-teams who had hopped the C-5 out of Rota, Spain, to Andrews. The grinding noise from the C-5's huge ramp opening up seemed to go on forever.

He was the only SEAL in the group, and he'd grabbed a crew birth and slept nearly all the way across the Atlantic. Still, he was exhausted, bruised, stiff and in one hell of a hurry to hold Morgan in his arms.

As he stood there, the sixty-five-pound ruck on his back, his AW Mag strapped upside down outside of it, the SIG riding low on his right thigh, Jake felt all his tiredness dissolving. The more that huge tail nose yawned upward, the more impatient he became.

Would Morgan be waiting for him in Operations? All incoming personnel transited through that building. Families were not allowed inside. They had to wait on the other side of it. He rubbed his jaw.

Jake had grabbed a quick shower at J-bad, climbed into clean cammies, hadn't shaved because he didn't want to miss the C-5 going out of Bagram in an hour. He'd managed to persuade a pair of Night Stalker pilots who were off duty to fly him to Bagram, a short trip. Luckily, the Army pilots, who worked with all black-ops groups, had been in the mood to do it after he'd told them he was going home to ask his girl to marry him. Even in black ops, romance moved mountains. Or in this case, his story touched two pilots, both married, into flying him to Bagram to catch that C-5.

The tail section finally locked. A buzzer sounded, alerting the men that they could now exit the cavernous C-5 via the ramp. Jake moved quickly down the long length of the largest U.S. military transport airplane in the world.

Outside, he could see the sun low on the western horizon. The late August heat and mugginess of summer hit him fully as he hurried down toward the concrete apron. Jake settled his black baseball cap on his head and craned his neck as he stepped onto the tarmac of Andrews.

His heart started a slow, urgent thud in his chest as he spotted Morgan standing, leaning against a cane just outside of Ops. He couldn't help grinning, knowing she'd somehow finagled permission to meet him out on the tarmac instead of inside the terminal. He started off at a slow lope toward her.

As he drew closer, Jake hungrily zeroed in on her face. Morgan was wearing civilian clothes, not her uniform. She was thinner, and that concerned him. She wore a simple pale pink blouse and dark green slacks. Her hair moved languidly in the hot summer breeze. His gaze moved to her left hand where she leaned on a wooden cane, most of her weight shifted to her right foot. He was going to put a ring on this woman's hand very soon.

He slowed, noticing her smile. Damn, Morgan looked so beautiful. As much as he wanted to, Jake knew he couldn't haul her into his arms and kiss the hell out of her. He stopped in front of her and gently framed her face with his hands. Her eyes shimmered with tears of welcome as she reached out, her hand sliding across his right shoulder.

"I stink," he warned her, his grin widening. "Even the C-5 crew wanted me put away in their quarters to hide me because I smelled so bad."

She laughed. "I don't care, Ramsey. You look wonderful to me. . . ."

"Good thing, because I'm going to kiss you anyway." Jake leaned down, curving his mouth hotly against her smiling lips. He felt her tremble, his hands tightening and angling her chin so he could kiss her hard and long. Morgan's fingers dug into his shoulder as he tasted her, absorbed her and inhaled her feminine scent. He groaned as she hungrily returned his welcome-home kiss. He couldn't feel her body against his because of the Kevlar he still wore. It didn't matter; she was here, with him, and he'd never wanted anything more in his life than that right now.

Jake heard the hoots, hollers and teasing of the Rangers and Special Forces guys trooping past them on their way into Operations. He lifted his mouth from Morgan's, drowning in the joy he saw in her lustrous green eyes. "I love you, babe. . . . It's good to be home."

"I love you, too," Morgan whispered unsteadily, barely aware of the men calling to Jake, razzing him. She knew it was in jest, that they, too, were all looking forward to coming home, meeting their wives or girl-friends who waited for them outside of Operations. She moved her hand to his face. "You look good with a beard. Do you know that?"

Jake chuckled. "Just get me somewhere where there's a razor. I can't stand the thing." He stood before her, absorbing her, sensing her joy. Jake lightly placed his hands on her shoulders. "Are you okay? How is your leg?" He stepped back to study the brace she had around it.

"I'm fine, Jake." Morgan couldn't stop looking up at him. His gray eyes were clear but bloodshot. He had to be more than exhausted. He'd lost weight, the hollows of his cheeks deepened. "Let's go. I have a car in the parking lot. I've got an apartment now. They finally released me from the hospital."

Jake carefully wrapped his arm around her waist, fully aware she needed enough room to walk slowly with the cane. "Thank God," he muttered. "Your place has a shower?"

Laughing, Morgan nodded as they made their way to the door. Two Rangers who passed them stopped and opened the doors for them. Morgan thanked them.

Within the terminal, Morgan knew the drill. Jake would have to sign out all his equipment, including his weapons. He'd take them with him once the list was handed over to an Air Force Tech Sergeant behind another desk. She went over to a group of chairs nearby, sat down and waited.

The noise in the terminal amped up as the men eagerly talked with one another. There was always teasing, laughter and black humor traded among the operators. Morgan watched as many of them had wives and sweethearts meeting them outside those doors. Many others, however, were going to be billeted nearby, catch a shower, some sleep, eat some American food and then be assigned to other flights leaving in a few hours from Andrews. The transports would head all over the U.S. to other major military

379

bases. There, those men, who she knew were as exhausted as Jake was, would finally get home.

Jake cut free of the red tape and hurried toward Morgan. She was the only woman in the terminal, and he saw many of the men look at her, longing in their faces for their own loved ones. She was like a beautiful flower in a sea of desert camouflage. He understood their staring at her. Reaching out, he helped her stand. Once she got her balance with the cane as an aid, Jake escorted her out those doors and into the suffocating heat and sunlight.

Because she was an officer, Morgan had been able to park fairly close to Operations. Jake stowed his heavy ruck in the backseat, careful with his sniper rifle. Morgan was already in the car, waiting for him. He slid into the passenger side of the black SUV and shut the door.

The air-conditioning was heavenly as he strapped in. She backed the SUV out of the parking zone and drove toward the exit that would take them on another highway toward Bethesda medical center. He waited until she was on the freeway before sliding his arm around her shoulders as she drove.

"How's PT going for you?" Jake asked, hungrily absorbing Morgan's clean profile and those soft lips of hers. As fatigued as he was, he was infused with a giddy sense of happiness that thrummed through him.

"Hard and painful, but I'm making good progress."

"I didn't think you'd be this far along." And he hadn't.

Morgan shrugged. "What else was I going to do? I wanted the hell out of that hospital. I've had my fill of them, Jake. The only way I could get out was to improve fast and show them I was no longer non-ambulatory." She glanced and met his gaze. He was grinning. So was she. "I managed to scoop up an apartment two blocks from the medical center. I'm renting this SUV for now. It works."

Jake moved his hand gently across her proud shoulder. "I'm glad. I know what kind of steel you have in that backbone of yours."

"I've grown to hate hospitals, Jake."

"Yeah, I know the drill." He sat back, allowing the air-conditioning to cool him. "I'm going to be damned glad to get out of this gear and climb into a shower."

"Yeah, you reek a little, Ramsey. But under the circumstances, I understand." Being out on a sniper op for a month, there was no luxury of getting a shower, shaving or anything else. It was a rugged, hard business, and only men and women with a certain kind of mental toughness could handle it.

Jake tipped his head back, closed his eyes and said wryly, "Like I said, the C-5 crew had clothespins on their noses every time I walked by." He chuckled.

"We've got some driving ahead of us," Morgan warned, glancing over at him. There were shadows beneath Jake's eyes. She saw the exhaustion in every line in his face. Right now, Jake needed a hot shower, a shave, food and then some decent sleep under his belt. It felt good she could give those luxuries to him. Morgan wanted to love him, but she understood the toll that an op took on a person. Loving Jake would come with time, and she could be patient. He was home safe and that was all that counted.

A while later, Morgan nearly cried out when Jake came out of the bathroom, a white towel wrapped low around his hips, his face clean-shaven, hair damp, and his chest still beaded with water. She had brought half a dozen fried eggs, bacon and toast to the dining room table when he padded out of the bathroom in his bare feet. There were wet marks on the wooden floor where he'd walked. She saw the terrible bruising across his chest. The dark hair couldn't hide the fact he'd been hit three times with bullets. Setting the plate down, Morgan swallowed hard as he ambled into the adjoining living room.

"Damn, that smells good," Jake murmured, moving over to her, giving her a kiss on the cheek. He wanted to do much more, but that was going to have to wait. Jake pulled out the chair opposite of where he was going to sit. "It's all right, babe." He touched his chest. "They missed me. Come on. Sit down. Talk to me while I eat."

Morgan was rattled. Jake could have died if not for the Kevlar vest he wore. She knew what a hit felt like. His comment about not ever wanting to leave her a widow again struck deep. As he sat down and ate like a starved animal, she fought back so many conflicting emotions. This all felt like a dream to Morgan. Jake and she were chatting as if it were the most ordinary thing in the world. But it wasn't. It was special, magical. She soaked up every second with him, her gaze never leaving his.

"How much weight did you lose?" she asked, her hands around her coffee cup.

"Probably twenty." He shrugged. "Guaranteed, I'm gaining it back in the next sixty days." Jake grinned boyishly over at her as he finished off the plate of eggs and bacon. He brought over a stack of toast, unscrewed the lid on the strawberry jam and picked up a knife.

"Sixty days?"

Nodding, he slathered a thick amount of jam across the first piece of buttered toast. "Yes." Jake lifted his head, his eyes narrowing on hers. "And I'm spending every day of it with you, babe."

Morgan stared at him, in shock. He seemed sincere, the earnestness reflected in his eyes and the stubborn set of his mouth. "It's like a dream, Jake."

"*You* are my dream." He bit into the toast and jam, savoring every bit of tart sweetness in it.

"After you eat, you need to sleep, Jake. You look like hell warmed over."

He snorted. "I'll go to bed as long as you're in it with me. You have no idea how many dreams I've had of us in bed together." He gave her a wicked smile.

"You're incorrigible," Morgan said, feeling the love radiating off him toward her. There were new, pink scars, along with deep bruises, on his tightly muscled arms. "I was given access to your op. I went over to

General Stevenson and asked her permission to get a copy of it. I read the mission report."

Jake grabbed a second piece of toast, piling on the jam. "Good, because you know I couldn't tell you anything."

"Yes," Morgan said softly. "I'm glad you got Khogani's younger brother."

"Makes two of us," Jake agreed, sitting back, finally feeling full. "I'm sure they'll find another leader. Like you said, nature abhors a vacuum. Someone else will replace them. Maybe another member of the Khogani dynasty will start it up all over again."

"Kind of depressing," Morgan said quietly, "but that's how it is the world over, for better or worse."

Jake looked contented, his eyes starting to droop closed. He set the toast on his plate, his long, scarred fingers laced across his flat, hard belly. "You're crashing."

Rousing himself, he muttered, "Yeah, I am. It's hitting me like a ton of bricks now." Jake roused himself. "Come to bed with me? Let me hold you? I'm too friggin' tired to do much else at the moment."

She smiled a little. "I'd love to, Jake. You've been in my dreams, too, you know?"

He got a little cocky and sat up. "Yeah?"
"Oh, yeah."

"What's the status on your leg?" he asked, pushing the chair away and standing. She still looked fragile to him.

Morgan knew why he was asking and slowly stood up, reaching for her cane. "I can bend my knee, which is a big improvement. But I can't have any weight on top of my leg."

Nodding, Jake walked around and pulled the chair back so she could turn with the aid of the cane. "Roger. Read you loud and clear. We'll figure something out. SEALs are pretty inventive." He slid his long fingers across her jaw and pushed a veil of red hair away from her cheek. "Besides, I don't have any condoms on me. Where would I use them over there? Only thing around us were those damned goats for four weeks, and they sure as hell didn't interest me."

Laughing, Morgan soaked up his unexpected touch. Her ear tingled as he gently eased strands of her hair behind it. "Ramsey, I swear to God, you're certifiable at times." She melted into that feral smile spreading across his face.

Jake felt a ton of exhaustion avalanching him. It was the emotional and adrenaline crash from the op, twenty-four hours of nonstop flying halfway around the world, and a month of sleep deprivation pushing him. "Come on," he urged, catching her left hand and holding it. "Lead me to the bedroom. I've got to crash and burn."

CHAPTER TWENTY-FIVE

It was so easy for Jake to turn over on his back, awaken and find himself lying next to Morgan. He barely opened his eyes, seeing a watercolor-pink wash of light around the bedroom window where the drapes were drawn. An incredible peace filled him as he felt Morgan snuggle into his arms, her brow pressed against his jaw. Her arm came across his hard abs. It was as if even in sleep, she felt his presence, wanting to be as close as she could get to him. Jake curved his arm around her shoulders, holding her close. He took in the scent of cinnamon among the strands of hair tickling his jaw. He slid his fingers slowly down her arm as she slept.

Jet lag, time differences, the decompression of suddenly leaving a war zone and having her soft, naked body against his, overwhelmed Jake. Morgan's breath was warm and moist, flowing across his darkly haired chest, her left arm curving across his hard, flat stomach. Closing his eyes, Jake simply savored all his senses where Morgan was concerned. His mouth quirked as his thoughts ranged from the first time he'd met this red-haired hellion at Annapolis.

Morgan's bright copper hair had stood out in that sea of plebes. Jake thought it was remarkable. She was the only person there who hadn't appeared scared by the screaming instructors. Her mouth had been determined, jaw thrust forward, green eyes narrowed. But no fear. God, she had no fear, and that beckoned to Jake. He'd never seen a woman *not* scared or fearful. Only now did he realize he had been looking through the filter of his chronically ill mother. Now he felt sad for the opportunity that had been there but he'd failed to recognize and grab. Whether he knew it or not, Morgan was a good dose of medicine for him in every way. It had taken him nearly a decade to figure it all out.

Lifting his right hand, he grazed Morgan's firm upper arm, absorbing the satin feeling of her flesh beneath his exploring fingers. She had never accepted his view of women. Not ever. When he'd finally met her in his third year and they'd come together like two colliding comets, his life forever altered. Jake slowly outlined each of her long, tapered fingers resting against his chest.

Morgan stirred. For just a second, Jake wanted to remember what had brought him to this moment, and he laid his hand gently over hers and waited.

Lying there, the pink color now flooding the room as dawn stretched across the East Coast, Jake's heart opened with a fierce love for this courageous woman whose spirit challenged him in every way. He found it so damned amazing and humbling that Morgan had never given up on him. Not then, not two years ago, and not recently.

Whether she knew it or not, she'd rescued his soul, infused new life into him with her body, her unbending spirit, and healed him with her incredibly loving heart. Morgan had the courage to meet him on the battlefield of life. She had not retreated emotionally from their heartbreaking past.

With a slight shake of his head, Jake felt like a man who had more luck than he'd ever deserved. Morgan was at his side. He had sixty days with her. *Alone.* He couldn't believe his good fortune.

The flush of pink dawn light flooded Morgan's shadowed face as he absorbed her softened, parted lips as she slept. Long, red lashes against her high cheekbones emphasized those pale freckles sprinkled across her nose and cheeks. His gaze lingered on her broken nose. Pain flitted through him as Jake leaned over, his mouth barely brushing that area, as if to try to remove the pain of that memory away from her. He'd caused her so much damn pain. He was going to spend the rest of his sorry-assed life trying to make it up to her.

Morgan roused from sleep, feeling Jake's mouth moving slowly from her brow, down across her temple, caressing her cheek until his lips lingered lightly over hers. Stretching languidly against his hard body, her softer curves perfectly fitting against his angled ones, she barely lifted her lashes. Morgan drowned in Jake's stormy gray eyes, feeling his breath mingle with her own. His mouth hovered a bare inch above hers. A lazy smile pulled at her mouth, and Morgan lifted her left arm and followed the line of his broad shoulder with her fingers. Wordlessly, she leaned up, a heartbeat of space between them, and curved her mouth softly in greeting against his.

Her world anchored as Jake kissed her. It wasn't a hungry kiss. It was a welcome-home kiss of the deepest, most wonderful kind. As their mouths moved and clung to one another, Morgan felt her heart burst open with such fierce love for this battle-hardened warrior that she wanted to melt into his body and give herself to him in every way.

Jake eased up on his side above her, his arm beneath her neck, curved around her shoulders. As she pressed against his chest, Jake groaned. He pulled Morgan gently against him, holding her tightly to feel the rise and fall of her breasts. He was more than mindful of Morgan's wounded leg, every gesture on his part designed not to aggravate it. She would let him know if she was in pain or discomfort. Jake wanted nothing to intrude upon this heated celebration shared between them.

Morgan reveled in his roughened hand trailing slowly downward toward her hip, his long fingers splayed out, easing her lower body against his own. She felt his erection press against her belly. Moaning, the sensation sent wild, flamelike sensations blooming throughout her lower body. She felt him leave her mouth, and she opened her eyes. The feral look in Jake's hooded gray gaze made her shiver with anticipation. Morgan knew that look so well, a man wanting his woman.

"Good morning," he said huskily, smiling down into her drowsy green eyes. He lifted a number of strands of crimson hair away from her cheek. "Before we get started . . ."

"I don't have any condoms, either, Jake." Morgan slid her fingers across his powerful shoulder to his neck and then came to rest against his jaw. "Why would I have any with me?"

His mouth pulled into a wry grin. "You had goats around here, too?"

She laughed, feeling the heat building between their bodies. "Something like that." Morgan saw Jake grow serious. They had never talked about children. About starting a family, and she could read the concern in his expression as he lay beside her, his fingers threading slowly through her strong, silky strands. She still didn't know where he stood with her. He'd loved her before and walked out of her life. He could do it this time, as well. "I don't care, Jake."

"What if it's the wrong time?" He was stunned by her answer. Before, Morgan had always been adamant about a condom and that she did not want to get pregnant. Jake saw her eyes grow warm with love for him. She reached up, her hand caressing his cheek.

"I love you, Jake."

He hesitated, shock rolling through him. He stared down at Morgan, confused. She had a military career path. She was fierce about proving women could handle combat. What the hell had changed?

The changes were coming too fast for him to adequately assimilate. An old pain rose up through Jake, the loss of Joshua. Was Morgan telling him she would willingly carry his child? The thought was as emotionally charged as it was freeing. The fearlessness was back in those green eyes of hers, silently challenging him. Telling him that if he loved her, the possibility of becoming pregnant and carrying his child was being gently placed before him to consider. Jake wrestled with her willingness.

"Are you sure?" he rasped, leaning down, meeting her lips, tasting her, skimming the warmth of her returning kiss.

"Never more sure, Jake. I want to love you with everything I have."

That was the answer Jake needed. "Then there's something I need to do first," he told her.

Morgan frowned, the silken moment broken. Jake looked like a man on a mission. A black-ops one that he knew about and she didn't. Carefully sitting up, she moved from beneath his arm as he rested his back against the headboard.

"What are you up to?"

Jake leaned over and opened the drawer

of the bed stand. "Well, I was waiting to spring this on you when you were at the hospital, but this unexpected op changed the course of my plans until just now. . . ."

Morgan's eyes widened as he produced a Ziploc bag. He placed it in her palm.

"This is for you, babe."

A gasp flew from her lips. There were two rings in the plastic bag.

"Jake!" Morgan jerked a look up at him as a boyish smile came to his mouth. It was a smile filled with love — for her. Jake took the Ziploc from her palm, opened it and pulled out one of the rings.

"Give me your left hand," he murmured.

Heart pounding with disbelief, Morgan placed her left hand into his large, calloused one. "Jake . . . I never expected this. . . ." And she hadn't.

He slid the gold engagement ring with four rectangular channel-cut emeralds onto her finger. "I was busy when you were at physical therapy getting the ring made by a jeweler in San Diego. I sent him the design, and he made it for you. I got them just before I left on the last op." Jake gave her a sheepish grin. "I kept them in my Kevlar pocket while I was in Afghanistan. When I was making a run to the rally point, all I was worried about were those rings. I didn't want to take a hit and have them destroyed. I did get hit, but not where the rings were. When I finally got on the chopper, I had Big open up my Kevlar pocket to make sure the rings made it, and they did."

Jake held her hand and looked deeply into her eyes. "I want to marry you, Morgan. I've never wanted anything more in my life. I love you. Will you be my partner? My best friend?"

His words were low, filled with emotion, his eyes locked on to hers. The ring tingled around her finger. His hand encased hers, warm, strong and so solid where she presently felt like an unraveling ball of emotional yarn. "Months ago you told me you were in a dangerous career and you didn't want me to be a widow again. What changed, Jake?"

He became pensive. "I had a lot of time out in the mountains to think long and hard," Jake admitted, sliding his fingers into her hair, moving it behind her ear. "I realized I'd said it because of my past. Not only would I leave you a widow, but I might lose you, too." He shook his head. "I had to figure it out, Morgan. I finally realized it was stupid to think that way. Both of us have always been risk takers. And I knew you were willing to take the risk on me regardless of my being a SEAL. I got clear it was me knee-jerking."

Jake leaned down and kissed her wrinkled brow, seeing the worry in her lustrous green eyes. "I'm clear now. I want to risk marrying you and settling down. Now . . . Will you marry me?" His mouth curved as he smiled down into Morgan's widening eyes that glistened with unshed tears.

"You know I will, Jake."

His smile increased. "Good. You can call your parents later and tell them you're officially engaged to this good-looking SEAL who thinks his world just got a helluva lot better because you said yes."

It made Jake feel good he'd decided to ask her to marry him now. Intuitively, he knew it would give Morgan a stake at looking toward the future. Their future. It would help her continue her amazing recovery even though he couldn't always be at her side to be a cheerleader and supporter.

"You're crazy! But I love you, Ramsey," she whispered unsteadily.

"I'm really a nice guy," he said, absorbing her strong arms around his shoulders. If a child resulted from their union, Jake was more than okay with that. He would not be like his father, a shadow in his child's life. He moved and smiled against her lips. "This is the first day of the rest of our lives together, babe." He helped Morgan to lie down beside him. Jake began a slow, concerted worship of her body.

Morgan closed her eyes, feeling the last of her fear dissolving as Jake's lips moved from her mouth, brushing small, light kisses down her slender neck. He nipped her flesh, kissing each spot, sending heat surging downward. Her breasts automatically tightened. Her nipples grew hard and achy. He outlined each of her collarbones with his tongue and lips, sensing he was memorizing her as he cherished her.

Jake had answered her question. Only he could honestly tell her if he was ready for marriage and fatherhood. And he was. As his lips followed the curve of her breast, her skin tightening, a soft whimper slipped from her lips. Morgan pressed her hips against him, feeling his need of her. Her fingers dug into Jake's shoulders as his mouth settled upon the first nipple, suckling slowly, sending slivers of living fire arcing hotly into her womb. Trembling as he curved his hand beneath her arching back, she strained against him, wanting so much more of him. Wanting him inside her.

Jake left her nipple and leaned up, grazing her lips, taking her mouth, tasting Morgan more deeply. She felt his calloused hand

slide slowly down her rib cage, fingers
outlining each one. Her flesh contracted
beneath his touch, more heat building with
each stroke. Her mind melted as his tongue
moved against hers, inviting her, challenging her. As Jake's hand left her side, her
breath hitched. His fingers moved against
her belly, sliding between her thighs, opening her. As he felt how damp, how ready,
she was, his mouth left hers, settling on the
other breast, his moist breath fanning across
the achy nipple. Groaning, she pushed
against his hand, wanting so much more.

Morgan's world turned molten as he took
the nipple, suckling strongly at the same
time as he eased his finger into her needy
core. A soft cry tore from her as her entire
lower body seized up, burning with fire,
mounting pressure making her twist in his
arms, bucking against his hand. Her hips
writhed against his hand, wanting him
deeper, and she made a sound of frustration.

He used his thumb to find that small pearl
of knotted, sensitive nerves at her entrance.
A keening sound caught in her throat, suddenly frozen against Jake, the scalding
ripples widening throughout her, making
her gasp. Morgan's entire body shuddered
with pleasure as it flowed outward like

molten lava. Jake growled, taking her mouth, absorbing her cries, continuing to milk her body, sending more sheets of liquid fire and searing pleasure throughout her.

Morgan felt diffused, her body glowing and throbbing as the last of the orgasm began to ebb. Jake smiled down at her, a pleased expression on his face, his eyes narrowed and intense upon her. He eased his fingers from her. Her entire body was damp, and she saw him give her a very male smile. She felt his hand curving about her breast, feeling his erection insistent against her belly. Unable to speak, only feel, he leaned down, capturing her lips, tasting her, cajoling her.

"We've just begun," Jake whispered against her mouth.

Morgan smiled up into his feral-looking eyes. "Fine by me," she managed, her voice sounding wispy, far away.

"I want you on top of me," Jake told her. "I'm not putting weight down on that leg," he told her, kissing her lids, her cheek and then lingering against her mouth. "All right?"

"More than all right." Morgan felt hot, throbbing sensations, and more than anything, she wanted Jake inside of her. Nothing would ever feel so right as that. "Help me?"

Jake nodded and eased onto his back. He spanned her waist with his large hands and lifted her over him as if she were a lightweight, but Morgan knew she wasn't. Jake made it so easy for her to slowly ease her left leg over him and straddle his body. He held her until she was positioned over him and then slowly allowed her hips, her core, to sink down upon him. The moment her warmth, her dampness rested against his erection, Jake sucked in a sharp breath. The sensations were scalding, sending him into pain so damned knotting he wanted to come right now. Controlling himself, Jake let Morgan to settle against him, get her balance, allow her leg to adjust to that position and get comfortable.

He watched her flushed face, saw her lashes drop, her lips part as she moved slickly against him. Her palms flattened against his chest. Hell, it was killing him, and he gripped Morgan's hips, drawing her down upon him, watching the pleasure come to her face. Nothing was more important than this, their intimacy, their pleasure with one another.

As Morgan eased forward, lifting her hips just enough, Jake shut his eyes, feeling himself pressed against her slick entrance. She decided how much or how little she would take him into her sweet, hot confines. His fingers dug into her hips as she sheathed him inside her. Jake groaned, lifting his hips, wanting her so damn badly. It felt good to be inside her, feeling her tightness, her body slowly accommodating him.

Jake didn't want to rush anything. Morgan's fingers dug into his flesh, and he knew it was pleasure, not pain, she was experiencing. Slowly, her body accommodated him and then relaxed, allowing her to draw him more deeply into her. He felt Morgan shudder as she took him all the way into her, felt her hips thrust forward, wanting all of him. Her moan of utter satisfaction combined with his growl.

The sizzling heat built rapidly, and as Jake pulled her forward, he could feel her building quickly. That was good because he was on the edge of losing it, wanting Morgan to come first, giving her the time she needed. But damn, it was difficult, and he grunted, willing himself to hold off. He sensed her so close, her hips ground down upon his, her breath coming in sobs, her fingers digging frantically against his chest. And then Jake felt her contract, felt that tightness around him, and he whispered her name, unable to control himself any longer, allowing himself to flood her.

Her keening cry mingled with his guttural snarl as the releases collided. She froze above him, and Jake took her hard and deep, prolonging the pleasure for her, feeling that tight, contracting grip around him, sucking every last bit of fluid out of him, draining him, scorching his mind, hurling him into heat and intense pleasure.

Morgan sobbed his name, collapsing against him afterward, her head against his jaw, her hands moving to his shoulders, clinging to him. Jake smiled and slid his hands from her hips up across her damp, long back, feeling her shudder in the wake of the last, powerful orgasm. Damn, they were so good together. So hot. He lay there, feeling scalded, sated and breathing in ragged gasps, holding her tightly against him, their hearts pounding in wild unison with one another.

Morgan moaned, limp in his arms. She nuzzled Jake's shoulder, barely able to move, feeling his calloused fingers gliding lightly down her spine. "That was so good," she managed, breathless, feeling him deep within her, feeling his strength already returning.

Groaning, Jake muttered, "I'm so damned

weak I can't move." He felt her barely nod, and he was content to hold her in the aftermath. Jake breathed in her womanly scent, strands of her hair tickling his jaw, and he closed his eyes, absorbing every second of it with her. Absorbing the moment.

Morgan was hot, sensitive and wild. And she was wearing his engagement ring. She was going to marry him. Jake's chest expanded with powerful emotions, his throat tightening as he realized this woman was going to consent to be his wife.

Morgan slowly lifted her head. She placed her hands on either side of his head, her eyes drowsy green fire, a look of satiation in her expression. Lifting his hands, Jake framed her face, gently drawing her down as he met her mouth.

"We're good together," he said, tasting her lips, feeling them pull into a soft smile beneath his.

She made a sound in her throat, agreeing with him.

"Want to get off?" he asked, concerned about her wounded leg.

"It's not happy," Morgan admitted, "but I don't care. There's other parts of me that feel wonderful. . . . It's a trade-off I was willing to make."

Jake eased Morgan off him and carefully rear-ranged her on the left side of his body. She lay there, smiling up at him as he leaned over her, kissing her for a long, long time.

The love shining in Jake's expression overwhelmed Morgan. Always, when they'd come together in the past, it was two sex-starved animals clashing, selfish and hungry. They had always taken from one another, rarely given. This time was so different. And yet, as Morgan lifted her hand, ran her fingers down the side of Jake's face, she understood they had both, for the first time, unveiled their vulnerable love for one another.

Before, they had protected themselves, never opening up to any degree with one another. It was still good sex. Great sex. But they'd shielded their emotions, never fully shared.

This morning, they had fully trusted one another, and it had left Morgan in awe. She could never give it words, but she saw the same realizations mirrored in Jake's clear gray eyes. She saw happiness glinting in them, saw it in the rueful curve of his incredibly male mouth. What they had was something so deep, so powerful and healing, that Morgan knew it would last them the rest of their lives. It shook her. It gave her a sense of trust in Jake she'd never had with him before.

After showering, Jake sat with Morgan eating a breakfast she'd made for them. She wore a pink silk robe over her naked body. Her red hair was deliciously mussed, and he wondered for the hundredth time why he hadn't married her a hell of a long time ago. He watched her pick up a white ceramic mug with those long, tapered fingers of hers. The satiation in her eyes made him feel good because he always wanted to please Morgan when they made love.

"Remember Afghanistan? Two years ago?" Jake asked, setting his empty plate aside. "We'd been making love off and on all night. I found some water. You managed to get a spit bath afterward?" He smiled in memory. It had been damn cold water, but it had been clean. He'd washed Morgan's back with a washcloth and the bar of soap he always carried in his ruck. Just the small moments, the touching, the intimacy that existed between them, had been so damned healing for him.

"Yes," she whispered. "I'll never forget those days with you, Jake." Morgan saw remnants of pain in his gray gaze. "Why?"

He took a deep breath. "What you didn't know at that time was I'd lost Amanda and

Joshua a few years earlier. I was so consumed with grief, I couldn't let it go. And then you showed up." Jake reached over, picking up her slender hand. "Those three days were amazing for me, Morgan. You were so damn tender toward me. Everything you did when we loved one another just kept tearing open that wound of grief I had inside me. I swore you somehow knew because the sex we shared was mind-blowing for me. You helped heal me, and you didn't even realize it. You gave me back my life, my reason to start to live again."

Morgan set the cup aside, her fingers tangled in his. She felt his pain, his loss. "Is that why we argued so damn much when we had to leave each other and go our separate ways with our teams, then?"

He grimaced. "Yeah. It was my fault. I was such a jerk to you, Morgan. And it will make you happy to know I've been kicking myself ever since because of the way I behaved toward you."

"I'd wanted a relationship with you, Jake. I wanted to try one more time. And when I brought it up, you flew into a rage. And I thought at the time, it was like a replay of Annapolis. I couldn't understand your angry reaction."

"Because I didn't tell you about the loss

of my family."

"Yeah." Morgan shook her head, regret in her tone. "And there I was, a bull in a china shop, accusing you of never being able to settle down, be responsible, never wanting to get married or wanting a family." Her voice broke. "I'm so sorry, Jake. I wish . . . I wish you'd told me. . . . I'd never have asked if I'd known."

"It wasn't your fault, Morgan. Those three nights with you made me vulnerable. I was raw with grief, but I didn't know it. Every time I loved you, I could feel the grief stalking me more and more. The first time we made love, I cried. I was embarrassed as hell because it came out of nowhere, but you held me. You made it okay." Jake shrugged. "The second night, I felt more of the grief coming to get me. I didn't want to cry in your arms again. Eventually, in the middle of that goddamn blizzard, I went outside, walked down to that stinking goat barn and cried for their loss. I was hurting so damn bad, I felt like raw meat, no skin, just wide open."

Morgan rubbed her face, tears in her eyes. "Damn, Jake, you should have told me. I had no way of knowing." And she hadn't. Those three nights had been heaven for her, opening her heart to Jake once again, dreaming once more of maybe having a relationship with him.

The morning after the blizzard had moved on and the two teams were about to leave, she'd triggered their hellacious, screaming argument that could be heard around the entire village.

"I didn't handle it very well," Jake admitted quietly. He reached out, enclosing her hand with both of his. "I guess I can use the old excuse that men don't know how to communicate or get their emotions the hell out of themselves and into the open. I was wrong in not telling you, and I'll be forever sorry for that, Morgan. I promise, in the future, if there's something bothering me, you're going to know about it. No more hiding. It didn't serve either of us, and it drove us apart again." God, he hoped she wouldn't cry right now. Tears were one thing Jake just could not handle. But of course, moistness came to her eyes.

"I wasn't exactly an angel in that argument, either," Morgan admitted, feeling the warmth of his hands enclosing hers. Hands that loved her so well, so completely. Working hands. Warrior's hands. "I was still working through Mark's death, too," she admitted, her voice strained. "Loving you helped release me, helped me to move on, and I'll always be grateful to you for that."

"We'd been mortally wounded," Jake said, shaking his head. "And neither of us had told the other. We were both wrapped up in our grief. Neither of us had the ability to see beyond ourselves or our suffering. Just chalk it up to being human."

"I didn't want to confide in you after what I went through," Morgan said. "It could have happened to anyone. We were both human in how we reacted. But I stopped trusting you and felt so alone."

Jake grimaced. "I owe you the whole explanation on my side of what happened that night back in Annapolis, Morgan. I'd just received word from the Navy that my father had died in combat at noon that day. They wouldn't tell me where or how he died because he was a SEAL operator. I was blown apart, Morgan. I felt like my whole world imploded on me, and I was in shock. I was at the admin office all afternoon and that evening trying to get information because in his will, I was the POA, power of attorney. I had to think through my own grief and loss to figure out where he'd wanted to be buried. Hell, I saw him so little, I had no idea what he wanted. It was a bad day for me. . . ."

Morgan ached for him. "Why didn't you

tell me this before?" And tears began to fall down her cheeks. All these years she'd accused him of running. Oh, God, she had been so wrong! So damned wrong.

Jake moved uncomfortably in the chair, not looking at her for a moment. "I was young. I was in shock, and I couldn't handle both crises, Morgan. I chose my father over you and that's the truth. I know it hurts you, but I was just too damned young to cope with all this hitting me all at once. In one day I lose my father and I get told by my roommate that I was almost a father myself."

Jake opened his hands, giving her a pleading look. "Looking back on it, and believe me, I've been so sorry for the way I behaved on that day, I'd have gone to you, Morgan. I should have gone to the hospital to be with you, too. My father was dead. He wasn't going anywhere. But I wasn't thinking clearly. I'm sorry. Sorry to my soul for what I did to you, Morgan. None of this was your fault. And the gossip that started around the Academy after you miscarried was that you lied to me about being protected. That ended up hurting both of us."

"It was hard on us that year," Morgan admitted in a raw voice. "I had to live down the gossip that I tried to get pregnant in

411

order to force you to marry me." She almost laughed because it was so absurd. Anyone who knew her knew she was at Annapolis to become an officer. "And I know, months after my miscarriage, you tried to approach me, but I was too angry at you. I just didn't want you in my life. I didn't want to hear what you had to say."

"Tell me about it." Jake's mouth quirked. "It took me three months to get out of my grief, Morgan. I'd buried my mother at eighteen. At twenty, it was my father. I was reeling. It's not an excuse, babe. It was life hitting me broadside. My grades fell, and I was struggling to even pass that third year. I was so damn close to failing." And he'd already failed her, as well.

"I know. I saw and I felt bad for you even though I thought you'd abandoned me. I knew you were hurting, but I never knew why. I could see it, but I was too angry. I didn't want to ever talk to you again, Jake."

"When we came back for the fourth year, I'd decided to stop trying to apologize to you," Jake admitted. "I felt guilty as hell, but you wanted nothing to do with me, so I gave up and let it go." He smiled sadly. "I never forgot it, and I'm glad we're getting clear on it now because I don't ever want to carry something like that in me again, Morgan. It damn near destroyed me. And look what it did to you. . . ."

She wiped her eyes with trembling fingers. "It wasn't your fault your father died, Jake. And knowing it now, I do understand. I can't even imagine if it had been my father who died suddenly and I had to handle it at Annapolis." Morgan sniffed. "I'm not sure at all I could have gone on like you did. I'd probably have failed and quit."

"Well," Jake groused, running his fingers through his short hair, "you love your father. I never loved mine and that's the truth. He was never around. He didn't want to take care of my mother, who was sick. He ran, Morgan, and I knew it even when I was ten years old. I owed him a responsibility because he was my father. I didn't owe him anything beyond that. He wasn't ever a father to me. He wasn't ever a husband to my mother, either. His real family was the SEALs, and he made it a priority over us. We were always second in his life."

Morgan's heart broke for Jake. She saw the grief in his eyes, heard the anguish in his low voice. "I wish . . . I wish so much we could redo those years. So many assumptions. So many mistakes . . . misunderstandings. . . ."

Jake gave her a rueful look. "Yeah, we've

had a few potholes along the way, haven't we?"

She gave him a grateful look. "You didn't run. You were ready to settle down because you married Amanda." Morgan shook her head and murmured, a catch in her voice, "I blamed you for so many things, Jake. And none of them were true."

Worse, she'd hidden his daughter from him for over two years all because she'd thought Jake was not responsible nor could he be relied upon. Morgan felt nauseated over her stunning mistakes. What would Jake think or do once he found out Emma was his daughter? Would he leave her because she'd hidden his daughter from him? Closing her eyes, Morgan felt dumped into the fires of hell. And they were all of her own making. She'd put herself into this position. There was no one to shoulder the blame but her.

Opening her eyes, her fingers tightening as he'd relaxed his hand, Morgan said, "I need you to fly home with me, Jake. Tomorrow? I want you to come home with me to Gunnison." *Come meet Emma. Your daughter.*

Jake smiled, opening his hand and holding hers. "It's about time I met your parents. I've spoken to them before, and I'd really like to meet the two people who created such a beautiful daughter that I'm in love with. A nice way to celebrate our engagement. I'm sure we can toss around some dates with them. Make them feel included."

Morgan's heart broke a little more. "I'll always love you, Jake."

"Well," he said, sitting up, holding her shaken gaze, "I intend to be a real husband to you, Morgan. I guess this is as good a time as any to tell you. I knew I was going to ask you to marry me. I wasn't sure what your answer would be, given our track record." Jake lifted one shoulder. "I was hoping like hell you'd say yes, forgive me for my past mistakes, and we could move on. I've only got six more months left on my contract with the Navy. I've already told the Captain of SEAL Team Three I'm getting out." He saw Morgan's eyes widen, her lips part in shock. He knew he'd get that reaction.

"I wanted to prove to you that I wasn't a runner, Morgan. That I took my responsibility toward you and any children we might have seriously. I would stay home. I'd be there for you. I'd be a father to our children. I didn't want to be like my father, Morgan. I wasn't going to be a shadow in your or our family's life. I wanted to damn well be

home for Christmas, celebrate Thanks-
giving, give you chocolates on Valentine's
Day. . . ."

"Are you sure about this, Jake? I know
how much you love being a SEAL." Morgan was shaken to her core. Jake lived
SEALs. Breathed SEALs. It was his family.
A second family that had embraced him,
supported him, and he'd finally felt as if he
belonged somewhere. Jake had had so much
taken from him as an innocent child, and
Morgan knew he'd found his family with
the SEAL team.

"Yeah, I'm sure." Jake watched her tenderly. "I finally got clear on that after you
almost died in that firefight, Morgan. I realized I was looking for a family. I was looking for you. I loved you. And when you
nearly died, so much of my old ways of
thinking and seeing the world shattered. I
realized I could have you if you'd agree."
How Jake hoped she agreed. "And I was
hoping you might want one or two kids with
me. But I would be fine with just you, babe.
You're my family now. The SEALs helped
me so damn much. They made a man out
of me. They made me responsible and
matured me. But that chapter in my life is
almost over. The next chapter I open up is

going to be about me marrying you, and we'll be a real family then."

CHAPTER TWENTY-SIX

When Jake stepped into the Boland house in Gunnison, Colorado, that late afternoon, he had a shock coming. Jim and Cathy Boland greeted him warmly. Jake noticed Morgan's father had gray eyes and black hair just like he did. The shock continued when he saw that his wife, Cathy, had red hair and green eyes, just like Morgan. As he stood shaking Jim Boland's hand, Jake wondered, what were the chances that Morgan would meet him and they would share certain physical traits?

They'd welcomed him. Jake felt their sincerity and gratitude for what he'd done to bring them into the loop when Morgan had been wounded. As they took him on the tour, Jake admired the four-thousand-square-foot, two-story cedar cabin sitting in the woods, surrounded by Douglas fir, outside of Gunnison. He held Morgan's hand as Cathy invited them through the kitchen and onto a huge sundeck outside the sliding glass door.

There was a redwood picnic table at one end and a number of chairs scattered around the deck. It overlooked a small pond that Jim Boland had landscaped and created. The place was peaceful, and Jake could feel himself letting down and relaxing. They stood along the railing, and Cathy told him how Morgan, when she was small, would go down to the pond and try to catch the frogs living among the cattails. He liked hearing about Morgan's growing-up years, the home at nine thousand feet, deep in the Rocky mountains.

"We're going to serve some iced tea, beer and snacks in a bit," Cathy told them.

Jake nodded and felt Morgan tug at his hand. He looked down into her pensive face, thinking about her as a rambunctious, curious child running free out in the mountains. It helped him understand her roots. And clearly, the deep affection and connection Morgan had with her parents was special. He'd never had it with his father and began to understand the depth of his loss in his own childhood.

"Come on," Morgan whispered. "There's someone else you need to meet."

Puzzled, he smiled and said, "Sure." Jake

excused himself with her parents and followed Morgan through the kitchen and into the foyer. She seemed nervous. Why? He could feel the dampness in her hand. When they reached the stairs, he knew Morgan would have problems climbing them because of her leg wound.

"Want me to carry you up the stairs?" he asked, grinning. Jake sensed she was anxious, which was unlike her, and he wanted to put her at ease.

"No. This is going to be slow," Morgan warned him. Placing her right hand on the banister rail, she used the cane to steady her left leg. "My PT guys have been challenging me on stairs for a while. I'll make it. Just stay behind me? Stay on my six?"

He grinned. "I like being behind you." He saw her blush as she glanced back at him.

"You promised to be good while you're here, Ramsey."

Chuckling, Jake said, "I'm black ops, babe. There's going to be places and times when I can touch you when no one else is looking."

Morgan shook her head, taking the shining cedar steps one at a time. "This is going to be like climbing a mountain," she warned him.

Jake slid his hand gently around her waist,

wanting to give her more support. "It's kind of like our life story, isn't it? We've had a long, slow climb to reach the top?"

Morgan stopped halfway up, feeling twinges of pain in her leg from the exertion and needing to rest for a moment. Jake stood on the same stair, his hand never leaving her waist, his expression wry. "You're right. Great symbol, these stairs. But it also says something else about us, Jake. We never quit loving one another no matter what kind of hurdles were thrown in our way, either."

He leaned over, caressing Morgan's lips, inhaling her sweet scent that was only her. She was relaxed here at home, not all buttoned-up and professional. In her purple tee and white summer slacks, she didn't look like an officer in the Marine Corps. She looked like a young, beautiful woman on the verge of flowering to him. Jake slid his fingers through her loose red hair, feeling the silky strength of the strands. Jake kissed her again, this time more slowly. As he eased away, holding her darkening green eyes, he rasped, "Life isn't easy, babe. It won't ever be." Caressing her cheek, he added, "Having someone at my side makes it a helluva lot easier, though."

"It does," Morgan said, her voice strained. "Come on. Six more stairs with me?"

"I should carry you."

"Not a chance, Ramsey. If you fall with me, you'll set my leg back by months."

He snorted. "Like I'd drop you?"

Morgan laughed a little nervously and made it to the second floor. "You've never dropped me."

Standing with her, Jake slid his hand across her shoulders, feeling the dampness on her skin, understanding how the stairs had challenged her fragile, healing body. "I didn't drop you coming out of that wadi. If there was anywhere it could have happened, it would have been there." He felt such a fierce love for her. They'd gone through so damn much together. Jake looked around. There were four doors along the polished cedar hall. "Where are we going?"

Morgan walked ahead, her hand settling on a brass doorknob. "In here." There was nervousness in her eyes, although he didn't understand why. Jake entered the room after Morgan. He closed the door behind him and turned around.

"I want you to meet Emma," she whispered, her eyes filling with tears.

Jake saw a little girl sitting at her small desk in the corner, coloring madly away with her crayons.

When Emma heard the door close, she

gasped, dropped the crayons and screamed, *"Mommy!"* She launched herself off the chair like a Harrier jump jet taking off from the deck of a Navy carrier.

Jake stood back, feeling powerful emotions sweep through him. He stood awkwardly, watching Emma fly into her mother's open arms. Morgan had knelt, smiling broadly, taking her daughter's full weight. Emma was dressed in a pink tee and bright red coveralls and had white shoes on her tiny feet. He stared down at her; it was as if a bomb went off next to him. Emma had black hair, huge gray eyes and a square face.

Jake's mouth went dry, and his chest tightened. His heart began a slow pound as he stared disbelievingly down at the child. Swallowing against a forming lump, Jake recalled Afghanistan over two years ago. His condom had broken. *Jesus.* Emma was *his* daughter!

He could see Morgan's mouth and nose in Emma's face, but there was no question of his genetic stamp upon this young, joyful little girl. His heart swelled powerfully with love for both of them.

Morgan released her daughter and gestured for Jake to come over and kneel down beside her. She saw the shock and realization in Jake's eyes. He'd put it all together, that Emma was his daughter. And then he hesitated, as if he was worried he'd say or do the wrong thing with his daughter. More than anything, Morgan saw love shining in his eyes for Emma. But would Jake ever forgive her? He had a right to be angry at her, too. She knew there would be long, intense talks alone, out of earshot of Emma. She had a lot of forgiveness to ask from Jake, too.

"Mommy, who's this?" Emma asked, thrusting her index finger toward Jake.

Keeping her hand around her daughter's tiny waist, Morgan smiled brokenly. Her voice grew hoarse with emotion. "Emma, I want you to meet your daddy."

Jake reached out, touching Morgan's hair, trying to communicate silently to her that everything was all right. He got Emma was his. He saw tears and anxiety in her eyes, as if she was scared he wouldn't accept Emma. Or that he was angry at what she did to him. Jake couldn't talk right now, not in front of the little girl. He leaned over and kissed Morgan's brow.

"She's beautiful, just like you," Jake whispered unsteadily, holding her gaze, watching her understand he wasn't angry with her. He knew why Morgan had protected Emma from him. So many damned mistakes and misunderstandings between them had forced her into this decision. Jake felt his heart tear over their jaded past with one another.

"She's yours," Morgan offered unsteadily.

He smiled a little, emotions running wild within his chest. His voice was low with emotion, and he smiled slightly. "Yeah, it's a little obvious, isn't it?"

Morgan nodded. "Just a little, Ramsey."

"It's okay, Morgan. Everything's going to be okay." Jake leaned over, kissing her brow, trying to ease the worry from her green eyes. "We'll talk this out later," he promised her gently.

Relief shearing through her, Morgan swallowed hard, wanting to cry but knowing she couldn't. Not right now. "Yes . . . later . . ." She turned her attention to curious Emma.

Jake watched his daughter studying him, a scowl on her little face, those huge gray eyes amazingly intelligent, missing nothing. Emma was so small and thin. And he was so damned tall. Maybe threatening-looking to such a little child. Kneeling, Jake rested his damp hands on his thighs, absorbing Emma's inquisitive expression as she tilted her face and studied him some more.

"Your daddy has been gone for a long time," Morgan told her daughter. "But he's finally been able to come home to us, Punkin'. . . ."

Jake smiled at his daughter. "Emma? I've been waiting for a long time to meet you. To hold you." His voice was rough-sounding because he fought back tears that wanted to come. Jake was afraid Emma would reject him. He opened his arms to her. "Can we say hello?"

Emma frowned and then looked up at her mother. "Why was Daddy gone so long, Mommy?"

Morgan moved her hand gently through her daughter's loose, black hair. It shone like a raven's wing, the very same color as Jake's military-short hair. "Your daddy is a very brave man, Emma. He's been away in another country." Morgan took Jake's hand and turned it over. "Look, do you see all these scars, Emma? Your daddy got those fighting in that war."

Emma was fascinated. She boldly moved forward, placing her little hand on Jake's hairy, darkly sunburned lower arm. Tracing the five scars she saw with her finger, she looked up at Jake.

"Do they hurt?"

Jake couldn't speak. His throat tightened. His daughter's gently tracing each scar disassembled him emotionally. She'd been so careful as she'd moved her tiny finger across each one. "Not anymore," he promised Emma, a catch in his voice. His daughter seemed so concerned. Jake knew he couldn't just reach out and grab Emma and hold her. He wasn't sure how Emma would react to him, but it was important that she make the first move toward him, not the other way around. Jake needed her to trust him.

Placing her finger into her bow-shaped mouth, Emma studied the scars as he patiently held his arm out toward her. She looked over at her mother. "Mommy, was Daddy in the same country you went to?"

Morgan nodded. "He was, Punkin'."

"And you got to see him?"

"A few times," she told her daughter, caressing her small shoulder. "He was gone a lot, Emma. Like me."

"You missed him, too?"

"Oh," Morgan said, laughing softly, "very much," and she shared a tender glance with Jake. He looked like a fish out of water. Unsure. Hesitant. Maybe afraid to make a mistake with Emma. Morgan wanted to tell him children were amazingly resilient and that he would make mistakes. But love between a parent and child would always smooth them over.

Emma leaned against her mother's right knee, studying Jake in the gathering silence.

Jake was sweating. His heart was pounding with fear of being rejected. Emma was just as readable as Morgan. She left nothing to question, and he managed a slight smile down at his daughter. "I'm sorry I couldn't come home sooner, Emma. I wanted to," he told her. His mind fled back to that Christmas in Afghanistan and those three miraculous days he'd spent with Morgan, renewing their heated connection. Those three days had been incredible, and they'd created Emma as a result. Jake studied Emma's scrunched-up face, and the corners of his mouth curved. Their loving one another in that desolate, desert country, with threat all around them, had produced this beautiful little girl. Jake absorbed her curious look, watching as she seriously chewed on her finger.

And then Emma pulled her finger out of her mouth and boldly marched forward, straight at him. She reached up with her thin arms, fearlessly met his eyes and said, "Daddy, I missed you. . . ."

Jake slowly closed his arms around his daughter, feeling her warmth, her vital force of life that sent his heart reeling with relief and love. He was so large against her smallness, her arms unable to span his torso. Emma laid her head on his belly, trying to squeeze him with all her child's strength. Closing his eyes, Jake felt tears burning behind his lids. He gently curved his hand around Emma, leaned down and pressed a kiss to her hair, which smelled like apple shampoo.

His heart spun with shock and joy; that this tiny creature would accept him just like that blew Jake away. Morgan gave him a reassuring look that spoke volumes. Emma, despite her age, almost three, was very old and wise, far more mature than her years as he'd just discovered.

Morgan slowly stood, smiling unevenly, trying to choke back a sob. It was so touching to watch them hug, and she pressed her fingers against her lips, trying not to make a sound. She didn't want this powerful moment to be broken. Morgan watched with joy as Emma pulled back, placed her little hands against his face, leaned up and smacked a sloppy kiss on his jaw.

"Goodness," Jake said happily, seeing affection in Emma's eyes. He felt as if he were staring at a reflection of himself. His daughter was unafraid, and he grinned as he gently scooped her up into his arms, settling her against his chest. Her small arms twined around his neck, and Emma sighed and rested her head against his shoulder.

Giving Morgan a glance, Jake saw tears running down her cheeks. Hot tears slid down his face, too. He was crying out of relief. Out of loss. Out of missing so much with the two women who were now permanently a part of his life. Emma nestled more deeply against his neck, closed her eyes, a content look on her innocent face.

His love overwhelmed him in the best possible way as he stood there, his daughter in his arms. Jake drew Morgan forward, sliding his arm around the woman who had carried his child in her body, kissing her for a long, long time.

Jake stood with his arm around Morgan's waist. Moonlight silently filtered through the curtains in Emma's room. She lay asleep in her bed, holding her favorite teddy bear, Boo, in her arms. They'd quietly come in to check on her before going to bed, and Jake found himself unable to leave. All he wanted to do was stare at the little tyke and absorb her into his heart. Emma had insisted he read her a story before she went to bed. Jake saw Morgan's spunk in her, the child knowing what she wanted and being fearless about asking for it. Jake had spent a half hour reading to his daughter, watching her eyes slowly droop closed, her arm around that old, almost-hairless teddy bear. He'd tucked her in, kissed her brow and quietly left.

"I think Emma is completely taken with you," Morgan whispered to him, resting her head against his shoulder.

Jake nodded, unable to speak. Much earlier, he'd taken Emma downstairs with Morgan, and they had all sat out on the sundeck with chips and beer. Emma didn't want to leave his side, stuck like glue to him, and Jake had found himself close to tears a number of times.

Jim and Cathy Boland appeared just as deeply touched. It was as if Emma had known he was her father, and she wasn't about to let him go. Probably for fear he'd disappear from her life again. So, she'd sat on his thigh, munching Fritos while he'd drunk his beer and talked with Morgan and her parents like the family they really were.

Jake took a deep breath and smiled down at Morgan. "You've got to be exhausted. Let's go to bed."

Nodding, Morgan turned and led him out of his daughter's room, and they walked down the hall to their bedroom. They each took a shower, after which Jake climbed into bed with her. Morgan wore a pale pink silk nightgown. Jake wore nothing. He saw the exhaustion in her eyes, understanding the stress the day had brought her. He leaned against the headboard and gathered her into his arms.

Morgan sighed, nuzzling against his jaw, feeling relief and contentment. It was nearly midnight, the moonlight spilling in through the curtains, the window open to allow the pine-laden air to circulate within the room.

She slid her fingers lightly across his deeply bruised chest. "Are you upset with me for not telling you about Emma?"

Jake captured Morgan's hand, placing his over it. "No," he said, kissing her hair. "When I saw Emma, I got it. I thought I was looking at myself for a moment." Jake slid his hand down her arm, her skin like velvet beneath his fingertips. "I understood why you didn't tell me, babe."

"Until yesterday," Morgan said, muffled by his neck, "I didn't know the whole story, Jake. I feel so bad. I kept her away from you for two years. I'm so sorry, Jake. I can barely live with myself for doing this to you."

He drew in a ragged breath, embracing her gently with both arms. "You were protecting Emma. You thought I'd appear and disappear in her life just like I had in yours. You wanted stability for Emma, not to be torn up emotionally all the time. I don't disagree with the decision you made, Morgan. And I sure as hell don't want you feeling guilty about it. All right?" Jake eased her away just enough to look down into her moist eyes. "I mean it," he emphasized. "We're both at fault in this. Emma survived just fine under your decision. She had your parents to give her the steadiness she needed in her little life. No harm, no foul, babe. We need to be looking at the present and what we're doing together in the future with her. Not chewing up the past again. It's done. It's gone. We can't go back and fix it or change it."

Morgan closed her eyes, her voice tremulous. "I was so afraid, Jake. I had terrible visions of you leaving me and Emma, not accepting Emma as your daughter. . . ."

Jake sighed and tucked her against him. "Silly woman. You can handle combat, but you can't trust me enough to know I'd see Emma and know without a doubt she's mine? And that I wouldn't put it together?" Jake touched her cheek, feeling the dampness of her tears. "Morgan, you nearly died. And it's been hell coming out of it. You're more emotional than usual and that's to be expected. I would never walk away from you and Emma. The only way that'd happen is if I were dead."

"I get it, Ramsey. I really do," Morgan muttered, wiping her eyes. "I feel like an emotional basket case on some days," she admitted softly. "I can't even blame my hormones this time around."

"It's okay," Jake reassured her. "Shock is hell. Most people don't realize what it does to a person mentally and emotionally. It doesn't end a day or a week or even a month later like everyone thinks. You're still going through the stages of it, and as you do, a lot of emotions are involved. They come and go. I ought to know. I've been shot at enough, wounded enough, to be an expert on it. Hell, I could write a book about it."

She snorted. "No kidding. Okay, I'll cut myself some slack."

"Good," Jake grumbled. Somehow, he'd handle her tears. He wanted Morgan to feel safe in sharing all her emotions, good or bad, with him from now on.

"Emma loved you on the spot. I swear," Morgan whispered, "she recognized you instantly as her father."

"I was never so scared when I realized she was mine. I didn't know what to do or say to her," he admitted, and Jake smiled down into her shadowed face. Morgan's hair hung in a dark frame around her soft face, and he threaded his fingers through that silky mass. "Thank you. I couldn't have done this without you."

"Emma's a bold little thing." Morgan laughed quietly, seeing Jake's hope and relief. "I knew if we handled it right, she would immediately accept you. Off and on, over the past year, she'd asked my parents where her daddy was. She knew my parents were not her mommy and daddy."

"God, she's smart," Jake muttered.

"Scary smart. She takes after you. What did you expect?" Morgan grinned. "In some ways, it's going to be just deserts for you, Ramsey. Because you're such an ongoing handful to deal with, Emma is going to test you in every possible way. She's like a wild mustang, free-ranging, independent and stubborn. Just like you."

Hearing her chortle, Jake gently pulled Morgan down beside him so he could kiss her. "Somehow," he rasped, "I'll be able to cope with Emma. I'll remember those times and feelings when I was young." He curved his mouth against Morgan's smiling lips.

Jake didn't want the kiss to end, but he knew Morgan was leaning toward him at an odd angle. He worried about the pressure on her wounded leg and eased away. Tucking her down beside him so she'd be comfortable, her head coming to rest on his shoulder, Jake felt her palm settle over his heart.

"I wanted to talk to you about some other decisions I'm thinking of making, Jake." Morgan moved away just enough to catch his downward glance. She opened her hand against his chest. "After getting shot in that gunfight, I began to want to reorganize my life."

Nodding, he caressed her hair. "Nearly dying has a funny way of doing that for most people," Jake agreed quietly, seeing the concern in her eyes.

"You had left for the second op," Morgan said, holding his stare. "I began to feel I needed to sort out my priorities, Jake. I missed Emma so much. I hated the fact I was overseas, and she was here. I didn't get to see her that often, no matter what I did to try and come home. To be her mother . . ." She reached up, caressing his jaw, holding his gaze. "I loved carrying Emma for those nine months, knowing she was your baby. I loved every second of it. And birthing her . . . well . . . I'll never forget that day. . . . I found myself crying endlessly because you weren't there to see her born. You didn't even know she existed.

I was so damned guilt-ridden, Jake, I could hardly bear it. Emma turned out to be so beautiful, so much like you, that every time I saw her, I wanted to find you. I wanted to tell you."

Jake drew in a deep, ragged breath. "I don't know how you did it." And he didn't. Morgan had strength far beyond anything he would ever understand. Her mother, Cathy, had that same titanium backbone, and she had passed it genetically on to her daughter. The woman he loved was the mother of his child. The power of it shook Jake to his soul. "I'm fine with you getting out of the Marine Corps, Morgan. Your priorities have changed." So had his, in the best of ways.

Morgan studied his shadowed, hard face. "Four months from now, my enlistment is finished," she said.

"If you want to stay home and raise Emma, I'll support you a hundred percent."

"Good, because that's what I want to do, Jake."

Jake held her gently. Her warmth flooded his heart. "You're one hell of a mother," he whispered against her hair. "Emma deserves to have both her parents around."

For a moment, Morgan wanted to cry with relief. "For so long, Jake, I've been at the point of the spear pushing women's rights. I believe in it with my heart and soul. After I had Emma, I began to change. Maybe it's hormones. Maybe it's something else. I don't know."

Jake smiled against her hair, holding her. "You spent eleven years in the military doing things no one thought was within the capability of women. You've more than proved yourself. Now it's time to move on. We have a daughter. And she's beautiful. God, what a heartbreaker she's going to be. . . ." He laughed quietly with Morgan.

"I'm not sorry to be leaving the military, Jake. I want to be here for Emma."

Taking her fingers, Jake pressed a small kiss on the tip of each one of them. "I have a family again."

Morgan moved her hand across his shoulder, trying to take away some of the pain she heard in his voice. "You've had so much taken from you, Jake."

His brow furrowed over the memories. "You're right. Holding Joshua brought me full circle, Morgan." Jake held her luminous gaze, feeling her love for him. "In that moment after he was born and I was holding him, I decided right then and there to get out of the SEALs and be a real father to my son. I wasn't going to be gone like my father was with me."

Grazing his jaw, Morgan whispered, "And then they were killed two weeks later. My God, Jake, that must have torn your soul apart."

"It did," he grimly admitted. Staring off into the muted darkness, he rested his hand against Morgan's slender neck. "I was in shock for the longest time." He leaned over and pressed a kiss to her hair. "When I met you that December in Afghanistan, I had never needed you more than then."

Morgan held Jake silently, eyes closed, remembering the first night they'd made love. "I'm glad we met there. I never regretted those days together, Jake. Not ever. . . . Emma was created by us then. How can we be sorry about that?"

He kissed her cheek and whispered, "Emma was a symbol for us even though we didn't realize it at the time. She was the best from both of us and she was created out of our love for one another. I have you. I have our beautiful daughter. What more do I need?"

The profoundness of his words rippled like warm waves through Morgan's heart.

Jake read her expression and saw her tears. He kissed her brow. "The team will be stateside and I'll be with you and Emma as much as humanly possible over the next six months. You know that, don't you?"

Nodding, Morgan brought Jake's hand against her heart 'and held it there. "We'll make it work, Jake. We'll find a house in Coronado. We'll be close to where your team is located. Your platoon remains stateside for the next eighteen months, and that's good news. You won't ever have to rotate overseas again, thank God." Morgan knew Jake had the sixty days of leave. They could find a rental, set up housekeeping and get everything in order before he had to report back for duty. The team would rotate out into the field for extended training exercises, and Jake would be gone for long periods of time. He'd come home on weekends whenever it was possible. And since she'd be with Emma every day, Morgan knew their daughter would handle his coming and going just fine. It was only for six months.

Sighing, Jake held her, their brows touching one another. "Emma deserves a father. You deserve a husband. You know I'll bust my ass to get home every chance I can, Morgan. You already know the platoon will be at various training sites while we refresh our skills."

Leaning up, Morgan curved her mouth

against his. "I love you, Jake Ramsey," she whispered. "We're a work in progress."

Squeezing her, Jake held Morgan for a long time, feeling her breath, inhaling her sweet scent. "You've given me back so much," he murmured against her temple. "When I lost Joshua, I felt like someone ripped my soul in half. I was completely devastated. I know Emma can't replace Joshua. But already, she's healing that deep wound in me, Morgan. I can't explain it, but she is. . . ."

"Emma heals everyone's heart," Morgan said softly, feeling Jake's loss. "If you let her, she will make your heart new just as she did mine. . . ."

CHAPTER TWENTY-SEVEN

"I don't want to lose you, Captain Boland."

Morgan sat in front of General Maya Stevenson's desk at the Pentagon. "I understand, ma'am."

"No," Maya said, smiling a little, drumming her fingers on the desk, "I don't think you do. I respect that you are not reenlisting. I support you going home to San Diego, buying a house and raising your daughter with Lieutenant Ramsey. And I'm not surprised that he won't reenlist, either."

Morgan tried not to show her reaction. "Then, ma'am, I don't understand what you're saying." Morgan had told her she would leave the Marine Corps when her contract was up. She tried to look beyond the carefully arranged expression on the General's face and couldn't.

"I'm going to throw you a curve ball, Captain. What if I make a call to the Commander of SEAL Team Three? And I asked that he hire you to work the SEAL intel desk at Coronado for the next six months while Lieutenant Ramsey is still in the military?"

Morgan considered the offer. "Ma'am, with all due respect, I couldn't do it full-time. I want to be home to raise our daughter."

"How about part-time? Three days a week? An eight-hour day shift?"

Morgan knew they could use two incomes to make ends meet. She and Jake had already talked a lot about their finances.

Maya smiled a little. "Consider the benefits, Captain. You'd have medical insurance. You'd be able to know where your husband was at all times."

It was an incredibly tempting offer. "That," she stumbled, "is very generous of you, General."

"And I want something else from you, Morgan."

"Ma'am?"

"You're in the catbird seat with your wealth of combat experience. I don't want to lose you, either. But what I need from you is something you can do from home. With your top secret clearance, you can read the sitreps, situation reports, from the field that are being filed by other women volunteers. I want you to read them, make comments and send them on to me. I need your eyes on Operation Shadow Warriors, Morgan."

Stunned by the offers, Morgan stared across the desk at the General. Maya Stevenson was well-known for not taking "no" for an answer. She was inventive and flexible, and she always thought outside the box.

"I'd like to do that, ma'am," Morgan said. "What I'll miss the most is the camaraderie I have with so many of the other women . . . and you."

Nodding and giving her a pleased look, Maya said, "All right, then, I'll set the paperwork in motion to hire you as a civilian working for me when the time comes. I'll get the Captain of the SEAL team on the horn and see if he has an opening for you. I'm sure he will. We always need good intel people. You'll be working five days a week. Three at Coronado for the SEALs and two at home for me. You'll be getting a good salary. I'll have my staff get everything together, and you'll come back here and we'll hammer out the details. If you like the package, like the salary, we'll shake hands and you can start to work."

Standing at attention, Morgan said, "Yes,

ma'am. I'd like nothing better."

The General gave her a faint smile, and then she dismissed her. Making a ninety-degree turn on her heel, Morgan left. In the outer office, Jake sat in civilian clothes, waiting for her, Emma on his lap. He rose when she stepped out of the General's office, pulling Emma into his arms.

"Well?" Jake asked as they took the steps together after leaving the Pentagon. "How did it go?" The late-September sunlight was hot and bright overhead. She was in her Marine Corps uniform of a simple tan short-sleeved blouse and dark green gabardine slacks.

Morgan smiled and waited until they were well away from the military people coming and going from the Pentagon to tell him the conversation. In the parking lot, she leaned over and kissed Emma's cheek and then slipped her hand into Jake's as they walked to the rented black SUV.

Jake opened the rear door and settled Emma into her car seat. And then he opened the door for Morgan, and she climbed in. He slid into the driver's seat and shut the door. They would catch a commercial flight at Reagan National Airport and have time to discuss everything on the flight back to San Diego.

"What do you think of the offers?" she asked, watching Jake's expression as he drove.

"More important, babe, what do *you* think? Is this something you'd want to do?"

"Yes," Morgan said, rubbing her hands together. "Best of all, Jake, I'd know where you are. I know you'll be stateside, but platoons can be out of touch with their family for two or three weeks at a time."

He grinned and reached out and squeezed her hand. "Even better, we can talk to one another on cell phone and Skype. You can tell me what kind of trouble Emma has gotten into on a daily basis." Jake gave her a wicked grin.

Morgan laughed. "Oh, I'm sure as she gets to know our new home, has thoroughly scoped out the large backyard, the eucalyptus tree where she wants you to build her a tree house, she'll be operational around the clock."

They had found a three-bedroom, single-story home near Coronado. A Lieutenant with SEAL Team Three had transferred out, and he'd rented them the house. It was only fifteen minutes to the SEAL facility at Coronado.

Jake nodded and said, "Emma takes after me. I remember growing up, my early years,

I drove my mother nuts. I was only three or four at the time. . . ."

Emma and he had become tighter than fleas on a dog. Jake didn't know how it had happened, but it had and he was grateful for his daughter's big heart. One day, Emma would know the whole story. For now, she was happy to have two parents.

"Yes, well, what goes around, comes around, Ramsey. Just remember that. Emma is a carbon copy of you in every way that I can see."

"Strong genes," Jake agreed, pride in his tone.

"Oh, I can hardly wait. Emma is going to challenge you like you won't ever believe." Their daughter was spectacularly intelligent, seeming to have all-terrain radar, could read their minds and was two steps ahead of both of them already.

"I remember," Jake said fondly, "as a young kid, before my mother came down with MS, I had trouble sleeping at night. She'd come in and read to me. I remember those times, Morgan." He glanced over at her. "I loved when she read to me. I like reading to Emma." Because Emma was like the Energizer Bunny, not wanting to go to bed at the right time, just as he had been as a young child.

Morgan chuckled. "I've got a better idea, Ramsey. While you're home with us, you get to read her a story every night?"

A grin spread across his face. "Okay. I know when I'm beat. Fair enough."

"I'm glad you and your mother had those early times together before she fell ill."

Losing his smile, Jake grew quiet. "Yes, those were good times I'll never forget." Now he could create happy memories for Emma.

"Emma can hardly wait for you to read to her," Morgan murmured, sliding her hand across his broad shoulder.

Toward the end of their thirty days spent with her parents in Colorado, her father had offered Jake a job when he had finished out his enlistment. Jake was an electrical engineer, and in her father's construction business, he needed one. Jake would make an easy transition from military into civilian life, thanks to her father. It also meant they would move to Gunnison, Colorado, and Emma would grow up with her grandparents nearby. They would be a family, and nothing made Morgan happier. Equally important, Jake now had a family, something he so richly deserved.

"I still can't believe all of this is happening," she told Jake. "I feel like I'm in a dream."

The pain from the past was still with him, but not as sharp as before. Jake nodded. "We've been downrange with one another, Morgan, but we had the heart and the steel spine to gut through it to the end."

"We've been downrange, all right," Morgan agreed. "What got us through it, Jake, was our love for one another. Love kept us connected through all those years."

Jake picked up her hand and kissed her fingers. "And I'm going to spend the rest of my life showing you just how much I love you and Emma." Jake met Morgan's glance, his expression serious. "Forever."

ABOUT THE AUTHOR

Lindsay McKenna is proud to have served her country in the U.S. Navy as an aerographer's mate third class — also known as a weather forecaster. She was a pioneer of the military romance subgenre and loves to combine heart-pounding action with soulful and poignant romance. True to her military roots, she is the originator of the long-running and reader-favorite Morgan's Mercenaries series. She does extensive hands-on research, including flying in aircraft such as a P3-B Orion sub-hunter and a B-52 bomber. She was the first romance writer to sign her books in the Pentagon bookstore. Today, she has created a new military romantic suspense series, Shadow Warriors, which features romantic and action-packed tales about U.S. Navy SEALs.

Visit her online at www.lindsaymckenna

.com, www.twitter.com/lindsaymckenna and www.facebook.com/eileen.nauman.